## PRAISE FOR THE NOVELS OF STEPHEN WHITE

*Line of Fire*

"Fans will love how the threads from the other books weave into a complex tapestry. Newcomers will find a compelling mystery set against the beautiful Colorado landscape amid raging wildfires." —The Associated Press

"*Line of Fire* is a Stephen White thriller at its best—a juicy and very complicated crime with characters drawn close to the heart. The ending is unforeseen, leaving loose ends to be tied up in the final mystery, which is now under way."
—*The Denver Post*

"Readers will watch—at times, completely mystified—as the careers of Alan and Sam begin to unravel. This is truly a perfect lead-in to what is sure to be a 'final act' of epic proportions for Stephen White's popular cast of characters."
—*Suspense Magazine*

"Longtime fans and newcomers alike will enjoy spending time in the company of the always hospitable Gregory. In an author's note, White explains why he's bringing the series to an end with the twentieth installment. There's one patient left in the waiting room, however. Let's hope it's a long session."
—*Publishers Weekly*

"A fabulous tale. . . . The action-packed thrilling story line is character-driven as the audience will feel Gregory's fears. With a great cliff-hanger . . . fans will enjoy this entry and look forward to the final curtain call." —*Midwest Book Review*

"[An] emotional, thrilling ride with all the elements of a good story—crime, sex, betrayal, friendship, love, lies, family."
—Doing Colorado

"White is a fine storyteller, and Gregory is a complex, compelling character whom fans have grown to love and respect. It will be hard for them to say good-bye, but at least his creator appears to be planning to give him a first-class send-off."
—*Booklist*

*continued . . .*

"White brings his own unique 'A' game to *Line of Fire* . . . put [it] on your must-read list." —Bookreporter.com

"*Line of Fire* is such a fitting book to begin the end—White ratchets up the tension, brings together a lot of series characters, and fearlessly takes his beloved characters to dark, unpredictable places. If this book is any indication, the Alan Gregory series will end with a flourish. Well done, Mr. White."
—Literary Treats

"White makes it clear that Alan's nineteenth appearance is his penultimate case; the next case will be his swan song. Judging from the risks he takes this time, fans won't want to miss the sequel." —*Kirkus Reviews*

### The Last Lie

"A satisfying page-turner." —*The Denver Post*

"Good action . . . an interesting mystery."
—The Associated Press

"With faultless pace, White excels at constructing tension-infused situations and multilayered, believable characters in this intricate narrative." —*Suspense Magazine*

"An intriguing thriller . . . action-packed."
—*Midwest Book Review*

"[White] holds readers in suspense . . . more twists and turns than the winding mountain roads of Boulder."
—Examiner.com

"Good action . . . an interesting mystery."
—The Associated Press

### The Siege

"Gripping. . . . The best and most interesting terrorism thriller I've seen so far." —*The Washington Times*

"Stunning . . . brilliantly conceived and executed . . . intellectually challenging and provocative."
—*Publishers Weekly* (starred review)

### Dead Time

"Gregory's (aka White's) use of his therapist skills to question witnesses and gather facts becomes almost hypnotically absorbing."  —*The Orlando Sentinel*

"Deeply layered . . . beautifully orchestrated."  —*Booklist*

### Dry Ice

"Guaranteed to keep readers glued to their seats."  —*The Denver Post*

"Entertaining and suspenseful."  —*Chicago Sun-Times*

### Kill Me

"A thinking person's thriller."  —Jeffery Deaver

"Big, provocative, and downright gripping."  —Michael Connelly

### Missing Persons

"A psychological thriller that will capture readers' interest until the very end."  —*Rocky Mountain News*

### Remote Control

"Dark and fascinating. . . . Stephen White writes thrillers of the first order."  —Nelson DeMille

### Private Practices

"Intriguing . . . and believable . . . will keep you guessing to the end."  —Phillip Margolin

### Privileged Information

"A dazzling new talent."  —Tony Hillerman

### Cold Case

"Entertaining, insightful, and enlightening."  —*The Denver Post*

# STEPHEN WHITE

# LINE OF FIRE

A SIGNET BOOK

SIGNET
Published by the Penguin Group
Penguin Group (USA) Inc., 375 Hudson Street,
New York, New York 10014, USA

USA | Canada | UK | Ireland | Australia | New Zealand | India | South Africa | China

Penguin Books Ltd., Registered Offices: 80 Strand, London WC2R 0RL, England
For more information about the Penguin Group visit penguin.com.

Published by Signet, an imprint of New American Library, a division of Penguin
Group (USA) Inc. Previously published in a Dutton edition.

First Signet Printing, June 2013

ISBN 978-0-451-41836-4

Printed in the United States of America
10  9  8  7  6  5  4  3  2  1

ALWAYS LEARNING                                                    PEARSON *to Stan Galansky*

# ONE

"Daddy," my daughter asked, "where is the red flag?"

It was a good question. And, unusual for Grace in her current developmental phase—technically, she was mid-latency, although I tended to think of her stage of development as the pre-devious—the query was posed without apparent subtext.

We were in the middle of a Sunday-night family dinner discussion about the danger posed by the tinder-dry grasses that carpeted the hillsides around our rural home on the eastern slope of Colorado's Boulder Valley. Lauren, my wife, was cautioning the family—mostly me—about engaging in any outdoor activities that might create even the smallest spark. Lauren's warning did have a subtext; she had already asked me—twice, she would be happy to note—to take my car in for a tune-up. The thing had backfired a couple of times over the weekend.

Grace's older sibling, Jonas, a boy who had antennae tuned to things dangerous or nefarious, real or imagined, responded to his sister in an I'm-the-big-brother-I-know-what-I'm-talking-about tone that a Red Flag Warning was in effect for all of Boulder. "And that includes us," Jonas stressed, in case his sister had forgotten where she lived.

Jonas had a subtext. He was on the cusp of adolescence; he almost always had a subtext. When he said "us" to Grace, he meant "you."

During other recent family discussions Jonas had produced ample evidence that his younger sister often managed to get herself excluded from general rules of family conduct, and he'd argued convincingly that her parents, mostly her father, let her get away with it. Where my personal parenting was concerned, Jonas had a valid point: I had a sweet spot for my little girl that could interfere with better paternal instincts. I had pled guilty to cutting Grace the undeserved slack and promised to work on it. Jonas seemed to be disarmed by my candor.

I decided to ignore the subtext Jonas included in his comment to his sister about the fire risk. I ignored it because I wasn't in a refereeing mood, and because Gracie wasn't involved in too many activities that generated sparks.

In reply to Grace's earlier question, I told her that I didn't think there was a literal red flag flying anywhere in town to warn residents about the extreme fire danger along the Front Range. In a preemptive effort to forestall whatever verbal jabs might come next from Jonas's direction, I added, "But your mother and your brother are right. We all need to be careful. It's very dry out there."

Jonas nodded in agreement. That, of course, worried me. Even his nods tended to have subtexts. He said, "It's a *virtual* flag, Grace."

Jonas had a way of rolling his eyes that could be so sly it was almost criminal. He did it then. Before Grace could react to the eye roll—I had no doubt she would react to the eye roll—Lauren jumped in. She said, "It's so dry. And it's been so windy. I never thought I would miss the summer monsoon season, but I do. Where were the monsoons this year? It's already Labor Day. Where is all our rain?" She sighed. "Maybe we'll get an early snow."

# TWO

My first psychotherapy session of the new week started routinely enough the next morning. But by 7:57—I noted the time as I pressed 911—I had my hands, one atop the other, between my patient's breasts.

At that moment, I would not have thought that my day could have gotten any stranger.

I would have been wrong.

Twelve-plus hours later I was exiting the elevator on the third floor at Community Hospital when I heard Sam Purdy's distinctive Iron Range patois.

"Hey, what the heck are you doing here, Alan? Is everybody all right?" Sam managed to extend the *o* in *doing* long enough that it deserved its own zip code.

"Yeah, we're all fine," I said.

I was as surprised to see my friend as he was to see me.

I moved in for a quick hug before I recognized that my impulse, as Boulder as the Flatirons, was not mutual. Embracing was a form of greeting that Detective Sam Purdy tolerated begrudgingly, almost never in public, and certainly not when he was on duty.

He was on duty. I could see the bulge of a shoulder holster beneath his sport coat. I stopped a few feet away while I explained that I was checking on a patient who had taken ill that morning.

"What about you?" I asked. "Are you here because of the fire?"

The fire was on everyone's mind.

He gave it some thought. "Indirectly," he said. He lowered his voice to a whisper. "So you know, it's even worse up there than they're saying on the news. I've heard reports that over a hundred homes have been lost already. It's completely out of control."

My office was only six blocks away from the sharp rise of the Rockies in west Boulder. I first saw smoke rising above the mountains late in the morning. Within an hour I could smell the smoke as well as see it.

The Red Flag Warning was no longer a fire drill.

My patients, scheduled back-to-back almost all day long, had kept me apprised of the fire's progress. In between sessions I used my phone to monitor the news online. The wildfire was being called the Fourmile Fire, named after its starting point up Fourmile Canyon above Wallstreet, not far from Gold Hill.

Each new patient I saw reported fresh bad news about

the fire's march and the horrendous damage it was doing. Although the blaze wasn't currently threatening Boulder proper, it was apparently devastating the rugged residential areas in the mountains above Boulder, especially up Fourmile Canyon and up Sunshine Canyon. The pioneer treasure that is Gold Hill had been spared, barely, but flames were consuming dozens of homes in the surrounding canyons and on the nearby ridges.

"You usually work this late?" Sam asked.

His curiosity seemed sincere, not always a given. "I worked late today, but not this late. The patient I'm hoping to see was having a procedure when I got here a couple of hours ago. Every thirty minutes the nurses tell me I'll be able to see her in another thirty minutes. I'm going to try one more time. If that doesn't work, I'll come back in the morning." I paused. "Have you heard about any fire damage near Left Hand Canyon? I've been trying to reach Diane all afternoon."

Diane was my friend and my longtime partner in our psychotherapy practice.

Sam asked, "She lives where, exactly? Pine Brook?"

I said, "No, Lee Hill. Near Olde Stage."

He nodded. "Then they were definitely evacuated. I haven't heard of any homes burning there yet. Farther up, yes. She's probably okay, so far."

Those reports had been consistent all day long. The homes that had been destroyed were farther up in the mountains.

But Diane being okay? That was a different question altogether.

A few years before, Diane had survived a devastating hostage situation outside Las Vegas. Her post-traumatic recovery had been tenuous at times, but I had thought she was turning the corner until the previous year's holiday season, when one of her close girlfriends was arrested for murder. Diane's decline after that fresh insult was precipitous. She began spending as though the recession never happened. She had almost stopped coming in to the office for work. I rarely saw her.

I didn't explain to Sam that I was as worried about Diane's emotional reaction to the fire as I was concerned about her safety. He would have lost interest.

I asked him what brought him to the hospital so late in the day.

"A John Doe was involved in a single-car accident on his way out of the hills. Car was packed full of shit, like he was evacuating. But his injuries don't add up. Pattern doesn't match the impact. Lucy and I are lending a hand because the department has everybody focused on the fire. Turns out your name came up at the scene. I was going to call you about it tomorrow."

"Yeah? How did my name come up?"

"No big deal. I need to see if you recognize somebody. We can do it in the morning."

I consciously allowed his big head to fade out of focus. The clock over his shoulder in the nursing station of the nearby intensive care unit told me it was a few clicks shy of nine o'clock. I was going to miss my kids' bedtime no matter what. I lowered my voice to ICU reverential. "Hey, I'm here. My tomorrow is crazy. If I can help, I'll help. No apologies necessary."

"I wasn't going to apol—"

"I know you weren't." I smiled.

"You sure?" he said.

I hesitated. Sam noticed the hesitation. He said, "You want to do your visit first? I'll be here a while."

My first patient that morning had been a forty-two-year-old woman who worked as a statistician at the Commerce Department labs on the south end of Boulder. Although she dressed the part—her work outfits nailed the nerd at the National Institute of Standards look—she was actually a generationally misplaced hippie. She spent a lot of emotional energy looking back over her shoulder at decades and opportunities she was sure she had squandered while following rules and guidelines her instincts had long told her to ignore.

She started that day's session by telling me she hadn't slept well. She punctuated the comment by pressing the side of her fist against the center of her chest at the top of her rib cage. Reflux, she thought.

"I had a dream, too. I should talk about that."

From another patient that transition might have sounded like a loose association. But not from her. She would never have wanted me to think of her as someone who wasted my time complaining about heartburn and insomnia. Or work, or friends. Or her husband. She wanted me to think of her as a patient dedicated to growth and change.

Ten minutes into our session she suddenly exclaimed, "Oh my!" in a high voice that caused me to think of Dorothy and of lions and tigers and bears. She—my patient, not Dorothy—sucked in a quick volume of air, held that breath, and pushed the knuckles of both fists into her upper abdomen. She closed her eyes in a tight wince. Moisture began shining through the powder she had dusted near her temples.

I thought, *Oh shit.* I had witnessed one heart attack in my life. What I was observing looked completely different from that earlier MI.

But it felt exactly the same.

I said her name as I stood to offer help. She began to stand with me but crashed to the floor before I got close enough to break her fall.

By the time I slid the coffee table out of the way and dropped to my knees beside her, she was unresponsive. I felt her neck for a pulse. I did not find one. I listened for a breath. I did not detect one.

I thought I was keeping cool, reacting well to the crisis, at least initially. I checked her airway before I called 911. Help on the way, I readied myself to start CPR.

I placed my hands between her breasts.

And that's when my progress stalled.

I was stumped trying to remember anything at all about a Bee Gees song that I was confident I detested. It was likely that I detested the entire Bee Gees catalog, but confirming that fact would have required a grand review, something I would be reluctant to do in any circumstance and not something that was a good use of my time given where my hands and my attention resided at that moment.

The specific Bee Gees song I was trying to recall had been featured in an online article that had identified it as the perfect song to recall in moments like the one I was experiencing.

*Oh God, what is it?* The song's lyrics had something-something in them about a mother and a brother that never made any sense to me. *Shit!*

*Two inches. One hundred beats. Yes!* The article suggested two-inch chest compressions with each thrust, and one hundred compressions during each minute of CPR. The purpose of that particular Bee Gees song was to help find the rhythm that would achieve that target pace of one hundred beats a minute.

Suddenly, I recalled the chorus: *Ah, ha, ha, ha, stayin' alive.*

The chorus led me to the beat: out loud, I started singing, "Ba, ba, ba, ba. Ba, ba, ba, ba," to time my compressions. When the clock indicated I was nearing four minutes of CPR, I paused and lowered my ear to my patient's mouth to listen for breath sounds while I spread my fingertips on her neck to search for a pulse.

I found neither. When the EMTs arrived moments later, I was feeling no confidence at all that my patient was, well, staying alive.

The instant the ambulance departed, I called Daniel, my patient's husband. I knew from her psychotherapy that she felt certain he'd been having a long-term affair with a woman who was a customer of his bicycle shop in Longmont. "I know who she is," my patient had told me. "She has this . . . great butt, and calves that are . . ." She did not finish that sentence. "Some of us can't spend all our time in spinning classes."

She and Daniel were discussing separation.

I explained to Daniel that his wife had collapsed in my office after suffering chest pains. I told him that her heart was beating and that she had begun breathing on her own by the time the ambulance left for Community Hospital.

Daniel said he was on his way there.

# THREE

---

I considered my options and decided that I didn't want Sam to be waiting impatiently for me to finish my visit. I would see my patient last, just before I headed home.

To Sam, I said, "I'm here, let's get it done. Who do you want me to eyeball?"

Sam hooked a thumb over his shoulder toward the ICU. I counted six occupied beds out of eight. He said, "He's the one in this little glass room."

Inside the isolation room I saw bandages covering many of the parts of a humanoid form that a bedsheet did not. I saw tubes and monitors and drains. I didn't see much of a patient. Some fingernails, darkened with dried blood, poked out from beneath a thick pad of gauze on one hand. I could see eyebrows, too. Dark. One undamaged cheek and eye, and a little more than half of a chin. The patient's neck was held rigid in a big plastic collar. What little hair was visible was curly and dark.

I was confident I was seeing man-fingernails and man-eyebrows. The rest of Sam's guy's face was obscured by tubes, large and small, and tape. Lots of tape. I counted a central line and a pair of visible IV lines, one in each arm. Two IV pumps. One was flushing a fresh bag of saline—*drip, drip, drip, drip*—as though the pump were keeping time to the Bee Gees anthem I no longer had a prayer of getting out of my head.

A second pump was locked. It was dispensing a measured dose of some narcotic in a fat syringe. Dilaudid or morphine.

Catheters snaked out from beneath the sheet to clear plastic drain bags hung on the side of the bed. One of the collection bags had to be for urine, but none of the fluid in any of the waste bags was even a close approximation of yellow. The absence of yellow fluid in any of the drain bags was not a good leading indicator about the state of the patient's kidneys or bladder. The deep-brown tones I spotted were not ideal colors for urine.

An EKG monitored the man's heart rhythm. Other than that flat was bad, I had no idea what the peaks and valleys dancing on an EKG screen indicated. The blood pressure numbers on the monitor were hovering on the low side of very low.

I went with the obvious. "He's not well. Is there an infection risk?"

"Nah. The iso is for us. Easier from a security point

of view. If they get a patient who needs the room, he'll get bumped. I'm thinking he's not aware of the upgrade."

I didn't argue the point; the guy looked like the definition of unconscious to me. "Is he sleeping? Sedated? Unconscious?"

"The paramedics originally thought he was slizzered. Now? An intensivist told the nurses that she thought this was the initial stage of coma."

"'Slizzered'? Is that what you said? That's a new one for me."

"Think drunk and simultaneously plastered on energy drinks. The alcohol-and-caffeine thing, or the alcohol-and-Adderall thing, or the meth-and-anything thing that the young and the stupid seem to favor. We round up slizzered kids every weekend on The Hill. Most of them don't end up looking like this, though."

"Never thought I'd be taking popular culture lessons from you."

Sam shook his head. "Right? Guess I have a finger on the pulse of today's youth."

I couldn't tell if he was serious. Prudence told me to live with the ambiguity.

Sam smiled in a wry way that got my attention. "I'm never sure what's important anymore. Things that seem crucial aren't. Things that I used to overlook? They come back and nip at my ass."

I thought Sam might have been offering the beginning notes of a philosophical reflection. Before I could encourage him to continue, a uniformed Boulder cop came through the door with two containers of coffee, one for Sam. She said, "Thanks, Detective. I needed that rest stop."

Sam asked about the fire. She told him it was "blowing up." Houses were still burning up Sunshine Canyon. She took a seat about ten feet away, facing the corridor that led to the elevators. Her chosen spot was midway between the entry to the nursing station and the door to the airlock vestibule of the isolation room.

"Guard?" I asked.

"For now." Sam pulled his phone from his coat pocket. He was a recent smart phone adopter and operated the thing with the fervor of a religious convert. In a matter of a few months—since the day he dragged me with him to Best Buy while he selected a replacement for his dead clamshell—he'd crammed the digital records of his life, both personal and law enforcement, into his new slab. I watched in admiration as he worked the device with the dexterity and assurance of a thirteen-year-old girl. I found it all extremely disconcerting.

Sam had selected a photograph for me to view on his phone. "Recognize that?" he asked as he turned the screen my way. The picture seemed to have been taken by the phone's camera; it had that sickly lighting that comes with close-up LED flash.

"You couldn't have just sent this to me?"

"Work with me here. There's protocol. We got no ID on our vic. Because the crash was in the evacuation zone, we have no forensics. We got no wits to what happened—"

"Are you thinking whatever caused his injuries wasn't an accident?"

"There was definitely an accident. But as compassionate a guy as I am, I don't tend to hang at the bedsides of traffic accident John Does."

"What then? Assault?"

"Assault implies motive. I don't know from motive. Civilians tend to miss that nuance. Let's start with battery."

"You're really going to diss me while you're asking for my help?"

"The cop at the scene thought the guy was beat to crap. Before the accident, during the accident, after the accident? Undetermined. If that's what came down, we're talking battery. One theory is that he was beat to crap—batterized—in one location, stuffed into the front seat of a car, and then the stuffer tried to rig things so that the car would go over a cliff. That would disguise said battery so that it did not look like assault. But the car found the trunk of a tree before it found the edge of the cliff."

"Sounds complicated," I said.

"First part may have worked. The rest? Best-laid plans and all that. I think I told you once that the second rule of criminals"—my ears perked up when Sam mentioned one of his "second rules"; experience told me I found them amusing—"is that they are always either smarter than cops give them credit for, or they're stupider than cops give them credit for. If the perp responsible for this is stupider than I think, he needs daily assistance figuring out which end of the spoon holds the soup."

I composed a mental picture. "You'll catch him?"

He shrugged. "Eh. Sometimes the stupid ones do such unexpected stuff that we end up a step behind 'em because we're using logic and they're not. That's kind of where you come in." I was thinking I should be offended. Sam went on. "See, the object in this freakin' "—Sam raised his phone—"photo was found near the vic. We don't have much else. We're four hours into this case and the trail is going cold."

I looked at the photo. "You found that on him?"

"Not on. Let's say it was close by."

"A car means registration. Registration means a clue. Identity."

He smiled. "Nice try. Car isn't currently registered. Possibly not even street legal. Last registered owner is twice this guy's age."

"Where is Lucy?" I asked. Lucy was Sam's partner.

"Even though she hates canvassing like she hates shaving her legs, she hates hospitals more than all that. She's out talking to people. Trying to find a wit, or a lead."

I reached out to adjust Sam's phone to get a better look at the photo. He yanked it back. He was protective of his smart phone. "Humor me, please, Alan. I have to do this the way I have to do this in case someday your wife or one of her DA colleagues or God forbid some member of the defense bar gets around to asking me some pointed questions under oath. So I say to you again: do you recognize any item in that photograph?"

The photograph was a close-up of a business card. Beside the card was a quarter. The quarter, I assumed, had been inserted into the frame to provide scale.

"You know that's my business card. Don't think it's my quarter."

Sam yawned. He'd had a surprising amount of dental work done in his lifetime.

"Figured," Sam said. "And, no, it's not your quarter."

"If you're hoping that's one of my patients sprawled out in there, sorry, but—"

He held up a hand. "I'm praying he's one of your all-time favs. Are you allowed to have favorites? Anyway—it would be a Vegas jackpot for me if it also turns out that you're busy formulating some magic exception to the doctor-patient confidentiality crapola that you usually use to tell me you can't talk to me about your work."

He smiled in a way that I'd come to recognize always meant something other than that he was happy.

"I want a name, Alan. Age. Phone number. Address. E-mail. Facebook friends. Twitter feed. Anything? Next of kin? Great. Significant other? I'll take a girlfriend or even a boyfriend—I'm becoming so damn open-minded, I'm good with either. Hell, I'm even good with both. Or maybe he has an enemies list he shared with you during a truly poignant session. That'd be like a wet dream for me."

Sam wasn't one for dramatic soliloquies. I savored what I was hearing. But in reply, I merely shrugged. Odds were that I didn't know the guy. And if I did know the guy, I knew him clinically, which meant I wouldn't be able to tell Sam anything due to Sam's recurring nightmare about my profession—doctor-patient privilege.

As much as Sam didn't want any of that to be true, Sam knew that it was all, likely, true. Even the fact that the guy in the coma was in treatment with me—if he was in treatment with me—would be privileged. If he was not a patient, if he'd never been a patient, I could tell Sam that fact. The null set was covered neither by my professional ethics nor by my legal responsibilities.

There had been a time, way back when Sam and I had first met over the death of one of my patients, when I didn't question the ethical mandates of clinical psychology. That day had passed. I wasn't sure that Sam had recognized the evolution of my ethical thinking. He hadn't shown any indication he had figured out a way to exploit it.

"The guy?" Sam said. "He's a mess. Closed head trauma. That's the biggie. They apparently used a fat bit in some big-ass Makita to bore a couple of holes in his skull to relieve pressure from a subdural or two. Internal bleeding in his gut. Something about one of his lungs. Fractures? Plural. Ribs? Yep. Collarbone? Yep. Dislocations, couple. Hip? Ankle? Some concern he may have lost the vision in that eye that's bandaged."

"Can I take a closer look? See if I recognize him."

"I didn't think you would bother. I'm getting all hopeful." He patted his chest with his open palm. "Like a little flutter in my heart." Sam took a step toward the nursing station. He stopped. "Oh, I forgot, he has a tat. You can check that."

"Tell me."

"Medium size. Tricep. Left arm."

"Of?"

Sam shook his head. "You know I don't get tats—I

mean, I don't understand tats, aesthetically speaking. Exactly what it was he thought was of such enduring value that he had it engraved in indelible ink on his freakin' arm? Well, I got nothing."

The tattoo rant was virgin territory, certainly a highlight of my miserable day.

Sam wasn't done. "It's some tattoo bullshit—a Siberian carving that represents ice-cold Satan. Or the Saturnian symbol for *namaste*. We uploaded the ink to iTat. We'll probably even get a hit on the specific parlor and a photo of the artist. Bet you a beer the guy has priors."

"The victim?"

"I was thinking the artist. Both."

"iTat?"

He raised his phone. "Latest law enforcement app. Just out in beta. You want a link? For that night when your sweet daughter walks in with her virgin ink."

My heart skipped a beat. Gracie? *Probably. Jeez.* "Sure. Send me the link."

Sam guffawed. "Joke, Alan. iTat? Come on."

I applauded. "Just to be clear, if it turns out I know him, I can't acknowledge it. You know that."

"Yeah, but I also know you have wiggle room. Maybe you can't talk to me, but you can go back to your files and call his emergency contact." Sam smiled that smile that confused me, the one that didn't mean he was anything resembling happy. "Then the emergency contact and I can have a chat."

Sam was a few moves ahead of me, not an unusual occurrence.

He went on. "Come on, I'll introduce you, or reintroduce you, as the case may be. Need to warn you, though—he's quiet. Makes no eye contact whatsoever."

The ward clerk didn't look up from the *Us Weekly* she was reading as she said, "I told you before, no visitors, Detective. No exceptions." She put her index finger down to hold her spot. From the photos, I thought the article was about the British royals. She looked up at Sam. Then at me. "Except for law enforcement. Is he law enforcement?"

Sam sighed again. He wasn't usually much of a sigher. To the clerk, he said, "Dr. Gregory's with me. He's an important part of my investigation."

I was suspicious. Sam rarely called me "doctor" unless there was an obvious pejorative context.

The ward clerk mounted an officious face and cocked her head to display it for Sam. I could tell she liked the officious face; she wore it as though it were a mask she was trying on prior to heading off to a costume party. But she worked the night shift, probably seven P to seven A. With the docs gone by six and the visitors out at eight, her opportunities to be officious during the quiet hours of her long shift were few.

I suspected that she secretly lived for moments like the one we were having.

I decided to intervene. I held out my hand. "Dr. Alan Gregory. I'm a psychologist. And—here's the good news—I am on the hospital medical staff."

She didn't shake my hand. She was disappointed at the unexpected turn of events. "Got a business card, *Dr.* Gregory? I have to write you down."

Sam chuckled at the business card irony. I gave the clerk—her ID told me her name was Imogen—one of my business cards.

**Alan Gregory, Ph.D., P.C.**
Clinical Psychology
*By appointment only*

I handed one to Sam, too. "Compare them," I said. "The one you found near your vic's body is my old card. From before I turned my practice into a professional corporation, a P.C. The one you have says Alan Gregory, Ph.D. Back then I was a sole proprietor. Now my practice is a professional corporation."

He said, "Way too much information, Alan."

The clerk said, "You're a Ph.D.? Not an M.D.," completely missing my point.

Sam smiled at his shoes. He pulled reading glasses from his breast pocket and stuffed them onto his face. The lenses were so filthy I had to fight an impulse to clean them. "How old is the old card?" he asked.

"Three and a half years. Four," I said.

"Ah shit, that's ancient."

# FOUR

"Do I need to gown?" I asked Imogen.

Imogen said, "Yes, and gloves. The M.D.s all know that."

Sam leaned in and whispered, "The one who was on before her said we didn't."

I took a thin gown from a tall pile and pulled it over my shoulders. I raised a mask by one of its straps and dangled it toward Imogen. I knew she had an eye on me.

Her peripheral vision was impressive. She said, "Nope. We got laminar flow."

Sam whispered, "Whatever that is." He pulled out his phone and started a Google search for "laminar flow." The reflexive Web searching was a new compulsion.

Sam gowned and gloved, too. The grand pastiche— the big pale-yellow sheet of fabric, the odd-toned turquoise gloves, and Sam's huge, slightly pink, fleshy head—left him looking like an artist's impression of a diseased manatee.

We crossed the small vestibule and entered the room. The left side of the man's face was uninjured. After checking to be certain Imogen wasn't watching, Sam pulled the sheet down to the guy's waist. John Doe's abdomen was swollen, bruised, and bandaged. His right shoulder and arm were covered with padding and immobilized by a sling, but the left arm was free. He wore a ring on the swollen pinkie of his left hand.

I didn't recognize the signet—nor did I see anything familiar about the left side of the man's face or the unbandaged parts of his torso. Sam lifted the man's left arm, exposing the tattoo, raising his eyebrows inquisitively. Sam had the kind of eyebrows that tested the nesting instincts of small birds.

"Sorry, Sam. I'm drawing a blank. Maybe a letter of some kind."

"What language?"

"Hebrew maybe. Cyrillic?"

"You just acting smart?"

"Yeah. I'm guessing."

"Figured. Give me your guess on age."

"Without the edema . . . I would say early thirties. Maybe late twenties."

Sam was holding his turquoise-gloved hands in front of him palms up, cupped one into the other, like a preacher who was standing outside his church greeting worshippers as they exited services during flu season.

"We done here?" I said. "Not that I'm not enjoying myself, but I could use some sleep."

He shushed me. I sighed.

Imogen stepped away in the direction of the waiting room.

Sam popped his head out the door to talk to the uniformed officer. He raised his phone. "I'm not getting a signal. Will you step down the hall and call Detective Davenport and let her know that the ID we were waiting on was negative? Thanks. She's waiting to hear." The officer pulled a phone from her belt as she, too, stepped away.

Sam stuffed a loose pillow from the bed over the microphone of the nurse-call contraption on the bedrail. He taped a doubled-over washcloth onto the microphone on the communications panel behind the bed. He looked in all directions for stray ears. He said, "Need to ask you something . . . off topic."

His voice had turned from businesslike to somber. I said, "Sure."

"Did Lauren say anything to you?"

"She's not catching tonight, Sam. I doubt she even knows about this guy."

Lauren was my deputy DA wife, which made her a County of Boulder prosecutor. Sam was my City of Boulder detective friend. Their paths and their jurisdictions crossed regularly, but neither their jurisdictions nor their interests exactly coincided.

I was mostly what they had in common.

Sam dropped the volume. "I'm not talking about Sleepy Doe here, I'm talking about . . . developments with our old friend Fred."

*Sleepy Doe?* Cops are nickname masters. The monikers often have the perfect touch of irreverence. "Fred?" I said.

"Come on. A little concentration, please. I'm talking about *Frederick?*"

*Oh God.* I gagged as though I'd just discovered a hair ball.

The isolation room in the ICU disappeared from my awareness and I found myself standing inside the lattice of an old aluminum phone booth that was missing not only its entire accordion door but also every pane of its glass.

The anachronistic booth was adjacent to an equally decrepit abandoned filling station on a rarely traveled road on a hillside outside of Los Alamos, New Mexico, not far from the home of a woman who bred adorable Havanese puppies.

Sam was on the other end of the call delivering, most reluctantly, a detail-deprived story about what he had just done inside a rented house outside the once-small Weld County town of Frederick, Colorado. His telling of the tale was obtuse enough that I'd had difficulty making sense of the narrative. That I didn't get all the progressions didn't faze Sam. His sole goal was that his audience—that was me, though he made it clear he would have preferred no audience at all—knew how the story ended.

On the walk back to the breeder's home, I constructed a few alternative scenarios about how Sam had ultimately coerced a woman named Justine Winter Brown—he knew her as Currie, and he knew her biblically—from point *a*, living, to point *b*, dead, and how he had managed to leave the body and the scene so that it would appear to any future law enforcement investigator that the death was the result of Currie's suicide.

Sam repeated his earlier question. "Has Lauren said anything?"

I had to be sure. I said, "You're talking about—"

"Yeah," he said. He didn't want me to finish my sentence.

Some weeks after Jonas and I returned from New Mexico with his new Havanese puppy—Callie then, Fiji later—Sam had dropped by the house with a public-record copy of Justine Brown's postmortem. The document included the Weld County medical examiner's conclusion about the cause and manner of her death. The manner was suicide. When I was done reading, Sam took the paper from my hands, shredded it into pieces, doused the scraps with lighter fluid in my grill, and set the scraps ablaze.

I tried to swallow down the acid in my throat, but I was parched from the imaginary hair ball. Sam and I hadn't talked about Frederick in years. *Have we ever talked about Frederick?* In the way that we talk about the Avs' defensive woes or the Nuggets' chronic problem with bigs? We had not. The sedate burg of Frederick, on a forlorn patch of dirt on the edge of the Great Plains, didn't invade too many of my day-to-day conversations.

I stammered. "No, Sam, she hasn't said—What would she—I mean . . ."

"What about you? You've never? Not once?" he asked. "I have to ask, Alan. To anyone? Not to your therapist? Or your priest?"

"Not once. I have never said a word."

"Lauren doesn't know?"

"Not from me." I wanted to tell Sam that it still broke my heart that I hadn't told her.

Sam joined me on the left side of the bed. He faced the nursing station with his hands still cupped in the I-may-be-a-man-of-the-cloth-but-I-want-nothing-to-do-with-your-germs pose. He was eager to know the moment either the uniform or Imogen returned.

Sam lowered his voice even further. "There's talk of reopening things."

*Shit.* "Why?"

He turned his head. Our eyes met. "New evidence of some kind. I'm thinking I shouldn't have used Tyvek."

"What?"

"I can't be spotted poking around out there. All I know is that something's up and there's a Boulder connection. Your wife is the deputy DA whose name is attached."

"She hasn't given me the slightest hint about it. What kind of activity?"

"Frederick is Weld County. That means I'm in the dark. The death took place just outside the city limits, so this could be in the hands of either a sheriff's investigator or an investigator from the DA. Weld DA is chronically short-staffed—they've been shanghaiing Greeley detectives for help with cases. I know a couple of those guys. If they're on this, I might be able to learn more. But now? I don't have shit. Thus, this conversation."

"I thought this was over. It's been years. Since . . . Adrienne died."

My dear friend and neighbor Adrienne had died in a terrorist explosion in Israel just before Currie's death in Frederick. The events were in lockstep in my memory.

Sam added to the night's heap of sighs. "Want to know the second rule of homicide?"

I said, "Sure." For the longest time Sam had referred to his peculiar tenets as "first rules." Since his return from a trip to Florida to attend his ex-girlfriend's daughter's engagement party—a relationship obli-cation that had unsettled him in profound ways I did not comprehend—I had noticed changes: The sheer number of precepts was exploding. And they had lost their primacy. They had become second rules. Not first.

Many were cop rules. Most of the rest were about sports, with a strong bias toward hockey. Some of the most memorable had to do with parenting, or women. The final few, save a stray or two, involved fishing in lakes, frozen and not.

I was also confident that, as often as not, he made the rules up on the spot.

Sam said, "The second rule of homicide is the body never stays buried."

"Last time you mentioned that one, it was a first rule," I said.

"I was cocky for a while," he said. "I had an experience that humbled me."

"The trip to Florida, right? That woman I met on the Mall? She's why you got humble?"

He shook his head. "Off-limits. I no longer assume that I know all the rules. I'm leaving room for important shit I might not know."

I wanted to know what had humbled him. My money remained on Florida and the woman who had surprised him in Boulder after his return. Her name was Deirdre. I gave some thought to whether or not Sam was in an introspective mood. I decided he was not.

"Anyway, I share the second rule of homicide with perps to try to help them deal with how discombobulated they are to be wearing my handcuffs while listening to my Grammy-winning rendition of Miranda. I tell them that the body never stays buried."

"The body in question that didn't stay buried? Currie's?"

"I'm talking metaphorical bodies right now."

I considered taking another shot, but my self-protective instincts were kicking in.

Sam said, "Did his eyes move? Do people in comas have REM sleep?"

The man's eyes looked still. "I don't think anyone's home, Sam."

He winced. "I thought using the Tyvek was genius. That night? I was worried about getting caught *that night*. The Tyvek was to keep my DNA out of that cottage and to keep her trace evidence off of me. Nothing works better for that than Tyvek. I didn't think enough about the long-term consequences. That the stuff never dies."

"Tyvek is the white stuff they use to make those indestructible envelopes?"

"Yeah. And to weatherseal the outside of new buildings. Can't tear it, can't burn it. Repels water, mold. Probably stops nuclear attack and locusts. When interplanetary archaeologists find the residue of this planet, they'll find all this shit we called Tyvek. It'll be a big deal a thousand years from now. Trust me."

I could foresee a second rule of interplanetary archaeology, but I kept it to myself.

"I borrowed the Tyvek jumpsuit I wore from a stash at a chaotic crime scene a long time ago. It was a someday-maybe thing. Even had a hood. Now? I'm sure it's the only possible evidence that could have survived this long."

"You think Weld County has it?"

"I'm thinking I'm not as smart as I thought."

"Are you going back for it?"

He didn't answer. "You're sure Lauren hasn't said anything? Not even a hint?"

"No. Lauren's in a good place. Her health has been stable. She's making plans for her daughter—Sofie, the one in Holland I've never met—to make an extended visit to Boulder. She's excited about maybe moving to town. I swear she drives by the *Camera* building every day either before work or after. She's been optimistic. A good change."

Sam changed the subject. "I don't know shit about real estate, Alan. But that big redevelopment? In this economy? Don't hold your breath. You guys are not moving to town for a long, long time. Maybe not ever, to that project."

I knew there was truth to what Sam was saying. Though I didn't want to admit it, the redevelopment of the prime land in downtown Boulder was a speculative play. Lauren, unfortunately, had grown completely cathected to the idea of living at Eleventh and Pearl. I did not want to be the one holding the pin when her balloon burst.

Sam said, "The good Lord knows I shouldn't be giving financial advice."

The good Lord did know that. Given that He probably didn't share Sam's recent humility epiphany, the good Lord might even consider it a first rule. Excluding the Commandments' prohibition about worshipping false idols, of course, the Lord had shown little use for second rules. I said, "But?"

"Unless you guys have a pot of gold you've never told me about, you'll be in way over your heads in that building. When it gets built. If it gets built."

"We're counting on Spanish Hills selling for a good profit."

"If Spanish Hills goes up in value, the place downtown does, too. You make more in one, you'll spend more in the other."

"You've given this a lot of thought, Sam."

"Not this. Chasing. I've given chasing a lot of thought. It's part of my humility thing. You're chasing, Alan. You're swinging at breaking balls out of the strike zone."

I made a noise that I intended to be an acknowledgment.

Sam wasn't done. "Your friend Raoul? It's his project, right?" I nodded. "Raoul's a golden boy. The goldenest boy in town. He's pretty, smart, charming, rich, successful. He's all tens. If I could think of more adjectives, he'd probably end up a ten-by-ten. That building where you want to live is being built for people like him and his ten-tens friends. And for a few suckers who think they're all tens, too, but aren't.

"Don't be one of them."

# FIVE

Imogen waltzed back into Imogen Central. She had a half-liter bottle of Diet Mountain Dew cradled under her arm and was using both hands to carry a small mountain of hospital food that was crowned with a bushel of french fries. The brief break from duty had done her mood good; she displayed a spring to her step I hadn't noticed earlier. Her hair was moving as she walked and her hips revealed a sashay that hadn't been apparent during her departure, when she'd marched away as though it were her sworn duty to keep a pencil from falling to the ground from between her butt cheeks.

Imogen glanced at us as though she was concerned that we coveted her meal.

Sam said, "Let's get out of here."

I said, "Don't forget the pillow and the washcloth."

"Thanks." Sam pulled the pillow off of the microphone on the nurse call contraption and then stuffed it right back into place. He leaned in so that his lips were inches from my ears. "My house used to have one of those whole-house intercom systems," he said. "Popular in the fifties and sixties."

I was befuddled by that headline, as though I'd somehow completely missed a clever segue. I was also mildly surprised at the bald facts. Sam's house was modest in all ways, and most certainly in size—a thousand square feet, tops. An intercom system was hardly a domestic necessity; a slightly raised voice would have sufficed for any routine family communication. I assumed Sam had a point to make, so I said, "Go on."

"The master panel is still in the kitchen, below the wall phone."

"You have a wall phone?"

"Don't get distracted, Alan. Not germane. The intercom system had a radio in it. Back in the day, you could play the radio in all the rooms in the house at once. AM or FM, like an iPod dock for the sock-hop generation. High-tech for its time. Folks who built the place probably listened to Elvis and Buddy Holly on it. Heard their first Beatles tune. Casey Kasem's Top Forty. Cool to think about. Fights used to be on the radio, too. Everybody could listen at once. Owners probably showed it off to the neighbors."

I didn't spot the allure of sitting in separate rooms listening to the same fight.

"Pay attention. Draw a picture in your head. There are four screws. Brass. One in each corner of the faceplate. Remove them." Sam's whisper was hoarse and reminiscent of the sick Brando in *The Godfather*—had Puzo set his story in Hibbing, Minnesota. "There's a sheet-metal box inside that holds the brains. Brains are busted. But the thing had transistors. Cutting-edge. Top of the box was louvered. Got all that? Even with transistors, it generated some heat, and—"

"There's a point, yes?" My whisper lacked character compared to Sam's. I knew that. An old girlfriend had included the fact that I was not a captivating whisperer on her list of reasons for dumping me. I'd been self-conscious about my whispering ever since.

"You'll need a way into the house. The key is in a magnetic key box that's stuck below the downspout extension by the back door. Can't see it, you have to feel for it."

"Downspouts are galvanized, Sam. Magnets don't work."

"They do if you use a strong enough magnet"—the word came out "maggot"—"and you put a big fat metal washer inside. Pretty smart, huh?"

"Genius."

He either missed or ignored my sarcasm. He said, "The faceplate is off. If you reach up and in on your left—it's easiest to reach in with your right hand—you'll be able to feel an S-hook. Grab it good. It's going to feel heavy. You let it slip and the next tool you're going to need is a sledgehammer or a Sawzall. With me?"

I said, "Yes," but it was a lie. My visualizing capacity was impaired by my fatigue, by the *bzzz-whrrrr* of Sleepy Doe's medical equipment, and by Imogen's determined assault on French Fry Mountain.

"The hook has nylon line on it. Once you have the weight on the line secure in your hand, reach in with your other hand to push the louver up. It's hinged."

"Why is it hinged?"

"I don't know. Fish up what's hanging on the line. Still with me?"

From a what-the-hell-are-you-talking-about perspective, I was completely lost. I was ready to go home, so I chose the path of least resistance. I said, "Sure."

"You're going to end up with a mesh bag in your hand. Nylon. In it is a piece of oilcloth wrapping"—his voice got even quieter—"a thirty-two Magnum. That's a revolver. Compact. Easier to handle than a thirty-eight." Sam paused. "It's had a tough life."

"Like you," I said.

He shifted his big head a few degrees so that he was looking me right in the eyes. We were six inches from iris to iris, no more than that. "You'll also find about a dozen rounds of ammo. A few spent shells. Three, four, five, tops. And a couple of slugs from that same handgun."

"Slugs?"

"Used bullets. Fired from that weapon."

I was hearing big news. Sam had just handed me a treasure map to a sophisticated hiding place where he'd stashed an unregistered handgun. Guns like the ones he was describing were called "throwdowns" by cops. Along with the .32, Sam had also collected and stashed ballistic evidence that he could choose to scatter—say, at a problematic crime scene—should he perceive a need.

I'm not as naïve about the lives of police officers as I

once was. Since I began to know Sam, I'd learned about the pressures and ambiguities in cops' experiences. Some cops have throwdowns. Some cops don't. I had considered the possibility that Sam had used a throwdown that night he visited Frederick. The woman who died that night was shot—at Sam's insistence, with Sam's assistance—through the brain stem with a slug from a handgun. Sam had either known Currie had her own weapon, or he had brought a handgun to the scene and then left it behind in order to complete the self-inflicted-gunshot ruse. The leaving-behind part would have been imperative, seeing that people who have shot themselves through the brain stem don't have the wherewithal, or the time, to dispose of a weapon.

I maintained my cool. I asked, "Why are you telling me this, Sam?"

"Take a look at Sleepy Doe. Shit like this makes me think about my mortality."

I did as I was told. Other than a twitch in Sleepy Doe's left eyelid, he hadn't moved a muscle since we'd entered. I was growing ever more convinced that Sleepy Doe was in the process of becoming Coma Doe.

I asked, "The thirty-two? Did you have one like it with you in Frederick?"

"Different conversation. Nobody's looking for the thirty-two in my intercom. Okay?"

"Is it registered?"

"I'm sure it was. Once. Not your concern." He leaned in closer to me. "If I ever—ever—get within shouting distance of having as little hope of getting my life back as

Sleepy Doe has this minute, I want you to know how to get to that thirty-two."

*Holy shit. Do not ask me to participate in your end-of-life bargain. I cannot go there again. I can't.* I said, "Sam. I don't want to talk about this."

"And I do? Here's my dying wish: I want you to pick your moment carefully. That's going to be the hard part. Finding the moment. But before, do your homework at a public computer. You're looking for directions on where to aim. I don't want to die in the hospital, so if we're lucky—you and me—I'll be home. I'll probably be a gork. You'll wear gloves—there are always gloves wherever there's a gork—and you'll wear long sleeves that you stuff down under the cuff of the gloves to prevent GSR getting on you."

"GSR?" The second I asked I remembered what it meant.

"Gunshot residue. Evidence. Don't wear a dress shirt. There's a gap in the sleeves on dress shirts. You take one shot. You walk out calmly. You ditch the gun over two blocks away. Keep it simple and natural. Wash your clothes. Even your shoes. Wash three pairs of shoes. Not just the ones you were wearing. Like it's a chore you do."

I was about to ask why I would own three pairs of washable shoes. I didn't. I said, "Shut up, Sam. I do not want to think about—"

Sam thought I was being squeamish. He reached up with his gloved hand and pulled my chin toward him. "Promise me you'll do this. I do not want Simon to spend his life wasting Sunday afternoons making obligation visits to his gorked father in some miserable fucking nursing home."

*God only really knows. Gork.* I removed the pillow from the microphone in an attempt to shut Sam up. I smoothed it and placed it near Sleepy Doe's head. I walked out of the room in a way that an observer might have described as "storming out of the room"—first stripping off the gloves, and then ripping off the gown as though the thing had been contaminated.

"Try Lucy," I said. "Maybe she'll help. Don't ask me again."

Imogen's mouth was full. She tried to mumble, "Do what?" but didn't quite manage it.

I left Sam in the ICU to return to the Coronary Care Unit for the final time that day. The nurse who had sent me away twice earlier stepped out of a patient room before I made it all the way to the nursing station.

I thought I was about to be sent away again. But her eyes softened.

She stopped walking. I stopped walking. She said, "I'm so sorry."

My shoulders dropped. I was stunned. I said, "Really?"

She offered an it-happens face. "She had a lot of muscle damage. Sometimes . . . people just have too much damage. I'm sorry."

*That could be a second rule of life. Sometimes people have too much damage.*

The nurse gestured down the hall. "Her husband is here. I'm sure he could use the support."

She excused herself and walked into another patient room. To her, ours had been a routine encounter in the corridors of the CCU. Not for me. I felt glued to the carpet.

I watched a woman emerge from the elevator vestibule across the corridor. She rushed into the arms of a man standing outside a patient room door. The man looked defeated.

He almost failed to catch her.

The woman said, "Daniel! I came as soon as I could."

# SIX

A guy sitting in the hospital lobby confirmed that Olde Stage had been evacuated.

"Lee Hill, too?" I asked.

"Yeah. Pine Brook. Wagonwheel Gap. Left Hand. It's bad up there."

A forced evacuation in advance of the Fourmile Fire would mark a fresh notch on Diane's recent log of trauma. I was no longer confident in her ability to bounce back. If she wasn't at the end of her rope, she could reach the end of the rope from where she was holding on.

If the fire took her house? *God.* I tried her cell again. She didn't answer, again.

I forced myself into the moment. My shock and sadness over my patient's death. The scope of the tragedy unfolding behind town.

Sam's damn intercom.

I didn't make much progress before Sam caught up with me. With texting and GPS, the game of tag was no longer the same challenge it had been when I was a kid.

He was waiting at my car. "Lucy dropped me off. I need a ride."

"You live three blocks away. You could be home already, playing with your vintage intercom."

"I'm not going home."

I didn't want company, but the police department was on my way. "Get in."

He got in. "Ophelia has my car. Hers is in the shop. All I need is to sit beside you while you drive home. Simon is with Sherry tonight."

Simon was Sam's adolescent son. Sherry was Sam's occasionally adolescent ex-wife. Sam, of course, was Sherry's occasionally adolescent ex-husband.

Ophelia was my delightful new neighbor. She was an emotionally mature, generous, intuitive, and amusing woman, adolescent in no way that I'd identified. From a developmental point of view, that made her a good choice for Sam.

He turned on the radio. I turned it off. Sam and I had starkly different assessments about Taylor Swift's entertainment value. I said, "Don't ever talk to me again about your dying wishes or the revolver hanging inside your damn intercom. Understand?"

"No," he said evenly. "I don't understand."

"I have some experience with this issue that I can't discuss. Okay? Now do you understand?" Sam would recognize my privileged-communication shorthand.

"I don't. I know you've thought about this. Tell me why I shouldn't bring it up."

"It's off-limits. Let it go."

Sam wasn't fond of my limits. "We could make a pact. Whoever goes first?"

"I swear I'll pull over."

He laughed. "And then, what? You think you can muscle me out of your car?"

I needed to change the subject. The alternative was opening a tender wound I wasn't prepared to reopen. "Since we're talking about awkward things, there's something I want to tell you. Please don't get weird about this, but Ophelia has a mole I don't like. She should have it looked at. You know, by a dermatologist."

"Really?" He paused. "Go on."

"That's the thing," I said. "I—It's—"

Sam said, "The one between her breasts? Way down there?"

*God.* "Yes. That one."

He waited ten seconds before he spoke again. I pretty much ran the light at Pine Street during the interlude. He said, "Red light. You're supposed to stop at those."

"I was distracted waiting for you to slug me."

"Ophelia has moles. But the one that worries you most is the one way down in her cleavage?"

In my defense I said, "The way she dresses? It's hard to miss."

Sam laughed. "Ophelia and her wardrobe, right? God, I think I'm falling in love with that woman, but that thing she has going on? I don't know how I'm ever going to introduce Sweet O to my mother."

I was relieved. "The first week after she moved in? I didn't know how to react."

"And then?"

"At some point it's like *National Geographic*. Piaget, accommodation."

"Yeah? You just stopped noticing? How do you spell 'Piaget'?"

I said, "Basically." Sam was already Googling "Piaget."

"Hasn't happened to me, thank God. But that spot— she had it checked. It's not a mole." Sam interrupted his search for twentieth-century French developmental psychologists and pointed his smart phone in a different direction. "I have a photo in Evernote. It's a . . . here it is, a seborrheic keratosis." He held up his phone. I didn't look; I feared he was displaying a frontal shot of Ophelia's actual seborrheic keratosis, on Ophelia's actual breast. "I looked it up on the Mayo Clinic site. It's no big deal."

"It's just a . . . thing? Good then," I said. "I feel better."

He said, "Accommodation? Really? Ophelia might be broken up that you stopped noticing."

"Well, maybe not completely stopped."

Sam laughed so hard that it rocked my little car. I waited until he settled.

"The patient I was visiting?" I said. "She died."

# SEVEN

Ophelia—from our earliest introduction in the days after her trailers were towed into Spanish Hills—seemed to live her life breasts-first. From the tai chi she practiced outside to greet the dawn on temperate mornings while wearing a wife-beater that had belonged to her mysterious ex, to the late-day, head-bowed, arms-up-and-out curtsies she did to pay homage to the dance of the sun above the Rockies, Ophelia insisted that her breasts be a primary component of her persona.

Our geographic circumstances—we were neighbors across a narrow lane—dictated that I was seeing Ophelia a lot, which meant I was seeing a lot of Ophelia's breasts. It didn't take long after I first made her acquaintance to become certain that Ophelia's daily revelations were nothing sexual. She had no intent to entice, or to flirt, or to seduce. What she did—for a reason that my Ph.D. in psychology was insufficient to help me fathom, and at the end of the day the reason was none of my business—was celebrate her upper body.

When I suggested to Jonas, my son, that he try not to stare, he reminded me that I had told him after we'd seen *Shakespeare in Love* together—an experience that had left both father and son surprised at the screen time devoted to Gwyneth Paltrow's uncovered breasts—that no one had ever been hurt by gazing at a boob.

He was right. I had said that then. And I had meant it. In fact, if I had second rules of parenting sons, the gazing-at-a-boob canon would have been in contention. But the parenting I had to do at that moment was about Ophelia, so I explained to Jonas that the issue wasn't the noticing of her breasts, but the staring at them as though he'd bought a ticket to a show and they were the only members of the cast.

"It's a matter of respect," I said. "Ophelia can dress how she pleases. I don't imagine she expects you not to notice her breasts, but I think she expects that you treat them as just a part of who she is, not all of who she is."

Jonas's bewildered face conveyed his impression that I had to be kidding.

I tried an example. "Your sister has pretty hair. People compliment her on it all the time. And then they move on."

Jonas thought about it for a moment. "I got it," he said. "I should just treat Ophelia's boobs like they're there. And move on."

"Breasts, not boobs. But yes," I said.

He took two steps. "Should I tell her they're nice? Like Grace's hair?"

I still had some parenting to do.

Sam's infatuation with Ophelia may have been part of a grand Cupidian design, but I had goosed the process along.

On a classic June Front Range evening, Sam had arrived at my house for a visit. The temperature hovered in the high seventies and the humidity was in the teens. I greeted him at his old Jeep Cherokee, my back to Ophelia's temporary residence. From his perch on the driver's seat, Sam had a clear view of my new neighbor's property.

He asked, "Is the county going to allow that?"

He was seeing Ophelia's trailers for the first time. The trailers—novel to him, but not new models, not even close—had been towed down the dirt and gravel lane two weeks earlier. The delivery had to have been an elegant elephant pas de deux.

"They towed them in while we were at work. We knew some equipment was coming, but we didn't expect the double-wide. Our new neighbor moved in the next weekend. She says the housing is a temporary arrangement until construction is finished on her new place. She's going to build a little farther up the hill."

"I don't think the county allows that," Sam said. "You can't do that here. Hell, you can't do anything here. This is Boulder." He began to pull himself from his car.

I'd known Sam a long time. Despite his law enforcement responsibilities he wasn't someone who gave a lot of thought to Boulder County planning, and if he did, his predilection would not have been toward enforcement. If Sam were developing a sudden interest in the issue I could shuttle him up Sunshine Canyon toward the mountain enclave of Ward, where building-code breaches and zoning violations were a competitive sport and as much a point of civic pride as the docile dogs that roamed, and owned, the center of town. A quick jaunt through Ward would reveal enough code-abusive dwellings to keep a platoon of inspectors busy until the return of Halley's Comet.

Sam blinked twice. And then he froze, one foot on the dusty ground, one foot in the old Jeep. I watched his head lock into place a split second before I heard a screen door slam.

Ophelia, proprietress of Casa de las Dos Casas—House of the Two Houses—had just stepped outside onto the little deck adjacent to the west side of her prefabricated abode. I looked over my shoulder as she combined a cleansing breath with the beginning of a long, deep curtsy in the direction of the gathering sunset. She was wearing her ode-to-whatever outfit—a long, gauzy skirt that skimmed the tops of her bare feet and a scoop-necked, sleeveless T-shirt that was a couple of sizes too large. The T had the faded numeral 23 across the front. The curtsy was elaborate; Ophelia extended her arms while pinching the hem of the billowing skirt fabric between her thumbs and index fingers.

"That's your new neighbor?" Sam asked.

I said, "Ophelia. I like her a lot. She's going to be much better than the last ones."

"Low bar," Sam pointed out. "Your last neighbors were murderers and rapists. And arsonists. And a lawyer. There are lifers in Cañon City who have cell mates who are 'better' "—Sam used air quotes for that word—"than your last neighbors."

The last neighbors had, during their exceedingly brief residence in Spanish Hills, caused my family and me more than a few heartaches. And they, collectively, committed a plethora of felonies, including the torching of the century-plus-old farmhouse that had once stood where Ophelia's double-wide was plopped.

"Want to introduce me?" Sam asked.

Ophelia was continuing her imitation of a statue of a woman doing a curtsy. Recent experience informed me that she could hold that pose for a long time.

I think Sam was transfixed by Ophelia from that moment on. Prior to that day, he had been hanging on to a long-distance love affair that ended the way cars run out of fuel on flat ground. Gradually. Sam woke one morning to the awareness that he'd been dumped a couple of miles back. The slow death of that love didn't ease his recovery from being dumped. His reaction to Ophelia was the first indication that he had any interest in climbing back into the relationship driver's seat.

Ophelia could have that kind of effect on a single man. Even at thirty paces, given halfway-normal distance vision.

"Sure," I said. "I'm happy to introduce you. I think, maybe, you'll like her."

"Maybe?"

"She's an independent thinker," I said. "There was a time when you might have had trouble with her . . . perspective on things."

"But I've grown?" Sam said, daring me to argue. He looked at me for a moment, which meant he looked away from Ophelia for a moment. I think he took his eyes from her just to prove to himself that he could. Then he said, "Should we, I don't know, give her a chance to . . . finish what she's doing? Maybe cover up a little?"

"You mean her breasts?" By then, I was no longer bashful about Ophelia's breasts. I had come to a certain acceptance that she wasn't.

Sam said, "They're almost . . . exposed."

I was tempted to point out to Sam that if the angle were a little better, or if he stepped a little closer, he would likely discover that all the important parts were indeed available for inspection. But he would learn all that himself soon enough.

I said, "If you're waiting for Ophelia to pull on a sweater, it's not going to happen unless a cold front blows through. That outfit is pretty much par for the course. I'm thinking winter may bring a change, a genuflection to the climate, so to speak. If this makes you uncomfortable, I'll get back to you come November, introduce you then."

"Really?" Sam asked. "That's how she dresses?"

"That's a casual look. She dresses it up when she goes out. But otherwise? Yes."

"Lauren doesn't care?"

"We don't talk about Ophelia's anatomy much, but as

far as I can tell, Lauren is pro-boob, and rather amused by it all. I think Gracie coming of age might prompt a maternal reconsideration. But for now, my wife is cool. The ladies get along well."

Sam said, "Sherry would have put blinders on me. She is so not pro-boob."

I smiled at the image of Sam with blinders. "This extended curtsy will last a couple more minutes. It's her personal homage to the evening celestial show."

"Like a spiritual thing?" Sam asked.

Sam was old-school. Where spiritual inclinations were concerned, he preferred organized religion—the more organized the better, as long as it didn't involve Catholics or Mormons doing the organizing—to any free-form spirituality. Especially to any of the out-on-the-edge spiritual movements he tended to trip over from time to time in Boulder.

Boulder had rubbed off on Sam. He recognized that an occasional meal could be composed without contributions from animals. He exercised outdoors. He had learned to appreciate the nuances of the local microbrews.

But New Age anything so wasn't his thing.

"It is spiritual," I said. "But not formal. She's not a Druid, or a Wiccan, if that's what worries you. What she practices seems to be within the realm of garden-variety Boulder spirituality."

"That's supposed to be reassuring?" Sam said. "Is she Tantric?"

*Tantric?* "Would that be good, or bad? From your perspective?"

He did a little two-step. I had no idea what that was about. He said, "I've been curious. I'll admit that."

"Maybe Ophelia's your girl," I said.

His phone appeared again. He said, "I can Google it."

"No need to do that for me," I said. "Want a beer? I'd love to hear about your Tantric inclinations."

I'd pushed him too far. He said, "Don't be an asshole, Alan. And yeah, I'll take a beer. What you got?"

A stop at Liquor Mart was on my to-do list. I said, "I think all I have left is some Karma that Lauren bought."

Sam glared at me. "Is there a beer called Karma?"

"Want one or not?"

"You're kidding, right?"

I wasn't. I herded him toward the door. "Are we done talking about zoning?"

"Think so," he said, stealing a final glance toward Ophelia.

We stepped inside to a pair of dogs eager to offer their canine hellos.

"What color is Ophelia's hair, Sam?"

"Not quite as dark as Lauren's." Lauren's hair was as black as Beelzebub's soul.

I was impressed. "Just checking," I said.

"Is she a big LeBron or Michael Jordan fan?" Sam said. "The twenty-three?"

"It's not about hoops. I asked once," I said, shaking my head. "She wanted to know who they were."

By the Fourth of July, Sam and Ophelia were an item.

That Independence Day we all gathered on our roof

high above the Boulder Valley to watch the celebratory fireworks displays. Me, Lauren, Grace and Jonas, and Ophelia and Sam. Sam's son, Simon, was with his mother.

Ophelia made homemade root beer for the kids. The adults were drinking beer or a devious and deceptive cocktail Lauren concocted with Peak Spirits Eau de Vie, a potion made from organic peaches, magic, and snow-melt on the Western Slope.

I counted eighteen different displays of fireworks visible from our rooftop that year, hardly a record. The fireworks we could see were clustered mostly to the north and northeast, toward the parts of Boulder County that were on the edge of the Great Plains prairie. The only display anywhere close to the mountains that year was the one at Folsom Field on the university campus.

A wet early spring and an unseasonably dry May and June had conspired to leave the foothills grasslands crisp, and the forests around them—scarred by acre after acre of beetle-killed pine—were tinder-dry.

Everyone without a serious DSM diagnosis was being compulsive about fire.

It could have been wishful thinking on my part, but I thought that even the smokers—the only class of serial litterers still on the loose in Boulder County—were tossing fewer butts from their car windows than they had in the past.

Red Flag Warnings were posted from Pueblo all the way north to the Wyoming border.

The soon-to-arrive monsoon season, with its daily afternoon dumps of tropical moisture from the gulfs of

Mexico or California, would be a mixed blessing. The intense bursts of rain would mitigate the aridity. But the thunderstorms would spawn fierce lightning parades that could provide ignition.

It turned out that the monsoons teased that year, but they never really arrived.

As Labor Day approached, Boulder's mountain backdrop was nothing but kindling.

Sam, the ace detective, had become my new occasional neighbor.

# EIGHT

In the days after my patient died firefighters struggled to tame the raging Fourmile Fire. Boulder held its collective breath. Everyone knew someone who'd been evacuated. Almost everyone knew someone who had lost a home to the flames. During the extended battle to control the huge perimeter each fresh gust brought a burst of anxiety to town. The danger posed by a simple shift in prevailing winds was palpable.

The Fourmile Fire was the unthinkable wildfire we had all been dreading. What scared us all even more? We all knew it could have been more devastating. Hell, no one had died. The fire could have consumed Gold Hill on that first day. Or it could have started miles closer to town.

Even worse? We all knew that the Front Range was as parched the day the Fourmile Fire was contained as it had been the day the wildfire started burning.

\*    \*    \*

On the evening that the end of the fire was in sight Lauren's mood was bright and she was more animated after work than I'd seen her be in a while. We were straightening up the kitchen after a supper of *chilaquiles*. She was loading dishes. I was washing pans.

The kids—back in school after their summer breaks—had descended to their basement domain. Jonas was undoubtedly doing homework. Gracie? Not so reliably.

If I had to bet, I would have bet that she was dancing, or thinking about dancing.

Lauren said, "Do you remember—it was a few years ago—there was a suspicious death in a rented house on a ranch outside Frederick? A woman in her midthirties."

After my conversation with Sam in the ICU a few days prior, the word Frederick got my instant attention. I inserted therapy-cool modulation into my voice before I said, "No, doesn't ring a bell. Why?"

"Sure you remember. It was the woman who we thought might have known Michael McClelland. She'd spent time at the state hospital the same time he was there?"

Michael McClelland had been my patient when I first met Lauren, years before. I eventually connected him to the abuse and death of his sister. He had retaliated by trying to rip apart the lives of everyone he felt was culpable for his subsequent arrest.

That meant Lauren, Sam, me.

His assault on us had been deliberate and relentless.

He'd orchestrated it first from his job in the Severe Storms Laboratory at NOAA, later from the Colorado state hospital in Pueblo, and most recently from the state prison in Buena Vista.

He had proven to be a brilliant, tenacious adversary.

I said, "I guess I was trying to forget."

Lauren explained. "Our office was involved briefly during the initial investigation because of the potential connection to McClelland. At the time she died the Weld County DA had some doubts about manner of death. The ME said suicide, but their investigators thought that the suicide appeared odd, almost staged. Didn't we talk about it?" I shook my head. "We didn't?" I was confident I would have remembered. "Anyway, the ME determination stood, and Weld County closed the file. This isn't ringing a bell?"

"Vaguely," I lied. "Frederick PD? Or Weld County?"

"Sheriff—the house is in the county, just outside the city limits. The evidence that perplexed them at the time was that the woman had gone through a progression of possible ways to kill herself that night—overdosing on prescription drugs and alcohol, slitting her wrists with a razor in the bathtub, maybe others, too—before she finally shot herself through the head."

I glanced at Lauren to see if she was watching me. She wasn't. She was closing the door to the dishwasher. I asked, "How would they know about the progression? Did she leave a note?"

"No note. Drugs on a table next to a glass of whiskey.

Antidepressants. Her bathtub was full and there was a solitary razor blade right there on the rim of the tub—the kind of blade no woman would allow anywhere near her legs."

Sam had once liked Currie. Perhaps it was the residue of that affection that inspired him to offer her a menu of ways to accomplish her demise. Sam had permitted her to pick her poison.

"No shallow cuts?" I asked. "No horizontal wounds?" I was asking about the razor blade, about signs of trepidation. I was asking questions that Lauren would expect a psychologist like me to ask.

Lauren took a seat at the counter across from the sink. She hadn't started the dishwasher. The damn thing was so loud it would have made our conversation difficult.

I assumed Lauren knew what I was asking with my questions about wounds. People making suicidal gestures that involve slicing a wrist often first make tentative cuts. The trepidation cuts are typically too shallow to do the job, or they run in a less lethal direction—horizontally instead of vertically.

"No," she said. "No blood at all. It was as though she rejected the prospect of cutting herself before she started. Have you ever seen that sort of thing? In one of your patients?"

"Can't say I have," I said. "Practice cuts, sure. But setting it all up, and then walking away to do something else? I don't think so."

As committed as I was to maintaining my grand lie with Lauren, I was not a capable liar. I wondered if she could sense how unconvincing I felt trying to preserve the pretense. If she was having any doubts about my act, she didn't share them with me.

She asked, "What about from your training? Is that a common thing for suicidal people? To show that kind of ambivalence about method? To literally set all of her options out in front of her? At one time?"

I had to force myself to think about it dispassionately. "At the end? Like you're describing? I would have to say no, it's not typical. The back-and-forth about method is common, but the ambivalence tends to be prodromal—it happens during the suicidal-ideation phase. When you interview people who have survived a serious suicide attempt, they almost always report an interval that included a mental rehearsal of how they planned to take their life. It's not uncommon for the person to try on different methods during the ideation/rehearsal phase. Eventually they settle on a method that feels right, or at least feels palatable enough to them that they become convinced they can . . . do it."

"Palatable?"

"Bad word. Possible. Doable. At the end of the day, if you can't swallow the pills, or make the cut, or jump off the bridge, or step off the chair, or pull the trigger, you can't kill yourself. If she intends to die, the method has to be something she can do."

"What do you mean 'if she intends to die'? Isn't dying always the intent?"

I shook my head. "It helps to think about suicidal behavior as having two pairs of defining variables. Picture a simple chi-square—a two-by-two graph. On one axis is the dichotomy of intent—the person intends either to die or to survive. On the other axis is the dichotomy of lethality—the person chooses either a method of high lethality or one of low lethality.

"The two-by-two chi square allows for four possible combinations." I turned over our grocery list and sketched a chi-square with four boxes. "People with low intent sometimes choose methods of high lethality. They can end up dying, almost by accident, because death wasn't what they were seeking. The opposite is people who intended to die, but they chose a low-lethality method. They're the ones who believed that five aspirin and two shots of vodka would kill them. But they end up surviving, again, almost by accident."

"You drew four boxes. What are the other two?"

I squeezed water from a rag to use to wipe the counter. "I described low intent/high lethality, and high intent/low lethality. The other two are low intent/low lethality, and high intent/high lethality. People in both those categories get the outcome they intended. Low intent/low lethality is the classic 'cry for help' suicide attempt—someone who intends to survive but is eager for someone else to know about the gesture. That person doesn't wish to die, and she chooses a method that makes death unlikely. High intent/high lethality is the guy who puts a shotgun barrel in his mouth and pulls the trigger with his toes. He intends to die and chooses a method that is damn near certain to do it."

"Where does the woman in Frederick fit?"

"Two out of the three of the methods you described were seriously lethal."

"Which one isn't?"

"Wrist cutting can go either way. Unlike, say, jumping off the Golden Gate, which involves little skill beyond resolve, wrist slitting takes steady hands to achieve a lethal outcome. It's quite lethal if it's done correctly. But she may have decided she wasn't capable."

"Does that mean she was demonstrating ambivalence?"

"Her? No," I said. "Not about dying. At the end, she chose to shoot herself in the head. That's not a method of ambivalent intent."

"But she was ambivalent about method? *How* to kill herself? Right?"

"Yes, but only about method. Is there something new in the case? Why is this coming back around?"

"There's new evidence."

"After all this time?"

"Happens."

"Significant?"

Lauren shrugged. "The woman had a visitor the night she died."

*Sam? Someone else? Shit.* "I don't see the relevance. From a suicidology point of view, the visitor could have been the precipitant for the suicide."

Lauren reached over her shoulder and literally patted herself on the back. "That's what I said. But the DA's investigator in Weld County told me to keep an open mind."

"The presence of a visitor might even provide a cogent explanation for the confusing suicidal behavior," I said.

"Really? Please, go on," Lauren said.

"The decision—to kill herself—may have been abrupt. Not premeditated. We mental health types like to think about suicide as part of a progression that goes from depression to hopelessness to suicidal ideation to suicidal planning to . . . finally reaching a decision to carry out the act. The last stage is the attempt.

"But there are exceptions. Sometimes suicidal behavior doesn't adhere to the progression. If someone visited the woman that day—"

"Night," Lauren said.

I'd known it was night. My misdirection was an intentional effort to augment my credibility about the ignorance I was feigning. I was operating well beyond my skill level.

"It's possible that the visitor was the precipitant. Maybe the visit had a great impact. The person may have told the woman something, or showed her something that caused acute distress. Maybe, you know, the person gave her some news that night, something distressing— something powerful enough to precipitate a suicidal crisis that was not present before the visit."

Lauren said, "It could have been a breakup. Or the person brought news of a death. Like that."

"Anything that tapped some preexisting vulnerability. We know that the woman had a tough mental health history, right? She had an extended stay at a state hospital. It's impossible to know for sure but the visitor might have been the precipitant."

"In that scenario, the progression you described earlier would have been compressed. Yes? She wouldn't have had an extended period of contemplation about whether, or how, to kill herself. The decisions—to kill herself and how to do it—could have been made on the spot. The mental rehearsal you were talking about could have taken place quickly. Hours, even minutes. But not days. Not weeks."

I let out some more line. "I see where you're going, but I'm not sure I agree. Remember her mental health history. She may have done some extensive contemplation about suicide beforehand but had not made a decision before that night. I bet if someone looked back closely at the victim, you might find a vulnerable individual who was predisposed to suicidal behavior.

"Most of us don't react to bad news by suddenly trying on a sequence of methods we could use to kill ourselves. But a psychological autopsy might reveal signs that this woman was vulnerable, or even inclined, to self-destructive behavior.

"In her suicidal process, all that may have been lacking was an acute precipitant. The visitor may have delivered that."

Lauren added, "She obviously hadn't decided on method, though." She walked back around the counter and started the dishwasher. The thing was on its last legs. We were using it more and more as a place to store dirty dishes. Neither of us wanted to take the time to research and buy a new machine. Or to invest the half day off work it would take to wait for someone to show up to install it.

She raised her voice. "This helps me a lot. The point of all this is that the Weld sheriff is asking us to check some things in Boulder as he considers reopening."

"What's the Boulder piece?"

"She lived here before she moved to Frederick."

I didn't know if that was news. "Reopening would mean what?"

"They're considering changing the determination of manner from suicide to homicide."

*Shit, shit.* "Homicide? I don't understand. Why?"

"That's what the investigator hinted at on the phone. Otherwise, why reopen?"

"Wow. They must know something else about that visitor."

"I think I agree. Description? Identity? A witness who saw something, or someone." I followed Lauren into the family room. She made the short trip without using her cane and with only a mild limp. "Elliot wants me to take a look at what Weld County has, but he's not gung ho about investing any more of our resources in this."

Elliot was Elliot Bellhaven, Lauren's boss, the Boulder County DA. "Should be interesting," I said.

"Can't wait," she said.

I was pretty sure she was being sarcastic.

# NINE

We had two dogs. Emily was a late middle-aged Bouvier des Flandres—a big, intimidating black bear of a Belgian herding dog. Fiji was a young Havanese. She believed herself to be of royal stock and deserving of the life of a princess, but she had the inbred attitude of a dog whose ancestors' job had been to protect a Cuban peasant's chickens from the local foxes. The Havanese was twelve pounds, give or take. For most of her short life the dozen pounds had consisted primarily of silky hair and relentless cuteness. Only recently had she shown signs of growing out of the manic part of her youthful personality. I was grateful.

Emily was grateful, too. She had suffered through Fiji's puppydom with profound reluctance.

I waited to phone Sam until I had the dogs out for their late evening stroll on the dirt and gravel lane near my house. Emily bounded off the moment I said, "Go." She had earned the right to accomplish rounds of her parish solo. I kept Fiji close. She had way too much confidence in her ability to go paw to paw with red foxes and raccoons. Coyotes and porcupines? I didn't even like to think about it.

"Got a minute?" I asked when Sam answered. "Or are you otherwise engaged?"

Sam's car was at Ophelia's. I didn't think that they were carnally occupied. Old used double-wides are not renowned for their insulation, thermal or sound. I knew more about my neighbors' intimate schedule than I ever wanted to know.

"What we do is our business."

"I'm down the lane with the dogs. Join me. It's important."

"Can Ophelia come?"

"Not that kind of conversation."

Two minutes later I heard Sam approaching. I heard him because he was wearing flip-flops, which I considered another sign of Ophelia's influence. Sam didn't yet wear flip-flops with aplomb. Each step came accompanied by a loud slap.

Emily bounded out of the blackness and blocked Sam before he got within twenty yards. The big dog's greeting took a good minute. Then it was Fiji's turn. Finally, mine.

"What's up?" Sam said. I handed him a beer and a bottle opener. "Appreciated," he said as he popped the top. I held out my hand to get my bottle opener back. Sam included the just-removed beer cap in the bounty. I pocketed it. If I hadn't been there I'm pretty sure he would have Frisbeed the thing into the tall grasses.

It might have nicked a piece of granite. Caused a spark. Fried the whole valley.

"What you said you were worried about in the ICU? Remember?"

He stopped the bottle inches from his mouth. He said, "We're not talking about my intercom, are we?"

"No. We're never going to talk about that again. Lauren got a call from an investigator in Weld County. She has a meeting tomorrow. They might have a new witness. Someone who saw a visitor. She thinks Weld wants to reconsider manner."

"Of death? Jesus." Sam lifted the bottle the rest of the way and finished half of the beer before he lowered it. "That's not good," he said. "What kind of witness?"

"She doesn't know."

Sam lifted one foot from the ground and wiggled his toes. He kept wiggling his foot until I looked down, too. He said, "Huh. I get blisters between my toes from these things. Does that go away? Or do the kind of people who wear these just live with it?"

Sam was talking about the flip-flops. The kind of people who wear them? I didn't want to know. I said, "The cool people get used to them."

He finished the beer before he mumbled, "Asshole."

I said, "You were thirsty."

"That wasn't thirst." He examined the empty. "What about time frame?"

"If you wear them every day, you should be good to

go in a week. Your toes will adjust. Your feet will feel liberated. When that day comes we'll have a ceremony and we'll make you an honorary Westerner."

"I wasn't asking about the damn flip-flops. What's the time frame for when the witness saw whatever the witness saw? Prior to time of death? After? That's important. Given my role in things."

"I didn't want to seem too curious with Lauren. When she senses curiosity from me, she tends to stop talking about her cases. She's most comfortable talking about her work when I'm helpful or when I seem only mildly interested. If I'm distracted, she stops. If I ask too many questions, she stops."

He said, "I'm the same way with civilians."

"Like me?"

"Yep. You be a civilian." He extended the hand with the empty bottle. I took it. I wasn't proud that I allowed Sam to treat me like his personal Eco-Cycle attendant. But he knew I wouldn't trust him to recycle the bottle on his own. Sam was not bashful about exploiting advantages. "I guess we'll know soon, huh?" Sam said.

"I will let you know if Lauren tells me more."

"Basically, what, you're playing dumb with her?"

"I am, and it's not as easy as you would think." Sam laughed. I went on. "Reading between the lines? It sounds like somebody is thinking the scene was staged. That the visitor arranged things to look like a suicide—a suicide where the victim couldn't quite make up her mind about which method to use."

Sam's expression told me he wasn't buying it. He said,

"My cop brain says that's bullshit. Why go to all that trouble? The self-inflicted gunshot was plenty believable. Skull bits and brain matter are compelling evidence."

"You staged it," I said. Injecting reality into the conjecture seemed appropriate.

Sam shook his head in a way intended to convey that I was an idiot. "But I didn't manufacture any of it. I gave Currie options. Door A was an overdose with a whiskey chaser. Door B was to slit her arteries in the bathtub. Door C was the gun. She couldn't decide. She peeked behind each door, but she couldn't pick. I told her if she didn't choose, I would. I wasn't eager to wait around for the drugs to work. I wasn't confident she could cut her wrists, and I didn't want to watch her bleed out in the bathtub, anyway. The single gunshot? I hated doing it, but it was the best option.

"To get rid of the evidence about Door A and Door B, I would have had to erase all signs of Currie's ambivalence, and that would have meant messing with what had become a crime scene. Detectives are pretty damn good at recognizing when someone has screwed around with a crime scene. So I left things as they were. I figured it would look like the home of an ambivalent suicide victim. It was what it was. The more I screwed around with the scene the more I increased the risk that someone would see evidence of my hand."

"And now?"

"Now? Apparently they think there's a killer who overstaged the set *after* he killed Currie. That's bad police work."

"But it isn't exactly in the realm of fantasy. The investigators may be able to convince the DA."

Sam sighed in a way that caused his cheeks to puff out. "I know, I know. The investigators may have the big picture kind of right, which worries me. I've been hoping all along it wouldn't matter—that the clarity about the way she died would supersede everything else.

"There's evidence that Currie was holding the gun that killed her. I made sure that her fingerprints were in the right places. Ballistics have to be consistent with a self-inflicted gunshot because that's what happened—if you leave out the part about my . . . insistence. GSR had to reveal that gunshot residue was deposited in the right places. Blood spatter was uninterrupted. I made sure of that. Unless the mystery witness was looking through a window to see what came down, I don't see my jeopardy in this."

"Her weapon? Or yours?" I asked.

He hesitated before he said, "Not mine."

"Are you really as . . . confident as you sound?" I almost said *complacent.*

"No," Sam said. He spent a long interlude staring at the western sky. Only the faintest evidence of the sunset was visible. "Truth is, I have been, up until this week. Confident. But now, not so much." He shook his head.

"I'm sorry," I said, "that I got you into this."

"Bullshit," he said.

My ears heard Sam's protest as genuine, and generous. He was telling me that he didn't want me to feel responsible. He knew I shared responsibility, but he wasn't comfortable with me sharing the burden. "McClelland was my fight," I said.

"That fight broadened to include cops, especially me, a long time before Frederick. And anyway, you didn't make me pick Currie. I've picked some good women in my life. And I've picked some less-than-good women. I made plenty of bad choices along the way that led me to that house, that night. No matter how I spin it, I feel the same way I felt then. I would make the same decision, again."

I was skeptical-plus. "I've replayed it a hundred times. Fifty of those times, easy, I tell Lauren what I've done. Keeping this secret eats at me."

"You're not thinking of talking, are you?"

I hesitated before I said, "No."

Sam glared at me before he walked ten feet away. With his back turned he said, "After we found her camera? With the pictures of our kids? I admit I went back and forth a bit, but I eventually convinced myself that I was out of time. That . . . that monster was going to hurt my son. It all began to feel determined, you know? What I had to do. When I drove to Frederick it was as though I knew"—he pounded his chest with one closed fist—"how things would end. The details were in flux, but the outcome? She was going to kill our children. I couldn't allow that. I knew when I got in the car that night that I was driving to that ranch to kill somebody who needed killing."

His voice dropped. "You know what that's called?" he asked me.

I did not know what Sam meant. I said, "No, I don't."

He faced me. "In my business, that is called premeditation."

Sam was spelling out the stakes for us. Murder one. High stakes.

He went on. "I had convinced myself that the system wasn't going to work for us, not in time. When she admitted she was going to do it—"

"Wait, Sam. Wait!" I hadn't heard that part before. "She acknowledged she was going to hurt them?" He nodded. "What did she say?"

"She said McClelland didn't consider them perfect substitutes, but they were good enough."

*Good enough?* "Substitutes for us? You and me?"

"You, me, and Lauren. McClelland wants us all. The way Currie put it that night? She said, 'If he can't kill you, he wants you to wish you were dead. All of you.' "

"God," I said.

"She wouldn't tell me how she was going to do it, only that it would be soon. Once I heard that? I'm okay with what I did."

"Do I hear a but in there?"

"This is God's truth—I was much more comfortable with what I did when I thought I'd gotten away with it than I am standing here right now knowing there's an outside chance I'll get caught. The consequences of not killing her? Unimaginable. The consequences of getting caught? God. I do not want to get caught. But I can live with it."

"We'll get caught together," I said. "I won't let you go down for this alone—"

"No," Sam said. His slumped shoulders straightened. His tone—the soft one we'd both been using to share our confidences—took on a framework of hardened steel. He pointed at the center of my chest. I thought he was going to poke me. He said, "No fucking way."

"This was my mess. Currie threatened my daughter. McClelland is my—"

"Currie threatened both our kids. I've been part of this since that first summer with McClelland in Aspen. Don't rewrite this history. I was there." I opened my mouth but didn't get a word out before Sam said, "You didn't go to Frederick that night. In fact, I think that travel and phone records will show you were in New Mexico. That, my friend, is quite an alibi. Use it."

"I am an accomplice. Both before and after the fact."

"Bullshit," Sam said. "And don't try to talk like a cop. You sound unconvincing."

Arguing the point was futile. I redirected him to the issue Lauren had raised. "Has anyone ever tied you to her, Sam? During the original investigation? Did anyone figure out that you and Currie had been going out when she lived in Boulder?"

"We were done by then."

"I know that. And you know what I'm asking."

Sam stuffed his hands in his pockets. "She'd given me a bogus name when we met. I didn't exactly introduce her around." He rolled his eyes. "McClelland must have known—he put her up to all this. When I've worried about any of this over the past few years, he's the one I end up worrying about. Not some unknown witness suddenly singing in Frederick. Fucking McClelland. He's who I worry about."

I woke with some regularity in the middle of the night with McClelland in my dreams, and a sharp fright in my heart.

His presence in my nightmares felt like the tip of a long blade pressuring the outer membrane of the pulsing muscle, threatening to pierce into the cavity where small cuts have big consequences. On the nights when my sleep was cut short by that blade, I didn't so much wake from a bad dream as much as I woke to the acknowledgment of a bad, bad reality.

My reality, as surreal as it was to me every time I faced it, was that I had a nemesis. My nemesis was an ex-patient named Michael McClelland.

In some of the dreams, McClelland held the blade. In some of the dreams, McClelland was the blade. In the dreams that woke me, Michael McClelland—by profession, he was a Ph.D. meteorologist, a severe storms specialist—was my Rasputin. No matter how many times I'd thwarted him with guile, force, dumb luck, or the leverage of law, despite whatever I'd thrown back his way over the years, he kept resurrecting himself and finding new ways to come back at me. And at mine.

Sam's seduction by Currie, her targeting of our children, and Sam's solo determination that the only clean solution was for her to die were all part of that most recent go-round with Michael McClelland. Since then, McClelland had been convicted of murdering a cop years earlier in Aspen. He was serving a lifetime-plus in the

Colorado penal system on the desolate outskirts of the mountain town of Buena Vista.

I didn't allow myself the luxury of believing that Michael McClelland was done with his Rasputin act. When I least suspected it, I knew he would come back at me.

The tip of the blade pressing at the membrane of my heart would never let up.

Sam was right that Michael McClelland knew that Sam had been dating Currie before her timely death in Frederick. Did McClelland ever believe the medical examiner's conclusion that his friend's death had been a suicide? Probably not. Did McClelland have evidence to the contrary? I could not rule that out.

If McClelland were to reveal to investigators reexamining old events in Frederick that the suicide victim had been romantically involved with a City of Boulder detective at the time of her death, that would certainly pique their attention. Throw in the new witness who had just maybe seen the wrong thing that night, and the dormant death in Frederick could come back to haunt Sam. And me.

# TEN

A gorgeous seventy-degree day in late September turned brisk as a fast-moving front left a hard freeze in its wake. By noon the next day the front had moved on to chill the Great Plains, leaving the skies above the Front Range the blue of possibility. The familiar respite of Indian summer seemed to promise a gentle and extended autumn.

A forty-five-degree swing of temperatures in fifteen hours? Welcome to Colorado.

I was seeing a new patient for a first visit. She had phoned the previous Friday, leaving a voice mail seeking an appointment. When I returned her call a few hours later we discussed potential times. She preferred to meet between midday Monday and midday Thursday, and not too early in the day, if that was possible. She sometimes worked late, she explained, and she traveled, sometimes on short notice.

She hoped that wouldn't be a problem. I was grateful for the latitude in her schedule; most new patients make a play for one of my always-in-demand prime-time appointments—early, just before work, over the lunch hour, or at the end of the workday. She and I settled on a late-morning time without much negotiation.

During the brief phone conversation, I had not inquired why she was seeking time with a psychotherapist, something many of my colleagues choose to do during the initial phone contact. Nor had I asked another common question—how she had learned my name. I tend not to do much initial screening on the telephone. Some prospective patients will volunteer a capsule version of what they expect their clinical story will be. If they do, I listen. Other patients are more circumspect during the first contact. To me, as a psychotherapist, both styles are informative, but encouraging a telephone rehearsal seems to risk diminishing the impact of the face-to-face version that is certain to come.

Amanda Bobbie hadn't inquired in advance about my fees or about whether she could use her health insurance coverage, nor had she posed any generic how-often-will-we-meet or how-long-will-this-process-take questions. I made a mental bet that she had been in psychotherapy before and that she knew how things worked.

In some ways a patient with previous therapeutic experience made my work easier. In some ways it made my work more difficult.

\*　　\*　　\*

Amanda was sitting in one of the pair of modern chairs that Diane had installed as part of a major waiting room makeover a few years before. The renovation was an early phase of Diane's attempt at psychological rehabilitation following the devastating trauma she'd suffered while a hostage in Nevada. I hadn't paid sufficient heed to Diane's coping at the time. My own life had been a mess then; I had missed the initial signs of her decline. It was a reasonable rationalization. It wasn't a good excuse.

In the intervening time, I recognized that the barricades Diane had mounted to deal with her suffering—denial, sublimation, suppression, you name it—had proven inadequate to the task.

The woman in the waiting room wasn't reading a magazine or flipping through content on her phone. She was sitting, contained, her back straight, her knees together, her gaze loosely focused on the cascades of water *shoosh*ing through the bamboo tubes in the too-big, too-loud water feature across the room.

Diane had been seeking Zen when she selected the big water feature from an artist out near Niwot. She hadn't found it. The Zen. Though she did find a way to install Class IV rapids into our diminutive waiting area, which was no small accomplishment.

There was nothing at all abrupt about the way Amanda shifted her eyes to me as I stepped through the door. "Hello," I said. "I'm Alan Gregory."

She stood. She said, "Amanda Bobbie."

She was somewhat younger than me—I was guessing early thirties. She'd applied almost no makeup that morning—maybe a little eyeliner and some lip gloss. I wasn't even sure about the lip gloss. An unfussy ponytail of long, dark hair terminated slightly off-center on the right side of the back of her head. She wore a sundress of pale, angled stripes that came together high on her waist. A thin jersey jacket with short sleeves made certain that any allure of the sundress was muted.

The impression was of someone determined to appear as though she could look the way she looked five minutes after she climbed out of bed. I had no way to know whether her appearance was truly that natural or whether the effortless look had taken an hour.

At the beginning of treatment, I generated hypotheses by the bushel and typically felt no urgency to test my theses. The accumulating theories were a reminder to me of all I didn't know about the person I was meeting. My reality? As with almost all things in psychotherapy, I believed that time would tell.

In my office, Amanda quickly assumed the same posture that she'd had in the waiting room. She had a choice between a seat on the sofa and on an upholstered chair. She chose the center of the couch, the only location that left her with no place to lean, or rest an arm. Few patients chose the center of the sofa.

The bright, palest-of-pale-blue eyes that had been focused on our mini-Niagara were now focused on me. There was, I thought, some warmth and softness in them. Amanda Bobbie wasn't afraid of eye contact. She sought eye contact. Some patients will challenge a new therapist with an overdetermined eye-lock; they employ it as a provocation in order to stake out territory, or as a competitive attempt to control the space and time of psychotherapy. Amanda wasn't doing that with me; if anything, her eyes invited a certain comfort.

I found it mildly disconcerting. We hadn't yet achieved that certain comfort.

My working theory was that I was in the room with a caretaker. *We're good.* That's what I decided her eyes were saying to me. *We're both good here.*

She took a sudden breath that lifted her shoulders about an inch. She then released the air from her lungs in a completely silent, extended exhale.

I wasn't sure if I had witnessed a gasp or a sigh. At the most basic level, being an effective psychotherapist is about paying attention. To be the therapist I wanted to be, my job required that I become an A student in the seminar that was being taught by, and about, Amanda Bobbie.

"Never, ever, expected to be here," she said. "Not *here* here. But anyplace like this with anyone . . . like you."

It wasn't an original opening. I made a mental note that—if Amanda Bobbie was being truthful, not a given in the work I do—it appeared I had lost my internal wager about previous therapy experience.

Had I walked into a social gathering with a room full of strangers, Amanda wasn't a woman who would have grabbed my attention. Not at first, probably not for a while. There was nothing about her manner or her features that demanded notice.

She wasn't, for instance, an Ophelia. I suppressed a grin at the realization that I had generated no initial impression about Amanda's breasts. *Large? Small? Attractive? Not? Shapely?* Nothing. I had no idea. Almost everything about Amanda whispered. Except maybe her serenity.

*Is the serenity a shell?* Back in that fictional room full of strangers, once I did get around to noticing Amanda, I suspected that my eyes would have been drawn back to her a second time, and maybe a third. My eyes would find her again because of her composure. I had enough self-awareness to know that her brand of confidence was a trait that captured my imagination in social gatherings. In that arena, where I can be guilty of a lack of poise, I often found myself drawn to someone who demonstrates it in spades.

I have a stock line I use during the initial moments with a new patient. I say, "How can I be of help?" I probably use the phrase with about half my intakes. The other half are either so relieved to be in the room with someone who will listen to them—or so anxious about being in the room with someone who will listen to them—that they enter my office in full verbal sprint, initiating their story before we make it down the hall.

Amanda was in a different minority. She started unprompted, but the crucial factor wasn't what she said— her words felt banal to me, though I was prepared to alter that impression as more data accumulated—but that she'd given us something unremarkable to talk about. I wondered if she was aware that she'd done it.

Her second line that morning—I offered no response to her first—was more revealing. She said, "I'm here today because . . . I have a friend."

# ELEVEN

*Really?* Early in treatment, I tend to be quite the philanthropist where benefit-of-the-doubt grants are concerned. Amanda's declaration caused me to reconsider my munificence.

I said, "You have a friend?" I tried to make the four simple words sound Swiss. Neutral. I probably didn't succeed. I find skepticism to be one of those infiltrates that is most difficult for me to couch.

Amanda's response was to flatten her lips into a thin line that barely curled up at each end, in the most subdued of acknowledging smiles. She raised her eyebrows, which served to widen her expressive eyes. "I know, right? I get no points for originality. I do not for a second imagine that I'm the first client to use that line here."

"No," I said, in lieu of the more pejorative *hardly.*

Parsimony seemed like a reasonable alternative to incredulity, or to my instinctive inclination toward sarcasm.

Parsimony was more Swiss.

Amanda continued. "Were I sitting in your chair, my tendency might be . . . I don't know . . . to be skeptical, or even disbelieving, if I heard those words about a friend from someone sitting where I am sitting."

What make therapy an art are the choice points. A simple reflection—*You're concerned that I might be disbelieving?*—was one option. A slightly confrontational backhand volley—*How would you choose for me to respond?*—was another. The therapeutic default option, silence, was always available.

In the earliest moments of a psychotherapeutic encounter, the most delicate things in the room are rarely content related. The fragility exists in the nascent relationship—the one, real or imagined, that is beginning to develop between psychotherapist and patient. The supposed facts are typically much less loaded with meaning than are the soft edges and gray borders around them that are about who stated the facts, how they were stated, who heard them, how they were heard, and with what expectations the speaker spoke the words, or the listener listened to them.

In shrink terms those fragile things, those poignant things—the carpet of eggshells on which the first steps of the therapeutic dance take place—are the stuff of process.

At the beginning the air in the consultation room— the process air—is either infused with the scent of trust or it is tainted with the tincture of its bitter cousin, mistrust.

Amanda may or may not have recognized trust as one of the components of our shared miasma, but she and I had already begun exploring trust—she of me, me of her.

My trust of her? I assumed some dissembling, intentional or not. Amanda had no reason to trust me. Blind trust was as illustrative of process as was a refusal to consider trust.

"Tell me," I said, "about your concerns for your friend." I was taking her at her word that her concern for her friend was real, and worthy of our time. She would either accept that as sincere, or she would not.

Amanda folded her hands, one over the other, on her lap. Only her pinkies, each adorned with a ring, intertwined. One ring appeared to be gold, the other a silver-toned metal. A ring on a ring finger, or the shadow of one recently removed, might have portended a story about a romantic relationship, a tale of satisfaction or failure, of safety, or loss.

The null set, the absence of that ring, told me little.

"I am worried about him," she said. "My friend." She shifted her shoulders back and forth. "He is someone I work . . . with. A successful man. A proud man. Although he is skillful and imaginative in his work, he is unaccustomed to certain personal challenges. Challenges that for most of us might be considered parochial. Those challenges upset his equilibrium. There are times I am not even sure he is aware he is off balance."

I was painting by the numbers on Amanda's portrait, assigning values and finding just the right hues to provide an accurate representation of her poise, and her presentation, and her manner, and her vocabulary, and her affect, and her mood. I made judgments about her intelligence—she had used the words parochial and equilibrium while describing her friend—and her relatedness, which seemed comfortable.

I was holding in abeyance other judgments. About her honesty. If we were indeed speaking about her friend, the proud man, I wondered whether we were discussing him so that she could seek help for him in his stead, or whether the focus on him was the most palatable way she'd found to begin the process of seeking indirect help for herself.

I wondered, too, if Amanda knew the answer to that question.

It was another early choice point for me. With a pointed comment or a question, I could have focused her on her friend, or on herself. She had revealed a working relationship without hinting at what either of them did for a living.

At the beginning of treatment, my question list was always much longer than my answer list. I knew the discrepancy would narrow if I avoided the temptation to throw myself in Amanda's path. I made the smallest of leaps from the parsed information she had revealed thus far. I said, "Something is challenging your friend's equilibrium?"

She said, "He has suffered losses recently. For him, they are difficult."

Loss is familiar clinical territory. A spouse, divorce or death. A parent, a friend. A child. *God*. A home. Lately, a job. Grief is one of humanity's great equalizers. I made another small, intentional leap as I reflected, "He has suffered a loss of someone close to him? That kind of loss?"

I watched some tautness appear in her mandibles. I suspected that I had leapt too far, or in the wrong direction, or perhaps just too soon.

"No," she said. But her head got caught in the gray area between a nod and a shake. "Money. His business. His money is his business, which is his life."

At this stage of therapy, I wasn't required to be right. But I couldn't afford to be consistently wrong. Amanda's sense of the value of the relationship between therapist and patient would be correlated with her perception of my competence.

Amanda said, "I may minimize his talents, they are considerable, but at the end of the day my friend is an investor, but also a gambler. His bets are on talent, on visionaries. On long shots." She closed her eyes momentarily as she lowered her chin to one side. "He's had a bad couple of years. The industry has retrenched. The economy? Right? My friend chose to invest his way out of trouble. Some of his moves were risky, even for him. They don't look good now. Many may prove to be complete losses. If that is true, he will take clients, partners, down with him."

In a town like Boulder, psychotherapists develop referral patterns. Subgroups of patients exist in odd employment or lifestyle clusters. One of my idiosyncratic clusters was composed of school administrators; in my caseload I was seeing three different assistant principals. Another cluster consisted of aerospace engineers. All but one worked across town at Ball Aerospace.

Another one of my clinical microworlds involved inhabitants of the esoteric world of VC. Venture capital. The VC cluster in my practice formed in a typical fashion. By chance, I treated an initial venture capitalist, a woman, who eventually referred another, a man. He referred two more colleagues, who each eventually referred a friend. A few members of the cohort stayed in therapy with me for a while. Others lasted only a session or two.

Before long, though, I had a view through small windows into a subculture of a subset of Boulder's moneyed class; they were men, and a few women, who provided seed financing for entrepreneurial endeavors using some combination of their own money and that of clients, friends, or family. Some functioned as scouts. Some as nurturers and mentors. Some were described by others as vultures.

The knowledge I acquired about the Boulder VC community from my clinical work complemented the knowledge I already possessed because Diane's husband, Raoul, was the unofficial dean of Boulder's tech VC group. During a dinner out with Lauren and me, Diane had referred to him as "Boulder's VC godfather." That night her indiscretion had earned Diane a pronounced frown from her husband.

I eased Amanda back to her narrative. "You are worried about your friend because of his financial losses?"

"He is unaccustomed to . . . failure. People recognized signs of reaching even before the latest misplays. I suspect few know how badly he is bleeding.

"He is flying out of town frequently. He wants others to think he has his eye on something they're unaware of, that he is doing due diligence on something they missed. Some of his colleagues may buy the charade—VC is as much about insecurity as it is about vision. But he is not scouting. He is praying for a score from a handful of still-viable bets that remain on the table. To stay afloat, he's been selling tranches of good positions he shouldn't sell. I am concerned that he has convinced himself that one big play he is contemplating will be the one that will save him."

I waited.

"It won't," Amanda said. "It's battery technology. Innovative, but vulnerable to competitors. Other start-ups are doing similar things with more secure financing and less restless talent. The patent barriers aren't insurmountable."

I allowed some of my incredulity to surface. I asked, "You came to see me because you're concerned about your friend losing money?"

She crossed her left leg over her right and tugged her dress to the top of her knees. "No," she said. "I came to see you because I am concerned he is going to kill himself."

In the early stages of psychotherapy new patients tend to discuss the issue of suicide, if at all, in euphemisms. Amanda earned points for frankness.

I had concrete questions to ask about her suspicions so that I could make a judgment about the risk of her friend attempting to take his own life, but they could wait. It was more important for me to see what step Amanda would take next. I said, "Go on."

"I am fond of him. I don't want him to . . . hurt himself."

*Fair enough.* At moments in therapy when truth finds focus, especially when it's associated with some meaningful application of insight, I usually feel a slight change in my clinical muscles. It starts with an initial lift—akin to the buoyancy I would feel as a young surfer the instant I knew I was in a wave, or as a young skier when I was able to balance my weight above my bindings and start to float in knee-deep powder.

I wasn't feeling that lift with Amanda. I wasn't convinced that her friend's vulnerability was the reason she was in my office. But my curiosity was piqued. *If a friend at risk of suicide isn't your motivation, what is?*

I said, "How do you hope I can be of help with that?"

She seemed taken aback by my question. Her chin actually snapped to one side as though she were pulling her face out of the way of a slap. "That's your job," she said. Her tone edged perilously near condescension, as though I were her plumber and she was reprimanding me for wondering aloud what I was supposed to do about her clogged drain.

Or, more to the point, her neighbor's clogged drain.

In a voice leveled to a micro-millimeter of flat, I said, "It's not my job."

I paused while her incredulity adjusted to room temperature. Once her disbelief had tempered, I asked, "Is it your job?"

"You are a psychologist. Trust me. He is at serious risk." Amanda's reply ignored my question—direct, and poignant with confrontation as it was—with ease. In case I had further misconceptions about my responsibilities, she clarified her perception of my duties. She said, "Your job is to help him."

"I don't think so," I said. I followed the words with a pause to allow yet another burst of her incredulity—sincere or not—time to ripen. "My job is to help you."

Her expression—I was far from confident in my ability to read it—progressed from incredulity to something akin to perplexity. She said, "Then help me help him."

"My earlier question—does it feel to you that it is your responsibility to keep your friend from attempting to take his life?"

Her eyes said, *Of course it does*. Her words? "I need your expertise. I can't—I need—I don't know how to get him to recognize that he needs . . ."

I allowed time for her to finish her thought before I said, "You believe it is your responsibility?" She nodded. "My experience is that psychotherapy by proxy can be a frustrating endeavor. Not only for the identified patient. But also for the intermediary. It usually proves much less salutary than the intermediary hopes."

"That's me? I am the intermediary?"

"I don't mean to be callous—I can feel your compassion—but keeping him alive is not something you can do." Light caught a tear on the surface of her left eye.

"But," she said meekly, "who else?"

The first progress in her therapy may have been reflected in the meekness of Amanda's defiance.

I said, "Please tell me about your concerns about your friend attempting suicide."

She said, "You will help him?"

I allowed time to pass before I said, "I remain interested in how I can help you."

"You will help me . . . help him?"

"I am here to help *you*."

Amanda looked down at her lap. "I am so confused," she said.

"That's not a bad thing," I said. I watched that tear escape. She caught it on the tip of her finger before it had traveled south even an inch. She touched the fingertip to her tongue. I asked, "Has your friend spoken of hurting himself?"

She looked away before she shook her head. "No." She raised a shoulder. "I keep orchids for him—long story—but he cares for them himself. We both know he uses the orchids as an excuse to visit. I find it sweet. But neglecting them? And he is neglecting them. I can't comprehend it."

Amanda might have picked up on a most poignant tell. Or not.

"Has he made any threats? Overt, or vague?" I asked.

"The day I called you? He left his briefcase open. There was a gun in it. I didn't know he had a gun."

*Oh.* The gun revealed many possible things. Amanda's friend might indeed have reached a determination about how he preferred to take his own life. The weapon could reveal that suicidal planning was well under way, or even complete. It certainly revealed, in a faint whiff of good news, that some small part of Amanda's friend might have been willing to leave clues that might raise alarm. Many people intent on killing themselves fail to give friends or loved ones any opportunity to intervene.

Or the gun left visible meant that Amanda's friend had left his gun visible. That was all. It might have been the cigar that was a cigar. "Let's talk about the help your friend might need," I said.

She comported her face into something that resembled a smile, revealing a dimple on her left cheek. But no twin on the right side of her face.

"Thank you," she said.

# TWELVE

Most people would choose a car to get to a place as far away as the town of Frederick. But I lived in Boulder. And I wasn't most people. Unless I had to transport something bulky, I rode my bike to places like Frederick.

In Boulder, few people would give my choice a second thought. Riding bikes long distances, even ridiculously long distances, was an accepted part of the culture. In Frederick? I suspected that the town's longtime residents would think me odd.

For a bicycling enthusiast, the ride was a mere jaunt. Twenty miles, maybe, one-way. Almost no vertical to speak of on the way out. The most moderate of climbs on the way back. I would hardly work up a sweat.

Although I was sure I'd been to Frederick before, I couldn't recall when I might have made that trip. Or why. I had no mental images of the town that weren't interchangeable with mental images of a half dozen other small towns east or north of Boulder. Maybe I was confusing Frederick with Erie, or Meade, or Dacono, or with distant memories of once-small towns like Superior or Lafayette that development and progress had forced big.

When I'd pulled up a map of the eastern border of Boulder County on my laptop, I was surprised that Frederick was located east of I-25, the north-south concrete spine that runs roughly parallel to the Front Range, border to border, from Wyoming to New Mexico. I would have placed the town west of the highway.

Sam Purdy, I knew, had been to Frederick. And Justine Brown had lived there. Most crucial? Frederick was where Sam had killed her. That murder was the reason I was riding my bike to Frederick that Saturday morning.

I've crisscrossed the High Plains north and east of my Boulder home on my bike more times than I can remember. Going from Spanish Hills, where I lived, northeast toward Frederick meant a trip from Boulder County into adjacent Weld County while sharing long straight county roads with speeding commuters, distracted carpooling parents, impatient big-rig drivers, and whatever motley collection of agricultural vehicles and equipment might be required that particular day to allow a rancher or a farmer to move from this field to that pasture, or from this silo to that market.

The more substantial the road, the more diligent was my attempt to avoid it on my bicycle.

The City of Boulder was often renowned as a bicycle-friendly environment. I knew few experienced riders who shared that assessment. After many years pedaling Boulder's roads, I didn't consider Boulder to be bike friendly; on a good day it was, maybe, a little more bicycle tolerant than other places.

One of the places that the city was more tolerant was the eastern, more rural part of Boulder County.

Another of those places was just about anywhere in rural Weld County. I knew from experience, and from a few square meters of accumulated road rash, that I would need to be watchful on my Frederick jaunt, a route that would carry me quickly from barely bicycle-tolerant territory to likely bicycle-intolerant territory.

The moment I turned toward the east I felt a blow of wind in my face. The bone-dry grasses in the adjacent fields rustled with the breeze. By the time the mammoth form of the interstate loomed in front of me, the wind was a constant in my face. I was grateful that the blow would be at my back on the ride home to Boulder.

Before I'd left the house, I spent about ten minutes online tracking down the precise location where Currie and Sam had spent her final moments alive, together. Meager press accounts of the initial investigation of her death revealed that my destination was a ranch just past Frederick off County Road 16, a street that the not-too-numerous urban dwellers of Frederick knew as First Street.

I crossed I-25 and then pedaled through Frederick. I knew what was expected of me. I slowed. I stayed right. I stopped at stop signs. I obeyed traffic lights. I yielded even when I had the right-of-way. A couple of minutes later, I turned onto the country lane that was my destination. I rode the entire length of the lane, which dead-ended at the northernmost of the three properties that used the road for access. Two of the three properties were on the west side, one at each end. The third was on the east side, a little less than halfway between the county road and the dead end.

Although I hadn't been able to locate the address of the house in my online search, I could tell from a news photo that my target was the solitary farm on the east side. The photo taken from the lane on that clear day showed no mountain backdrop. In rural Frederick, on a clear day, no mountain backdrop on a north-south road meant that the camera lens had been pointed east.

I rode back slowly along the length of the lane, eyeing a barn and corrals, which said ranch. But the adjacent land was cultivated, which said farm. I thought the field was planted with a late crop of alfalfa, but I wasn't confident. At the Boulder farmers' market, I could discern Italian parsley from cilantro, or pea shoots from garlic scapes, at twenty paces. I didn't like what it said about me that I couldn't identify acres of my neighbors' crops.

I stopped to focus on the cluster of buildings—homes, and barns, and outbuildings—that marked the heart of the property.

"You looking for the rental?"

I spun on my saddle to see who had spoken. The speaker was a young woman in her midtwenties. From her outfit—linen pencil skirt, tailored blouse, fashionable flats—I was guessing maybe a real estate person, but not a local.

I opened my mouth to say I wasn't looking for the rental, but beside her I caught sight of a clean, crisp FOR RENT sign nailed to a fence post.

The woman said, "You're quick. I only got it up on Craigslist last night."

She stuck out a hand. "I'm Isabel Kane. Izza." In flats she was only a few inches short of my six-two.

She'd spoken with the wind at her back. I wasn't sure I heard her correctly. "Izza?"

"I-z-z-a," she said, as though she'd spelled it too many times in her life. "Isabel was my mother's idea, but my daddy thought it was too formal."

I shook her hand. "Alan," I said. As I omitted my last name from the introduction, I realized I was setting the table for the possibility that I was about to tell Izza Kane a lie, or two, or three. A lie, or lies, that would prove vulnerable to a Google search if the searcher had knowledge of my last name.

Izza said, "Did you see the sign at the corner? It's not very big. I tacked it up this morning, then drove all the way to Greeley before I realized I left my cell phone here." She made an exasperated noise. "But now I'm here to show you around. Life is funny, isn't it?"

Izza had intriguing eyes and wavy, barely red hair that the wind was blowing away from her face. Her skin was flawless. Her body was athletic, but she was a step or two shy of toned. I had an impression that she fought her weight—a battle she was currently winning. I also suspected that months went by when the pencil skirt and her favorite jeans never made it out of Izza's closet.

"Do you always ride your bike when you're out looking for places to live?" She smiled. Two of her lower teeth were crooked.

"I like to ride," I said. "And I like to ride in the country. I wasn't thinking I wanted to live this far north, but I thought I'd see what the area is like. Now that I see how close it is to the highway, it doesn't feel that far north. I do like the open space. I could get to Denver fast, be back home after a short commute."

"I'm an honest person," Izza said. "If the wind wasn't blowing from the east like it is, right here where we're standing we would be hearing the big rigs on 25. Inside? No. Windows are double-glazed. But when the wind isn't upslope? The truck noise is real. A Denver commute? Stay away from rush hour. The other side of 120th is a pain in the butt."

"I could live with all that, I think. And I like being around horses."

I had leapt from misleading Izza to lying to her. I don't actually dislike horses, but my feelings about them are closer to neutral than to general affection. The lie had been unnecessary, and the moment it escaped my lips, I recognized the door I had kicked open.

"We used to keep a lot, but we're down to a few. Do you ride?" Izza asked.

*That* door. "Used to, a little. Had an incident. Maybe someday I'll get back on."

Izza crinkled her nose. "I'm the same about bikes.

Sorry," she said. She grabbed her hair to keep it from blowing into her face. "You want to get out of the wind, see the place? It's nice. Everybody likes it. It's always just a question of money. It's nicer than other places out here, but people feel they shouldn't have to pay for nice."

"Is it ever a question of whether people want to live in . . . Frederick?" I said. "Sorry."

She laughed. "Don't apologize. I grew up here. I moved away."

I stepped off the bike and rolled it beside me as we walked onto the property, past a big midcentury single-story house and around a large barn of a much older vintage. On the other side of the barn was a small house. Unremarkable. Shingle roof. Siding. Concrete walk. No garage. I hadn't even noticed it on my ride.

"My grandma lived here. Daddy built the bungalow for her when I was a little girl. I was maybe five or so. I used to get in trouble playing in the construction before it was done. Grandma Bridget died the day George Bush, the second one, was reelected." She made a face I could not interpret. "So there you go," she said.

I wondered if Izza meant that Grandma had died with a smile on her face, content with the results of our democratic process, or that she had expired with grave disappointment at the electoral judgment of her fellow citizens. I didn't ask for clarification. It didn't take much intuition to surmise that politics in Frederick and politics in Boulder involved making selections from two entirely different food groups.

I said, "I'm sorry. Were you close?"

"She raised me. With my dad. My mama left when I was little. A toddler. She's in Florida."

I said, "That must have been hard. To have your mom leave that young."

"Barely even remember. It was always just me and Daddy and Grandma. But you can't want to hear about me and my family stories." She waved an arm out in front of her. "We pay electric, but you buy your own propane. No a/c, but you can see there's a swamp cooler on the roof. It does a fine job most days. We keep it working, don't worry. There's always a day or two each summer where evaporative cooling's not enough, but . . . Anyway, six-month lease. I'll negotiate a deposit. But I need two good references, and I'm going to run a credit check. All that's nonnegotiable. Pets?"

She made a face that suggested that she was hoping I didn't have pets.

I asked, "Is that a deal killer?" I was looking for an out.

She rocked her head from side to side. "It's been a problem. When we had more horses. Probably depends on the pet. If it works, it works. Is it just you? Do you have a roommate? Or a . . . significant other?"

"It's just me," I said. Another lie. I told it cognizant that my cropped riding gloves concealed my wedding ring. I was wishing I had actually seen that Craigslist ad.

"You never answered my pet question," Izza said.

"I was kind of thinking about getting a dog. Not right away, but . . . soon. Living out here, it'd be nice."

"Ah," Izza said. Her cell phone rang. "Puppies and

horses aren't always a great mix." She stepped a few feet away from me before she answered her call. The gusty breezes were coalescing into a steady wind; she used her free hand to corral her hair. I could tell from the bits of conversation I could hear that she was making arrangements to show the cottage again that evening.

"Some competition," she said to me, wiggling her phone as she stepped back toward the door. "You may have to act fast. Shall we go inside?"

# THIRTEEN

While Izza was on the phone I had been trying to imagine how Sam had chosen to approach the cottage the night that Currie had died.

I couldn't see Sam driving onto the property in clear view of the ranch's main house, knowing what he was about to do. Nor could I see him parking his Cherokee on the lane in front of the ranch and then sauntering in the open toward Currie's home. Not with suicide and homicide on his mind.

The cottage backed up to the edge of the huge cultivated field, separated from the crops only by a narrow dirt road that provided farming equipment access to the fields. If Sam had chosen an inconspicuous location to park out on the county road near town, he could have walked the third of a mile or so to the dirt access road, which would have taken him directly behind Currie's cottage.

I decided that's what he did. With the big barn providing a visual barrier blocking the cottage from the main house, Sam had approached Currie's place on the field access road, without ever becoming visible to anyone in the ranch's main home.

He had probably exited that same way once his ex-girlfriend was dead.

I followed Izza inside, eager to visualize what had happened between Sam and Currie in between Sam's arrival at this house and his departure a while later.

"Partially furnished, as you know," Izza said.

I didn't know. I forced my attention back to the moment. "You never know what that means," I said. "Sometimes 'partially furnished' means a beat-up old couch and maybe a wobbly table in the kitchen."

Izza stopped two steps inside the door. I stopped beside her.

"With us, it means no bed, but almost everything else. I don't like used mattresses. It's just not sanitary." Izza exhaled in a way that accentuated the discomfort she felt about the old-bed issue. "If you don't have your own bed, you're going to have to get one. There're ads in the Sunday papers almost every week. Decent deals. They all deliver. Couple hundred bucks for a full. More if you want a queen. Bedroom really can't handle a king. If you're that type. The king type."

I was tempted to ask what type that was, but I didn't.

The front door opened into an L-shaped combination

living room and dining room. A slice of the kitchen was visible on the far side of the room.

*Currie died in this room.*

"Oak floors, like the ad says. Good windows, like I said already. The fireplace works, but it's not very efficient. Keep that flue closed or you'll have trouble staying warm on cold nights. There's some firewood out back, been there a couple of years. Elm, I think. Maybe some ash. Nice and dry. You'd be welcome to it.

"We replaced the dishwasher about—oh, I don't know—six months back. Not top-of-the-line, but not a cheapo, either. Do you cook?"

I was distracted. My attention was focused on the circuitous route that Izza chose as she walked from the front door toward the kitchen. She bypassed what would have been the most direct path from where we were to where she was headed.

"I do cook," I said. "It's kind of a hobby."

*Currie died right there,* I thought. *In the area between the dining room table and the sofa and chairs in the living room. The part of the room that Izza circumnavigated.* I wondered where Currie had been standing. Where Sam was. What direction the barrel of the gun had been pointing. Which way the blood had splattered.

I corrected myself: *spattered.* Other liquids splatter. Blood spatters. *Thank you,* Dexter.

I replayed the first conversation that Sam and I ever had about Currie's death. I'd been in a derelict phone booth in an even more derelict filling station in the hills above Los Alamos, New Mexico. Sam had been at a pay phone in Boulder. Somewhere near Ideal Market, or maybe across Alpine near the Boulder Wine Merchant.

Sam had mentioned whiskey and pills on the table. I looked at the dining table. The table was solid and simple—dark stained oak that showed the wear of fifty years of dining. I imagined an amber pill container and a bottle of bourbon. A solitary glass. In my imagination I made it a highball glass, with etched vertical flutes.

Had Sam said Jack Daniel's? I thought he had.

I clarified the image. I made the whiskey a square bottle of black-labeled Jack. I screwed the lid off the bottle and set it on the dark wood.

I poured a double shot into the highball glass. I doubled the double.

"You coming?" Izza said. "Hello."

"I am. Sorry—I was imagining what it would be like. You ever do that?"

Izza shivered, her arms covered in gooseflesh. "Yes. Sometimes," she said.

My question had rocketed her someplace she didn't want to go.

I took the same wide route around the center of the room that she did. She was rubbing her arms. "Nice," I said. I stood beside her in the kitchen doorway. It was a good-sized room with plenty of counter space. A big farm sink. That new dishwasher.

"Grandma was a baker," she said. "It was built like this

for her. She didn't care about much else in the house, but she cared about this kitchen." She smiled. "And she wanted a deep bathtub. She took long soaks. That's what she called them."

The kitchen had its own table and chairs. The table was a linoleum-topped model with three chrome diner-style chairs with vinyl cushions. I could almost feel that vinyl sticking to my bare skin on hot summer nights.

During that phone conversation from New Mexico to Boulder, Sam had said that the whiskey and the pills had been on the *kitchen* table. He hadn't meant the oak table in the other room. I rearranged my imaginings.

The black Jack and the drugs reappeared in front of me as though I'd Photoshopped them into the frame. In real life, I didn't know how to Photoshop. In my imagination, I was a wizard.

*Did Sam and Currie sit here for a while, in the kitchen? Did they talk, discuss her options? The mess she was in? Did they share some of the bourbon?*

I decided they didn't drink together. Given the threat she represented, Sam wouldn't have been comfortable with that.

I didn't mentally Photoshop a second highball glass into the picture.

I wondered if Currie believed that she could somehow thwart Sam's plans. Was she seducing, or dissuading, or plotting her big escape while they sat at this table and talked? Perhaps she had a counterattack in mind? A quick move for a kitchen knife?

Or was Currie accepting her defeat, feeling the mantle of martyrdom, or the weight of her approaching death, as she sat with Sam? Was this where she admitted that she indeed planned to kill our children?

I tried to feel some compassion for her. It gave me pause that I was unable.

I realized time had passed. Too long an interlude for a potential renter who should have been doing nothing more than taking a quick look at a cottage kitchen. I tried to recover. I said, "Just seeing myself here some morning. Having coffee. Maybe some pancakes. A nice breeze from that window. In winter, I could see the sun rise."

"You're up early," Izza said.

I smiled. "Sometimes."

"Me too," she said. "I like the quiet. The bedroom? Shall we?"

She blushed at her own words before she rushed ahead of me out of the kitchen.

"Onward," I said. I was apparently tamping down any incipient discomfort by adopting the absurd pretense that I was a Christian soldier.

# FOURTEEN

The hallway was short. I held back. "Just a sec," I said. "I want to see that deep bathtub you were talking about."

She had a puzzled look. "Men don't usually care much about the bathroom."

Sam had told me that the tub was full during his visit to the cottage.

He had also described a fresh razor blade resting on the edge of the bathroom sink. Lauren had said that it was a single-edged blade. I imagined one like the ones painters use to scrape stray streaks or splatters from glass. Sam, I was sure, had added the blade to the tableau. One of the options for Currie was to make a precise vertical cut, or two, into a visible vein in her wrist.

I didn't know the progression of events. Had Sam started running the bath after he arrived? Or had Currie been drawing her own bath at the moment he surprised her? The plan for the evening, either way, would have required that Currie accomplish the tough cut and bleed out into the tub.

Did Sam consider making that cut for her? It would have made for a most intimate murder. His ex-lover would have been naked in the bath. Sam would have been kneeling beside the tub holding her forearm rigid. The hand in which he gripped the blade would have needed to be steady.

If Currie struggled, she would have ended up with bruises from his grip or random slashes from the blade. Sam would have been concerned about premorbid bruising or awkward cuts showing up during a post.

No, the razor option would have had to be Currie's wish. Her show. Sam would have had to wait while that played out. I wondered how long it had taken for her to decide she couldn't do it. Had she undressed? Or entered the tub? I didn't know. Sam would not show patience with her indefinitely. He would have been concerned about how long it would take for Currie to bleed out. The variables, of course, were the chosen vessel and the quality of the cut. Artery? Should be quick. The pump that was the beating heart would do all the heavy lifting. A dripping vein, though? That would mean a slow death. Sam would not have wanted to watch.

And he, literally, didn't have all night.

The edge of the sink was adjacent to the bathtub. Grandma's soaking tub was narrow but deep. Well-scrubbed stains around the drain were evidence of decades of struggle against the high mineral content of the local water.

"Nice tub," I said.

"Told you," Izza replied.

I gestured toward the stains. I said, "Well water?"

She nodded. "Couple of big cisterns, too. Plenty of pressure. We get the stains everywhere. If I still lived here I would use one of those water filter things. The pitchers? For drinking? All the fracking I hear about has me worried, too. That big Wattenberg Field? It starts right near here."

"Good idea," I said. "I can get one of those filters."

All the damn fracking had me worried, as well. But I didn't say that.

I didn't recall Sam mentioning the bedroom of Currie's house. It hadn't been on the itinerary of the tour he'd described on the night of her death. I didn't step into the bedroom because I didn't see a need. From the doorway, the room appeared small and barren. As promised, it lacked a bed. A too-small-for-modern-needs closet was on the far wall, door open. A solitary nightstand appeared to have been built from a kit. The dresser was beat-up honey oak—a Sears or Montgomery Ward catalog model from early in the last century, long before this house was built.

"I'd recommend an area rug over there," Izza said. She pointed across the bedroom. Her breathing changed. "But maybe that's just me. I hate getting out of bed in the morning and putting my feet on the cold floor." I didn't reply right away. She shifted her weight from one foot to the other.

I felt the awkwardness between us again. I stepped back toward the living room, stopping at the edge of the spot that we'd both avoided earlier.

Izza was half a step behind me—for the first time I could detect a sweet scent from her. In a voice that was halfway to a whisper, she said, "Somebody died here. I don't *have* to tell you that, it's not a legal requirement, but I think you sense it. Like I said, I'm an honest person." I turned my head, trying to keep my expression neutral. "Do you feel something?" she asked. "Here? In this room?"

"I'm not sure," I said. "Every old house has a spot where someone has died. Maybe that's what I feel. Nothing . . . bad. Nothing that bothers me."

Izza swept her right arm in a large circle in front of her. "Someone died *right* . . . here. Gunshot. Suicide." She strung out the long *i* at the end of the last word for a good two seconds. It gave me a chill, the way she highlighted the sound, as though she were determined that the *i*—the very personal pronoun—embedded in suicide not be forgotten.

"On this spot." Izza touched the tip of her index finger below her chin, pointing it slightly upward. She pressed hard, deflecting her flesh inward.

I was grateful that she didn't mimic the actual gunshot.

As I stood in that forlorn Los Alamos phone booth, Sam had left me with the impression that he'd aimed to impact Currie's brain stem with the slug. I didn't doubt that he'd aimed well. My mental clip of the night's events had

Currie dead before gravity finished drawing her all the way to the floor.

I said, "Earlier, when we walked through? You walked around this area as though you wanted to avoid it. Did you see it? I mean afterward? What happened?"

"No. I was at school. At UNC. A few days later, the propane guy was here, topping the tanks, checking the lines. He smelled something coming from the cottage. He told Daddy that he thought there might be a dead animal under the stairs in back, or in the crawl space. Daddy saw the body on the floor when he looked through the front window.

"Everybody was gone by the time I got here. The cops. The coroner. The body."

"Did you know him?" I said. "The tenant who died?" Then I offered a prophylactic, "I'm sorry, you know. If you did."

"It was a woman. New tenant. Couple of weeks is all she'd lived here. She was somebody Old Elias met at a horse show. She mentioned to him that she was looking to live on a ranch. Hoped to get a horse. He told her about the cottage and that he thought there was a vacancy coming up. She came out to take a look. Daddy was still involved then. He liked her. Heck, everyone around here liked her. I'd only met her once. She was busy in the corral, working one of the boarded horses. She did it for fun. Daddy said it was like having a free hand living on the ranch, said he was sure she was going to be the best tenant ever. And then . . ."

I gave Izza a moment to complete her thought before I said, "With the smell . . . bad enough to get the propane guy's attention, she must have been dead for a while."

"Three days, they told us. But Elias Tres, bless his heart, said it was four. So . . . let's say it was four."

Izza had mentioned Elias twice. "Elias is . . . ?"

"Oh, sorry. The big house at the corner? Across the way. You passed it on your way in. With all those gables?"

I shrugged. It hadn't made an impression.

"It belongs to Old Elias. Big Elias. Elias Tres is the one who said it was four days, not three, that the body had been there before the propane guy smelled it.

"Big Elias is . . ." Izza didn't finish her thought. "Elias Tres?" She beamed. "He'll talk to anybody about anything." She shook her head and smiled. "I swear that boy'll make your head spin."

"The Eliases are father and son?" I asked.

"Grandfather and grandson. Elias Tres's father was an Elias, too, so there were three. But nobody ever called him Elias. Everyone called him Segundo. You know, second. The second Elias." Izza blinked quickly, turning her face away from mine. "Segundo was killed in Afghanistan, on his second tour. A marine. He'd survived one terrible year in Iraq. Having him back here after that was a blessing. And then . . ."

She was rushing the final thoughts from her mouth, as though she knew if she didn't hurry she would never get the words out of her body. I thought I saw the shimmer of tears forming in Izza's eyes before she turned away.

I made an assumption that a story of Segundo's death would have a special chapter, written just for her. Or just about her, and the meaning of her loss. Every soldier who died for the rest of us left unwritten chapters behind for survivors like Izza, stories that the rest of us rarely took the time to know.

I was curious about Izza and Segundo, and what they'd shared that ended with his death. "Segundo's death touched many people?" I said, hoping to draw her out.

"Oh yeah. That little boy still doesn't accept, in his heart, that his daddy isn't coming home. I mean, he knows. But . . . he doesn't. Does that make sense? It is so sad."

I pushed. "Is Elias Tres's mother in the picture? Is it just the two Eliases?"

Izza said, "No, she's long gone. She and Segundo never should have married. She got pregnant in high school." She shrugged her shoulders at the mundanity of the story. "I used to babysit Tres. But not so much since Segundo died."

"Is Big Elias married?"

"He was." She smiled an uncomfortable smile. "He's a hard man. People say he scared her off. I don't know. That was right after I was born."

I waited for Izza to offer more. She didn't. I told her I understood. I didn't.

Izza said, "Elias Tres was called Tercera when he was a little boy. Like his daddy was Second, Elias was Third. But after Segundo . . . didn't come home from Afghanistan, Big Elias decided he didn't like Tercera. As a name.

"One day he told Megan down at the bank that he

thought it sounded gay—he called it 'queer,' of course."
Izza rolled her eyes. "And that day he began telling
everyone to call his grandson Elias Tres. For three. Uno,
dos, tres? Like that?"

I finally understood the genesis of the little boy's
name. In my mind, I switched the spelling from Elias
T-r-a-c-e, which is how I'd been mentally translating the
sound, to Elias T-r-e-s.

I decided to see what a hard turn would do to Izza's
composure. "Had to be upsetting for everyone," I said.
"The suicide? Does anyone know why she did it?"

Izza wiped at her eyes before she faced me again. The
tears, I thought, were complicated. They had started
when the conversation went to Segundo's death, and ac-
celerated when I asked about his son's family.

"No one knows. It surprised Daddy and he probably
knew her best. Him and Elias Tres. Tres was down here
whenever she was here, is what I understand. But he was
only five then. Is that right? Oh, ask him. He'll tell you
for sure. Down to the number of days. Hours. What the
weather was on his birthday. Who came to his party. That
boy." She smiled before she tightened her jaw. "It was a
difficult time."

*Is Big Elias the new witness? Is the boy?* I wondered.

"Difficult how?" I asked. Izza shook her head. I
changed my tack. "Your father lives in the larger house on
the other side of the barn?"

"When he's well enough. He's sick—in and out of the
hospital a lot."

If we were in my office with her, I would have said,

*Tell me about your father,* or more simply, *Tell me.* Instead, I resumed my fact-finding. I asked, "Did she leave a suicide note?"

"I wish she did. What she left was a mess to clean up, some sad people, a brokenhearted little boy, and a whole lot of questions that will never get answered."

I gave her a moment. "And a long story you feel compelled to tell when a nosy prospective tenant starts asking too many questions?"

"That, too," she said. "You got me talking." She wagged a finger at me while she forgave me with a small grin.

"I'm sorry," I said. "I should mind my own business."

"What do you think? About the place?"

"I like it. But it sounds like I may have only a few hours to decide if I love it."

"It usually goes fast. The rent is fair." She raised her arms halfheartedly and wiggled her hips. "And the landlord is a gem." She ended her jig, looked down at my feet, stepped back, and tracked her eyes all the way back up to mine. "Can you drive a tractor? If you can, there's a way to get a break on your rent. Daddy's no longer able to move the snow off the drive. If you could do that, it'd be great. But you will have to be able to drive the tractor."

"Could you show me how to do it?"

"I could try."

I waited for her to meet my eyes. "Izza? Is there anything I need to know about your father?"

"Daddy?" She hesitated before she said, "No," in a way that I didn't find entirely convincing.

"Any neighbor issues? With Big Elias?"

She began leading me toward the front door. "Nothing that you have to concern yourself with."

"You're sure? I don't like walking into . . . situations."

She turned away from me before she said, "Daddy and Big Elias were friends. Now they're not. It is what it is. They're old. They get cranky." She looked up while she nodded, as though she were convincing herself. "Daddy's sick. No worries for you."

Before we stepped outside into the wind, I asked, "What are you studying? At UNC?"

"Criminal justice," she said.

# FIFTEEN

"The last time didn't go as I thought it would," was how Amanda began her second appointment. It was the first Monday in October. "I had an expectation that you would tell me what to do. I thought my time was going to be about helping my friend."

She paused. She crossed her legs. She touched her hair. Her posture didn't waver, not even a little. The silence between us grew to twenty seconds, then thirty.

"But you—" She stopped herself. "You kept insisting that it was about me. That what I was talking about, my concern, was about me."

I could have offered her encouragement. I didn't. I didn't want to interrupt; that was part of it. I was also curious about the process, what would emerge next.

Amanda said, "My brother died when I was fourteen,

almost fifteen. He was sixteen when he died. Almost seventeen."

She smiled, the solitary asymmetrical dimple emerging for half a second.

My instinct—human, not therapeutic—left me tempted to say, "I'm so sorry." I didn't. Her words felt like preamble. Something about the way she began the narrative— the "almost fifteen" and the coy smile—left me with a hunch that the story about her brother's death wasn't entirely about her loss.

I thought, *This feels like last week.*

"He was diagnosed with non-Hodgkin's lymphoma when he was fourteen." She reached up, her fingertips grazing a hollow on the right side of her neck.

I guessed that she had absently touched the location on her body where his first lymphoma was discovered on his. I kept the guess to myself.

"Your brother was diagnosed young," I said. I had treated a couple of non-Hodgkin's patients for therapy over the years. The disease is relatively rare in younger teenagers, especially among non-African-Americans.

"Yeah. His cancer was aggressive. The treatment, too, right from the start. Chemo. Radiation. Surgery. His spleen was removed. God. I didn't even know what a spleen was. The doctors were able to slow the growth at first, the spread, the new tumors, but they never really got the cancer under control. We'd have a few weeks of hope here and there, and then . . . a new lymphoma. He never really had a remission. The cancer was the first thing we thought about when we got up, and the last thing we thought about when we went to bed. He was sick from the day he was diagnosed until the day he died."

I had my eye out for strands—perhaps one that would be as fine as spider's silk—that might tie the story of her brother's illness and death to the concerns that Amanda had voiced during our last session about her friend.

"We were living in Texas. In Austin. We'd just moved there like a year before for my dad's work. From Ohio. He'd been unemployed—he was always unlucky with work. He got the job in Texas managing a big truck repair shop. Things were okay, then *bang*! Cancer. My brother was being treated in Houston, at MD Anderson—it's a big cancer center at UT. At first, he and my mom traveled back and forth for his treatments. I would stay in Austin, sort of look after my dad."

Amanda made an incongruous face. I filed it. I began to wonder whether this story was about her sick brother or her feckless father, or both.

"The last year, my brother stayed in Houston. Eventually, I went, too, to help. Money was a problem. My mom had to get a job down there. She worked nights. Cashier, waitress. I'd stay with my brother while she worked. I enrolled in high school there. I didn't fit in. No one else had a brother who was dying."

I said, "You had been sort of caring for your dad in Austin. Then you began caring for your brother in Houston." I was restating facts she had shared, but by juxtaposing them I was highlighting her roles.

She heard that part. "My dad was a mess. He needed my mom. Not me."

Were the larger story not so grand, I might have encouraged a detour to reflect on the mess her father was in, and her inadequacy to help. But the larger story about her dying brother was that grand, and any detour determined by me was perilous.

I said, "What you're describing must have been very disruptive. To move twice, for the reasons you had to move, to leave your friends and school behind each time. To feel the"—I chose the next word I spoke after some deliberation—"obligation to take care of your brother. I can only imagine how it felt."

"It wasn't an obligation," she said. "I felt better in Houston. I belonged there."

Amanda did something then that I would become more familiar with as I got to know her better. She bit down gently on one side of her lower lip. The asymmetry was a stark contrast to her almost perfect comportment. I thought she looked ten years younger when she bit down on her lip. I imagined I was seeing the girl who'd been in Houston.

"My brother had a lot of B symptoms by the time that I went down to help. They were my job. The B symptoms."

"B symptoms?" I said. I didn't know the term.

"Secondary symptoms. They got worse when the lymphomas got worse. God, let's see, he had abdominal pain. Awful back pain, itching, oh, the itching, fever, sweating. Night sweats. Muscle aches. I would do what I could.

"We were living at Ronald McDonald House. We had

a little two-room suite thing. That was home. My mom and I had fold-up cots. In the evenings, my mom was gone. The nurses were great, but they had other patients. My big brother—my big, strong, tough brother—would . . . cry from the pain sometimes. He'd weep."

Amanda bit down on her lip again. "He didn't like narcotics. He would take them sometimes, he had to, but he hated the way they made him feel."

I was beginning to sense the psychological terrain that Amanda was crossing, and was beginning to make some tenuous guesses about the reason she was crossing it that day with me. I was wary though, skeptical that what I was seeing indicated progress; patients without a significant psychotherapy history rarely demonstrate evidence of that kind of forward motion early in treatment.

She went on. "I started hating the sun going down. Mom would be at work. Often, by the time it was dark my brother would be in agony. I did what I could. I did what the nurses told me to do. They said to stay positive. To distract him. To make him laugh. Towels in ice water for his forehead. Hot packs for his gut. Creams on his skin for the itching. This medicine. That medicine. We played cards. I sang to him. I read to him. I was, like, Ronald's apprentice clown. On bad nights? Nothing helped for more than a minute or two. Five, if I was lucky."

Amanda's shoulders sank. She seemed to deflate. "It was," she said, "exhausting. Everybody who was staying in Ronald's place had cancer. Or something just as bad. Everywhere I looked I saw sick kids. Cancer. Cancer. Cancer."

"Everybody?" I said, repeating her word. "You felt as though you had it, too?"

"We all had it. He was the only one who was going to die from it. But we all had cancer. We felt its ups and downs. We felt these big forces, too. The things that could change a good day into a wreck, or a hopeful week into a crisis. Or any kind of future into a fantasy." She stopped abruptly. "He'd have a good morning one day and I'd convince myself he was getting better. Then there'd be bad labs or a bad scan. Hope? *Poof.*"

Amanda shifted the focus of her eyes about twenty degrees away from mine.

I thought they were aimed vaguely, or specifically, in the direction of her past.

"Anyway," she said. "One night I was out in the kitchen, a big communal space where family members would get together and cook and talk. Hoping I would see somebody I liked. A little break. Eventually it was time to go back. I walked in without knocking—before I left he'd started drifting in and out of sleep, and if he was asleep I didn't want to wake him.

"He moved his hand the second I stuck my head in the door. I could see the outline of an erection below the sheet."

Amanda took a quick breath before she continued. "I was a young girl—I hadn't seen an erection, not in real life. But I knew about them. I looked away, at his face. That almost made things worse, because I could see his embarrassment. He raised his leg, bending the knee between me and his boner, but it didn't hide . . . anything.

His dick was pointing up toward his belly button. I was kind of embarrassed for him, so I just pretended nothing was different. I did what I did—I wiped his forehead. I gave him ice water—he always liked fresh water.

"And then I sat down beside him, and I took his hand—the same hand he'd been using to touch himself—and I probably began telling him about something funny that happened. I would make stuff up to distract him or get him to laugh.

"I remember thinking his eyes got sad as he watched his erection fade away below the sheet."

# SIXTEEN

The sudden interjection of the sexual into the dialogue of psychotherapy is one of the unexpected forces that can completely change the energy in the room. When the sexual interjection comes from the point of view, and in the distant voice, of a fourteen-year-old girl witnessing an erection for the first time in her life, the change can feel profound.

I prepared myself to be buffeted, though it didn't happen the way I expected.

Amanda said, "As his dick got smaller, his pain got worse. He couldn't hold his legs still. He started shifting around, trying to get comfortable. Couldn't. He folded his pillow. He did it again. Rolled on one side. Then the other.

"The erection thing was distracting me, of course. I kept sneaking looks at it until it was gone. It felt like it was all in slow motion. Later, I knew more about teenage boys and erections, but that was my first and it felt like the world had slowed to a crawl."

Amanda's comfort discussing her brother's erection was remarkable. I tried to make sense of it. I failed.

"Everything that night felt new to me. Powerful. Amazing. Fascinating."

*Not erotic? Or stimulating? Frightening?* I kept the questions to myself.

"Then I thought, *Oh my God!* Despite my ignorance—oh, I was ignorant—I saw the connection. I knew what he'd been doing while I was out of the room. He'd been masturbating as a way to distract himself."

She wrinkled her nose. "It made perfect sense. I'd done it, too. Not because of pain, physical pain, but I'd masturbated when I wanted to be, or needed to be . . . someplace else. Boredom, being annoyed with my friends or my parents. Whatever. I had done it. I knew why he was doing it."

She said, "I asked him if he wanted me to leave. If he wanted some time by himself. I told him it was okay if he did, that I understood.

"We weren't a family open about much. Certainly not about sex. I couldn't remember a single conversation I'd had with my mom about masturbating, or about boys, or erections. That I was even hinting about it to my brother must have . . ." A fresh tear formed in Amanda's right eye. "He told me that he knew he could trust me."

She wiped the tear and closed both eyes. "That," Amanda said, "was a gift. Right? When he said that he could trust me. Big gift."

She pulled back that one side of her lip and bit down gently before she spoke again. The act left her face pleasantly vulnerable, and completely disaffected. "But he was still embarrassed. He pretended he didn't know what I was talking about. I almost said, 'Uh, your boner,' but I didn't. He made a joke about something. I didn't leave.

"We tried to have a regular night. We watched *ER*. We had this contest where we'd try to find all the medical things they got wrong in the show. I read to him. He listened to music. He was all Aerosmith and Pearl Jam. I hated Steven Tyler, and Pearl Jam made my eyeballs ache. It was just another bad night for us."

I was cognizant that Amanda's narrative had a momentum that hadn't crested whatever incline it was ascending. I couldn't see over that ridge, so I chose silence.

"Around eleven is when he would try to sleep. That was a Mom rule. She wanted him asleep when she got back. She didn't do much that was selfish, but that was a selfish rule. She was so exhausted after work that she wanted to come back to some calm. I turned off the lights, like I was supposed to. That night he was too miserable to sleep. He was *writhing*. His stomach hurt, his back hurt. When I asked him where the pain was he just waved his hand and his arm over the middle of his body."

Amanda leaned forward a few inches. She interlaced the fingers of her hands, with her palms toward me. She closed her eyes.

I felt as though I were standing right behind her as she approached that crest. She was able to look beyond the top of the ridge, but from where I was standing behind her, in her shadow, I still could not see what she saw.

"I couldn't take it any longer. Watching his misery. Listening to his misery. Smelling—yes, I could actually smell his pain; don't ask me how, I just could. For the first time, I knew—I was naïve, but I wasn't stupid—I knew I could help."

She unlaced her fingers. She opened her eyes. She dropped her shoulders.

"I wasn't a bad girl. I knew the rules. All of them. Mom's rules. God's rules." She laughed. "I even knew Ronald's rules. I knew the big unspoken rules. I knew what I was thinking was something I wasn't supposed to be thinking. I knew it was something . . . I was supposed to think was unthinkable." Her voice had taken on an unmistakable Texas twang that I hadn't heard before. "And not just a little wrong. No, sir.

"Wrong wrong. Wrong.

"But it didn't feel wrong."

The Texas melody receded from her voice as quickly as it had materialized. "That night? In the dark? With his pain? He cries out. I swear the sound is like a squeal in a catfight. I feel it vibrate like my flesh is the skin of a drum."

I noted the abrupt change in tense, from past to present. I glanced at the clock. I hoped the remaining minutes would permit us some closure.

"I take a deep breath and I say a prayer that if God is having trouble with what I am considering, He needs to put down whatever else He is doing, and He needs to give me a sign. Something clear. If the nurse walks in, that's God being God.

"But she does not walk in. God is not giving me the don't-do-it sign.

"I give Him one more try. I whisper, 'God, last chance,' as I stand up.

"My brother hears that. He says, 'What?'

"I say, 'Just praying.' I sit beside him on his bed, and then without hesitating for even one single second I reach below the sheet and I put my hand on his dick. I begin to move my fingers. I go right at it. I don't let myself think. I just go."

Amanda grew quiet. She seemed to regroup. When she spoke again the present tense was gone. "It was a . . . gonzo moment. Touching a boy was all *so* different than I'd imagined. I almost stopped because of my surprise at how it felt. But I didn't stop. I just caressed his dick, or I did my fourteen-year-old clueless version of caressing his dick. I'm sure I was terrible at it." She shrugged. "There, in the dark, in Ronald McDonald House, I was giving my big brother a hand job. I mean," she said, "how . . . crazy . . . was that?"

Amanda continued to look past me. Was she afraid of what she would see in my face? Or was she disinterested? Was it possible that her life between that day in Houston and that day in my office had inured her to the odd majesty of her story?

"He was as overwhelmed as I was, I'm sure." She widened her eyes and laughed. The laugh was just a little trill. "I didn't know what I was doing. I'd never touched a penis and I don't know what I'd expected to happen, but I hadn't expected it to go from soft to hard as fast as it did. I don't know why, but I expected the process would take a while. Like dough rising. But it was more like biscuits popping out of a can. Like that."

Amanda stopped then, and she locked onto my eyes. "No judgment? Really?"

I was holding my facial muscles into a configuration that I hoped would appear neutral. Accepting. I had a lot of experience with that particular expression and I had some confidence that I could pull it off. The truth was that I had little to disguise. Judgment about Amanda's behavior wasn't on the list of things I was feeling.

"Well, he stopped me. Not right away, but almost right away. Five seconds? Ten. He grabbed my hand through the sheet and he held it there. He didn't pull it away, though. He held it right where it was, wrapped around his dick. He said—I can still hear him—'You do not have to—'

"I put my other hand on top of his hand. I was holding his hand, he was holding my hand, and below the sheet my other hand was holding on to his prick, which was still getting hard. I told him to shut up. It's something I never said to him, so that got his attention almost as much as what I was doing. I told him I knew I didn't have to do it. I was using the voice I would use when we were arguing about something and I would be telling him I didn't care if he was older, he couldn't tell me what to do. It was a funny moment, looking back.

"My girlfriends in Austin were doing stuff for boys

already. Hand jobs. Some of them were giving them to boys they didn't even like, just to do it. We talked like hand jobs weren't that big a deal. Girls only a little bit older than us were doing a lot more. Oral sex. A couple girls I knew were screwing older boys."

Amanda curled her lips, top and bottom, inward for a moment. She held them there, pressed together while she searched for something. She wetted her lips with the tip of her tongue before she resumed speaking. "I knew I was touching my brother sexually. But I wasn't doing it . . . to touch him sexually. I was doing it to help him deal. It is so hard to explain, even now. This isn't a story I have experience telling, but I can imagine it must sound pretty crazy.

"In the rule book of life—the rules of my family and my church and my school and my town and even of freaking nature—what I was doing was wrong. I knew it was somebody's definition of incest. I knew that other people"—she spoke "other people" in a breathless, dismissive rush as though the couplet was a profanity she found as offensive as any in the language—"would be appalled, my motive be damned.

"And I knew that if we were caught my brother would be blamed, even though it was me starting it, me doing it. But after living on my own with my dad in Austin for so long I was becoming the girl who was good at not getting caught. I expected to get away with it. I considered it a challenge. That was the girl I'd become."

At that moment I began to consider the possibility that Amanda's story was heading in the direction of a conclusion that included the part about her not getting away with it. I wondered what form the apprehension would take. What the consequences she suffered would look like. What fallout, perhaps still radioactive to that day, she would be putting on display there in my office so that we could, together, find a way to accelerate the half-life of the decay.

"And if I didn't get caught? If I just kept helping him until the end? That would be great. The end was coming. I knew that. The end would be the end of his life."

She lowered her head for a few seconds. "Later I thought about him being sexually dependent on me, on his little sister. That wouldn't be good, right? But who else was going to get him off in Ronald McDonald's freaking house in freaking Houston, Texas? So what if he gets hooked on his sister giving him hand jobs?

"He was dependent on narcotics. Why weren't they worried about that? Because he was dying. That problem would die when he died. I felt the same way about what I was doing. He was dying. His death would end any consequences."

*For him,* I thought. *But what about for you, Amanda? This is about you.*

Amanda was telling me this story so that she could explore the cave where she'd stashed the memories. The question in my head about the consequences for her would eventually be addressed. Until then I would trust her to do this exploration her way. I found her willingness to risk that vulnerability remarkable.

Amanda adjusted her weight on the sofa. She folded

her hands in the same chaste manner she had the very first time she sat across from me.

She said, "That night? I lifted his hand away from my hand. I stood up. I checked the door. I checked the time to make sure that my mom wasn't due back. I pulled the big heavy chair all the way around the bed, so I could sit with my back to the door so that I would be screening him if anyone walked in. And then I sat down, and I started touching him again. He was still hard.

"After a minute or so his body began to relax. His legs straightened. His shoulders fell back against the bed. His breathing became regular. Different, but regular.

"It changed him. I could see it. I could feel it. I could smell it. The writhing stopped. He became still. Quiet. I wasn't trying to make him come—he would sometimes, especially at the beginning when I didn't know what I was doing. The point was to prolong the distraction as long as I could. To allow my caress to become the focus of everything for him. When I had my hand on him he would go to a different place. For him different meant better. I felt like I had the power to lift him up and take him away.

"That night I became my brother's hand job fairy." Amanda smiled her one-dimple smile. "Truth is, it was never a big deal for me, some huge burden I carried around. It wasn't my dark secret. I knew right away that first night, in my heart, that I was helping. That's all I cared about. I had something special I could do that made a difference. No one else could do it, or would do it. It was me, or it was nobody.

"He slept better. Laughed more. My mom noticed the

change. On her days off work, when she was caring for him, when he and I had no real time alone, she would ask me what my magic was with him. She told me once that she wished she could duplicate it.

" 'No magic,' is what I told her." Amanda paused before she added, "There were times I thought she knew. She'd look at me a certain way. Open her mouth to say something and then . . . not say a word."

I gave Amanda time to feel whatever she was feeling. She held my gaze for about half a minute before she became entranced looking out the window. I wondered if she realized she was gazing south, toward Texas. "I never told her what I was doing." I watched the muscles in Amanda's jaws tighten before she added, "I can't tell how you feel about all this. I thought I'd be able to tell."

"Is that important?" I asked. "How I'm feeling about what you're telling me?" I was redirecting her to our process. I was curious if she could spot the progression in her words. From wondering if her mother knew to wondering how I felt.

"Of course it is. I don't know you, so I can't trust—is that the right word?—how you feel about it. If you're appalled, then I'm not sure that you will be able to help me. So yes, it's important. God. Yes."

"You're concerned that I might be appalled?"

"No," she said. "Not really. I don't want any judgment from you to get in the way."

"A moment ago, you expressed concern that I might not be able to help you. Help you with what, Amanda? What exactly are you here seeking my help for?"

She didn't move. I said, "Last week it was to help your friend. This week? What?" Silence. I said, "Today is about you. Just like last week's session was about you. Last week wasn't about your friend. This week is not about your brother."

She nodded. Her lips flattened into the most bittersweet of smiles.

"One hundred days after the first night I touched him, my brother died."

Amanda began to gather her things. I hadn't noticed that the time was up. She hung her jacket over her arm. She hooked the handle of her purse in her fingers. She said, "My friend? The one I am so concerned about? From last week?"

"Yes."

"This economy? A while back, I lost my job. Was unemployed for a long time. I've been putting together gigs to keep going. My friend is one of my gigs."

I nodded. For young people disadvantaged by our stagnant economy, gigology—piecing together jobs—had become part of the culture of adaptation.

"The job I do for him?" She paused. "I'm his companion. He pays me . . . to be with him."

My breath caught in my chest for a split second, as though the power serving my grid were suddenly interrupted and my nervous system suffered a rolling brownout.

My eyes flitted to the digital clock behind Amanda. In that brief instant, the numbers changed from :44 to :45. The session was over.

Amanda stood. I got to my feet a second after she did.

My balance felt just the slightest bit compromised, which was likely Amanda's intent. She had saved that last bit of news until the end of the session for a reason.

We stood there, two feet apart, eye to eye, for a few seconds.

She said, "Now you will get some time to decide how you feel about what I do for a living."

I opened my mouth to reply—aware of the overt challenge inherent in her timing. My instinct was to find some magic reply that would shed some light on the dynamic between us. I found nothing.

Amanda said, "Thank you." She made a graceful pirouette before she walked toward the door. She pulled it closed behind her.

# SEVENTEEN

I spent the remaining moments before my next appointment, an initial session with a new patient, trying to clear my head so I would be ready.

I had no way to know it, but no amount of preparation would have left me ready for him.

The intake session started off not unlike many other first appointments.

The moment the man sat down he said, "How do I start?"

That was how I translated what he said, anyway.

The words in that first quick sentence came out as a mashed-syllable mumble—"Howdeyestrt." He spoke as though his last stop before my office had been an extended visit with his dentist, a practitioner who favored massive doses of Novocain. I had to replay the speech sounds in my head a couple of times before I felt that I comprehended the noises my patient was making.

I could have said nothing in reply. Or I could have suggested he begin anywhere he liked. Instead, I rolled out my well-practiced opening line.

I asked him how I could be of help.

He didn't have a ready answer. He stuck his tongue against his cheek far in the back of his mouth on the left side.

My initial impressions of the man included that he was anxious and that he was not a typical patient for my practice. His presentation had an edgy, muted hipster vibe that would hardly stand out on the sidewalks of Boulder, especially on The Hill, but if putting food in my children's lunch boxes depended on my maintaining a vibrant hipster caseload, my kids would have been hungry. Mid- to late-twenties guys like my new patient were not the bread and butter of a Boulder psychotherapy practice like mine. I could recall only one quasi-hipster I'd treated in the previous couple of years. He'd agreed to see me for four sessions only because his parents were threatening to kick him out of their guesthouse if he didn't go to therapy for at least a month.

He made a consistent argument to me that his presence in a therapist's office was ironic, because he didn't have any problems. Initially, I was content to point out that, despite his protests, he had at least one very concrete problem: his parents were threatening to kick him out of his house if his lifestyle didn't undergo metamorphoses.

He and I had made some progress over our four sessions. I had ended up liking him quite a bit. By the end of the month he'd found a job. He told his parents he was working in a used-record store, but what he was actually doing was selling medical marijuana. He told me he was also thinking about graduate school.

That one previous hipster psychotherapy experience left me curious whether my new patient's appearance in my office that day might have been somebody else's idea. Perhaps a parent, growing tired of his living in the basement. Or the court, growing tired of a swelling misdemeanor rap sheet. Or whatever physician had treated him for the apparent injuries he'd recently suffered.

From his physical appearance—he was healing from a slew of injuries—I suspected he had been in a bad fight, and lost, or a bad accident, and had been lucky to survive.

I reminded myself to keep an open mind.

His reply to my query about how I could be of help was, "Igothrtanaformiafir. Oocanprolleetell. Broakmyfash."

I leaned forward and asked him to please repeat what he said, as slowly as he could. I explained that I was having trouble understanding him.

He took a deep breath. Exhaled. Inhaled again. He said, "Sorry. The olds tell me I mumble when I'm nervous. And it's hard to talk now, with my jaw. I mumble even more."

*The olds?* I thought. Back to the Urban Dictionary. *Is that me? Huh.*

He then repeated what he had said before, forcing unnatural pauses between the words. "I got hurt during the Fourmile Fire. Among other things, I broke my face." He waved at his jawline, then tugged at his hair, which was cut at various lengths, depending on the location of the nearest head wound.

I was relieved that he could temper the mumbling with some effort. I had begun to fear that his speech difficulty was going to be a constant part of our time together.

I had no idea at that point that as far as my fears went, that particular one was completely overdetermined.

When he'd made the appointment with me on the phone, he'd used the name Ricky Contreras. To me, it was just a name.

During the first moments he was in my office, as I struggled to make sense of his pressured, garbled speech, I considered the possibility that his speaking pattern was the result of the poor grasp of English of a nonnative speaker—Contreras can be an ethnically Mexican name—or was a consequence of his apparent recent facial injuries. My gut instinct said that neither was the correct explanation. Although mumbled and rushed, Ricky's English wasn't accented or flawed. His sentence structure was fine.

Even after I had managed to get him to acknowledge his tendency to mumble when anxious, and after I had asked him to slow down and repeat his reasons for coming in for therapy, Ricky's speech sped right back up.

Trying to comprehend the staccato bursts of syllables

as they piled up on each other like railcars in a train wreck required that I use all my brainpower to reverse engineer the sounds into something that might resemble words from an English-language dictionary. I then had to break the words apart into sentences that I might comprehend.

I steeled myself. Listening to him for an entire forty-five-minute session was going to be exhausting.

Ricky Contreras had been injured the first night of the Fourmile Fire in an auto accident. That fact alone should have made me suspicious, but it didn't. I had still not made any connection between him and the unconscious man that Sam and I had visited in the ICU. I did not make that connection until he rolled up his shirtsleeves and exposed a distinctive tattoo on the underside of his left forearm.

*Ice-cold Satan,* I thought. *The Saturnian symbol for* na-maste.

That is the moment I realized that I was sitting a few feet away from Sleepy Doe.

Rick explained that it was his reputed unconsciousness in the days after the accident that motivated him to seek help from a therapist. His physicians' descriptions of his absent consciousness, he told me, never felt accurate to him. He was, in fact, certain that he had clear memories of things that had happened in the ICU during the time when he was supposedly in a coma.

He admitted he was having some trouble, still, sorting out what might have been real about the experiences he was recalling from his first few days in the ICU and what might have been the result of imaginings caused by his head injuries.

He told me he was hoping I could be of some help sorting all that out.

I had grown so anxious by then that I was reminding myself to breathe. To buy myself some time to ponder the mess I was in, I asked, "Since your discharge, I assume you've followed up with a neurologist?"

Rick had. The outpatient neurologist had, in fact, recently assured him that his recovery was on track, and perhaps even ahead of schedule. The doctor expected a complete, or near-complete, recovery to what Rick called "pre-morph-ed" neurological status. I made an assumption that my new patient had meant "pre-morbid," but I didn't correct him.

It would not have been a therapeutic thing to do.

# EIGHTEEN

Ricky Contreras left my office abruptly after only twenty minutes. He apologized for the quick exit, said he had another meeting he had to attend.

That is what I thought he said, anyway.

"But this was helpful," he added.

I wasn't accustomed to patients deciding when a session was over. I told him I would have to charge him for the full time we had scheduled. He asked how much he owed. I repeated the number I had given him on the phone when we'd scheduled the appointment. From his pocket he pulled a wad of bills wrapped in a purple broccoli band, and he peeled off enough cash to pay me.

Actually, he included forty dollars too much. I pointed out the overage, fearing that he intended the extra as a gratuity.

He told me he didn't have any small bills and he would like me to hold on to it, apply it next time.

"You would like another visit?" I said while trying to disguise my amazement.

"Absolutely," he said. "Now that I've gotten to know you a little, I have some questions for you."

I wasn't planning to work that Friday, but I made an exception for Ricky Contreras. We picked a time in the afternoon.

*Holy shit, holy shit, holy shit.*

Sam had previously invited me—it was more like a summons—to meet up with him over my lunch break. He had spent his morning at the Justice Center, across Canyon Boulevard not far from my office, waiting less than patiently to testify at an assault trial. That's why he had insisted that our rendezvous take place on the Boulder Creek trail near the criminal courts. I didn't often cross Canyon during a workday; most days the road felt like too daunting a barricade for pedestrian transit and offered too little reward on the other side.

I was feeling an acute need to tell him about the brand-new problem I feared we were facing—the fact that Sleepy Doe, who became Coma Doe, had tracked me down—but Sam already had an agenda in mind for our meeting. Sam's goal was to chastise me about my decision to visit Frederick.

I acquiesced, listening without much rancor to his partisan redescription of my supposed sins. But I felt that the tenor of his conclusion, "Don't do it again, Alan," constituted an unnecessary provocation.

The directive was particularly unpalatable because Sam delivered it in his cop voice, not his friend voice. The general "it" he was referring to was my cycling sojourn to Frederick and my extended encounter with Currie's landlord-once-removed, Izza.

"That's an order, Detective?" I said. I didn't even try to disguise my sarcasm.

He sighed at me. "Do not go back there. Under any circumstances. You don't know what you're doing. What you're getting into. Who might be paying attention to you in that location." Sam shook his head in a way I construed to be demeaning. "There are a lot of moving parts to all this. Don't—Just don't. What kind of name is Izza anyway?"

Sam's question about Izza's name was not born of curiosity. His current stress level was causing a regressive reversion to cranky, narrow-minded Sam, questioning anything he didn't understand or endorse. He could have just as easily framed his rant with a pointless demand to know why people were no longer named Tom or Mary. Or Sam.

"It's short for Isabel," I said, wondering why I bothered. "Some of what you're saying about my trip to Frederick may well be true. I'll give you that. But—"

"You'll give me that. Gee, thanks. I—"

"Think, Sam. Damn it. What's the harm? I have a much better understanding of what happened that night. The terrain. Who the players are. How it went down."

Sam was waiting to pounce. I hadn't recognized that the demeaning act I had just endured had actually represented restraint on his part. "And you think that's a good thing? Are you really as simple as you sound? You act as though you're the only one on the planet with eyes and ears. You need me to walk you through some of the absolutely catastrophic ways this could go wrong?"

"I'm not asking for your imprimatur. Maybe I do think that what I learned is a good thing. And was worth the modicum of risk I took."

"Imprimatur? *Modicum?* You kidding me? If you think using ten-buck words makes what you did more reasonable, then you're an idiot. This isn't about what facts you know, or might learn. This is about what facts *they* know. And I'm still trying to discover what facts they know. What information the sheriff has now that he didn't have when Currie's body was found. What this purported new witness of theirs saw."

At times, when Sam got impassioned he could sound as though he'd just stepped out of northern Minnesota for the first time. Other times when Sam got impassioned he could sound as though he'd spent his whole life in Des Moines. This was an example of the latter. The Iron Range patois was absent.

"Try this on: now that word of the reopening of the investigation is spreading, the investigators could be using rumors as bait, and they may have set up surveillance to see who shows up in Frederick to sniff around that bait. Did you consider that? That somebody might have watched you pedal into the middle of that mess in your weird little biking shoes and your chartreuse frigging helmet?"

I considered my new helmet to be more of a fluorescent green but decided not to press the point. I didn't like the sound of the police-setting-a-trap part of Sam's speech.

I said, "You think the sheriff might know I was there?"

"No, all I was thinking was the sheriff might know *someone* was there." Sam's tone revealed a worrisome combination of disbelief and disgust. "Because it didn't enter my dim-witted brain that you would use your real name."

"I did not. Well, my first name, yes. But that's it. I left Izza, the landlord, with the clear impression I lived and worked in Denver. That I would commute if I rented the place. She doesn't know who I am. Or where I live."

Sam took two more steps before he spied the soft underbelly in my story. He stopped, already shaking his head in anticipatory dismay. "And later on, did you get back to her? To Izza? About not renting the cottage?"

"She asked me to let her know, one way or another."

"Dear God above, please tell me you didn't."

*I am an idiot.* I said, "Okay, she has my cell number from the text I sent."

"Yeah, she has your effing cell number."

"I'm sorry. But it's not that big a deal. I was a pretty convincing prospective tenant. There is no reason for her to be suspicious of me. And, to be positive about all this for just a minute or two? A second perspective on how this went down could be a plus."

"Yeah? 'How this went down'? That hasn't been a big question mark for me, seeing that I was there. I haven't forgotten what happened. In fact, I will never forget what happened."

Despite my hard-learned experience that contentious discussions with Sam when he was in a dyspeptic mood rarely got me anywhere, I pressed on. "But you don't know who else might have seen something the night you were there. And that is a big deal, given what's going on with the investigation.

"For example? There's a little boy who lives at the end of the lane, the end that's closest to town. I didn't get a last name, but I know which house it is. Kid's name is Elias Tres, like Elias the Third. Oh, and this is an interesting thing—he disagrees with the coroner's finding about time of death. Izza gave me the impression that everybody in Frederick believes the kid's version. They all think the medical examiner got it wrong."

"Everyone believes the kid? That's what Izza says?"

Sam was skilled at condescension. I had to give him that. I said, "Apparently."

"Does Izza say the boy thinks the death was sooner or later than is in the record?"

"Tres thinks that her body was there a day longer than is in the coroner's report."

Sam took a couple of steps without adding anything demeaning. I saw progress.

He said, "I always assumed the coroner had it right. The date. I don't think I checked. Maybe he got it wrong. That could help. If the record is wrong."

"See?" I said. I was scoring that as a point for me. Sam might still have an advantage on the scoreboard, but I was no longer being shut out.

"Could the new witness be that kid?" Sam asked. He had his phone in his hand; I half expected him to use Google to search for the answer. "How old?"

"I don't know for sure, but young. Izza described him as a chatterbox. Likable. He lives with his grandfather. His father died a while back in Afghanistan. Izza called the grandfather Big Elias, or Old Elias. For what it's worth, I think Izza may have had a thing for Elias Tres's father, the marine who died. People called him Segundo. He was the second Elias. *Segundo* means 'second' in Spanish."

"I know that," Sam said.

Sam didn't know that, but I let it slide. Bilingual, Sam was not. Yes, he knew *cerveza* meant "beer." But when Sam said "gracias," the word never came out of his mouth the same way twice and rarely came out sounding the way a native Spanish speaker might appreciate. On a good day, Sam could order a Tex-Mex meal without embarrassment. That was about the extent of his Spanish language skills.

"Huh," Sam said. "A kid? Under ten? Over ten? You really don't know?"

"From the context, I would say he's under ten. I got the impression he was only around five at the time of the . . . death. What I learned is going to give me an advantage when I'm talking with Lauren, Sam. When she mentions something about the case—and she will—I'll be able to understand the context, tell whether it's important."

"Sometimes I'm pretty sure you have brain damage, Alan. Anybody ever recommend you get fitted for one of those protective helmet things?"

I took a deep breath and soldiered on. "Where did you park that night? I assume you didn't drive up to the house and park on that road in front of the ranch. That would have been careless. You know, for an experienced detective like yourself."

He glared at me. Early in our friendship, I would retreat, and cower just a little, when Sam descended into his intolerant zone. In recent years, as I began to stand my ground with his inner bully, he wasn't quite sure what to do with me.

He said, "You don't need to know where I left the car. Anything you don't need to know, it's better that you don't know."

I waited to shrug until I was certain he would witness my shrug. I said, "We don't know what this supposed new witness saw that night. Could have been you, could have been your car. If the Jeep was parked a ways from the lane, then we're talking about a whole new range of possible potential witnesses. That's the type of thing I was hoping to narrow down by going out there—who could have seen you? Who might the witness be? So that's why I think it would be helpful for me to know where you parked your damn car."

Sam stuffed his hands into his pockets. He stayed silent as we approached a young mother who was pushing a twin stroller in the opposite direction. The stroller was one of the long narrow ones, not one of the side-by-sides. It had as many moving parts as a space shuttle. I suspected it cost as much as my first two cars, combined. The babies, most definitely fraternal, were asleep. The woman's eyes widened as she moved closer to us. She lifted an index finger to her lips, imploring us to stay quiet while we passed.

Once we were downwind of the trio, Sam said, "Nobody saw the Jeep. Okay?"

"How can you be sure?"

"I'm sure. Let it go, Alan."

I knew I was pushing my luck, and that I hadn't started the conversation with much good fortune to spare. To maintain any credibility in the discussion of Frederick with Sam, I would have to convince him I had something important to add. I said, "Based on what I saw out there—the geography of that part of Frederick—I think you approached the cottage on foot down the dirt service road that runs north and south adjacent to the fields. Behind her place, on the east side? You know that road?"

He levitated one of his bulbous eyebrows. "Yeah? Go on."

"I see you parking someplace else—maybe even in town, it's not that far—and then walking down the state road until you got to the little ag access thing. I can't see another way for you to have approached the cottage without being obvious. I don't think you had any good choices, but I think that was the best of your bad choices."

Sam raised both eyebrows. "Is that what you think?" he said. "That I didn't have any good choices that night? What a revelation."

My dime lost, I threw down my dollar. "The other approach—driving or walking down the lane that cuts off from the state road—would have left you visible to anyone in a few different houses, or to anyone who happened to be driving to or from any of the farms or ranches on that lane." I no longer felt any confidence that Sam was paying attention to my conjecture.

After a few more steps he said, "Stay out of this, Alan. You're smart enough to be dangerous. You're not smart enough to be helpful."

I chose to ignore the insult, which, from Sam, was tepid. I said, "It is what it is. I'm an accomplice. You are not going to change that by wishing it were different. If you get caught, I get caught. You can't protect me."

His voice took on a chill. "Could you possibly be as cavalier about this as you sound? We're not talking about a slap on the wrist. We're talking your career, gone. Your house, gone. We're talking every penny you've ever saved for your family, for your wife's old age, and for your kids' college gone to lawyers. Then we're talking about first-degree homicide. That means life in prison, or worse. You know about the worse?"

"I've covered this ground a hundred times in my head, Sam. It's not abstract for me. The alternative? That woman was threatening our children. That woman was planning to kill our children. That damn woman had already broken into my daughter's bedroom and destroyed her security and molested things that she loved. That bitch had already photographed our children—yours and mine—in places where they were most vulnerable to her.

"You want to talk about my vulnerability now? It's a fraction of the vulnerability we had then. You told me that we had nothing to take to the police. No evidence to implicate her. You told me you acted that night because the only alternative to her death was living with the threat she posed to our children.

"Well, I prefer this vulnerability to that vulnerability. You did what had to be done. I supported you then. I support you now. I am all in. I will stand by you. And I will be grateful to you. Forever."

I was proud of my speech. I'd said what I needed to say.

Sam wasn't so impressed. He stopped walking. In a modulated voice devoid of antagonism, he said, "What you just said is lovely, poetic bullshit. Pure, righteous rationalization. You think any prosecutor or any jury is going to care *why* I did what I did that night? Or *why* you allowed yourself to become an accessory to murder *after* that night? They won't *care*. No one will give a shit.

"Why? Because cops and prosecutors know what I know, what every homicide detective knows: the eloquent righteousness that is spewing from your mouth is the final excuse of the vigilante. The difference between you and me? You won't ever hear me feel or sound as self-righteous and self-satisfied as you. Two reasons. The first is because I know nobody cares.

"The second is more important. It's because I don't plan to get caught. You? You talk like you're rehearsing the soliloquy you plan to give at your sentencing hearing. Jesus. I, on the other hand, don't plan to have a sentencing hearing.

"You're out biking around the county like you're invisible and invincible. If I'm a cop trying to break this thing, you are my damn wet dream." He tightened his jaw before he continued. "Don't screw with my plan, Alan. My plan is simpler than your plan. *My* plan is to not get caught. Do you understand what I'm saying?"

He didn't want an answer. I didn't have one. We were finally on the same page.

I thought he was done. I was wrong. He said, "With all your good intentions, you're going to end up leaving us both on the wrong side of some high fences and thick walls in Cañon City or Buena Vista."

His phone chirped. He checked the screen. "I'm the next witness. I have to go. You know, be a cop." He pocketed the phone before he put both his hands on my shoulders. "Don't fuck this up for me. The stakes are too high. If you do fuck this up, and the state doesn't kill you, I will kill you." He smiled at me, as a friend. "I'll do it more slowly than they will. And I will enjoy it more than they will."

Sam began to walk away. To his back, I said, "There's a new development. Something else we need to talk about. It's important. It may end up having some bearing on Frederick. Indirectly." He barely slowed down. I called out, "I realize that this may not be the best possible moment, time-wise."

He laughed loudly enough that I could hear him even

with his face pointed away from me. He turned briefly. "You're right, it's not the best moment for me, time-wise." He raised his phone, the contemporary equivalent of tapping the face of a wristwatch. "We'll talk about your news some other time."

I yelled, "What about tonight?"

"Working."

"Tomorrow?"

"Working."

He kept walking.

"It's important," I yelled. "Really important."

Sam waved.

# NINETEEN

I was ambivalent about postponing the next conversation I had to have with Sam. Although the topic was urgent—even critical—I had not yet figured out how to share with him the news that the newest addition to my clinical practice was Coma Doe.

I was bound by professional ethics. And legal responsibilities. The fact that I was seeing Coma Doe for therapy was privileged information.

Although the news about Coma Doe was something I could not hide from Sam, I was also concerned that Coma Doe could be waiting for me to get careless about his confidentiality. If he discovered me sharing clinical information cavalierly, with a single phone call he could make my life even more complicated than it already was. I had to be clever, or at the very least smart, about how I was going to bring Sam up to speed.

\* \* \*

After Sam returned to testify at the Justice Center, I crossed Boulder Creek and followed Arapahoe up past the Foot of the Mountain Motel to Eben Fine Park. Each of those locations reminded me of a previous serious mess I'd gotten myself into. I comforted myself that I somehow escaped the mortal perils I'd felt during those episodes. I tried to feel reassured by the fact that I'd survived each one. None of it worked. I felt as vulnerable heading back toward downtown as I'd felt walking away.

I tried to clear my head, forcing myself not to perseverate on the mistakes I might have made on my visit to Frederick, or on any review of the mistakes I might have made in my initial, abbreviated meeting with Coma Doe.

I refocused, determined to think through the powerful session I'd just had with Amanda, and the provocative way she had chosen to end the hour.

She had deliberately used the word "companion" to describe her relationship with the man she had previously identified as her boss. Her specific challenge to me at the end of that morning's session had been to decide how I felt about, as she put it, what she did. As I walked back to town on Pearl Street, that is what I was pondering.

*What does a "companion" do?*

I was assuming that Amanda was telling me that she was acting as a paid companion to the man whose professional life was falling apart. The one who was, possibly, contemplating suicide. I was also considering the likelihood that her companionship with him took multiple forms, and that some of those forms were intimate. Or—if not intimate in the psychologically meaningful way I usually defined the word in my office—at least sexual.

I was having a hard time arriving at any other conclusion than that Amanda was telling me that she was, for want of a better word—and that morning I lacked that better word—the man's mistress. But Amanda had obviously considered there to be a better word, the one she had used with me. That word was "companion."

Was the difference in vocabulary one that made a difference? She hadn't said she was the man's lover. She hadn't even led me to believe that he was married, or involved with another woman. Amanda had not chosen to identify herself as his "mistress"—a word I would have construed to mean something specific—nor had she chosen to define herself as his "courtesan" or his "concubine." Had she used either of those last two nouns I would have simply gone online and researched contemporary connotations. The ancient definitions in my head—part geisha, part something else—probably didn't have any application to whatever relationship she was having with the troubled venture capital guy.

Amanda had identified what she was doing as companionship. She had clearly described the man as her employer. The variable that differentiated mistress from employed companion? I was assuming that money was changing hands. Hell, she had identified her service to the man as one of her gigs.

I revisited her challenge. *How do I feel about it?* I was having trouble generating much moral outrage about her employment.

When I let my mind freely wander the psychotherapeutic terrain, I noted how easily my focus skipped between the current arrangement she had with her employer and the earlier one she'd had with her older brother when she was just shy of fifteen years old. The creation of just that gestalt—the current figure, companion, superimposed over the earlier ground, hand job fairy—could have been Amanda's intent.

I was acutely aware that Amanda had chosen, consciously or unconsciously, to present those two chapters in her life to me in a particular order. The order of the narratives made it difficult to view her recent adult—"adult" in all its connotations—choice absent the context of her earlier, immature, adolescent decisions.

*How do I feel about her work?* As part of the companionship arrangement, she was earning money. As part of the arrangement, she was likely making herself available for sex. If *a* was true, and *b* was true, then *c* was also, likely, true.

*C* was that Amanda was functioning, in a broad context, as a sex worker. An escort. A prostitute. Her challenge at the end of the session left me wondering whether she anticipated that I would feel some negative judgment about that profession.

I had scant context to help me understand the work Amanda was describing.

Not many months before, I had been seeing a Denver banker for therapy for what he self-described as an addiction to "hobbying." The term was new to me at the time, but the hobby he was seeking help arresting was a lifestyle that included frequent visits with prostitutes. The therapy had been short-lived, and I considered it less than successful. Despite the fact that his hobby was costing him up to a thousand dollars a month that he said he couldn't afford, I had always considered his desire for change to be tepid at best. I told him once, just before he abruptly stopped therapy, that his anxiety appeared to be almost entirely about being discovered or caught.

"Of course," was how he replied.

I wasn't confident I had been helpful to him, but during the brief treatment, I had managed to learn a lot from him about a microworld about which I had previously known almost nothing.

The women he visited, and paid for sex, were never "hookers" to him, or "whores." My patient didn't troll for streetwalkers. He had always referred to the women he made "dates" with as "escorts," "providers," or "ASPs." Adult service providers. He had always spoken of the women with respect. Occasionally, I thought, with reverence.

*Was,* I wondered, *Amanda one of those women? An ASP?*

I wasn't sure. My ex-patient had paid various providers for short increments of their time. An hour or two. An evening. When he traveled, he would occasionally splurge for an overnight date. Although a couple of women became what he called ATFs—his all-time favorites—he mostly preferred variety.

Amanda was not describing much variety. I was suspecting that Amanda's commitment of time to her employer was much longer in duration than an evening or a night. Did that change things? Did the extended time commitment Amanda made cause her to be something other than a "provider"? I did not know.

I cut back toward my office when I got to Sixth.

My next session with Amanda would likely provide new pieces for the puzzle and new data to remedy my ignorance.

I literally stopped in my tracks when I recognized that Amanda's revelation in the last moment of our time together that she was a paid companion had almost completely overshadowed what had been one of the most poignant sessions I had experienced in my office, ever.

*Talk about process. Lord.*

As I walked up the driveway toward the back door to my office, Sam texted me.

**Some asshole busted into my car. Where the f were the f-ing cops??? Do you know a good glass place?**

Before I felt any compassion for Sam's situation, I felt some selfish relief that he'd discovered the burglary after our earlier conversation, and not before.

# TWENTY

I continued to leave Sam messages trying to find a time to talk about Coma Doe. No luck.

The next afternoon, Diane invited me to join her to look at a downtown flat after I was done with work. She actually used the word "flat" in her invitation, which made me wary—it was not exactly a common term in the local real estate vernacular.

The invitation came in the form of a handwritten note she attached by tape to the door to our shared bathroom. She was confident I would see it there; after practicing together as long as we had, Diane and I knew each other's intimate patterns as well as would a longtime married couple.

One night the previous spring when the four of us— Lauren and I, Raoul and Diane—had been out to dinner,

Raoul had waited until the ladies excused themselves to the restroom before he told me that Diane often referred to me as her "work spouse."

I replied that I wasn't sure whether to feel honored or offended.

At first, he said he hadn't known whether to be threatened by my status. But he ultimately decided that it was cool.

That Raoul might feel even a twinge of threat from me was the stuff of revelation, though I was unconvinced about his sincerity. "Work spouse? Really?" I'd said.

He allowed that sometimes it was "work husband" and occasionally even "city spouse." He said that one—"*ciutat cònjuge*"—was his favorite, and probably the most accurate. The translation, I assumed, was into Raoul's native Catalonian tongue.

Unsure of the accuracy of the translation, I asked, "That's not some kind of Mediterranean homie insult?"

In response, Raoul smiled a smile I envied. The envy was pure. I envied Raoul's smile the same way that I envied Derrick Rose's dribble drive or Brian Greene's grasp of cosmology.

"Hardly. I am grateful to you. You are a great friend to my wife. Through some very difficult times. Her wounds are not always easy."

"I adore her, Raoul. She is my dear friend."

Diane's real estate invitation included a short, desperate postscript. It read, "Please don't say no please please please." I suspected that Diane's flat-shopping summons was part of my city spouse responsibilities. I understood that I would decline at my peril.

I texted Lauren that I would be home a little late. As explanation, I used the solitary word Diane. She texted me back that my penance would be picking up dinner.

Diane was waiting in her office at the end of the day. She knew I'd say yes.

"We walking or driving?" I asked.

"Four blocks," she replied.

Diane was either implying that four blocks was a dreadful hike or that four blocks was a mere jaunt. I didn't care whether we walked or drove, so I made a guess about her preference. "Let's just walk," I said.

"I think I'd rather drive," she said. "I'm in heels, and the place has terrific parking. How great is that?"

Years of friendship had left us with few secrets. Although Diane would often appear to be interested in appearing accommodating with me, she had a controlling side I knew well. I'd been aware of her self-centered streak from the beginning of our friendship, but as we aged together as partners and friends her controlling, self-focused alter was becoming a more dominating presence.

For my part, I was yielding to her wishes more than I did when we were younger. In that sense, we were coconspirators. I liked to rationalize that I wasn't enabling her, but rather that I was exhibiting compassion. For Las Vegas, initially. But more recently, for the pain Diane had suffered watching the family of her longtime best friend disintegrate the previous year.

Diane had not recovered from the traumas of Las Vegas. She had not been able to digest the crimes her friend had committed to protect her family. My longtime friend was becoming a poster child for the consequences of repeated trauma.

I asked, "Are we meeting Kevin?" Kevin was Diane's real-estate-agent-slash-friend. Once she demonstrated the first inclination to move to town, Diane had proven to be an ambivalent house shopper; her insistence on seeing everything—not an exaggeration—and her refusal to commit to anything caused her to burn through Realtors at a rapid clip. Diane had earned her reputation.

Kevin was a recent acquisition. He'd already hung around longer than most.

Diane whispered, "Kevin gave me the lockbox code," before she returned her voice to its normal pitch. "The owners are in Slovakia. No, Slovenia? Far away. Raoul would know which was correct just by looking at the couple from across the room. If he heard them speak, even just a sentence, he would know what village they're from. Drives me nuts. Anyway, Kevin says the listing agent knows about us stopping by. We can inspect at our leisure."

"Kevin gave you the code?" I wasn't accustomed to real estate agents sending buyers on solo property-hunting missions armed with lockbox codes to private residences. "The place has no alarm?"

"Kevin doesn't think it's set. It wasn't when he showed it to me."

"I don't think I wanted to know that."

"Don't be such a good boy, Alan. It's a tough market. People have to be flexible if they want to sell. Kevin has a charity thing tonight. He knows how interested I am in this place. And anyway, who, I ask, is more trustworthy than me?"

I was way too experienced with Diane to disagree with her self-assessment. I said, "This is a good idea? Yes?"

She asked, "What is three percent of two point seven million?"

Lauren often reminded me that she found me annoyingly good—the amalgam of compliment and criticism completely intentional on her part—at doing arithmetic in my head. The posed problem—Kevin's half share of a likely 6 percent real estate sales commission—wasn't much of a challenge. "Eighty-one thousand dollars," I said. "Is that exactly how trustworthy you are?"

Diane grabbed her things. Over her shoulder, she said, "At a minimum."

I said, "I thought you and Raoul were going to rent while the *Daily Camera* project gets sorted out. Buying means a big change in plans."

"I'm impatient." Diane had not always been so impatient. She knew that. I knew that. I wrote the change off, too, to Las Vegas and PTSD. She said, "I've looked and I've looked. There's nothing to rent downtown that's right for us. Now I'm thinking we'll buy, then we'll sell again once the redevelopment is done and the market has recovered. Maybe even make a little money on the flip. Then"—she widened her eyes—"we can move into my new sky palace at Eleventh and Pearl."

Considering his wealth, Raoul was a simple man. He showed no inclination toward accumulating stuff, or collecting things, and had an aversion to purchases that might complicate his life. Despite his money—I didn't know the extent of his fortune, but I assumed that it had grown large enough that at any given time he didn't know the extent of his fortune, either—Raoul possessed few of the accoutrements of the wealthy. He and Diane owned no second home, not even a condo in ski country. No time-share jet. No yacht on call in St. John or St. Tropez. Diane didn't flaunt big jewels. Their home in the foothills was of modest proportions, especially considering the extent of their financial resources.

Buying a multimillion-dollar temporary downtown home—excuse me, flat—sounded like the exact kind of thing Raoul would consider an unnecessary complication.

I said, "Raoul's on board with this? It doesn't sound like his kind of move."

Diane exhaled audibly through her nose. I translated the sound as exasperation. "Raoul's in Chicago. Again. He told me I could find someplace for us to live in town. If I decide this is the place, I'll convince him there isn't an alternative. That's the way it works for us. As a couple."

I put my arm around her. "You mean once he understands that he has a wife who has reached the absolute end of her tolerance for living in the mountains?" Diane looked up at me. I could see all the years of our friendship reflected in her eyes. I said, "I was talking about the Fourmile Fire. I know how frightened you were."

She nodded, then she said, "I don't even like to think

about that." She looked away for a second, then back. "The truth? It's more like Raoul has a wife who's in danger of becoming a complete bitch. I swear, if the *Daily Camera* thing falls through, if . . ."

I hugged her with both arms. She curled into my body like my daughter, Gracie, did after she'd endured one of her rare bad days.

"How're things with you?" Diane asked.

I was taken aback. Since Las Vegas, Diane's self-focus almost never swayed. In her unique variant of PTSD, she had become post-traumatically narcissistic. "The kids are good, Lauren's health has been stable. No complaints." *That I can tell you about.*

"Work? Your practice? Therapist friends tell me things are slow. You getting new referrals?"

"I've picked up a couple of new patients recently. I'm doing all right, given the economy."

"Interesting patients? Will they stick around?"

I was wary. The last two questions were not things I recalled Diane wondering about before. I shrugged. "Interesting? Sure. Long-term? Who knows? Too soon to tell."

"I'll send some more your way."

*More?* I didn't recall recent referrals from Diane. "I know you will, Diane. You know I'm grateful. You want me to drive?" I asked as I was locking the door to our building.

"Nope," she said. She climbed into her Saab convertible and lowered the top.

# TWENTY-ONE

The flat of Diane's of-the-moment dreams turned out to be a what-the-hell-were-they-thinking thirty-six-hundred-and-change-square-foot two-story renovation of an old commercial building that was less than half a block from Pearl on the other end of the Pearl Street Mall. The neighborhood was a thriving part of downtown with some of the city's best food and most interesting shopping.

Diane's estimate of our trip had been four blocks. I was tempted to point out that had we driven only that distance from our office we would have been less than halfway to the flat. I didn't.

The building that was our destination had been an unremarkable two-story, Depression-era, commercial brick rectangle in a downtown Boulder location that had gentrified in many interesting ways, including a good selection of urban housing. Diane pulled into a reserved parking space from the alley behind the building. I had already made a decision to keep any less-than-exuberant first impressions to myself. Were I to proffer discouraging words I would need to be willing to absorb the consequences. I was tired. I wasn't willing.

Diane said, "There are three more parking spaces inside that garage door. That one, see?" She pointed to an industrial-size overhead door that faced the alley. "And this guest space outside. So, parking for four cars? Three indoors, and heated? That's pretty great in this part of town. You have to admit."

"It is," I said, seizing the opportunity to be agreeable.

The alley behind the building would be dark at night. I could see no convenient path leading from the guest parking spot around to the front door of the flat. A visitor would be required to make a long walk around the building. Guests might not be thrilled with the access. I kept those thoughts to myself.

A fussy, anachronistic doorway in the middle of a street-level retail façade marked the dwelling's sidewalk entrance. The door was sandwiched between a showroom for a company that was selling geothermal heat-exchange equipment and a business that appeared to be the eponymous gallery of a local artist I'd never heard of. Her stuff seemed technically proficient but a tad floral for my tastes. Since Diane was more comfortable with floral than I was, I thought she might appraise the gallery space as a distinct neighborly asset.

Diane fumbled with the digital lockbox for a moment. Her first attempt at entry failed. She stomped her foot and cursed. Diane then hummed for a few seconds before she sang a little song—"*Who you gonna tell? Everybody. What you gonna sell? Sell me, baby!*"

The memory cue did the trick for her. She entered another code. The compartment of the device opened, yielding Diane a pair of house keys on a small ring.

Inside the front door was a narrow landing that led to an even narrower staircase that my internal protractor told me was way too steep to meet Boulder County's exacting building code. For two point seven million dollars, I'd expected to see an elevator.

Diane hiked up her skirt and trudged up the stairs. I followed, counting fourteen treads. It would be a lot of climbing for an elderly guest.

The apartment was big and featured great views of the city and the mountains. The apartment was also—I tried to find another word but couldn't—garish. The word fit the décor of the apartment the same way that "tawdry" fits the atmosphere in the French Quarter in New Orleans.

What flavor of garish? If I closed my eyes I could imagine a South Beach condo after a redo by a design-challenged second cousin of Gianni Versace.

Diane kicked off her heels. I pulled off my loafers. I stayed close by as Diane played tour guide. The owners had poured a mess of money into a gut renovation of the public rooms on the second floor of the existing structure. Diane explained that the homeowners had managed to exploit planning loopholes by expanding an existing rooftop shed into a copper-clad third story that included dual master suites. They had topped the new addition with an expansive rooftop deck.

She traipsed around the flat at a rapid clip. I trudged behind as my impressions hardened like quick-curing concrete. Diane's monologue was upbeat and enthusiastic, but I thought she was parroting a sales spiel she'd heard earlier from Kevin. Her enthusiasm was intended to convince me to like the place so that I would do her the deep favor of convincing her to love it.

I could already tell that she would require some convincing. Diane didn't love the flat. She wanted to, but she didn't.

We ended the tour back in the long, narrow living room that had a great view of the Flatirons. I waited.

"Is it too much?" she said just a moment before she collapsed beside me onto a tangerine leather sofa that was ten times firmer than it appeared to be. She literally *thunk*ed as her butt hit the cushion. "Did I mention that the furniture is included?"

"Good news, or bad news?" I said with a friendly smile. A fake-fur throw that was draped over the back of the sofa—I hoped it was fake fur—was high on my list of potentially bad news.

She looked around the big space once more, allowing her eyes to settle on a variety of expensive touches that raised questions of taste. Either my taste, or that of the designer responsible for the flair.

"I admit there's a lot going on in here. Right? Isn't there?" she said. I was hoping not to be required to provide an answer. Diane and I had a history to consider; we had demonstrated an inability to discuss interior design without clashing. She went on without my two cents, as I hoped she would. "I know—there is. And there's a tad too much . . . bling in here. Shiny, sparkly stuff. It's not exactly Boulder. But since Kevin showed it to me the first time, I've been asking myself if that's such a bad thing. There's plenty of Boulder right out there." She swept an arm toward the windows.

The Boulder that was apparent out the window was a relatively charming, redbrick, late-nineteenth-century pioneer downtown. A few of the old buildings were Victorian treasures. A few of the more recent were architectural travesties.

"There's a lot of color in here," I said, leaving it up to Diane to decide whether the bouquet of brilliant hues was a good thing or not. "And tile. Hectares of tile, it seems. You like the tile?"

"With waves," Diane added as she got swept up in the design-critique momentum. "Right? Blingy, colorful tile with waves. On the walls? The ceiling even. There's tile on the ceiling, right?" I looked up and nodded. "Did I miss an entire design trend?"

I considered it unlikely that Diane had missed a design trend. But I reminded myself why I'd been dragged along on the errand: to be a friend, not a design *mevin*.

"And why did they put the kitchen off by itself like that?" she asked. "It doesn't relate to anything. Who does that anymore? Resale might be sketchy with that kitchen."

I didn't have an answer for the hide-the-kitchen decision. "The place is big, and it is downtown," I said. "You want big, and I know you want downtown. That rooftop deck? Wow. The views? Think about the parties."

"But," Diane said, "there's no hot tub up there—Raoul wants one—and no shade. The chinooks will probably blow any patio furniture that's not bolted down all the way to Limón. And why didn't they run the elevator up there? I don't understand that—it would be really convenient not to have to carry everything from the kitchen to the roof."

Diane wasn't a cook. It had been a long time since she'd carried much. Any concern she was expressing about convenience was for the caterers she would hire to staff the parties. Still, I gave her points for consideration.

I said, "Arriving guests can't really use the elevator at all, can they? I assume it opens in the garage somewhere. I didn't see an elevator in the front foyer."

She rolled her eyes and nodded. "Behind the staircase that leads to the garage from the front, there's a door. It's disguised. The elevator is through there. Hardly ideal. But it's an old building and . . . there were compromises."

Compromises sounded like it had been one of Kevin's words.

I was waiting for Diane to acknowledge the reality that this flat would not be her temporary downtown home, though I wasn't sure she would arrive at that conclusion that evening. I said, "You doing okay, Diane? I've been worried about you. You're working less and less. I don't see you much."

She paused and waved her left arm at the wavy tile. "I want this place to be the one that will get me out of the hills. I *need* it to be the one. Raoul's on the road all the time. I can't stay up Lee Hill by myself any longer. It's making me crazy. All alone, with the fire danger? I need to make us a home . . . he wants to come home to."

Something had been making Diane a little crazy. But it wasn't just Lee Hill. "You think Raoul is staying away because, what, you're so unhappy with where you live?"

"No. Because I'm a bitch." She smiled. But the smile was halfhearted. She said, "I want to be able to walk out my door and be someplace. To see some people. Not deer—I am so tired of deer. And that damn fire, Alan? Fourmile. God, it scared me to death. Can I tell you something I haven't told anyone?"

"Of course."

"When the fire first blew up, and we got the reverse 911 telling us to prepare to evacuate? I say 'we' but it was me. Raoul was in California trying to outbid some ex-Google people for some social networking start-up. When I was ordered to evacuate, I kept going back and forth between how awful it would be to lose our home and"—she shook her head—"thinking how great it would be to just be done with it." She lowered her voice. "I actually thought about setting the grasses next to the house on fire before I drove away." She wanted something from me right then. I wasn't sure what. "Is that awful of me?" she asked.

I was at a loss. Of course it was awful of her.

"No comment?" she said.

"You're feeling desperate," I said.

"Was that a question?" She wrinkled her nose at me. "I'm baring my soul here."

"I know how desperate you are. How strong was the urge?"

"To become an arsonist? Meh. I've had stronger. But who knows about the next fire? Who knows then? Now I've had time to think about it. To actually plan my arson, buy a half-decent flamethrower at Army Navy Surplus."

I checked her face to be certain she was kidding.

She said, "Do you think the *Daily Camera* site is ever going to get redeveloped? Be honest with me."

The *Camera* site was the primest of prime blocks in downtown Boulder. Raoul was part of an investment group that had purchased the land with plans to redevelop it into a mixed-use bonanza. Lauren and I had tentatively agreed to buy one of the condominiums in the new building. The idea was for Diane and Raoul to live somewhere above us in a hyper-luxe penthouse.

"Of course it'll get done. Soon? You know how soft the real estate market is now. Financing a project that size has to be almost impossible in this environment. Raoul knows all this better than I do. Ask him."

"What Raoul knows is that I'm a mess. Fragile. I don't think he's being honest with me about the prospects for the new building, but he's saying basically what you're saying, what everybody says. It's all about the market and the financing, and that kind of sucks now. You and Lauren are still going to move there? Right?" Diane offered a hopeful smile that almost instantly deteriorated into something fearful. "And don't even think about lying to me. You are going to be my new neighbors, right? I need to count on that."

I finessed a reply. "The economics are much more precarious for us than they are for you and Raoul. Lauren and I will reexamine the moving decision once we get an idea about a timeline and firm numbers about cost. We want to move, but it's going to be a close decision, one way or the other."

Diane leaned into me. "I need this . . . whatever this is . . . to be the place, Alan. This flat has to be my transition. I need today to be the day I begin to find my way out of the damn mountains." I felt a shiver move through her. "But here I am sitting in this expensive fruit-salad-in-a-metallic-bowl apartment. And I don't know."

Diane's hope was in pieces. But she was desperately trying to hold on to it. To me, it was as though she were trying to embrace an armful of packaging peanuts. I placed my arm around her shoulder and squeezed her. "There will be another something to look at soon, Diane. You'll see."

She shook her head. "No!" she barked. "There won't. There isn't anything else. I've looked. I know."

My truism had been intentionally banal, not the kind of reassuring, hopeful appraisal that I thought would be vulnerable to argument. I was taken aback by her vehemence.

After a stop at Zoe Ma Ma to grab takeout for the family, I sped toward home. The flashing lights that distracted me in my mirror as I cut south on the Foothills Parkway pretty much guaranteed that we'd be eating cold food for dinner.

I'd been going fifty-three in a forty-five zone in a location that I knew drew rush-hour traffic patrols like free beer draws college students. I knew better.

My phone rang as I was turning off South Boulder Road onto the winding lane that was the last leg on the way to our Spanish Hills home. Even though the odds of any traffic on the lane were low, I pulled over. The speeding ticket was still sizzling in my pocket.

The call was from Diane. I tried to be upbeat. "Change your mind about the flat? Convince yourself that all that bling is you after all? And this time you want me to talk you out of it? Am I right?"

She said, "Alan, I need your advice."

"Don't buy it, Diane. It will be a bitch to unload when you're ready to move again. Other than the view, and the fact that it's within spitting distance of Frasca and Cured and Snooze, it doesn't have a lot of charm. People are not going to line up to take it off your hands. Don't forget that kitchen that's off by its lonesome."

"I know. It's not about the flat." I heard something somber accompanying her words. I wondered if it had been there earlier and I had missed it. "Sorry," I said. "What can I do?"

On a rushed exhale, she said, "I think Raoul is . . . involved with someone."

I changed the phone from my right ear to my left ear. Changing ears with the phone is something I did when conversations took unexpected twists. I never really understood why I did it. It was as though my right ear had untwisty listening abilities that my left one lacked.

I said, "Excuse me." It was something else I did when conversations took unexpected twists. I had a little more insight into why I did that: I said excuse me so the person would repeat what they said so that I could be sure I heard it right the first time.

I suspected both habits were annoying to whomever I was speaking with.

Diane responded by becoming more graphic. She said, "I think Raoul is fucking around."

Not screwing, fucking.

From Diane's lips, an important distinction.

# TWENTY-TWO

I handed Lauren my speeding ticket—I had a fantasy that since she was a well-connected deputy DA she would tell me in an offhandedly affectionate way not to worry about such a mundane thing, that she would have an assistant take care of it when she arrived at her office in the morning. But like many of my marital fantasies, that one didn't come to fruition. She did offer a consolation prize—a soft, wet kiss on the lips that lingered for a second or two beyond the usual greeting peck—before she said, "Major bummer. Though I can't believe you were speeding on that stretch of Foothills. There are always cops there. You know better."

I did know better. I told Lauren I had to go back out to see Diane.

"Can't wait?" she asked, already knowing my answer.

Lauren and I had both been alarmed by Diane's deterioration after her friend's arrest for homicide the previous winter. Though less traumatizing than her own hostage experience, the recent tragedy had seemed like the proverbial straw. Diane was struggling to hold on.

I shook my head. I promised to fill Lauren in when I got back home.

I lifted the traffic ticket off the counter. "Any chance you can help with—"

"No. No chance," she said with a smile.

Diane and Raoul lived in what residents of the Front Range call the foothills. In most other parts of the country, our foothills might be called mountains. Front Range foothills life provides a residential experience that is comparable to mountain living, but with training wheels. Elevation—with all the positives and negatives that altitude brings to the home-owning equation—is present in the foothills, though to a lesser degree than in the real mountains. Wilderness experience is plentiful in the foothills, too, though it tends to be less in-your-face than in the high country. Requisite gorgeous mountain and canyon views are present in both locations. Overall, when the foothills are compared to the high mountain communities in Boulder County—up Sugarloaf or Magnolia or Coal Creek, or near Nederland, Gold Hill, or Ward—the foothills provide a less challenging lifestyle.

One primary reason for the reduced challenge is that foothills communities tend to be much closer to urban centers than are mountain communities. From Raoul and

Diane's home north of town, for example, I could be in the urban edge of Boulder in minutes. Fewer than five certainly, fewer than three if I broke a traffic law or two.

Lee Hill was, however, a long way from my home in Spanish Hills; if a square were superimposed over residential Boulder, Lee Hill and Spanish Hills would be found in opposing corners. The distance between our homes meant that I didn't pull into the steep driveway behind the Lee Hill hogback until almost nine o'clock.

Diane had not turned on any lights for me. That evening's moon was either hidden behind clouds or it was in one of those phases that render illumination inconsequential. Once I stepped outside I was standing in the kind of absolute dark that city dwellers—and edge-of-urbanity dwellers like me—tend to forget exists.

I stumbled twice on my way to the door. At the threshold, I couldn't see the doorbell, but I could make a guess about the location of the door. I knocked.

I ended up knocking a few times. I pressed the lever on the door handle. The door opened. I stepped into a dark foyer. My eyes, accustomed to the complete absence of illumination outside, found the light washing in from the distant kitchen to be more than adequate for navigation.

I called Diane's name over and over again as I walked toward the source of the light. Finally, I heard, "Alan? I'm back here. Just a second."

*Back where?* I wondered. The house was built just below the peak of an uphill slope, with the main rooms on the upper two floors enjoying views both east and west. I had never known there was a "back here" anywhere in the house. The bedrooms were on the highest level. I had never seen a basement.

Diane emerged from the short hall that led from the kitchen toward a room that she and Raoul used for watching TV. She was dressed in the same clothes she had been wearing earlier during our visit to the downtown flat, but had changed from heels into the kind of furry house slippers that guests are usually not permitted to witness.

Diane's were a shade of green that would flatter only a frog.

Her eyes, in Christmas-color contrast, were red and puffy.

I stepped forward to offer a hug. She stopped me, not with a greeting but with a hands-in-the-air question. "Why can't I get on the Internet?" she asked.

Diane was a digital illiterate. It was a state of ignorance that caused her no dysphoria. Given the typical, sometimes incomprehensible nature of her technological queries at our office, I found myself impressed that she had asked the question about Internet access with such, well, clarity.

"What are you trying to use to get online?" I asked. I was aware that with my question I was not only complicating things but was also granting Diane the benefit of some significant doubt. The primary grant I was making was that she had understood what her original question meant.

A befuddled stare was all I got back. I went back to the beginning. "Are you trying to use a computer to get online?" I asked. "Some other device? Did you get a new smart phone?"

Diane's lower lip began to quiver. I pulled my own mobile from my pocket as I moved in and wrapped my arms around her. As I hugged her, I checked the screen over her shoulder to see what kind of signals my phone was receiving. It turned out that I was getting between one and two bars from some cell tower, but no Wi-Fi signal.

I said, "We'll figure this out, Diane. Don't worry. Show me what you have."

She took my hand and led me to the TV room and then through a door that I had always assumed led to a closet. It didn't. It led to a spacious utility and storage room. At the back of the room was a glass door to a temperature-controlled wine cellar.

Diane flicked on an overhead light and pointed toward a bare concrete wall on the left side of the room. Along the wall was the electronic equipment that provided the digital brains for the home. Alarm panel. Satellite TV decoders. Landline telephone boxes. DSL modem. High-speed router. Backup hard drive.

On a plywood table below the equipment sat an open laptop. A cable—it looked like USB—was strung from the backup hard drive to the laptop. "What's that for?" I asked.

"I was trying to use it to make it . . . work. The laptop. I was thinking if I got it closer to the . . . you know . . . those things, those boxes, then it might work. Better. At all."

"And that gray cable? That's for . . . ?"

"I saw Raoul do that once when we couldn't get on-line. He hooked it up like that."

Diane's explanation made no sense. If Raoul had been troubleshooting the Wi-Fi, he would have been using a Cat 5 cable, not a USB cable. And he would have connected it from the laptop to the router, not from the laptop to the backup hard drive.

I said, "Are you certain that he connected the laptop to the backup hard drive? To that box? Like this? Or did he, maybe, connect it to the router—this box, here—with a different kind of cable than the one you're using?"

She shrugged her shoulders. I might just as well have been asking her if her abductor's spaceship had been equipped with hyperdrive. "Maybe," she said.

"Well, we can work this out. Right now? You have the laptop connected to the backup hard drive. That's not going to help you get online."

She shrugged again. One piece of good news was that the modem in the setup was the same model I had at home. I recognized that one light on the panel that was supposed to be solid was instead flashing. "May I try something?"

"Please."

I am not reliable tech support, but I have a reliable strategy for establishing how little I know in a circumstance like the one I was facing. I disconnected the power cable to the DSL modem. I counted to thirty. I plugged it back in.

We waited. When the modem cycled back on, the light that had been flashing went solid. "I think you're golden now," I said. "You're cooking with gas."

"Is that good?" Diane asked.

She thought I was talking in some tech code.

# TWENTY-THREE

We settled in the kitchen. Diane had been making tea before I arrived. I finished the process and carried two mugs to the table.

"Want to talk about it?"

"The Internet? Or my fucking husband?"

If it were really my choice, I would have picked the Internet.

I asked, "What makes you think Raoul is involved with someone?" My use of her earlier words was intentional.

Diane's eyes flared fire. "I was in for my annual Pap yesterday. My gynecologist is a friend. She called me tonight personally to tell me I have"—Diane emitted a growl like an unhappy terrier—"an STI. Actually, she said I have two STIs, that I might have had them for a while." She growled again. "Two!"

Before I could say *What?*—that is something else I do

when I'm flummoxed during a conversation—Diane burst into tears.

I figured that STI stood for "sexually transmitted infection" and that it was synonymous with the more familiar STD, or "sexually transmitted disease." I was hoping that Diane's STIs were the kind that could be cured with a course of antibiotics, though I knew that remedy would address only the bacteriological part of the current problem.

"I didn't even know I was sick. But my doctor said many women don't."

I was nodding a lot, hoping to keep Diane talking. I was also hoping to dissuade her from crying. I could tell she had cried plenty; a break in the tears wouldn't hurt.

"What is 'a while'?" I asked. "Weeks? Months?" I was realizing that I was in a phase of my life when STDs weren't part of my experience. I treated a caseload that didn't raise venereal disease issues much in therapy sessions, and I hung out with friends who didn't often discuss the clap or its cousins. I was, I feared, becoming STI ignorant. Since I hadn't studied STDs in a while, I didn't know how long it was common, or even possible, for women to remain asymptomatic with a garden-variety infection. "Did your doctor say anything about that?"

Diane opened her eyes and spread her hands wide simultaneously. "A long time," she said. "But I don't know." Diane was able to recall only one of her two diagnoses. She was pretty sure she had chlamydia. I was left to hope that her second diagnosis was equally treatable.

I'd read bad things recently about drug-resistant gonor-
rhea.

"I need to call her at the office tomorrow. You know
what? I should make a list of questions. What else should
I ask her? I should get a piece of paper or I won't remember. I was trying to look stuff up online. That's why I
need your help figuring out how—"

"I'll double-check your Internet access before I go," I
said. I rested my hand on top of hers on the table. Diane's strong hand had held mine through many crises
over the years. I feared that I might be failing to provide
whatever comfort or support she needed from me. I
found it heartbreaking to feel the vulnerability that was
radiating from her.

"She called in antibiotics. Said I have to tell anyone
I've been . . . intimate with about . . . my infections."
She looked at me with doleful eyes. "'Intimate'? She
means sex, right? My gynecologist is asking me whom
I've been fucking? Has my life come to this?"

Diane inhaled suddenly and held the breath. Her eyes
went wide. I flashed on my recently deceased patient's
expression in the instant before she collapsed on my office
floor.

Finally Diane exhaled. She looked away. I was still
taken aback by Diane's use of that particular profanity. It
wasn't like her to choose the word fuck to describe intercourse. On rare occasions she might spice a conversation
with the word in less literal contexts, but in sexual terms
she was much more likely to use a less controversial coital
verb.

In the current context, I was not inclined to offer a single argument that the profane choice was not the most fitting one.

She added, "I don't want to tell Raoul. Do I really have to tell Raoul?"

I opened my mouth and closed it. I had been proceeding under the assumption that Raoul was playing the role of the bad guy in the current tale. Bad guys typically know that they are the bad guys. "If he's really having another relationship," I said, "then I would imagine that he's the one who infected you. Right?"

Diane looked puzzled, as though she were trying to do multiplication in her head and wasn't confident about carrying numbers. Her lips were parted and her eyes looked blank.

"Our marriage isn't . . . simple, Alan. Not how it seems. I think."

"Whose is, Diane? Marriage is hard."

She shook her head, rejecting my banality. I moved to an argument devoid of blame and responsibility. "If only one of you gets treated, you'll just pass the infections back and forth again. Right? That won't work."

"If we have sex," she countered.

*"If we have sex"*? I made a quick assumption that she was implying that she was so angry or so hurt that she never planned to have sex with Raoul again. I recognized the statement for what it was: Diane was understandably furious. I tried to clarify. "Raoul and you are not . . ." I was at a loss about how to finish my sentence. I actually visualized that roster of coital verbs.

Diane, however, was ready with a conclusion. She said, "In the same time zone with much frequency. These days. My husband is well-endowed, Alan, but not across-state-lines well-endowed."

*Well.* We had just edged over the imaginary demarcation between me being uncomfortable with the conversation and me being certain I had just learned more information about the intimate details of my friends' marriage than I ever wanted to know.

Though, given Diane's precarious emotional situation, I did find the cogency of her retort impressive.

I tried to recover my bearings before she flooded me with new, unwelcome revelations. I said, "You're saying that you guys aren't—"

She winced. I really did not want to be having this conversation with her. Given all that she'd been through in the recent past, and all the sequelae that I had witnessed to the Las Vegas trauma, could I believe that her marriage might be fraying a little? Of course I could. Did I believe that the marital fabric was actually torn? No, I did not.

Raoul and Diane had one of those relationships that made people believe in marriage. They had one of those marriages that I had relied on as a model to quell the doubt that threatened to consume my own relationship during difficult times.

Did I have any desire to know anything about the frequency with which she and Raoul had intercourse? *Please.*

Diane said, "It's not been a good time. For us. There

have been problems. He's probably made some mistakes. Since . . ."

"Since . . . ?"

"The truth is I haven't been the same since . . . And Raoul has had a hard time dealing with my . . . Oh God. Oh God. Reaction? Withdrawal? How about anxiety? Depression. Call it whatever. We adjust. We do the best we can. And now there's this *Daily Camera* development problem, which was supposed to be a solution and not a problem at all, but instead it's become part of this big . . . problem I'm having right now. See? Do you see?"

She glanced up at me with eyes pleading for understanding.

"The truth? Raoul doesn't understand the urgency of my need to move. Not really. He likes this house. He"— her voice began to rise in volume and pitch—"doesn't understand why I feel so strongly that I have to just get the hell out of . . . this place. Right now!"

I was, I admit, wondering how Diane and I had moved from the discussion of a truly acute crisis—the sudden introduction of multiple STDs into her marriage—to what felt to me like the subacute crisis of moving from the foothills into town. I was about to point out to Diane that it might be helpful to talk a little more about the venereal issues that were on the table in front of her than about a long-term real estate issue that would likely prove immune to a course of antibiotics.

I had to be missing something. I asked, "Did your doctor say anything else?"

Diane's response? With a motion as natural as a kid

tossing a softball across the room to a friend, she flung her mug of tea against the stone hearth of the breakfast-area fireplace. The tea splattered. The clear glass shattered.

For a few seconds, I sat stunned. My next instinct was to jump up and do something. Run to her. Ask her if she was okay. Start cleaning the mess, something. But I didn't. I sat. The only thing I moved was my mug—out of her reach.

"All right," I said. "I get it. You want to move. I already knew that. I suspect that Raoul knows that, too. Raoul is doing what he can to facilitate the move. Yes?"

*What,* I was wondering, *does this have to do with Diane's STDs?*

"He says he understands. He's . . . supportive. Tonight? He told me to see if the owners of the flat would lease it to us for a year. Kevin said the place has been on the market for seven months, with no real offers, and he thinks the sellers are motivated. They've already dropped the price almost ten percent. Raoul thinks they might be getting desperate enough to consider renting instead of selling. He thought it would be a good interim solution for . . . me. He said 'us' but he meant me.

"In another year, he thinks the questions about the future of the *Camera* development will be resolved. And renting in a great location, even if it's someplace that isn't perfect, would get me out of"—she looked around for something else to throw; I fixed both my hands around my mug—"this house that much faster. Definitely before next year's fire season."

Although I hoped that a resolution was on the horizon, I wasn't focused on the potential short-term solution to Diane's housing problem. I was more interested in the rest of her conversation with her husband. I asked, "You spoke to Raoul tonight?"

"Yeah. Before Tara called." She saw the puzzlement in my eyes. "Tara's my ob-gyn. I called Raoul to tell him about the place near the Mall. I got his voice mail, of course. He's in Cleveland. He called back and told me I had to look past the problems with the apartment. To begin to view it as . . . a temporary solution. He called it a bridge."

She'd spoken the word Cleveland, her husband's midwestern location that night, with abject wonder, as though she considered the fact that he was spending the night in Cleveland to be akin to learning that he was bunking down on Jupiter.

"This is my fault, Alan. I used to be fun. A fun wife. Wasn't I fun? I was, right? I used to be a lot of fun. Raoul didn't used to go to Cleveland."

*Fun? This has to do with fun?* "You were fun. You are fun."

"No. I'm not fun. I'm this far"—she held her two index fingers a few millimeters apart—"from being a complete bitch."

"Diane, no. It is not true. And it's not your fault that you have—"

"It is. True. And it is my fault. Not just now, but since . . ."

Vegas? Or since her girlfriend's arrest for murder? I

didn't know where Diane would assign responsibility. "You've been through a lot, Diane. It would be the same for anyone who went through what you've gone through. Give yourself a break."

She waved a hand at me, dismissing my attempt at comfort. "I know I'm not handling things well. I haven't been able to move on. It's been hard for Raoul. I don't want to travel. Plan things. He's been patient. Raoul has. But he's not patient anymore. He's in Cleveland. I have to do something."

"Are you getting any help, Diane? Seeing someone?"

I had asked Diane the same question a few times before. She'd brushed me off every one of them. I waited for her to answer.

"I tried," she said. "It didn't work. Therapy is bull-shit."

I weighed her assessment of our profession for irony. I found none. "Hey, Diane—"

"No!" she said. "Cleveland, Alan?"

She was looking at me as though she wanted something from me. *Does she think I know something*? I said, "He's looking at some start-up there, right? The next Facebook or something? The next PayPal? That's what he does. That's why he's in Cleveland."

"Is there someone in his life? Do you know?"

Her question did not seem perfunctory. I said, "I don't have that kind of relationship with your husband. We're not that open with each other. He cherishes you. I have never had a moment's doubt that he loves you . . . deeply."

She countered, "He's never given you any reason to . . ."

She did not want to hear that Raoul and I had a relationship that did not include sharing indiscretions, nor did she want for me to tell her what she already knew: that Raoul understood that my allegiance to Diane would always be stronger than my allegiance to him. I offered an unequivocal "No, he has not."

"And he's never introduced you to some woman? One you were curious about? Wondered if he was . . . hitting that?"

*Hitting that?* "Never. Women flirt with Raoul all the time. You see that. He is never anything other than a complete gentleman every time it happens. He loves you."

"Of course. It's all in my head."

I didn't bite. "Is there something else to this? Another piece that you want to tell me?"

"Things were fine. For a long time. Now it's a mess." She stood. She said, "I'm tired."

I embraced her. "You need to talk with your husband, Diane. Soon."

When I am on my game clinically, I can be astute. I can take almost invisible threads from a patient's life, almost undetectable affective lint from a patient's story, and weave the wisps of psychological reality into a lifeline that can guide her back to the place and time where the fabric began to unravel.

When I'm dense, though, I can be a master of obtuseness. In those instances when I—ultimately—recognize my density, the awareness of my blindness often comes with a comical stumble and a clunky *aha* moment.

I had one of those as I was driving in the dark down Lee Hill from Diane's house, approaching the location of an auto accident that years before had claimed the life of a patient of mine. The culprit that distant night was a sharp curve and wet roads. And an evil hand.

The woman who died had, literally, been my introduction to Michael McClelland.

*Thread and lint.*

The curve in front of me in the night, the memory of arriving on the scene of my patient's death, was as fresh in my mind as that evening's visit to Diane's garish flat.

From out of that darkness came the thought, *Diane referred Amanda to me.*

*Oh my God.*

I failed to brake in time to finesse the curve. To grab the last of the narrow shoulder I was forced to oversteer. My tires squealed. I wondered if centrifugal force would work to my advantage. Or if my late braking would prove to be a fatal error.

*Diane was the one who referred Amanda to me. She knows Amanda.*

*Diane thinks that Amanda is involved with Raoul. She has thought it all along.*

The car held the curve.

I exhaled into the last segment of Lee Hill, a straight shot to Broadway.

*Is Diane counting on me to discover—what—the evi-*

*dence of the affair? Is that why she sent Amanda to me for therapy?*

*Diane, please, no.*

Diane did not return my calls or my e-mail the next day. She didn't come into the office on Thursday, which was one of her few regular workdays.

I was tempted to check in with Raoul to discuss things as his friend, but I didn't know what I would say. If I were offering someone else advice about what to do in the situation in which I found myself, my counsel would have been to stay the hell out of the middle of other people's marriages.

I decided it was wise counsel, or as wise as I was capable of giving right then.

The referral source for any patient rarely felt like a crucial fact in my work. But learning the identity of a referral source wasn't trivial, either. In its simplest form, knowing who had given a new patient my name provided one new data point in the sociogram of the patient's life; I would be able to identify at least one person in that patient's near or extended social or professional sphere. Like all professionals running a small business, I endeavored to keep an informal accounting of the people in the community who were sending me work.

On rare occasions, learning the identity of a referrer might provide a warning sign that an ethical conflict, usually a conflict of interest, might be lurking out there.

I tried to recall everything that Amanda had said about

how she had heard of me. I thought I had asked about the source of the referral and that she'd said that she'd heard my name mentioned in the micro-community in which she worked. I had accepted the statement at face value.

I didn't recall asking her for a specific referral name. The truth was that, from almost our first moments together, I had been distracted by Amanda's stories. Was it possible that one of the things I had been too distracted to learn was the source of the referral? Sure it was. My interaction with Diane raised concerns that my failure to identify the person who had given Amanda my name had left me vulnerable.

Could Amanda be involved with Raoul? Might she know Diane socially? Was it possible that she initially heard my name from Diane in a nonprofessional context? Or even from Raoul?

*God.*

# TWENTY-FOUR

I was outside with the dogs on Thursday evening when Sam arrived to spend the night at Ophelia's. He had taped cardboard over the opening where his front-seat passenger window had been.

I had devised a scheme to let Sam know that Coma Doe had shown up in my office. For my plan to work, I needed Sam's cooperation.

He began bitching about his week even before he killed the engine. I expected the break-in of his car to be the first headline, but he started his kvetching with the judge's decision to call a motions hearing in the assault trial earlier in the week. It soon became clear that Sam wasn't as interested in my empathy about his shitty week as he was interested in my advice about the evening ahead.

Ophelia wanted to go back downtown for dinner at

Oak. That meant Sam would miss at least the first two periods of the Avalanche game. If I hadn't needed his help the next day, I probably would have pointed out that the Avs were a work in progress. But I did need his cooperation, so I tried to convince him that he might enjoy a date with his splendid girlfriend. I also told him I thought he would like Oak, even though I wasn't at all confident Sam would like Oak.

Sam was skeptical. "You think? It's not too . . ."

I guessed where he was going. "Boulder? No. Oak is Boulder enough for the rest of us, and old-school enough for you."

He grunted. How Boulderish something might or might not be was not an increment of measure that Sam trusted. Oak? Sam was wary of organic food. I wasn't eager to learn that he also had some odd bias against Oak's penchant for local sourcing.

"How much time do you have before you need to leave?" I asked.

He checked his phone. "Need to leave in an hour or so. Why?"

"I'd like you to tell me a story."

"Which story you want? You having trouble sleeping? Simon used to think I was best with the ones where I got to do animal voices."

I smiled, putting effort into making the smile appear less than gratuitous. "The night of the Fourmile Fire? The assault—excuse me, the battery—you were helping investigate that night? What actually happened to that guy? What was the outcome?"

"This is important?"

"Might be crucial," I said.

Sam's eyes told me he was suspicious, but he began the story without demanding to learn my motivation. He pulled himself up onto the hood of his Cherokee as he said, "It starts off as your basic wildfire evacuation story."

The car that Sleepy Doe—Coma Doe—was driving out of the path of the Fourmile Fire the night he ended up in the ICU was a 1960 Ford Thunderbird. The car belonged to Coma Doe's then-girlfriend's father, who was out of town.

Although Sam had quickly established some storytelling rhythm, I interrupted when he mentioned the T-Bird. "Did the girl's father collect classic cars, or was it just that one?"

"I think that was the one and only. Can I go on now?"

The mystery of how my business card had shown up at the scene of the crash was solved. The T-Bird, I was pretty certain, belonged to an ex-patient of mine, who had inherited it from his mother. He'd actually driven it to a session to show it off to me after her death. At that time, years before, he'd been married and had a daughter around Jonas's age.

He'd been seeing me to deal with the complications in his life caused by the fact that he was gay. He thought his mother's death might help him open the door to the closet.

That information was protected by therapeutic privilege. Telling Sam that I knew the solution to the business card puzzle and then not telling him said solution would be tantamount to taunting. I didn't want to go there. I said, "Please go on. Sorry to interrupt."

Sam sighed but proceeded. The girlfriend's father had begged her to find a way to get his T-Bird to safety. Problem was, his daughter worked at the Denver Tech Center, well over an hour from Boulder; she could not get back to move the T-Bird in time.

She enlisted the help of the guy she'd been dating. That was Coma Doe. She asked him to fill her daddy's iconic square T-Bird with a list of stuff from her room that she wanted to save and then to drive the car down to town.

"The trip was complicated by animals," Sam said. "One domesticated. One wild."

"Don't feel any obligation to do the animal voices," I said. "I'm not Simon."

"Gotcha," Sam said.

The domesticated animal was Coma Doe's then-girlfriend's four-year-old English bulldog, named Henry. The wild walk-on was a good-sized buck with an impressive rack that was escaping the fire by crossing a two-lane road in the Boulder foothills in the dark.

Coma Doe spotted the buck in the Thunderbird's headlights. To avoid a direct impact he reacted with a reflexive turn of the steering wheel. A split second later he accompanied the evasive steering with some emergency hard braking.

I raised a finger to indicate I had a question.

Sam made a guess: "Skid marks confirm the evasive maneuvers. He turned before he braked," Sam said. "In that order."

"Were there hoof marks to confirm the presence of the buck?" I asked.

"Right front quadrant of the T-Bird clipped the deer," Sam explained. "Busted the car's headlight. Busted the deer's femur. First responders did the humane thing, destroyed the buck not far from the scene."

I said I was sorry to hear that. Sam, who grew up shooting deer for recreation, and for dinner, shrugged. His shrug, I thought, lacked a certain compassion.

He wanted me to keep in mind that the old car, though a beauty, was blessed with neither antilock brakes nor electronic stability control, since neither had been invented back when John Kennedy was elected president. The absence of those features—in addition to the driver's unfamiliarity with the model, and the radical steering maneuver, and the hard braking, and the off-center impact with the hindquarter of a big deer—complicated any efforts the driver may have made to regain control of the car.

The result was that the T-Bird was fishtailing erratically as it crossed the road.

I asked, "Confirmed, once again, by skid marks?"

Sam said, "Yep, we got data. And an expert to interpret it." He also had a caution for me. "Right about now that bulldog comes into the story. The bulldog's entrance involves some unavoidable conjecture. The conjecture is supported by facts, but accident re-creation is not an exact science. Certain shit happens off camera. Just does. Flying bulldogs? Sometimes you got to have faith."

I told Sam I could live with a little flying-bulldog conjecture.

The accident re-creation guy surmised that when Coma Doe hit the brakes to avoid the buck, the rapid deceleration of the Thunderbird caused Henry the bulldog—despite his significant mass, or perhaps because of it, Henry was not immune to the laws of physics—to be launched from his temporary perch on the backseat of the T-Bird. At the instant of Henry's precipitous takeoff, he became a fifty-eight-pound canine missile.

A mere fraction of a second after launch the bulldog projectile smacked Coma Doe so squarely on the back of his head that it might have appeared that the driver's skull had been the precise target programmed into the bulldog missile-guidance system.

The sudden deceleration of the car, along with the brute force of being struck on the back of the head by the solid torso of a bulldog with a healthy appetite, caused Coma Doe's head and face to begin to fly forward at alarming speed. The acceleration of the upper portion of his body did not abate until it met the rigid, uncushioned plastic and metal of the most definitely non-impact-absorbing steering wheel of the up-until-that-moment almost cherry Ford Thunderbird.

As a result of the flying bulldog trauma Coma Doe suffered the first and second of his multiple closed-head injuries that night.

*　　*　　*

I was confused. I said, "First and second?"

"Henry was uno. Turns out a whack on the back of the head by a flying bulldog is good for a decent concussion, at a minimum. Who knew?" he said.

"And the second?"

"Our boy's faceplant on the steering wheel. That impact caused a second concussion, along with a broken jaw and a laceration or two. By then, the poor guy's brain was sloshing around in his skull like an apple in a barrel at a Halloween party."

"Whiplash?"

"You betcha," Sam said, moving his own head all over, as illustration. "This way, that way. Every damn which way."

Sam's whiplash description had an odd, "Old McDonald Had a Farm" cadence that distracted me more than a little. "Go on," I said. "Please."

Coma Doe had been wearing his factory-installed lap-only seat belt, but shoulder restraints, headrests, and air bags had been no more of a consideration on the date the Thunderbird was manufactured than was an iPod dock, a rear-seat DVD player, or a digital navigation system.

The fishtailing Thunderbird, suddenly pilotless because of Coma Doe's dual head traumas, crossed the single lane of oncoming traffic, hopped off the raised shoulder, and descended into a shallow but wide roadside culvert. The car exited that drainage airborne, covering an impressive distance of almost twenty-three feet before it touched down again, front tires first.

At that point, the car, pristine but for the busted head-light, was on a route that would lead it to become air-borne yet again. The second flight would have exceeded the seven-plus yards of the first by a considerable margin, since the takeoff would have involved a high cliff and a deep ravine.

That flight never happened. Instead, the front end of the Thunderbird butted head-on at an estimated thirty-eight miles an hour into the unyielding trunk of a once stately lodgepole pine. The tree suffered no consequen-tial damage from the impact because the evergreen had already been tortured to death by an army of life-sucking pine beetles.

The doctors who treated Coma Doe later surmised that microseconds after the Thunderbird met the tree trunk, his skull endured the third of the three distinct closed-head injuries it suffered that night, and the second in a row that involved the remarkably unyielding steering wheel of the Ford classic.

"Henry?" I asked.

"By that time he was safely pinned on the floor behind the front seat."

"Well," I said. "At the end of the day, no assault, and no battery?"

"Right, if you don't count Henry," Sam said. "Now tell me why you wanted to know."

"During our walk the other day? I told you there was another thing I needed to talk to you about," I said.

"Yeah?" His phone was in his hand. He glanced at the

time. "Is this going to be one of your long explanations?" He sniffed his left armpit. "I should shower."

"I need you to be sitting in my waiting room at three thirty tomorrow afternoon. I have something I need to hand to you. At that precise moment."

Sam reacted as though he thought I was kidding. He said, "No way," slid off the hood of the Cherokee, and directed me to bring whatever it was home with me. I could give it to him then. He promised me that he would be back at Ophelia's.

I said, "This is time sensitive. It's important that you see what I have to show you at that precise moment on Friday afternoon. And that I hand it to you personally."

He checked the time again, sniffed his armpit again. He said no, again.

I reemphasized the importance. He sighed. He asked if his partner Lucy could do it. I told him that wouldn't be a good idea on many levels.

Sam interrupted again to remind me of a previous visit he'd made to my office, one that hadn't gone well. "That one time I fell asleep in your waiting room reading a magazine, you told me you didn't want me to wait inside for you ever again. You said I scared one of your patients. Which I don't think was my fault. You guys have that waterfall in there that, I swear, would put anyone to sleep. It's like hanging out at the base of Niagara."

"It was one of Diane's patients who complained," I said. Other than that minor detail, Sam's story was pretty much true. The scene had not been idyllic, with Sam's snoring being what it was, and with a disgustingly distended rivulet of drool seeping from the corner of his mouth all the way onto a so-where's-the-actual-swimsuit photo in the *Sports Illustrated* annual swimsuit edition. "We'll consider this to be a one-time waiver to the no-waiting-in-the-waiting-room policy."

"Why?"

I said, "Please, Sam? Read between the damn lines. Be there on time. In fact, get there a few minutes early. And stay awake, even alert."

He looked over my shoulder, smiled, and waved. My back was to the double-wide. I assumed he was waving at Ophelia. Given the time, and the altitude of the sun in the western sky, she had likely just stepped outside to perform her evening salutations. I knew specific times of day when it was better that I didn't attempt to make eye contact with Ophelia. I raised my hand to add my greeting, but I didn't look over my shoulder.

I said, "So you know, I won't be free to talk tomorrow until five fifteen."

Sam spotted the discrepancy. "You want me there before three thirty—being alert and all—while I'm waiting to get whatever it is you want to hand me, but I can't actually talk to you until later?" I nodded. "And I'm supposed to listen to that waterfall without falling asleep and offending somebody's patient?"

"You'll only be there a few minutes. I'll come out to hand you . . . something. Then you're free to do what you wish. If you can come back at five fifteen, that would be great. By then, all will be clear."

He said, "You promise me, here, today, that this will make sense? And that I'll understand the importance?"

"That's the idea."

He was staring over my shoulder at Ophelia, the tension in his face melting away. Sam was falling in love with a terrific woman. As an observer of the nascent romance, I found myself delighted for him. If he wasn't such a big, pale, freckled polar bear of a man, I am certain that the whole romantic thing would have been cute to watch develop.

"Okay," he said. "I'll be there."

"One more thing," I said. "Under no circumstances can you speak while you are in my waiting room. It's crucial that your voice not be heard. Not a sound."

He mimed a lip-zip. Then he said, "I'm out of here. I have to get ready for my date. My pits smell like they defrosted too long on the counter."

# TWENTY-FIVE

Late the next day, after my last appointment was over, Sam fell back onto my office sofa so hard the big piece of furniture slid a couple of inches as it absorbed the energy of his collapse. I had almost concluded he wasn't going to show up.

By the end of most workdays Sam looks like he's fought above his weight class for a few rounds. My impression was that he looked even more beat-up than usual.

I took the seat on the other end of the sofa and waited for him to start the conversation. I was waiting because the ruse I was using to convey privileged information to Sam left me no other choice. The choreography was complex. I was doing it the way I was doing it only because the alternatives seemed worse.

"Worse" meant possibly illegal. Definitely unethical. My chosen path? I didn't think it was illegal. Technically, anyway. Unethical? Let's say I wouldn't have wanted to put it up for a vote to a jury of my professional peers.

My biggest fear was that my plan would prove ineffectual.

The awkward choreography required that Sam take the next step. He obliged. "Wow," he said. "I admit I did not expect to see what I saw at three thirty."

I was relying on Sam recognizing that my hands were tied, and that they were tied right over my lips. He didn't disappoint.

He said, "I saw him. And I've been around you long enough to predict that from this point forward you are going to be of no help to me in the what-the-hell-does-that-mean part of this conversation."

"Help with what?" I said, underscoring for Sam the determination of my feigned ignorance.

"I'm talking implications, not facts. You can talk implications with me, right?"

"Not really. But I will provide whatever vague guidance I can."

"You're worried about this asshole's confidentiality?"

"Not at all," I said. "I'm worried about being tricked into breaching it. That would be an unforced error on my part."

"Gotcha," Sam said. "Okay. Then this is going to be worse than I thought—and where you and your job and me and my job tend to collide, I usually find myself thinking of the worst right off the bat." He stood. "There's an ice-cold Hoss with my name on it over at the West End. Want to join me?"

A beer sounded fine. "Just one," I said.

"One? In a fine bar, the first brew is there merely to make introductions to the second."

By the time our butts were balanced on the two stools at the end of the long bar of the West End Tavern, the tension between us was easing. Coma Doe was a common adversary. We didn't have energy to waste fighting each other.

Sam ordered me the promised Hoss—a local lager that earned its spiciness from a pinch of rye. I liked it. He also offered me some Beer Nuts that had been stashed in his sport coat pocket in a ziplock bag that was opaque from advanced age and, likely, some other prolonged abuse that I didn't want to contemplate. My estimate was that he had stashed the bag, and the enclosed nut fragments, in the recesses of that coat during the extended investigation into JonBenét's death.

I declined the snack. I asked about his Cherokee. "You never said—did the thief get anything from your car?"

"Nothing to get," he scoffed. "He probably got scared away. Courthouse parking lot? Either he is really stupid, or my colleagues in blue are really bad at what they do."

"Any video surveillance?"

"Useless. Shows a human-shaped blob next to my car. Big help. Why do surveillance cameras always have such crappy resolution? What's the point?" He paused as though he thought I must have had the answer. I didn't. "Just saying," he said.

"How bad is the estimate on the window?"

He nodded. "Not too bad. Nice people. Thanks for the referral." Sam was done with small talk. He said, "We should probably focus on this afternoon. Coma Doe."

At the prearranged rendezvous I had made the short amble from my office to the waiting room to greet Rick Contreras, aka Coma Doe, the patient I had seen for the first time a couple of days before. In my hand I was holding a white business-size envelope containing a single sheet of paper. I nodded a quick acknowledgment to my patient before I walked across the room and handed the envelope to Sam.

I said, "This should be all you need. Thank you so much for coming by."

Sam took the envelope without comment.

I turned. "Please come on back, Rick," I said. I used his first name solely for Sam's benefit. Rick tossed his magazine to the coffee table, stood, and preceded me down the hall. I was tempted to risk one more look at Sam's face, but I didn't.

Sam placed the bag with the vintage Beer Nuts between us on the West End bar. He then reached into an inside pocket of his jacket and pulled out the white envelope. He unfolded the solitary sheet of paper and smoothed it out on the bar top. "It's either invisible ink," he said, "or it's blank."

"Invisible ink is beyond my skill set. Consider it the latter."

"The medium is not the message?" he said. "Damn."

The McLuhan reference was welcome. Sam was a smart and witty man; it was one of the things I appreciated about his company. "If anyone ever asks, you will be able to explain—with complete honesty—that the reason you came by my office was to pick up an envelope."

"And if someone asks—let's say while I'm under oath—what was in said envelope?"

"'It was so unremarkable that I don't remember' should describe the facts."

He rolled his head as though he were stretching his neck. "Nice," he said.

"I try to keep it simple."

Sam laughed. "Since when?" He took a tiny sip from his glass, as though he were checking the lager for poison. "The guy? That's a hell of a scar."

I was determined not to respond directly to any question that might reflect on my patient's identity. Technically, confidentiality forbade it. Practically, I was worried about a trap. Either way, Sam had the identity question nailed.

He raised the Hoss, exhaling with a long *ahhhhh* after he drank nearly half of it in one extended go. He replaced the glass on the bar with a *thunk*. I half expected the remaining beer to geyser up and fly out of the glass. It didn't.

Sam ran his cold fingers over his Guinness record–sized forehead. It had been my friend Adrienne who had once pointed out to me that Sam's forehead was the shape, and a good approximation of the size, of the state of Nebraska.

"Him? In your office? I did not see that coming. If I'd

given it any thought, and I didn't, I might have thought there was a minuscule chance he'd show up sometime, in some way. But I wouldn't have guessed he'd show up that way, with you. Any chance this has to do with that old business card, and not with the conversation you and I had in his room at the ICU?"

I considered how I could reply. "If I were to guess?" I said. Sam turned his head to look at me. "I would guess that it had nothing to do with any old business card."

He threw some Beer Nut debris into his mouth. He'd had to dig around among the dried-up peanut skins to retrieve enough meat to make the toss worth the effort. He mumbled a profanity describing a frank sexual improbability before he added, "Depending on what the guy knows, this could be . . . an awkward development."

"Yeah."

"It's safe for me to assume that he did not introduce himself as Coma Doe?"

He did not introduce himself as Coma Doe.

My second session with Rick Contreras, the one that came immediately after Sam's cameo appearance in my waiting room to receive the envelope, was less about subterfuge and more about threat.

I had already concluded that Rick had been taking my measure during the first visit. Going into that second session, I anticipated that the assessment phase was over and that something more provocative than the fact that he had identified me as someone who had visited his room in the ICU was coming my way.

I didn't see any indication that Rick Contreras had recognized Sam in the waiting room before the session. If he had, it would have provided clear evidence that his investigation into what he had heard, or thought he had heard, during his comalike state was more advanced than he was letting on. When I had implored Sam to sit in the waiting room, I did so counting on the fact that there was no way that my new patient would recognize him. To the best of my knowledge Contreras had never seen Sam— Coma Doe's eyes never opened while we were with him in his isolation room in the ICU—and although he may have heard Sam's voice as we talked that night, he could not have matched it to Sam's voice that day in my waiting room. Sam had adhered to my admonition not to speak in the man's presence.

"Here's the thing," is how Contreras started that second meeting. "Do you mind if I cut the bullshit?"

He was working to control the mumbling. I was grateful for that. The content? My heart left its canter and started to gallop. I told him I didn't mind. I preferred it.

"I know you were in my room in the ICU after the accident. Shit, man, you left your business card for me. And I know—I know, see, because I *remember*—that you were there with a cop. I know you guys talked while you were in my room. I don't pretend that I remember everything, but I remember pieces, big pieces, here and there."

I used every bit of my self-restraint to maintain therapeutic neutrality in my expression. Inside my head? Pure chaos. Moments-after-the-big-bang chaos.

"Important pieces. You know what I mean?"

I didn't respond. It wasn't tactical. I was incapable.

"You asked me last time how you could be of help. Well, I need you to tell me what you know about that cop you were with in my room."

I continued to try to keep my cool as Rick slowly turned over the cards in his hand. Rick seemed to be interpreting my silence as strategic. The reality was more mundane; my vocal cords felt temporarily paralyzed by what I was hearing.

"Okay," he said. "You're wondering why you should help me? Here's why—because if you help me, I'm not interested in you. You help me, you skate. I'm interested in him. The cop. And what he did . . . that thing you guys were talking about."

*"That thing"? Maybe he doesn't really know.*

Coma Doe smiled right then. I realized he'd suffered some damage to a cranial nerve in the accident. His smile was one-sided and kind of evil.

"I'm in legal trouble. Not your concern. But to make my legal trouble go away, I need to develop some . . . information that might interest the district attorney. What do I know so far? I know"—he pounded his chest with the thumb side of his closed fist in a way that startled me—"that if it turns out I can finger a dirty cop I will have me some top-notch scratch for negotiating my way out of my mess.

"So my offer to you is this: You tell me what I need to know about that cop friend of yours, and what he did, and I'm out of your face. And I'm out of your life."

*If only it were that easy,* was what I was thinking. I was

also determining that my new adversary wasn't Einstein, but neither was he a dunce. He'd come up with a plan that was, unfortunately, plausible. I didn't think it would work, but I could see how he would think it would work.

"Listen, figuring out this puzzle of mine won't be that hard," he said. "Like I said, I heard important pieces that night. But I don't remember every little detail. I've already followed up on some big pieces, done some investigating on my own."

He stopped. I considered the possibility that he was waiting for me to fill in some blanks for him. I waited, too.

He wanted to know what I knew. I wanted to know what he knew.

The only good news? I was more experienced at enforced silence than he was. Outwaiting him was not much of a challenge. He said, "You know—just say, for an example of what I've learned—how many of what they call 'unattended deaths' there have been in the little town of Frederick, Colorado, in the recent past? Say, four years? That a good number?"

*God, he isn't bluffing.* At that moment all the doubt that had been supporting my denial evaporated. *He did hear us that night.*

Contreras knew about Frederick. *Shit. Four years?* Had Sam or I mentioned a time frame in regard to Justine Brown's death? I couldn't remember. *Damn.* Had we mentioned her name that night? I couldn't remember that, either. *Shit.*

What precisely had we said that night in the ICU? I

couldn't recall. Not to save my life. And saving my life, and Sam's, seemed to be the stakes that were on the table.

For the next thirty seconds I didn't move a muscle that wasn't under control of my autonomic nervous system.

"Exactly seven," he said. "Unattended deaths. In Frederick. Colorado. Lucky number, huh? Only three of those even required investigation." He rolled his thumb into a tight circle with his index finger, leaving the other three fingers extended in case I was having trouble with the arithmetic.

I noted that he spoke the name of our state "Col-o-*rad*-o," emphasizing the third syllable in a sound that rhymed with *sad*. That particular accenting was more common among new arrivals, visitors, and nonnatives. Rick Contreras was a transplant.

He folded his pinkie down. "One death was a fifty-one-year-old rancher who had a heart attack in his barn while he was loading hay bales into the back of his pickup truck. His body was found in the back of the truck by his wife. Tragic." He folded his ring finger down. "The second was an elderly woman who died from a brain hemorrhage, perhaps while she was sleeping. She was in her bed when her daughter came by to deliver some groceries." He paused, pursing his lips together in a way that caused his recent facial scars to whiten from tension. "Nice way to go. Just my opinion."

The last finger to remain unfolded was flipping me off. It was intentional, I thought, and juvenile. "The third? The third death was the most interesting to me, and I mean that because of what I heard that night in the ICU. It was a woman who killed herself with a single gunshot to her head. Her body was found in a little rental house on a farm just outside of town. That death? For a while at least, it was the talk of the town. People still remember it. Turns out they're eager to talk about it."

He smiled that lopsided, cranial-nerve-damaged smile. I couldn't help myself; I got distracted trying to figure out which cranial nerve had been injured. He yanked me back to the moment when he said, "But I'm wondering if she really killed herself. Even after all this time, there seems to be some doubt in town about that.

"In case you're wondering, that's the one that got my attention. That supposed suicide. The one you guys were jabbering about in my room."

Rick, it turned out, had spent a few hours in Frederick already. He wanted me to know what he knew, and he wanted me to know how easy it had been for him to learn what he knew.

He'd chatted up a butcher and a cashier at a grocery in town. He had a long discussion about the benefits of vegetarianism with a girl at the counter in the coffee shop—she was the vegan; Rick was a pescetarian. And he'd even managed to get a bartender at one of the town's saloons to tell him stories about the shit that he and his buddy Segundo used to pull before Segundo became a marine.

The cover story Rick Contreras was telling the Frederick locals was that he was a criminal justice student at

Metropolitan State College in Denver. My gut seized as he filled out the details of the ruse he had manufactured. The fact that he stumbled onto such a fine fake story left me with no doubt that his quest in Frederick, and the story he was telling me in my office, would eventually reveal that he'd been in touch with Izza Kane.

Her truth, and Rick Contreras's fiction, would leave them with ever so much in common. *Mostly unanswered questions about the death of Justine Winter Brown. Currie.*

The specific story Rick told to anyone who seemed even the slightest bit interested during his visit to Frederick was that one of his professors at Metro had given the class an assignment to reinvestigate a death that the authorities had originally identified as suspicious. Each student was to reinvestigate the available public facts and come to an independent conclusion about the case, writing an eight-page paper about how he or she reached their conclusion.

The specific cases were assigned to the students at random. Rick had been assigned a case in Frederick. A suicide.

The butcher had grave doubts about the Rockies' bullpen but knew nothing about the suicide. The clerk at the grocery store had been in town for only eighteen months. Her truck driver husband had left her after nine of those months. She didn't think she had ever met the dead woman and didn't think she could be any help with his school paper.

As an unwelcome aside, Rick described the clerk as "ripe." He maintained she would be his "for the price of a cheap motel." My countertransference for my new patient was already in need of some repair. That little aside didn't help. I was tempted to point out that his cranial-nerve-damaged grin was on the evil side of attractive. I didn't.

With the waitress in the café—a woman who reminded him of his father's baby sister, his aunt Tawny—he struck gold. She knew the whole story of the suicide and recalled a wealth of details, including the dead woman's first name, Justine, and the fact that she had a way with horses. The waitress drew him a little map to show him precisely where the property was—"You can walk from here, hon, take you no more than three minutes"—and she explained how he could tell exactly which house was the specific cottage where the woman died.

Once Rick got the bartender in the saloon talking—the key was a compliment about the man's cowboy boots—the man told him all about his high school friend Segundo, and Segundo's little boy, Elias Tres. The bartender told Rick Contreras that if he was smart he would focus his story on that little boy—that would get him an A on his paper for sure. "That kid is a trip," is what the bartender said about Elias Tres. "Nope, make that a trip and a half."

The bartender then warned Rick off trying to talk to Big Elias. "I wouldn't recommend that. Don't even say hi. Odds are he'll take it the wrong way."

# TWENTY-SIX

"I followed him, of course," Sam said. "After you were done healing him. You are one precise shrink, by the way. It was forty-five minutes on the nose that you spent with the guy. What do you get a minute? Three bucks? Four? Five? More?"

I didn't reply. Sam wasn't curious about my fees. He was strip-mining for raw material for future ridicule.

"I waited that whole time. Outside, in my car. I didn't sleep. I spent those forty-five minutes pondering what this might mean. And then he came out. He walked to his car a little farther down Walnut." Sam raised his beer but didn't drink. "He went to McGuckin. Bought P-traps. Three of them. Who does that who's not a plumber? Then he went to Liquor Mart. Jägermeister. Who still drinks Jäger? Then he stopped and got gas on North Broadway. I ended up getting worried he'd notice the same car behind him for so long, so I made an executive decision to break off the tail.

"When I was on my way back over here, I pulled up to a patrol car in the Ideal parking lot. I got the patrol guys to run the plate for me from their vehicle computer. Turns out that the car he was driving isn't registered to any variation of the name you used to greet him. So—if it ever turns out that you get curious about such things— you might want to consider the possibility that he didn't use his real name."

Sam gave me a moment to reply. When I didn't—he had to know I wouldn't—he said, "I assume psychologists, like you, ask a new patient for a home address?"

I said, "I know I do." I could have found a way to give Sam the address the man had given me, but I was presuming it was fake and that there was a chance I was the only one to whom he'd given it. If Coma Doe spotted me, or anyone else, showing any unusual interest in the address he'd provided, he would know who was responsible for the attention. That would be me. I wasn't at all interested in getting compromised that easily for so little potential gain.

Sam hadn't really expected me to spill the address. He said, "Do psychologists, like you, reputable doctors, ask their patients for identification? A picture ID?"

I decided I could answer Sam's question. I didn't waste much mental energy deciding whether or not I should. Given my mood at that time—modulated rage mixed with a gut-wrenching sense of vulnerability for me and my family—I wasn't so much searching for ethical brakes as I was searching for ethical license.

"I don't," I said.

Sam scratched the back of his neck. I lost a second or two trying to interpret the gesture before I decided his neck itched.

Sam hunched forward, flattening his forearms on the bar. He said, "My doctor makes a copy of my driver's license." He spoke the final words into his almost-empty pint glass. The sound that reached me rumbled and echoed.

"That's because you let him. I don't."

"You don't do it? Or you don't let your doctor do it?"

"Both. Neither."

"You just decline?" Sam seemed to be having a revelation.

I said, "I just decline."

"Okay, do psychologists, like you, ask new patients for a Social Security number? I'm thinking for insurance. Or to track down a guy who skips on his bill? Or even just for the hell of it?" He smiled. "Because people like me let you."

"I don't do insurance billing for my patients, so I don't require that kind of information. I've never yet sent a client into collection, don't think I ever would, so I don't have a need for Social Security numbers."

"No collections? Your patients all pay?"

I chuckled. "Almost. I don't chase down the ones who don't. I eat it. My policy about patient information? Any-

thing I don't require, I don't collect." I glanced over.
"There have been times in the past when certain authorities have become overly enthusiastic about examining my
patient files. If I don't collect something, then nobody
can discover it."

Sam returned my glance. He winked, acknowledging
that he thought that I'd played that card well. We both
knew that Sam had been one of those overly enthusiastic
authorities taking a peek at my off-limits patient files.

Then he said, "Bottom line, though? A patient could
lie? About his or her real identity? Place of business? Living situation? You would have no way to know?"

"Patients lie to me every day. I'm sure I miss most of
it. Has it happened about identity? Sure. The patients
who pay by check? I see what's printed on the check. But
a patient who doesn't?" I shrugged. "A patient could
mislead me about who he is. Where he lives. Other
things."

Sam nodded. He dug around in the pathetic bag for
the last of the Beer Nut crumbs. He tilted his head back
while he poured them into his mouth from the thumb
side of his fist. He said, "It's completely possible that you
may have had a patient, even as recently as this afternoon,
who was not exactly who he said he was?"

I sniffed the air for rancidity while I weighed Sam's
question for ambiguity. For me, ambiguity meant license.
I was comfortable with what I detected.

"I would say that was possible. Given whom I saw this
afternoon."

Sam raised his empty glass and narrowed his eyes as

though squinting would make a fresh brew magically appear. He asked me if I wanted another. I shook my head. He caught the bartender's attention, pointed to his glass, and held up his pinkie. I almost missed what he said next because I was wondering why he used his pinkie.

"So here's what else I did today while I was out in my car waiting for you to finish up with that patient in your office. I tracked down Coma Doe's real name."

The more Sam said the name Coma Doe, the more he compressed it into a solitary word, Comadoe.

I was tempted to ask for Comadoe's real name but decided I was better off not knowing. If I saw him again, I might use it inadvertently. That wouldn't be good.

I said, "If you have his real name, I presume you ran it. Or you tricked a colleague into doing it. I am kind of curious if the guy has a record." I recognized that it was the kind of question that Sam would get around to answering on his own.

"Guy is not much of a driver. That's for sure. Speeds a lot, school zones even, and he isn't at all fond of stop signs and red lights. But more important, he has a few drug priors. Two for possession when he was still an asshole kid. His parents lawyered him right up back then and he got deferred prosecutions. But he was a slow learner even before that night his brain got beaten around like it was a hanging curve thrown to Albert Pujols."

"Yeah?" I said. "You got more?" Sam, it seemed to me, was investing a lot of energy in waxing his board. I was interested in coaxing him back into the water, watching him catch a wave.

"He deals. When he was young, weed to his friends. Later, he was busted for intent when he was old enough to know better. He copped a plea on that one—charge was changed to possession. Substance was"—Sam did a drumroll on the bar top—"meth."

Sam was back in the water, paddling into a swell. "This next part is interesting. See, there's a pending charge from the night of the Fourmile Fire. Serious shit."

*Some good news?* "For?" I asked.

Sam again tapped his fingertip on the blank sheet of paper on the bar. He was using the doubled-over empty envelope as an ineffective coaster for his sweating glass.

"In the T-Bird he crashed that night? Turns out a K-9 discovered meth in a nylon zipper bag in the trunk. Ounces. O-Zs. For a guy with his priors? Could be real time."

"Yet," I said, "he's out and about, not incarcerated. He could even be visiting psychotherapists."

Sam smiled. "It appears that there are complications with the investigation. Having to do with proving possession of the meth."

"You want to tell me about the complications?"

"I'm deciding."

"While you decide, how is Henry doing?" I said. "The bulldog?"

"Thanks for asking," Sam said. "Henry spent that night in a temporary shelter with all the other dogs rescued from the fire. Was returned to the girlfriend the next day no worse for wear. Want some irony?" Sam was a fan of irony. "The back of Comadoe's head probably saved

Henry from a trip through the windshield of the crashed T-Bird. Comadoe may be a true hero in the bulldog underground."

I was relieved about Henry. I also thought that, as a breed, bulldogs were too wise to pin a medal on the chest of someone like Comadoe.

# TWENTY-SEVEN

Sam went on. The anticipation of that second beer was bringing out the storyteller in him. "The first night of the fire was crazy for us, for law enforcement. Certain protocols were . . . suspended in order to keep personnel available to smooth the evacuation and to assist the firefighters. That's a roundabout way of saying that the car Comadoe crashed was left at the scene overnight. No tow trucks were being allowed up the hill, so the car wasn't towed to impound until midday the next day. That has created some chain-of-custody problems, seeing that the meth wasn't discovered in the trunk of the T-Bird until a sniffer dog went batshit at impound eighteen hours after the crash.

"The detectives Lucy and I were helping that night have a tough nut. They have to prove that Comadoe knew the meth was in the car and that it was under his personal control. Those unresolved issues are why he hasn't already been charged with a new drug felony, and they are why he hasn't already been picked up for violating probation on his intent-to-sell plea bargain. With me?"

I nodded. Sam nodded right back at me. "For reasons that I hope are obvious, it's just not prudent for me to snoop around the edges of that drug investigation, but let's assume the worst for Comadoe. There are two reasons I want to assume the worst. One, just for argument's sake. The other because, well, it makes me feel better.

"If we're presuming the new meth charge is righteous—that the drugs in the trunk were his; that the quantity constitutes intent-to-distribute, which it does; and that the good guys, the cops, can prove it all to the DA's satisfaction. Which I'm not sure we can. But I don't think Comadoe believes that.

"If all my presuming is true? Our boy looks like toast and he's feeling all kinds of vulnerable right about now. Comadoe's never done real time. Yeah, yeah, he's survived a couple of sleepovers at County, but nothing scary. I'm sure he's heard stories about what big-boy prison is like, and I'm thinking he's a little anxious about his peculiar vulnerability. Those curls of his? That cute little tat? All the unmarked flesh begging for clink ink? I would say our boy is feeling a little desperate."

*So that's what Rick was alluding to with his comment to me that afternoon about dirty cops.* I looked at Sam. I thought I was following his reasoning, but to be certain I said, "If Comadoe is desperate, he may well be looking for some leverage. Something he can barter to make his drug problems diminish. Maybe another plea bargain."

Sam began to tap the bar top with his index finger. No particular rhythm emerged before he said, "Since another plea is unlikely, is that supposition based on what I told you? Or is that a conclusion based on something you may have heard, you know, elsewhere?"

During that afternoon's session, Rick Contreras had indeed described himself as a desperate man. Although he hadn't mentioned the meth in the trunk of the T-Bird, he had suggested that his only way to avoid serious incarceration was to begin to fulfill a lifelong dream of ridding the world of "dirty cops" by pointing out "one or two" to a suitably grateful district attorney.

As allegory, Comadoe related a quick story about the first time he was busted when he was sixteen. He was the passenger in a friend's pickup when a cop car came out of nowhere with one quick pulse-elevating burst of siren, lights flashing. His friend told him to roll down the passenger-side window and flick their weed out at the next curve.

During the ensuing traffic stop the driver engaged in a one-sided discussion with one of the two officers about probable cause. The argument didn't turn out the way the driver hoped. The kids were each patted down. Somehow, during the search, the same bag of weed that the young Comadoe had tossed out the window had ended up back in the inside pocket of his jacket.

"Dirty cop, right," was my new patient's conclusion about the law enforcement sleight of hand.

I had sensed no indication that Comadoe was aware of the irony of the circumstance he was describing.

Comadoe told me that ever since that experience he'd had a fantasy about making things more fair. Getting rid of the dirty cops. He was, he said, basically a go-along, get-along kind of guy. A don't-prosecute-victimless-crimes, no-collateral-damage, leave-well-enough-alone kind of guy.

Dirty cops, he maintained, upset that natural order. They "skewed everything." His analogy for the problem had to do with tilting a pinball machine. "Same thing."

He stood. I thought he was going to leave abruptly again, as he had during the first session. "You willing to help me?" he asked. "Or not?"

I did not know what he was asking. "Recover from your trauma? Absolutely."

"No. Help me nail that cop you were with in my hospital room."

"I don't understand," I lied.

"You can't tell anybody what I'm saying, right?"

I thought about his question. I thought about misleading him with my answer. I gave him an honest reply. "Basically, no. But there are exceptions."

"Like?"

"If you're planning to harm someone. Yourself, or someone else." He'd asked for an example. I had offered a less-than-comprehensive list of exceptions.

"That's not this. Now tell me you understand," he said. "Yes or no?"

"Your psychological reactions to your injuries are understandable," I said. "I think I can be of help in sorting them out."

"Don't bullshit me. I've been watching your eyes. Your face. To try to decide if you know. If you remember. Well, you do know. And you do remember. So decide whether you're going to help me."

At that moment I was grateful that patients did not have a right to take a therapist's pulse. My one-twenty-plus would have revealed more about my state of mind than I wanted Comadoe to know. I did not know how to react. I said, "Would you like to set up another appointment, then?"

"You kidding me? I don't care about you or your help. I don't know—yet—how things came down with that dead woman. I think you do know. That's the help I want."

I said, "I think I made clear how I can be of help. The rest . . . is not clear to me."

"You got balls, man," he said. "I'll give you that. Call me if you see the light. I did not make you as a hero. If you fall when he falls, it's not on me."

He walked out.

How did I read Comadoe's exit?

He was telling me he would spare me if I would help him set up Sam.

And he was reminding me of the consequences of not complying. What Comadoe didn't understand were the consequences I would suffer if I did comply.

\* \* \*

I couldn't directly answer Sam's question about what I'd heard from Comadoe and when I heard it. But by not replying at all, I was able to convey to Sam what he needed to know.

"Thought so," Sam said. Over the years, he'd developed certain skills reading me.

The bartender delivered Sam's second beer. Sam gestured at the wall and asked her if she would switch one of the TVs to *SportsCenter*. Our lives were in the balance, our families' futures were on the line, and Sam wanted to check the early hockey scores from the East Coast.

He dropped his voice in volume and imbued it with a certain confessional timbre. "Since this afternoon, I've been wondering what the guy might have to barter. So," he said, "I've been thinking back to that night in the ICU. Let's say Comadoe wasn't actually in a coma. Let's say maybe he was just . . . I don't know, sleeping. Drifting in and out. A post-concussive state. Drugged even. Let's say during the drifting he heard . . . shit that was being said in his room. Or at least parts, fragments. Like when you and I were there. Depending on what he heard, or thinks he heard, that could create a serious problem for us. Should he decide to exert his, what did you call it? Leverage."

I could tell Sam wanted a verbal indication that he and I were assessing the risks the same way. I probably should have thrown him a simple, "Go on." Instead I said, "He could have actually been in a coma, like the intensivist said. There are reports of coma patients hearing what was going on. It's relatively rare, but that rare phenomenon may well turn out to be a crucial part of our current dilemma."

Sam repeated the word. "Dilemma." He drenched it in sarcasm. He had dropped his head down as though it were too heavy to hold upright. His face was parallel to the bar top, hovering two inches above his beer glass. He rotated his head a quarter turn to look at me, which left his ear hanging close enough to the foam of the fresh beer to allow him to listen to the carbonation combusting, were he so inclined.

"One of us"—Sam paused for effect—"made a point that night of announcing his name and his professional status to the clerk on the unit. Imogen. That was her name, if you forgot. If I remember it all correctly, one of us even gave her an effing business card. That business card may have made it easier for someone like Comadoe to track down the identity of his two visitors."

Sam was blowing smoke. I said, "He could have just asked her who I was, Sam. She would have told him."

Sam wasn't in the mood for a mitigating-circumstances defense. He held up his hands. "Just saying."

"Our problem isn't what the guy might have heard from the ward clerk. Our problem is what he might have heard when certain people were talking in his room."

"You think he heard enough?" Sam asked.

"I think he heard enough to find out enough. If he's smart and he's motivated. Pure guess? I'm thinking he's no genius, but he's smart enough. You've already amply described his motivation."

Sam took a measured sip of his second beer. I was waiting for an indication that Sam understood our vulnerability.

"You ever think about living in another country?" Sam asked.

"Excuse me?" I was sure I had misheard him. If the conversation had been taking place on the phone, I would've switched the receiver from one ear to the other.

"You heard me."

If I'd heard him right, Sam understood our vulnerability. I decided to be vague so I wouldn't sound like an idiot. "Like?" I said.

"I don't know. South America."

"That's not a country."

He shot me a *fuck you* look. "Argentina then. That's a country. Turns out I have, like, this standing job offer down there. Good job. Pays well. In the security business, loosely defined."

From a pure news-value perspective, it was as tantalizing as hearing that Sam had been invited to be on *Dancing with the Stars*. "Really? Because of your language skills? Or is it your well-honed cultural sensitivity?"

It wasn't an ideal time for my sarcasm, but the target was too tempting to resist. In almost any circumstance when cultural awareness was imperative, Sam could be counted on to be an Iron Ranger. All else was unnatural to him.

Sam didn't bite. He said, "I did something for somebody once, somebody with influence. That somebody is, like, eternally grateful."

"Yeah? I'd love to hear about it. What did—"

"Can't. Don't ask again. Just answer my question—you ever think what it would be like to live in another country?"

"When I was younger. Kidless. Sure."

"Want to think about it now? This person is so grateful, I could probably get you some work, too. Though I don't know if they even believe in shrinks down there."

I was tempted to explain that psychology wasn't a religion, and I wasn't a priest. But the truth was that psychotherapy was quite popular in Argentina. Still, the futility of proceeding with the argument loomed, at least with Sam. I closed my mouth.

*God, Sam is talking about going south of the border.*

*That* kind of going south of the border.

I had images of us as Butch Cassidy and the Sundance Kid. And immediately considered that their trip south of the border had not ended well.

I lowered my voice. "So, Argentina doesn't have an extradition treaty with us? I assume you've checked."

"Yeah, I checked. And, actually, they do. Which is a problem. So Buenos Aires isn't really option numero uno." Sam pronounced it *you-kno*, even though I knew he knew how to say it correctly. "It'd be someplace else down there. Somewhere smaller, and maybe a little more banana-y." He sat up straight for a moment, as though good posture was something he would need to demonstrate in his new career. "Think about it. It's a real option."

*Banana-y?* That was the cultural sensitivity I was concerned about. I said, "Not a lot of hockey in South America, Sam."

He stared at me with *you imbecile* in his eyes, in neon. I chose that moment to get up to pee. He grabbed my arm. "Did he hear enough?" he asked. "Comadoe?"

"Sometimes people hear dots. And everything depends on their ability to connect those dots. If I were us, I would be worried that Comadoe heard some dots and was born with some of those dot-connecting skills."

Sam was ready for my return. "So when would you guess might be a good time for me to be parked nearby your office again? Don't worry. I won't come in. I'm assuming that the onetime pass to your waiting room will not be renewed."

I wanted to tell Sam everything I'd learned about my new patient, but I didn't think I could. Not ethically. I had, of course, considered and reconsidered tossing ethical considerations to the wind—Comadoe was not a real patient; he was a fake patient making a real threat—but I hadn't reached the point where I would be cavalier about discussing our time together. I could see reaching that destination soon enough, but arriving there would still require some deliberation.

A tiny part of my reluctance was that I continued to cherish the ethics of my profession, but the bigger part was that I didn't trust that Rick Contreras was setting a trap only to catch Sam. I had to assume that, as a backup, he was setting a parallel snare to catch me. Getting me to start abrogating my professional responsibilities had no-

where near the cachet of implicating Sam in a felony murder, but if I fell for Comadoe's simple ethical trap, it
could cost me my career and my livelihood. I was confident that I could toe an ethical line and still manage to
communicate to Sam the essential things he needed to
know about the man who wasn't really Rick Contreras.

I said, "Sometimes I see patients only for a couple of
visits."

Sam nodded, lowering his voice in pitch and in volume. "We have homework, both of us. We need to write
down a transcript of everything we remember saying to
each other while we were in that asshole's hospital room
that night. Every last word. Unless we can remember
what we talked about, we really have no way to know
how vulnerable we are.

"I'll do mine tonight. You do yours as soon as you can.
Let me know when you have it. Then we'll use our combined recollections to fill in the blanks. And don't use a
computer. Single sheet of paper, not part of a pad or a note-
book. Something burnable or shreddable would be best."

My cell vibrated. Lauren was probably wondering
where I was. I retrieved the phone from my pocket and
looked at the screen.

It was Izza, not Lauren. The new prospective tenant
for the cottage had failed his credit check.

**Red flag from Experian from a previous landlord in
OK. He hadn't even told me he'd lived in OK. Ru interested? Can I tempt u?**

Izza had followed the question mark at the end of the
last sentence with an emoticon that I couldn't interpret.

My interpretation skill with emoticons was pathetic. It was a source of significant amusement for my children. They had even begun creating nonsense emoticons to spoof me.

"Do you have to go?" Sam asked.

Sam would not be happy to learn that I'd just heard from Izza. Despite his discomfort with my involvement with her, I felt that Izza was one of the few advantages in my arsenal.

"Soon," I said.

# TWENTY-EIGHT

Leaves were falling from the lesser trees. The elms and ash were tougher. They wouldn't shed their foliage until winter screamed its arrival.

Amanda arrived for her session dressed for fall. And knowing where she wanted to start. "I work for two men. They know that they do not have exclusive access to my time. Neither knows the other's identity."

She had cut her hair. Her ode to autumn was jeans, boots, and a bulky cotton sweater. The trimmed hair fell just beyond her collar; the familiar ponytail look was no longer in the cards. I thought maybe she'd had some color done, too. What had been a deep mahogany brown seemed to approach the hue of the blackness of the leather of her ankle-high boots.

I didn't know how an escort should look. I tried to turn the equation on its head. If I were a man looking for an escort, how would I expect her to look late in the morning on a weekday, while visiting a therapist?

Answer: not like an escort. That was how Amanda looked: not like an escort. I allowed for the likelihood that I crossed paths with escorts—adult service providers—at other times in my daily life, and that I never knew it because I had no way to know it. I assumed that was the way that the women preferred it.

Amanda said, "I've been doing this for just shy of a year and a half. I consider myself a novice. I know a few girls in the business, but I don't feel much in common with traditional escorts, and I doubt that they consider me one of their own. It's a volume thing, mostly." Her face showed some consternation. "And sugar babies are definitely suspicious of me."

*Sugar babies?* I began keeping a mental list of things to look up later on Urban Dictionary. Urban Dictionary was becoming my new go-to Web reference.

She sighed. "The men? My gentlemen. For one of them? I am a constant in his life. We go out often, discreetly. He visits me at my place.

"Where do I fit for him? For him, I try to be an island of calm, of predictability, in what feels to him like a most demanding world. He likes women. Women adore him. But he doesn't *get* women. Women are work for him. I try to make that part easier."

Amanda narrowed her eyes. "It might be tempting to think that I am talking mostly about sex right now. But I am not. Sex is part of it. A necessary but not sufficient part. But the piece that I make easier? That's not the sex. I make the rest of being with a woman easier for him."

I considered replying. Saner instincts prevailed.

"I have also—but this is less common—joined him in other cities on business. We have taken a couple of brief holidays together." She smiled her one-dimple smile. "I recruited him. I convinced him of the potential advantages of the arrangement. After witnessing his misadventures over the years, it was not that difficult a case to make."

She made firm eye contact and nodded succinctly. We were moving on.

"My relationship with my other current gentleman is almost the opposite. Logistically, in terms of what he needs, everything. The circumstances could hardly be more different. He lives in the area, but I see him, almost exclusively, when he is away on business. I fly to meet him somewhere. We don't travel together. I've never been on the same plane with him. We have separate rooms in the hotels where he stays. On rare occasions I see him here, but always at the home I rent. He parks in my garage. We do not go out. I bring food in. Or he cooks. He is a good cook."

She swept her hair to one side with her fingertips. It didn't stay where she was encouraging it to go. Amanda was still getting used to the new haircut.

"I don't know how much detail is necessary. Or appropriate." She looked at me with wide eyes. "You probably don't, either, do you? Shut me up if I go too far."

I didn't shut her up. I knew I was allowing Amanda to lead me in over my head, but I kept following. I also knew I was curious about facts, which was not always a useful place for a therapist to be.

She said, "Girls have rules. My rules are simple, as far as that goes. This is how it works: I am a student. Mutual respect comes first. School comes second. Each man knows he is involved with a full-time student who is serious about her studies.

"They are aware that they must arrange for my availability in advance. Seeing me always requires at least an hour's notice—I need the hour to prepare, to get pretty, to preserve . . . my allure. For an extended trip out of town, if I have to juggle my school schedule, or exams, I might require a month's notice. The men do not come to my home uninvited. Ever." She raised her eyebrows and looked to the side. "That's about it.

"Beyond those basics, I am as accommodating as I am able to be. At the end of the day, the thing that the gentlemen are most appreciative of is that I am . . . accommodating." Amanda narrowed her eyes, repeating her earlier caution: "Again, I am concerned that you think I am speaking about sex when I speak of accommodation."

I suspected she was seeking acknowledgment. I didn't offer any.

"In my world the difference between a pro and an amateur isn't just about the sex. A talented amateur can manage the sex. It's about attitude, about the before, and the after. And the sex." She wrinkled her nose. "I have sex rules, too. Things I . . . don't do. That's common, in the business. Do you need to know those?"

Was I curious? Sure. But Amanda's sex rules sounded

like a distraction trap to me. I replied that it was her call. She said she would think about it. She knew she was tantalizing. I knew she was tantalizing. We both knew control of the session was up for grabs.

I had expected Amanda to begin the session by renewing her challenge that I communicate to her how I felt about her work. I reminded her of her earlier comments before I said, "You seem to expect that I will misunderstand the work you do."

"I guess I do. I presume that you're not . . . familiar. Perhaps that is an error."

Her words were intentionally coy. I left her musing unaddressed. She hadn't expected an answer; she had been making a point.

I thought I saw a flash of surprise in her eyes at the first question I did pose to her that day. I asked, "You're in school? I didn't know." Her surprise, I guessed, was that my question had not been about sex.

"First time around, when I was younger? I was a finance major. My work background, before, is in financial analysis. Up until the economy tanked I was a freelance consultant doing due diligence, mostly on the acquisition side. I had a dozen or so reasonably reliable clients, big regional law firms and VC outfits. But the bottom fell out in 2007 when IPOs and M and A—I'm sorry, initial public offerings and mergers and acquisitions—disappeared to almost zero. I burned through too much of my savings before I finally threw up my hands and tried to find a corporate job. Waiting was a major mistake. By the time I got serious, in 2009, no one was hiring.

"I'd been dreaming about doing something else for a while, so I decided to treat the economic downturn as an opportunity to reinvent myself. I wanted something more oriented to people than to numbers. You know what? Turns out I am good with people. Now I'm studying management at CU; I'll get my degree in the spring. I have a position lined up in Atlanta with a girlfriend from my consultant days who started a corporate training firm. Fortune 500 clients. Lots of travel." She smiled. One dimple.

The smile faded. She crossed her legs. She made the act of crossing her legs seem like punctuation, which left me wondering what would come next.

"This job? I had done work for one of my gentlemen's businesses. I knew he was physically attracted to me, but he had always treated me well. In late 2009, when I was desperate about finding a real job, I ran into him at an industry meeting in Palo Alto.

"A girlfriend and I were in the City for dinner, on the Embarcadero. He was there, too. George. With an attractive woman. We ended up in the bar waiting for tables. George excused himself to take a call. After a few minutes chatting with his friend, I realized she didn't know him. At all.

"She was funny, and she was smart—educated smart, well-traveled smart, literate smart—but George hadn't revealed the first thing about his life to her. I tried to pick up a first-date vibe from them, but that wasn't it.

"I found myself wondering if George had hired an escort. After they got a table, I didn't give it another thought.

"A couple of months later, almost the same thing happened in Las Vegas at another business thing. I was still unemployed, still networking. A group of us had left the Mandalay Bay, where the meeting was being held, to check out the new Wynn casino. George was at a bar across the lobby talking to a woman. She got up and headed toward the elevators. A few minutes later, he did the same. Again, I thought, *Huh, escort.*

"Grown-ups, you know? Doing grown-up things? Not my business.

"It's an hour later, two hours later, George takes the seat next to me at the blackjack table. My friends are playing craps. I have the end stool at the only small-stakes table in the room, nursing a rapidly diminishing pile of chips.

"George gives the dealer some hundred-dollar bills. Eight, ten. They come off a pile he keeps unfolded in his inside jacket pocket. The bills are so crisp the dealer has to peel them apart to count them. George pushes a couple of stacks of chips in front of me, tells me he doesn't like to gamble alone. I ask if his friend would be joining him. He makes eye contact. Shakes his head.

"He knows I know. He doesn't care. He was telling me she was history. And he was telling me he trusted me knowing that."

I thought of Amanda's brother. His trust that she wouldn't tell. How much that meant to her. I filed it.

"We played blackjack. George won, I lost. Without giving it enough thought, I placed a big bet: I said, 'She's lovely, George. Beautiful. But you can do better.'

"He didn't respond at first. After another hand he said, 'You think I want better?'

"I said, 'I think you're missing my point.'

"We played cards for most of an hour. George continued to win, mostly. I continued to lose, mostly. He flirted a little bit. I flirted back a little bit less. When it was time for me to go, I thanked him for his generosity and returned the rest of his chips. He cashed out. He tried to give me some of the remaining money. I declined. We shared a cab back to the Mandalay. Then we shared an elevator up into the tower. I got off first, of course—his suite was on a higher floor.

"I knew how little savings I had left. Maybe three months, if I was careful. I opened Excel on my laptop. I stayed up for another hour and I ran numbers. I had no trouble conjuring a plan that would work for me, one that would give me the financial freedom to go back to school. The dollar number I came up with? It would be inconsequential to George.

"That was the easy part. The math, and the money. I pulled a chair over to the window and I stared down the Strip. I forced myself to examine my recent romantic history—actually, almost all of my romantic history—and I tried to be honest with myself about whether I could really do what I was contemplating doing. Not perform the job I had in mind; I knew I could do that. I wondered if I could tolerate the job. Emotionally.

"I wasn't sure that I could. To make it work, I decided I would need to have a buffer—some insulation—in place. Why? I knew George could be serious trouble for

252 • Stephen White

me. Other than his age—he's older than I am—he was the kind of man I'd always gotten into trouble with in relationships. He's comfortable with power. I love that in a man. I love his . . . complete assurance about his place in the world. He expects people to make room for him. And they do. I find that sexy as hell.

"If I let my guard down, I knew that in a week, or a month, or a few months, I could end up the proverbial smitten kitten, completely attached to George. Maybe even in love with George. Vulnerable, with a capital *V*. Stupid with a capital *S*.

"But I'm a realist"—Amanda offered the one-dimple smile—"or at least I am until that moment that I'm smitten. And that side of me knew that George wasn't going to get attached. No matter how good a companion I turned out to be. No matter how tantalizing a courtesan I became."

I wondered if her name was Amanda. I hadn't wondered that before.

"And thus the need to find a buffer. I went back to the laptop and I altered my new business plan to make room for two Georges. I redid all the numbers. Came up with a set of guidelines that I could live with that would allow me to juggle two men, even three, and still allow me to have the life I needed as a student. The numbers worked; I knew that by graduation I would be able to put aside a decent cushion to replace what I'd spent. Cover my tuition and expenses. Enjoy a few luxuries.

"I presented the proposal to George over a late breakfast the next morning. His initial reply? 'I have no interest in being a sugar daddy. For you or anyone else.'

"I said, 'Good. I have no interest in being your sugar baby. That's why this will be business. A deal, with parameters.'

"He chuckled. 'Parameters? Like rules? The other girls have no rules. They are younger and more beautiful.'

"George wasn't belittling me. He was doing what he does—identifying weaknesses in my proposal. I was judging that George trusted the young women just enough to . . . rent them. George would not put enough faith in unfamiliar drop-dead-gorgeous young women to lease one. For that he would want emotional maturity. Some experience in her life. Some intuition about his life. And discretion that would last longer than a date.

"I told him we both knew I was attractive enough for him. I told him he deserved a girl who wasn't pretending to enjoy him because she was hoping he'd leave another hundred on the table before he walked out the door.

"He was far from convinced. Commitment, he thought, even a business partnership, would bring potential problems. 'I know that what I'm doing is not ideal. Every decision has trade-offs. That is life. Certain risks are unavoidable.'

"I said, 'Those trade-offs? Ten girls? Ten potential problems. The right girl? No potential problems. No trade-offs.'

"Either way, with his escorts, or with my proposal, it was pay-for-play for him—a clean business transaction. I had to offer something different. With value added. I said, 'The big difference? If you yearn to slide behind the wheel of a familiar Ferrari, you won't find it waiting for you at Zipcar. For the quality you want, for the sincerity you deserve, you will need to commit to a lease. Why? Because what you really want is not available by the hour. You know that.'

"He found my analogy amusing. By nature—by *character*—George is not a deliberator. VC is a gut game. At the venture capital stage of a business's genesis, there are few numbers to analyze. Consulting about risk was *my* job. I had convinced George that his downside was limited.

"We closed the deal before he flew out of town that day. We agreed on a three-month trial—he called it his test-drive. If he liked it? Annual mutual renewals. He shook my hand and said, 'We have a deal, Enzo.' Enzo Ferrari. He still calls me that."

I thought Amanda looked wistful at the memory of how it all happened.

"I didn't see George again for almost three weeks. I actually met him for the first time—as his companion—at a hotel in Salt Lake City." She smiled, perhaps at the irony. "My anticipation as that first night approached was electric."

I was captivated by the story. I was aware that could be a problem.

"George had only a couple of rules—some reasonable limitations on the other . . . man. My buffer. And on any personal relationships I might have that could undermine my value. A few cities he didn't want me to visit while he was there. Places where he has family. A meeting I couldn't attend anymore because it was one where men took wives."

"George is married?" I asked. I immediately questioned why I had asked it.

Amanda's eyes, I thought, hinted *yes*. She said, "So that was how my life changed." She shrugged. I wasn't sure how to read it—I couldn't tell whether the shrug was an it-was-no-big-deal kind of shrug. Or whether it was a you-never-know, life-is-a-funny-thing kind of shrug.

I said, "Later? You found your buffer?"

She looked away from me for a quick second. "Just in time, really. Within days of beginning to see George, I knew I had been right about my vulnerability. Each time I was looking forward to the next time. I came this close"—she brought her finger and thumb a millimeter apart—"to being smitten.

"It wasn't as easy as I thought it would be to find another man."

I couldn't wait to hear the rest of the story. *God*. Amanda had me, I feared, precisely where she wanted me. It was not anywhere close to where she needed me.

I asked, "The man with the handgun and the orchids? George, or the Buffer?"

She shifted her weight. She didn't answer.

# TWENTY-NINE

I spent much of my professional time listening to people tell stories. Most of the storytellers believed they were relating nonfiction. A few probably were. But the majority told me stories that they had unconsciously edited through the subjective filters of personal experience, memory, and psychology.

While few of the stories were tedious, most were more mundane than the storyteller thought. Even among those that weren't banal the majority were as familiar to me as the furniture layout I spied in front of me each day from my consultation chair. Only a tiny fraction proved novel. A rare few were captivating enough to make me want to sit forward on my chair and not miss a word.

Amanda was reintroducing me to captivation. Each time she began a story I felt the allure. That day's story was replete with magnetic themes—of vulnerability, and survival, and human weakness. The story featured potentially destructive forces, passion and danger, and it carried undercurrents of the tantalizing, of generous hearts and of endless money, all disguised as abundant power. And sex.

A more objective part of me—the part of me that was being paid to be objective—knew that the story Amanda was telling about herself and George and the Buffer was not the only completely captivating story I'd heard from her lips. I had not forgotten what a rapt audience I had been for the tale of the Orchid Man with the Handgun, or for the Hand Job Faerie of Ronald McDonald House.

Amanda had managed, thrice in three sessions, to do something that most patients didn't accomplish even a solitary time in a year of Thursdays at one forty-five: Amanda had made me her grateful audience.

My training, my experience, and the compass in my head—the things I relied on to tell me the difference between north and south, right and wrong, therapeutic and not—all chided me about my responsibility to resist her undertow. I had a clinical obligation to escape whatever riptide Amanda was creating and to guide her to shore.

That's where we would do the work. Onshore.

But, in that moment, in the room, in the therapy, with Amanda, I was in danger of convincing myself that the undertow was integral to the treatment. The undertow, I was arguing, was *process*. And process was, of course, paramount.

The reality? To be an effective therapist with Amanda that day, I did not need to know additional intimate details about Amanda's life with the men who paid her for accommodation and companionship and affection. And, yes, sex. Not right then, certainly. Maybe not at all.

To be an effective therapist for Amanda, what I needed to know more about was the storyteller. To be an effective therapist for Amanda, I needed to understand the advantage she accumulated by telling me captivating tales.

As a young, inexperienced therapist, I likely would have misperceived the process. I might have convinced myself that by learning about the sex and the money and the power I would somehow—osmosis, maybe—learn what I needed to know.

She sensed something had changed. Intuiting alterations in the atmosphere in a room where she was alone with a man had to be a well-honed skill for someone living Amanda's life. She glanced at me quickly before diverting her eyes. Amanda's glance was her way of taking my temperature. She was determined to understand the reason for the sudden thermal change.

I did not know what advantage Amanda was seeking with me that day, nor did I know why she needed it. Process in psychotherapy, if it had value, mimicked an important process that occurred in a patient's life. I leaned forward, dropping my elbows to my knees. I kept my gaze on Amanda until she felt it. She knew something was up.

"What?" she said.

Psychotherapy rarely yields benefits when a patient is content. For the first time in almost three complete sessions Amanda was experiencing psychological discomfort. She reacted by trying to steady herself. "Watch what you wish for, right?" was what she said, while she rolled her eyes in a self-mocking way. "Juggling two men turned out to be much more difficult for me than—"

I didn't want her escape to be so facile. By raising both my hands and turning my palms toward her—I did it slowly—I threw up an impediment. Her next word caught in her throat. I shook my head. I said, "You tell great stories, Amanda."

She tilted her head a few degrees to the dimple side. Her expression hinted at offense. "They are not . . . stories," she said. "What I am telling you is all true."

"You tell great true stories, Amanda."

The offense dissipated. It was replaced by something else, something I hadn't seen before. She pursed her lips to speak but reconsidered. I thought I was witnessing wariness. Wariness might have been progress.

I said, "I could listen to your stories all day long." I allowed a moment for that thought to impact her. "For us? Here? That may be a problem. I'm thinking that, in your life, it may also be a problem." Her expression told me nothing. "I could let you tell me more stories. About wealthy and powerful men, and young beautiful women, and fancy casinos and five-star hotels."

I allowed her to digest what I was saying. I half expected that she would have a response. Something surprising for me to consider. And because I would have to consider it, it would serve as another distraction. I hoped I would recognize the reappearance of the resistance in a new form.

Resistance is what psychotherapists call the phenomenon of warding off conscious awareness of potent issues in therapy. Amanda seemed to be busy doing just that.

When she didn't respond, I said, "And then, after you tell me more stories? After I let you captivate me more? Our time will be up, and you will go home. You will come back next time armed with another story. I'm guessing the next story, like the one about the orchid man and his gun, and about your brother and his pain, and about George and being smitten, would have high stakes about your life and about someone else's life. The story would be about interesting people doing interesting things." I paused. "But I am concerned that is not a productive way for us to work."

She smiled just enough to reveal the solo dimple. "They are not stories. They are *true*," she said. She was concentrating so much meaning into that solitary word— *true*—it was as though she were a cook desperate for me to recognize that the sauce she was plating had been reduced to its very essence. She wanted me to judge her experience, her reduction, to be as savory as she did.

Why? I didn't know. We weren't there yet. "I don't doubt," I said, "that your stories are true."

"These aren't just stories. This is my . . ." The sentence rolled to a gentle stop.

I sat straight. I kept my eyes on Amanda's. My eyes were kind because I was feeling kind. She grew uncomfortable again, either because of my attention or because of my kindness. But most likely because of whatever pressure she felt on her resistance.

Amanda wasn't accustomed to that pressure. Not with me.

The moment that the power in the room shifts in psychotherapy is, like the moment that a rising tide begins to ebb, often subtle. It can take time for therapist and patient to recognize the alteration. But that day we both felt the fresh tilt to the room.

In psychotherapy the same steps often must be repeated time and time again before the patient can comfortably recognize the progression. Repetition wasn't necessary that day. Amanda said, "Usually, I can distract a man. Any time I choose."

*I bet you can,* I thought. "I've been conspiring with you. Letting you distract me," I said. *That has been our process.*

"Until today," she said.

"Until just now," I said. I was wary of her insight. A doubting part of me felt as though she were tossing me a bone. I allowed the silence to settle before I stirred things up again by asking Amanda a question I should probably have pressed before.

I said, "Why are you here, Amanda? In therapy?"

Her hands were on her lap. She joined the tip of each index finger to the tip of the same hand's thumb, completing two tiny circle shapes. The orbs intertwined. The gesture puzzled me. I fought the temptation to divert some energy making sense of it. I filed it.

I said, "With me? In therapy. Why?"

Well more than a minute ticked away. The silence was hers to break. Or not. If nothing else happened to advance our work that morning, we'd already had a valuable session. If she chose continued silence, I was content to let the time expire.

I began to think that was what would happen.

As the session neared its end, she stood. With a tone as poignant and vulnerable as that of a new mom offering to allow a stranger to hold her baby, she said, "What if he hadn't died?"

Amanda's last words of the hour reverberated in my head for the rest of the day. But I didn't begin to comprehend what she'd meant until I was on my way home.

I was less than a mile from my office on Ninth, waiting to turn onto Baseline at the foot of Chautauqua. To my right, the western sky was in pre-sunset splendor, with hazy pastel ribbons floating above the Flatirons. The driver of the car behind me honked twice, impatient for me to force my way into traffic.

The impudent honk echoing, I understood what Amanda had meant: she had been talking about her brother.

*Her brother is the "he."* What if he had started responding to the chemo? What if he had been the beneficiary of some medical miracle? What if his lymphomas had vanished? *What if he hadn't died?*

The horn honked again. In the rearview mirror, I could see that an elderly woman had raised an arthritic fist at me for missing an opportunity to pull onto Baseline. I waved a casual apology. Seconds later I slipped into a too-narrow break in traffic.

Straight ahead, to the east, the sky over the Great Plains was growing dark. I checked my mirror. The gray-haired lady in the oxidized Honda Accord had forced herself into the tiny slot in traffic right behind me. She was tailing me as though we were at Daytona and speed meant all.

*What if her brother hadn't died?* What if Amanda had ended up being a sexual partner for her slightly older but physically recovered teenage brother? What if he had wanted—even insisted—that their sexual relationship continue? Or what if he had insisted that their relationship mature—if that was a word that could be used—sexually?

What if he had threatened her? What if the power—in her naïve fourteen-year-old eyes, the power had belonged to Amanda—had shifted to him?

My question to Amanda at the end of the session had been: *Why are you in therapy?*

Her answer had been: *What if he hadn't died?*

My new question to her—the next time we met—would be: What was it about her brother not dying that motivated her to seek my care?

*And why did you call me the day you did?*

*And why . . . me?*

The woman honked at me again. I had no idea what I

was doing to displease her, other than honoring the speed limit.

*That's it. Of course,* I thought. *It's not about me. It's transference.*

"If not me, then who?" I said aloud.

The Honda was so close to my bumper, I could not see its license plate in my mirrors. I was beginning to get annoyed.

# THIRTY

Lauren and I didn't often shop together for groceries. Marketing was a chore we split, not one we shared. When she asked me if I'd go with her to Whole Foods the next day, on Friday afternoon, I agreed. The trip, she promised, was for things we couldn't wait to get on Saturday at Boulder's glorious farmers' market.

Even during times of the day when the rest of Boulder wasn't particularly frenetic, the long block of Pearl in front of Whole Foods was sclerotic with traffic. When Whole Foods was busy—and on any random Friday afternoon it was—the store became a kind of crowded that caused me to question whether I really needed to eat that day.

It took ten minutes to find a place to park. I did a valiant job, in my appraisal, of hiding my aggravation at Lauren's timing for the outing. Her equanimity about it all perplexed me. She was either feigning patience for some reason I couldn't discern, or she'd been rendered copacetic by her delight at having my company. I was hoping that the latter was true. Regardless, I was determined to maintain a veneer of calm to disguise my aggravation.

She grabbed a minicart from near our car. The handle provided her with something to lean on, literally, during what I was beginning to think would be an extended sojourn in Whole Foods land. "You have the list?" she asked.

I held it up, proudly. Even when I made grocery lists, which wasn't usually, I had a tendency to leave the list behind where I penned it. The utility of a grocery list greatly diminishes when it is left on the kitchen counter. That I had not only contributed to assembling the list but had also brought it along while shopping was a rare constellation of events. Not lunar-eclipse rare, but still. I was feeling good about myself.

Inside the store we joined a herd heading toward produce, where we became trapped behind a trio of large carts pushed by people visibly indecisive about lettuce. Each in turn fingered a big plastic clamshell of whole butter lettuce. None selected the butter lettuce. I took a deep breath. I counted to ten, then twenty, while I waited for the ambivalence to sort itself out. So that I didn't exacerbate the congestion in the leafy greens area, I squeezed in beside my wife. She hooked her right pinkie over my left.

"You're being good," she said. "Keep it up, and I'll get you a treat when we check out."

I liked that she had recognized that I was being good. I pulled my trapped pinkie free and used that hand to lightly cup the right cheek of her fine butt. I whispered that I could wait for my treat until we were home.

She laughed and whispered that she was thinking more along the lines of a granola bar.

Whatever she might have intended to act as segue to what came next, I missed. I was knocked more than a little off balance when she said, "That case in Frederick? Weld County kicked a piece our way. They think that the woman who killed herself had been romantically involved with a cop, maybe even a Boulder cop, before she moved to Frederick."

I tried to keep my cool. I said, "How do they know that?"

"An acquaintance, a neighbor, said she'd been seeing a cop. That's it."

"Yeah?" I said. I didn't think I could manage much more of a sentence than that. Since Lauren was busy looking for a route out of leafy greens, she didn't seem to recognize my apoplexy. I tried a diversion. I said, "The dead woman may have been acquainted with Michael McClelland while they were at the state hospital. Right?"

"Yes. *May* have been acquainted. There's never been any proof. Could be nothing more than temporal coincidence—they were there at the same time. We have no evidence they even met."

A tiny gap opened as a man with shoulder-length white hair, a tattered AC/DC concert T-shirt, below-the-knee cutoff jeans, and a beat-up pair of forest-green cowboy boots chose baby spinach over arugula and aimed his cart in the general direction of the berries. Lauren jumped into the opening.

"Has anyone spoken to him?" I asked as we were forced to a stop just shy of our goal of lemons. "McClelland? Whether he knew her?"

"We won't tip our hand with him. He's too slippery to use for a fishing expedition. It would blow up on us, and he'd end up with an additional advantage."

"Is it possible that McClelland has a hand in this? The suicide? Everything?"

I knew Michael hadn't been a player in that part of the extended drama, but I threw out the possibility to Lauren hoping that even the potential of McClelland's participation might add a complication that could be a valuable distraction to the Boulder investigators. One that would lead away from Sam Purdy.

"Given our personal history with McClelland, Alan, I never rule him out. No indication of his involvement surfaced during his Pitkin trial. And there have been no new red flags from prison since his conviction. He could have found a way around the correspondence monitoring— hell, he probably has—but . . ."

She let the thought drop. I said, "How is the relationship the woman might have had with the Boulder cop significant? The relevance escapes me."

"We don't know. How do I read it? The Weld County sheriff seems to suspect that the suicide was really a homicide. Throw a cop into that mix? Especially one from another jurisdiction? And if they can develop something that makes that Boulder cop a plausible suspect, then this suicide-turned-homicide becomes a very big deal for them."

"Yeah," I said. My stomach was beginning to hurt.

Lauren said, "I want some of those fried potatoes. The ones that you bake first? Will you make some?"

"The ones that look like latkes?"

"Those."

I kissed her lightly on the lips. "Your wish is . . ." I stepped away from the safety of the cart determined to grab potatoes and make a quick return.

Lauren's revelation meant that two different posses were riding after Sam.

Comadoe was trying to find someone in Frederick who could place Sam in town the night of Currie's death so he could serve Sam up as a sacrificial lamb to keep himself out of prison. And now the Boulder DA's investigators were trying to find out which Boulder cop had been romantically involved with Currie before she moved from Boulder to Frederick. If either posse proved successful the entire ruse about how Currie died—the carefully constructed suicide house of cards that had insulated Sam and me since he had assisted Currie in her death—was in serious jeopardy of crumbling. If Sam were caught in the law enforcement net, or in Comadoe's amateur snare, I would be trapped, too. The consequences would be life-altering for everyone in Sam's orbit and everyone in mine.

A kid pushing a cart for his mom crashed into the back of my legs as I bagged some purple potatoes. He hit me hard. His mother apologized to me.

The kid told her that it was my fault for not moving.

I had some thoughts that I managed to keep to myself.

Lauren said, "We still need lemons. I'm heading over to citrus. Stay close."

I thought I would brine and sear some scallops to go with the fried potatoes, which meant dealing with the throngs lined up at the fish counter. Lines and Lauren's MS didn't get along, so I joined the fish queue while Lauren parked our cart out of traffic in a sedate cul-de-sac near an apparently undesirable end of the dairy cooler.

I phoned her after about five minutes. We could see each other. I still had the list in my hand. She waved at me when she spotted my name in caller ID. I asked, "Are couscous and quinoa in the same location in the store?" I knew one, quinoa, was a grain and one, couscous, was a pasta, but I also knew that they were both little tiny hard food balls that became edible only after spending time in hot water. My question was really whether their tiny hard roundness was a sufficiently compelling shared trait to place them in close proximity in a grocery store. I didn't get to hear Lauren's answer; it was my turn with the fishmonger. I said, "Got to go," and pocketed my phone.

I ended up with some fine-looking scallops. I carried the package over to the eddy where Lauren waited and tossed it into the cart. I said, "Even with the addition of a Boulder cop to the puzzle, it doesn't really explain your department's interest in an old suicide in Frederick. I'm thinking that you're not convinced that Michael McClelland is really on the sidelines."

She looked over at me, a rueful smile on her face. "When has that particular assumption ever served me well?" she asked. "Us well?"

I touched her arm. "Hunch? Or fear? Or do you have some evidence he's pulling strings from prison?"

She said, "Fear, so far." She grazed my fingers with hers. She gestured down the long aisle that ran the length of the back of the store. "Are you ready to deal with the cheese people? And with the olive guy?"

"I thought you liked the olive guy."

She began to push the cart toward the far side of the store. "You know, there are days that I just want to buy olives. I don't want to discuss them. I don't want to know their lineage or what kind of weather they endured. He likes to discuss his olives. For me, this is one of those I-just-want-to-buy-them days."

I offered to deal with the olive guy after I tracked down the quinoa. She could do the cheese. She thought about it for a few seconds before she told me she was a big girl and she would deal with the olive guy.

Lauren ran into a couple of her friends before we made it ten more feet. Once I recognized that the three of them wanted to talk, and not just say hello, I excused myself. They were still together after I located the quinoa. I retreated to buy a smoothie at the front of the store. I lucked into an empty table by the window. I called Sam.

"Yeah?" he said. "I'm working. Not everybody takes Friday off."

I said, "The sheriff knows that a cop, maybe a Boulder

cop, was in a relationship with . . . that woman before she left town and moved to Weld County. How careful do you think they were? The possible cop and the woman who moved away?"

He laughed at me. In a mock-conspiratorial whisper, he said, "You really think our phones are bugged? If our phones are tapped we're already screwed."

I moved on. "Okay, how careful were you with Currie?"

"You asking about condoms?"

"I'm trying to gauge how down-low you guys were."

"We were discreet, but not as down-low as I would have been had I known things were going to end up with her . . . killing herself. Early in our relationship I didn't foresee the killing-herself scenario. If I had, I think I might have passed on the romance."

"Best guess? Will the investigators be able to identify you?"

"It's possible. We met at her place sometimes. I didn't wear disguises. She had neighbors. We met at my place sometimes. I have neighbors who might remember her face or her car. Do you know who's going to be doing the looking? Did Lauren say?"

"Boulder DA is investigating at the request of the Weld County DA. I would guess it'd be one of the in-house investigators. Abrams? Or maybe Otero. If it's important to you, I can press her on it."

"Let it go. I don't want to draw any attention. What's that noise? Where are you?"

"Whole Foods, God help me. On Pearl. McClelland's the other wild card, Sam. Lauren says that it appears he's on the sidelines so far. He must know about you and Currie. If he decides he can bring any of us down by disclosing what he knows, then—"

"Yeah. We have to assume he knows, but there's nothing we can do about it. He'll play the card when it suits him."

"Is there a way to reach out, to express our . . . concerns?"

"Concerns about what?" Lauren said. She slid onto the chair across from me.

"Sam says hi," I said. I did not want to answer Lauren's question.

She grabbed my smoothie and took a long drink from the straw. In a stage whisper, she said, "You think we can finish up? I'm pretty sure I'm getting tired. But I got the cheese *and* the olives."

"Bye, Sam." I killed the call.

"There was a little too much rain in Greece," Lauren added. "For the olives."

I told Lauren to sit and finish the smoothie. I would check us out.

She told me not to bother to pick out a granola bar.

# THIRTY-ONE

Jonas was learning how to play the stand-up bass. My son was slight in build, like his birth father, Peter. Jonas's bass was tall and portly. The height dwarfed him to such a degree that the match of child and instrument felt wrong. Jonas was, I hoped, pre-growth spurt, which meant I could hold on to my dream that he'd eventually grow into his bass.

Jonas's feel for the instrument seemed intuitive. He had a connection with the sound he was creating that he didn't have with a football, or a basketball, or a soccer ball, or a Frisbee, or for *World of Warcraft*. He had a feel for the thing that he'd never displayed for his dead father's power tools. I knew how proud Adrienne would be that the genes that had left her so musically handicapped during her life had managed to combine with Peter's to translate into recognizable musical talent for their solitary offspring.

The music instructor worked from his basement apartment in a little house near Folsom and Mapleton. The teacher was a rabid vegan in his late twenties who had gently asked Jonas to consider wearing only certain shoes, leather free, to his lessons. Jonas was fond enough of his teacher that he had acquiesced to the shoe restriction without too much complaint.

Before that Saturday lesson, instead of taking Jonas to Snarf's for his favorite corned beef sandwich, I had taken him to get falafel. He had not kvetched. On the first pre-lesson falafel journey, I'd explained that the culinary choice was a gesture of respect for his teacher, who would be offended by the aroma of meat, corned or otherwise, on his student's breath.

Jonas was wise. He'd asked, "This wouldn't be an issue in most places, would it? Whether I eat meat? What shoes I wear?"

Jonas had never lived anywhere besides Boulder. How would he know that Boulder was "other"? I was impressed.

"Exactly," I said. "Everywhere isn't like here." I managed to speak that sentence with a straight face, cognizant that I was edging into world-record understatement territory.

My mobile rang two seconds after Jonas finished dragging his heavy instrument through his teacher's door. I stayed parked at the curb while I looked at the screen. I mumbled, "Shit." *Answer? Don't answer?* I answered.

"Oh good. Alan? I hoped this number would find you. It's Izza. Is this a good time? How are you?"

She asked how I was in the hyper-sincere tone people use when they wish to convey that they care about the reply. In another circumstance I might have been touched. Instead, I winced. I did not want Izza to care about me, and certainly not sincerely.

"Good. How are you?" I included no hyper-sincerity in the reflexive volley I sent back over the airwaves. I was concocting a list of all the ways that Izza calling me on my mobile phone could portend bad things.

I considered telling her I was married. I was also preparing myself for the complications that would ensue if it turned out she didn't give a rat's ass about my marital status.

She said, "When I Googled your number, it said that this is a Boulder cell. I didn't have you for a Boulder guy. But the bike, right? Your funny shoes? I should have guessed. Are you on Facebook?"

"So, what's up?" I said, trying to be polite without replying to her Facebook inquiry or sounding happy to hear from her.

"You can probably guess. I want to tempt you one more time," she said, pausing just long enough to allow the word tempt to begin to ferment. "There's a new renter in the picture. I know I'll rent it soon, that's not the thing. But—I'm being honest here—I'd rather rent to you. I can cut the rent fifty dollars if that helps. I can go all the way to eighty if you do the winter snowplowing we talked about. That's a great deal. I know this market, and that's a bargain. I haven't had good luck renting to students."

*Students?* The word unsettled me. I thought, *No.* Then I thought, *Damn.*

"The new potential tenants are . . . students?"

"Stu-*dent.* Singular. He says he is, but I don't think he's being completely honest with me. He told me he attends Metro and, get this, he has the same major I do, but when I tried to get him to talk about his classes he didn't seem to know what he was talking about. I mean, the most basic things just went right over his head. I don't like liars and I think the guy might be lying."

"Really? What makes you concerned?"

"He was hurt in an accident recently. He's really . . . bruised and cut and battered. Said there was no alcohol involved, but . . . I'm not sure I believed his story." She paused. "My experience is that students have parties. Horses and parties? Not a good match. Horses and drunk twentysomethings? Never a good match. And with my dad sick right now . . ." Izza sighed. "Please? Can I twist your arm? Take another look?"

I was thinking, *Comadoe.* I said, "You'll run a credit check on the guy, right?"

"Sure. As soon as he e-mails me the application."

Izza was gauging my interest in renting the cottage, of course, but she was also gauging my interest in her. I could almost smell her uncomplicated vulnerability through the phone. I could have wasted some energy being flattered, but a much healthier part of me wanted to advise her to keep looking to her contemporaries for a romantic match. I wanted for her to believe that she would eventually attract a boy who had some maturity to spare.

My protective impulse meant that I was becoming distracted by Izza's sweet nature. Although that may have been a generous inclination, I couldn't afford to let it get in my way. Not if Comadoe had located ground zero, as I feared he had.

The danger was that Comadoe might soon trip over the first and the third living Eliases, and the second dead one, and God knows what he would discover after that.

Maybe even Sam's ever-elusive Tyvek jumpsuit.

I said, "Okay, I'll come by and take one more look at the place."

"That would make me so happy," was Izza's reply.

The vegan bass teacher—more precisely, the bass teacher who was a devout vegan—didn't live far from Sam's house. I didn't call to tell Sam I was stopping by.

That was probably a mistake.

"Hey, got a second?" I said when he threw open the door of his North Boulder bungalow. He was glaring at me through the storm door as though I were trespassing on his stoop while attempting to sell him anything other than Thin Mints.

"We're the kind of friends who show up at each other's front doors unannounced? When did that happen?"

I laughed. "You've basically moved in next door to me. And you're offended that I knock on your door once? Be gracious. Invite me in."

He said, "I won't be gracious." He allowed me to squeeze past his belly to enter his living room. He said, "It's not always this clean. In fact, it's never this clean."

The caution was appropriate. Sam's place was neat. And it was clean. Entire sections of the original oak floors that hadn't been exposed to daylight in well over a decade were free of the piles of crap that had been accumulating since well before his wife Sherry left him. The mess was not Sam's fault alone; neither Sherry nor Sam had ever displayed a dominant neat gene. I said, "Is your mother coming to visit?"

"No, she would find this very concerning."

"Then what's up?"

"Ophelia wants to see where I live. She's never been here. And she wants to meet Simon. I agree that it's time for her to meet Simon. I offered to bring him up to the DW. But she—"

"The DW?"

"The double-wide."

"That's what you call it? We call it Casa de las Dos Casas."

Sam stared at me as though he was sorry for me. "What?"

"House of the Two Houses. Jonas made it up."

"That's clever," he said. He meant if Jonas really made it up. If it were my creation, Sam's praise was of the ironic variety.

"You were saying?" I said.

"O wants to see my home. Not my house, my *home*. I straightened up a little. Made it all a little more presentable."

"This is false advertising. Like wearing Spanx on a first date. Are you really going to pretend to Ophelia that—"

"What are Spanx?"

I didn't want to go there. "Google it. With an *x*."

Sam pulled out his phone and started to do just that. I'd meant later, but I should have known better. I continued with my original thought. "Are you going to do anything to prepare Simon for Ophelia's . . ." I was looking for a way to finish my sentence in a way that Sam wouldn't find provocative.

Sam said, "Breasts. Am I going to prepare Simon for Ophelia's breasts? I probably should. The best that could happen is that he'll stare and be speechless. The worst? I don't like to think about it. I was actually going to call you, thought you might have some guidance for me."

"Because I'm a psychologist? That would be a first."

"Hardly. Because you have a teenage son who has already had to adjust to Ophelia's wardrobe." Sam found the link he was looking for on his cell. He rotated the phone to show me a photo. "Really? Men wear these Spanx things?" he asked. "They come in big sizes?"

I could tell he was intrigued. "Men do. As for size? I would imagine XXL is Spanx's sweet spot."

He shrugged. He put the phone in his pocket. I was pretty sure he'd left the browser on the Spanx link for future reference. "Simon has no choice but to deal, right? I mean with Ophelia? He'll have to see her for who she is. Get to know her as a person."

I smiled. "Eventually, sure. But at his age? With his testosterone levels? I think it's reasonable for you to expect your son to drag his eyes north when he's addressing her. Settle for that."

Sam had a lower bar in mind. "Even the first time?"

"He should make an effort, Sam."

He turned his back to me before he said, "I haven't slept with her."

I offered up a befuddled, "Excuse me?"

"I haven't slept with Ophelia. I've slept *beside* her. We've messed around. But no . . . sex."

"Is it important I know that?" I was hoping it wasn't.

"Currie?" Sam said. "We're in this god-awful mess in Frederick because I did not use good judgment about sex. Now I'm going slow. Going fast created problems."

It was true. Sam's sexual judgment had proven problematic. The ladies loved him, which baffled me. He loved them right back, often indiscriminately.

"Ophelia?" I asked. "She's okay with your . . . pace?"

"She's a patient lady. She has some things in her past, too. I don't know about them yet, but there's big baggage of some kind. That twenty-three on her shirts?" he added. "I think that's history. It has something to do with something."

I was suspicious that I was witnessing a Clinton/Lewinsky splitting of hairs. It wasn't adding up for me. I said, "Sam, we're, like, neighbors. I hear things."

"Oh crap." Sam's ears turned red. He walked into the kitchen, opened the refrigerator, closed it, and returned to the living room. "What you're hearing?" He held up a hand. "That wasn't a question. Don't tell me. See, Ophelia and I may not be having, like, cocktails, but that doesn't mean we don't enjoy . . . other adult beverages."

282 • Stephen White

Despite the obvious peril to my well-being, I smiled. "Did you just come up with that? This minute?"

"Alan, don't."

"Say no more. We're already well into way-too-much-information territory." I added, "Going forward? If you feel any compulsion to let me know when the sexual drought ends, that'd be a good time to rethink your instinct. I can live a long time without knowing."

# THIRTY-TWO

Sam came perilously close to a cleansing breath. He said, "Why are you here, Alan?"

I sat. "I'm pretty sure Comadoe is trying to rent the cottage in Frederick. That means he's connected a lot of those dots."

Sam stood. He stuffed his hands into the back pockets of his jeans. His pale face began turning red. Sam's complexion was never far from red. It almost always bore a preparatory glow, so the transition from standard-issue pale pink to almost-alarming red didn't take light-years to develop.

"You know this how?" he asked. "You see him again?"

I told him about the call from Izza but left out the part about Jonas's vegan bass teacher. Social controversies could sidetrack Sam. He had recently dragged me into a meditation about whether the *B* and *T* parts of

LGBT really deserved equal billing with the *L* and the *G*. During the harangue, he never once said the word *bisexual* or *transgender*. *B* and *T* was as far as Sam could go.

Sam's reply to my news about Izza and Comadoe was, "This isn't good."

"Comadoe has a record, right? Does that mean he's on probation? Or parole?"

Sam said, "Probation." He nodded again. The second nod was more definitive, which meant his head was developing a metronome-ish sway. Given the raw heft of his cranium, and the whole objects-in-motion physics thing, the momentum concerned me. "Yeah, probation, probably. And with new charges pending? Interesting. Good, Alan. I like where you're going. His probation officer likely has him on the shortest of short leashes. If he doesn't, he should. If he doesn't, I can ask him to."

I said, "By going to Frederick to look at a house, could he be in some kind of violation? I was thinking that he might not even be allowed to live outside the county without permission. Is that possible? Does it work that way?"

"If he hasn't told his PO what he's up to? That he's moving? Sure, that's possible. But it doesn't matter if he's in violation. What's important is if I can convince his PO that he's in violation. They're not the most trusting souls on the public payroll. How hard can it be to convince a PO that a drug-dealing asshole is a deceptive drug-dealing asshole?"

I considered it a rhetorical question.

He said, "I'll think on this. Since you're here, I want to show you something." He walked into the kitchen. I followed. He stopped in front of the control panel for the luxury intercom system he'd described to me that night in the ICU, the system that all the neighbors would have envied in the fifties. He held a screwdriver in his right hand.

"Sam, I told you I don't want to be any part of your end-of-life scheme. I don't care what's inside that—"

He ignored my protests. Sam had a number of moods of which I wasn't fond. That one jumped up near the top of the list.

"Four screws, like I said." He popped out the quartet of brass screws. "Then you have to pull off these knobs. I may have forgotten to tell you about the knobs. Then the faceplate comes off—it'll just dangle down from the wires. See?"

Sam was one of the few people who knew that I had accidentally shot my father when I was a child. *Could you really have suppressed that?*

I tried once again to convince Sam that I was not a good choice to be his death buddy. "Sam," I said gently, "no."

I had an additional explanation for my reticence, one with more recent echoes. But confidentiality forbade me from revealing that I'd had a patient who had hired someone to kill him if he ever got sick or disabled, or that the entire episode that had ensued had saddened and ter-rified me and left me with great apprehension about that phase of anyone's life. Especially that phase of the lives of people I loved.

I had no good options to use to deter Sam; I didn't want to revisit my role in my father's death and I didn't want to dance around what I couldn't reveal about my dead patient. "Sam, I'm sensitive about this. I'm not at liberty to tell you why, but you should pick someone else to help you with your plan. Lucy or Sherry. Someone more comfortable with the issues—"

"Here's the S-hook, up here on the left. Give me your hand." He took my hand and forcibly extended my fingers so that I had no choice but to feel the contours of the exposed curve of the S-hook. "You can push up on the hinged top of the housing"—he used my knuckles to do the pushing—"and then you can pull up on the hook. Grab it. Go ahead, grab it. Got it? Do it. It's important that you can do this when the time comes. By definition, I'm not going to be around to hold your hand."

"Sam, I'm not pretending I don't want to be involved. I don't want to—"

"I'm not asking you to shoot me. Not today, anyway. I want you to know where shit is. Life is complicated. People change. Circumstances . . . evolve. This is a precaution. It's like me telling you where to find my will. Now pull."

"Where's your will? Let's start there."

"Pull."

I pulled. As Sam had promised that night in the ICU, I felt a significant amount of weight on the other end of the nylon line that was attached to the S-hook.

"Keep pulling," Sam said. "You almost have it."

The hook slipped from my fingers. As the hook rattled toward the housing, Sam gasped. He transitioned from gasping to cursing me with such alacrity that gravity had not even succeeded in yanking the heavy weight at the end of the fishing line down to the floor plate inside the wall before he finished the initial profanity.

"Did you do that on purpose?" he said.

"Hardly," I said, but I chose not to initiate a discussion of my unconscious motivation. I did reach in to see if there was anything left to grab. Unfortunately, there was. The hook had caught on the lip of the housing. I was tempted to flick it right back off and let Sam's hidden pistol clank all the rest of the way down inside the wall. Instead I grabbed the hook for the second time and began to methodically fish the line back out of the wall. "No harm, no foul," I said.

Sam called me an asshole before he cautioned me that getting the bag out of the opening wasn't as easy as it looked.

The nylon mesh bag contained the promised handgun wrapped in oilcloth along with a small cardboard box of ammunition. "Okay," I said. "Can I put everything back?"

Sam said, "Lauren's gun is a Glock. A nine-millimeter. You know how that works. Or at least you should. This is a revolver, a thirty-two. Different animal. A good blend of size and power. I want to show you how it works, how to load it, how to fire it."

Sam knew I was not a gun guy, though he had apparently repressed why I wasn't a gun guy. He certainly wasn't allowing my bias to dissuade him from continuing with his Jack Kevorkian tutorial.

He tugged open the top of the mesh bag and removed

the oilcloth. He set the package on the kitchen counter reverentially, as though it were a religious relic or an archaeological treasure. Or, who knows, a loaded gun.

He unfolded the oilcloth. Inside was a hunk of Colorado red slate. On the slate, someone had traced the outline of, I was guessing, Sam's .32.

Sam glared at me. I shook my head.

He checked the box of ammunition. The box contained nothing but stones.

I followed him as he hustled out the back door and dropped to his knees beside the downspout extension on the northwest corner of the bungalow. He lowered his head all the way to the soil so he could peer under the bottom edge of the galvanized spout extension. He said, "The magnet that holds the key case in place under the downspout has been turned almost a hundred and eighty degrees."

I wasn't about to pursue an argument about how he could possibly know that. I said, "Which means . . . what?"

"Someone turned it. It can't rotate on its own. It's a strong magnet."

In life I go for the obvious. Outside of my office, anyway. Hoofprints mean horses, not zebras. A cough means a cold, not lung cancer. Common things happen commonly. Rare things happen rarely. I said, "Simon probably locked himself out of the house. When he replaced the key, he put the magnet back differently."

Sam thought about it for, say, five seconds. "Simon has used the spare key once. That one time, he left all the pieces on the kitchen counter for me to put back in place. He's a teenager. He leaves stuff where he uses it. Milk on the counter. Doesn't close cereal boxes. He's never capped the toothpaste in his life."

"That night in Comadoe's room? We definitely talked about me killing you"—I smiled for his benefit—"when the time comes. With your unregistered, illegal handgun. And we talked about exactly where I could find said gun in your kitchen."

By the time I had reached the last sentence I was talking to Sam's back. He was on his way inside the house.

Sam lifted his butt up onto the kitchen counter right beside the Colorado slate. He said, "The asshole knows my name. He knows where I live. He has my house key. We have ample proof he heard what we said that night. And now he's carrying an unregistered weapon that has my prints on it."

"I'm sorry, Sam."

"What is he up to, Alan? Until I'm sure of that, I can't risk putting his PO on him. This may change everything. How much worse can this get?"

*Oh*, I thought, *let me count the ways.*

# THIRTY-THREE

I found out part of the answer to that question an hour later when I met up with Lauren at the farmers' market downtown. We were wandering the crowded paths hand in hand, lost in the fog of lovely aromas—a poetic pastiche of fresh bread, Palisade peaches, and Rocky Ford melons—when Lauren spoiled the moment by telling me that one of Currie's old neighbors at her apartment in Boulder had a crappy cell phone photograph of the guy Currie had been dating before she moved to Frederick.

Lauren's legs grew tired before we made it across the market. She found a bench. I delivered her a cold drink and a toothpick with a hunk of perfect cantaloupe before I headed out to collect the best end-of-summer fruit I could find. I had plenty to choose from. Colorado doesn't get enough credit for the quality of its late-summer bounty.

While I waited to pay for a bag of peaches, I pondered why the dense crowds at the farmers' market were so much less aggravating to me than the dense crowds at Whole Foods. I had reached no conclusion when I phoned Sam with the news about the photo.

The photograph Lauren had described was taken outside Currie's apartment, near the complex's pool. The view was from behind a couple that was sitting close together at a table beneath an umbrella. The guy was wearing a baseball cap. The photograph was replete with shadows and bad angles. I asked Sam if any of it sounded familiar.

"It's possible. Does Lauren know it's me?" Sam asked.

"If she does," I said, "she's not letting on."

"Did she say anything new about the witness? Or what the witness saw?"

"In Boulder or Frederick?"

"In Frederick."

"Not today."

"You still think it's the kid? Tres."

"Yes."

"What does he know? How believable is he?" Sam wasn't asking for my conjecture. I listened to him breathe until he said, "No one can tie you to this, Alan."

I knew we'd have this conversation at some point. I pressed the phone tight to my ear. I cupped my hand around my mouth. I said, "No, Sam. No."

"Good," Sam said. "Then we agree."

He hung up. When I returned to her bench, Lauren took one look at the distended bags I was lugging and wanted to know what we were going to do with all that fruit.

I drove to Frederick the next morning. I told Lauren I was going to see a guy about some bike parts he was selling. Few things in this life bored my wife more than listening to her husband discuss bicycle pieces.

Maybe the Broncos. It would have been a close contest.

My wedding ring was in the coin pocket of my pants.

Izza was working outside when I arrived. She was wearing jeans and cowboy boots and two different strapped tanks layered over a purple bra. The bra straps were more substantial than the straps of either of the tanks. She wore a beat-up baseball cap of the Tulsa Drillers. The cap was almost as well-loved as her boots.

If the look she was going for was cowgirl-femme, she was nailing it. I hoped it was her routine weekend-morning-doing-chores-for-her-dad outfit and that she hadn't glammed it up for me.

I said hello from ten feet away. She stepped in close to me as she stripped off a pair of leather work gloves. I thought she might be moving in for a hug, but she stopped just shy of invading my comfort zone. She placed her hands on her hips girl-style—her thumbs hooked forward, her fingers extended on her upper butt cheeks.

"Good decision," she said. "Coming back out here. You won't regret it. Maybe when we're done, I'll introduce you to Daddy. He's having an okay day."

She gestured toward the larger of the two residences on the property. I hadn't noticed when I drove up, but sitting in the shadows of the front porch was a man in a wheelchair. I waved.

He didn't wave back. "What would you like to see?" Izza asked.

"You said I'd be able to hear the truck traffic on 25 if the winds were different. You were right, I can hear them downshift on that hill."

"I am," she said with a smile, "an honest woman. What will it take to sell you?"

I waited for her to end the sentence with another word or two. She didn't. I said, "I'm more interested in seeing how it feels out here. Just . . . being here. Being in the house."

"How it feels . . ." She laughed. "Should have guessed—you're from Boulder." She planted both her feet. "Well, Mr. Boulder, I have a deposit check in my pocket from a cute young married couple from Cheyenne. Their references are good. Experian says their credit is fair. And they both already know how to drive that tractor.

"So this is it. Love it today, or leave it today."

My heart soared. "What happened to that student who was so interested?"

"I sent him on his way. He lied to me. That's all it takes."

In my head I started singing the chorus to Leonard Cohen's "Hallelujah."

My celebration was short-lived. Izza said, "Now he's

interviewing everybody in town about that poor woman who died. I hope he finishes soon. I don't trust him."

My phone vibrated in my pocket as Izza led me toward the cottage for my final look around. I asked her for a moment and wrestled the phone from my pocket.

Despite the good news, pessimism remained my companion. I expected the call to be from Comadoe, dropping the other shoe. Upping the ante. Raising the threat level.

But the call was from Amanda. I waited as she left a voice mail, then told Izza I needed to listen to a work message. I stepped down the walkway and turned my back.

"The Buffer just fired me," Amanda said. The short sentence was followed by so much dead air that I almost stopped listening to the recording. Then she added, "I'm so worried. I hope he's okay."

That was it. I continued holding the phone to my ear while I considered how to respond. Amanda hadn't asked me to return her call. I decided not to do it. Whenever I could, I tried to give patients the message that I believed they could cope with difficult news without my intervention. Her call didn't constitute an emergency.

I stuffed the phone back into my pocket.

"Ready?" Izza said.

"I am," I said.

On the way home I left Sam a voice mail. I told him that the guy wasn't going to rent that place after all but that he wasn't done nosing around town.

I ended with a question that I knew Sam couldn't answer. I asked, "What if he does? Figure it out?"

# THIRTY-FOUR

Amanda was traveling the next week. Since the Buffer was out of the picture, I figured there was a good chance she was on the road with George. She and I didn't have another appointment scheduled until the week prior to Halloween, when we were scheduled to meet twice to make up for lost time.

The days leading up to Halloween were warm and dry. Although the holiday had a well-deserved reputation for attracting winter weather, I was ambivalent about the front that was threatening the state from the northwest. A storm would certainly complicate trick-or-treating for the kids, but a generous dump of snow might mitigate the persistent fire danger.

I didn't hear from Comadoe during the time Amanda was out of town. I couldn't decide whether that indicated he'd given up on me, which was potentially good news, or that he was busy plotting his next move against me, which was potentially bad news.

Amanda didn't comment on her time away.

She offered no preamble at all before she said, "I never offered him a future. That was never going to be part of what we were doing."

A patient will sometimes elect the pretense, either as a conscious act or not, that the precise point where a previous psychotherapy session ended has nothing at all to do with where she chooses to begin a subsequent visit. Other times the opposite seems true. She will begin the subsequent visit as though the continuity is as unfractured as a mother's love. When the latter occurs, the first sentence spoken in the new session can feel like a seamless continuation of the final sentence spoken at the conclusion of the previous hour.

I said, "To be sure we're on the same page, you are talking now about your brother?" Amanda's unique ministrations to her brother had been the topic at the very end of the past session, two weeks before.

"My brother. The hundred days." She shook her head, as though trying to clear a thought, before she said, "The distraction I provided came in the form of sexual arousal." She raised her chin and looked off into the distance toward some shadow of the complicated past she shared with her older sibling. She bit down on her lower lip before she said, "But there was never any promise beyond that. My sexual involvement with my brother stopped right there."

I wasn't sure what she was defending or where she was

going. That day's session was young. I trusted she would find a way to help me understand.

"A few years after he died, when I was in college, I had a psychology professor who gave a lecture on the nature of human communication. He considered himself an Ossorian, if that means anything to you. He maintained that most promises between people in relationships aren't verbal. His thesis was that promises in relationships, intimate or casual, are often not spoken.

"He believed that the simple act of behaving in relationships—by behaving, he meant being, acting—constitutes a specific promise to the other person. How we behave in a certain situation in a relationship becomes an unspoken commitment to the other person to—I want to say this part exactly right—to act in a similar way . . . in similar circumstances . . . in the future." She took a deep breath before she added, "*Unless.*"

I was intrigued. "Please go on."

Amanda explained that the unless part was what captivated her. She said that her professor presented it as the most powerful of communication qualifiers, because it was never predefined. It was a wild card. The unless could and did change with each new nonverbal commitment between the people in the relationship.

I waited for her to ask me what I thought of the hypothesis. She didn't.

"I was dumbfounded after that lecture—what he was saying explained everything to me. About my brother, his death, what I did with him, for him—about that whole surreal hundred days. Although I'd never known how to understand it, or how to talk about it with my brother, I knew from the first time I touched his dick that I was making a promise to him, and that an unless was always part of the promise.

"Until I heard that lecture, I didn't know how to frame it. When I gave him the first hand job I was making a promise to do it again, and again. I knew it wasn't just once. He knew it wasn't just once. I was promising to give him handjobs whenever he was in pain. But . . ." Her eyes filled with tears. "There had to be exceptions. Right? Limits. Unlesses. That professor helped me understand the unlesses. I would continue to give my brother handjobs to help him . . . unless.

"Unless there was someone else in the room with us. Or about to come into the room to interrupt us. Unless we were caught. Unless, unless, unless. We never talked about it, but all along I felt that we had an understanding— that we both knew about the unlesses. Maybe I wanted to believe that he saw things the same way I did. Maybe I wanted to believe that the promises we were making to each other were mutual.

"But there were moments when I sensed that we didn't see things the same way." Amanda smiled at me, the smile reflecting something rueful in what she was thinking or feeling. "I was young. God. He was, too. My big brother, even at the very end, was clinging to hope. There was a part of him that hung on to the belief that he was somehow going to survive. Despite his prognosis. Despite his decline. Despite all the grief that he could see in everyone else's eyes.

"Part of me came to fear . . . I hate that I felt this . . .

that he had another hope that was keeping him going—that he was also hoping that he and I had a future together."

The room became so quiet I could almost hear her pulse accelerate.

"He never said anything, but I think he had fantasies that he and I could be more than brother and sister. More than friends." Her shoulders sank. "But that was never part of my promise." The rueful smile made another brief appearance. "Maybe I should have seen it coming, but I didn't. I didn't know much about the power of sex for boys. Especially vulnerable boys."

Amanda's eyes glistened. She swallowed away a tear.

I asked, "The unless? That was what you were referring to the last time you were here? At the end of the session? By making the decision to comfort"—I intentionally used her word—"your brother sexually, the commitment, the nonverbal promise, that you were making to him was to provide him that same kind of sexual comfort in those unique 'similar circumstances'? Do I have that part right?"

She began nodding even before I finished my thought. "Yes," she said. "Exactly."

"And the unless? The crucial unless—unspoken—was unless he lived? Unless he survived. Yes?" She nodded. "Amanda, is there some currency to those feelings, something that still resonates in your life? Today?"

She began rejecting my thought even before I finished articulating it. "No one else is dying. Now. In my life. That I know of."

She had not yet mentioned the voice mail she had left me. The Buffer. Her fear of his suicide. Being fired by him. The dangers of the smitten kitten.

She shifted her weight. She began to smile but bit down gently on her lower lip to contain the breadth of the grin.

I asked, "What was that? What was going on right then?"

Not even a heartbeat later Amanda said, "No one is dying." She sighed a shallow sigh that felt to me like capitulation. She said, "I don't know how I'm supposed to look at this. My life. What I do. When I was fourteen, with my brother, was I a slut?"

I weighed her words for facetiousness. No, that wasn't it. *More distraction?* That felt right. I waited. *The resistance is coming, the resistance is coming.*

"Now? I guess I am a prostitute. It's always seemed to me that adult relationships, romantic relationships, involve a negotiation about sex. Money is part of the negotiation, directly or indirectly. There are studies, right? Or is that a rationalization? I don't know."

I felt the therapeutic momentum evaporating. I opened my mouth to interrupt her, to challenge the resistance, but I lacked confidence in my appraisal. I said only, "You've given this a lot of thought?"

"I receive money. I engage in sex. So what am I?"

It felt insincere. I tried to bring her back. "You were talking about your brother's death. About now. About an example of unless."

"Okay, fine," she said. "Unless. It was the unless that made it possible for me to be generous with him that way—sexually." Her voice took on a sudden edge. "I was offering him nothing that would endure. My sexual relationship with my brother never existed outside the walls of Ronald McDonald House. Even at fourteen, I knew I was making a commitment to give him hand jobs to help with his pain. But that was all.

"His promise to me? His promise to me was . . . to die."

Her words sucked the oxygen from the room.

"That was our bargain." Tears flowed down her face, but Amanda didn't sob. "Even as that kid, that girl, I knew that being a sexual partner for my brother was dangerous. Not in the way I might understand it now, but I knew there had to be limits to what I would do for him. Could do. Without . . . damage."

I risked an inquiry. "Damage?"

She gave no indication that she heard me. "One night, less than a week before he died, I couldn't get him hard. That had never happened before. His cock was just fat and heavy. I couldn't help him." She inhaled deeply and held her breath for an extended moment. "He asked me to use my mouth. Not my hand. 'Try your mouth,' he said. Just like that. Like he wanted me to hand him the remote."

Amanda stared toward me, but not at me. Her eyes were focused on a distant place. I guessed Texas. MD Anderson. Ronald McDonald House. The smell of chemo. The texture of cheap hospital sheets.

She said, "My brother wanted me to give him a blow job."

# THIRTY-FIVE

Amanda's eyes focused on something even farther away. Although I wasn't completely convinced the emotion I was seeing was genuine, I was far from convinced that it was contrived.

"I couldn't do it. I didn't even think about doing it. It was instinct. No less an instinct than the first time I reached below the sheet to touch him. I knew—at that moment I knew—that there were limits to what I could offer him.

"I told him no—I wouldn't do it. It felt awful. Selfish. Even cruel. It was like refusing to call the nurse when he needed morphine. Do you see?"

In the room, at that moment, I didn't know whether she was asking the question of me or of her brother. Because of the raw power of psychotherapy, of transference, I knew the distinction was unimportant. I had no plan to reply.

"I had believed I would do anything for him. But it all changed right then. Right then, there were limits in place. Limits I hadn't known about because I didn't understand the unlesses. I couldn't articulate them."

"That particular unless?" I asked.

"What the hell would happen between us if he didn't die?"

Saying the words seemed to deplete her of an essential force. I watched her fall into an involuntary emotional retreat. Her eyes searched the distance for a horizon she wouldn't find. Her breathing grew shallow and disappeared into her gut.

"Where did you go just now, Amanda?"

A full minute later she said, "I didn't go. I came back. To now."

"Tell me about that. About now."

She found my eyes again. "This is about me, right? Me? That's what you said. Me? I still provide comfort to men. It still involves sex. It's gone well beyond hand jobs, of course, and I've discarded all of my reluctance about blow jobs. But it's still about relieving pain. The pain isn't physical, but call it anything you like—loneliness, isolation, inadequacy, failure, fear. Exhaustion. I provide distraction for men who want it, who think they need it. And who can afford it. Sometimes the distraction is sexual.

"I tell myself I act generously, but the question of the limits, the unlesses, is a big deal for me. That hasn't changed since Houston."

She finished as though she thought something had concluded between us.

I wasn't so confident we'd reached an end. I said, "Amanda, go on."

My words jostled her, as though she were in the fragile moment when she was first waking, and we were sharing only a fraction of the same reality.

"With George? Right from the start, from the first night in that hotel in Utah, when we had sex we were together completely. It was as though we were there for nothing else. The sex was that right, and that consuming.

"Later—this part is just as true—when we would have breakfast together, or watch a movie in the hotel room, we would eat and talk and laugh as though we were there, together, with each other, for nothing else. Our time— our nonsexual—together time was completely consuming, too.

"Our relationship isn't easy to define. It's time for money. But it's not. It's pay to play. But it's not. George pays me to complete him. And I try to do that. I let him pay me to complete me. Yet I fight that with all my will. Where is the balance? Where am I in this?"

It seemed to take all her energy to complete her thought. I wanted to see if she could take another step.

"Does what you just described between you and George feel real?" I asked.

My question invigorated her. I suspected she had anticipated it. She said, "Is this real?"

She meant the therapy. I was instantly wary. I said, "Distraction, Amanda?"

The shorthand worked. She said, "Of course it's not real. George never disappoints, because I have no expectations beyond a semiannual wire transfer. I never disappoint him because I'm adept at reading his expectations, and because I'm good. There are no broken promises, spoken or unspoken. We both know the . . ."

Amanda's shoulders sank. Her eyes closed. I recognized her trajectory. I thought I should shut up. I didn't shut up. I said, "You both know what?"

Amanda gave her reply some consideration before she said, "Before I found and recruited the man you call the Buffer, I entertained selecting other men. But they didn't view the arrangement the same way I did."

I felt a distraction approaching the same way I can feel a semi approaching too close when I'm on my bike on a narrow road. I didn't have to see it to know it loomed.

"One of the men told me that for what he would be paying, he didn't think he should have to share me with another man. He wanted all of my time. From his perspective it was a question of what he was 'getting for his money.'

"I asked him, 'All of my present time? Or all of my future time?'

"I knew him well. He was a trader. A present-value thinker, more of an arbitrage guy than a value-added guy. He wanted the time he wanted, and he wanted the services he expected me to provide during that time."

"Sex?" I said. I recognized I was enabling. I was guilty of distracting Amanda with my ignorance. I was distracting her during her distraction.

"Yes, sex. But don't underestimate the other. Sex without the other? Doesn't work. The other without sex? Doesn't work, either. Women know that. Pros and not.

"I explained to him that he was misunderstanding the nature of my proposal. 'What you will get for your money,' I told him, 'is not a complete claim on my present but a partial claim on my future. My present is valuable, my future is invaluable.'

"He never understood what I meant."

I said, "I am interested in what you meant."

"I'm paying you to be interested," she said. Though her tone made clear that the statement was at least partially banter, her words carried the echo of the earlier tease, an echo I would ignore at my clinical peril. "Is this when I should wonder if that is why you're interested in me? Because you are being paid?"

Debating her analogy—comparing the sexual interest she showed in her clients to the clinical interest I showed in her, my patient—would take us far afield. To acknowledge the issue, yet to chart a path past it, I said, simply, "Touché."

"Indeed," Amanda said. "Touché." She adjusted her posture as she accepted that I wouldn't bite at the bait. She hadn't been prepared for victory; she'd only been prepared for battle. The battle, one I refused to engage in, had been the point.

She said, "Had he shown any curiosity about me and my life, I would have told him that I charge what I charge because of the way I value my future. What each of my gentlemen pay for so dearly are my lost opportunities—" She stopped abruptly. "The things I might never experience because of my decision to be a paid companion."

I wasn't sure what she meant. I said, "Please go on."

"While I am working there are other experiences and opportunities that will not be available. Either during the time I am with a client physically, or during the time that I am merely waiting to be with him the next time. Do you see?"

"Not yet," I said. "All jobs require us to trade certain freedoms for the chance to earn income. We all lose opportunities."

"What is different are the opportunities I relinquish. The lover, or husband, I may not find because our paths did not cross. The child, or children, that I may not bear because of that lover or husband that I did not find. Most jobs don't require those kinds of trade-offs. This one does. At least for me."

Amanda's voice was becoming fragile. I was unfamiliar with the texture, though to my ear it sounded sincere.

I wasn't convinced by her argument, but my conviction wasn't the point.

A solitary tear wended from the outside corner of her right eye before it took a detour toward the lobe of her ear. "And that is what I would have told the uncurious man to explain why the price for my time is high."

She brought her lips together and looked at me, unblinking. The trail of the tear left an uneven scar where it had traversed the blush on her cheek before it disappeared beyond her jaw. "Your future," I said. "The one you may never know?"

"Yes." She seemed to recompose before my eyes. Her voice rediscovered its confident timbre as she said, "My present? Or the part of it I choose to give to my men? It's much less dear. Like all jobs, it involves time. Mine involves sex, too. I don't find sex mystical. Once I choose a man, and I choose to give my time, I accept that I am yielding opportunity. That is my sacrifice. But the sex I consider to be almost gratis. I know it is a big part of what is expected of me, but I do that part of my job . . ." She lowered her voice in volume and allowed it to settle into a husky place before she said, "Because if I've picked the right man, I don't mind it, and often I enjoy it."

*Oh God,* I thought. *I am allowing her to do it again.*

She'd switched her train to a set of parallel tracks so she could tell me a story. A good story. A novel story. Maybe even a true story. Certainly, a distracting story.

I backpedaled. "Earlier in the session? You started telling me about the . . . now. It felt to me as though you were about to go someplace important."

"But I distracted us?" she said.

"Perhaps." The clock over Amanda's shoulder told me our time was short.

She said, "Yes, the now." She bit down on her lower lip in that vulnerable way that magically subtracted a decade from her face.

Cognizant that the clock was ticking, I said, "Yes?"

"Now . . ." She looked away. She looked back. She said, "Now? I am pregnant."

My lips fell open a centimeter as I considered the possibility that Amanda was playing me again. But when I recognized that the sigh that followed her admission that she was with child seemed to empty every part of her but her womb, I knew that her announcement had not been a ruse.

*Is the baby the Buffer's? Is it George's? Is there another man?*

When she looked up at me her eyes were swollen with possibility, good and bad, her lips flattened into that no-man's-land between frown and grin.

Then she said, "After my brother died, my daddy got a friend of his who owned a funeral home to go down to Houston in one of their retired hearses to get the coffin. We caravanned back to Austin. When I first saw my daddy again—he'd stayed behind, he was waiting in front of the funeral home—I tried to smile for him, to be strong.

"He held me at arm's length, one of his big hands on each of my shoulders. He said, 'Baby girl, last time I saw you, you looked different. Younger. Know what? I'm thinking that when your brother left us, what he did was that he took one of your pretty little dimples with him to heaven, to remember you by.'

"He leaned in then, and he kissed me, just a feather touch, right here." Amanda's fingertip tapped lightly on the cheek that had sacrificed the dimple to her brother's memory. "He said, 'Now you only have one dimple left.'"

*More distraction?* I had no way to know. The clock was ticking.

"To prevent this?" Amanda said. "Double precautions. Sometimes triple. I'm on the pill. For safety, I insist on covers. Always."

I didn't know what that meant. I said, "I'm not familiar with that term."

"Covers? Condoms."

I learned something every day.

"One of my gentlemen had a recent vasectomy. That should make him triple-safe, right? How's that for a complicated unless?"

"The father?" I asked.

"Depends what failed, doesn't it? Did the vasectomy not work? Did the cover fail? Did my pill have an off day? Those are all unlesses, aren't they?" she said. "I don't know who the father is." She pursed her lips to empty her lungs in an extended, silent blow. "And I am not sure I want to know right now."

"When?" I asked.

Amanda shrugged.

"The last time we met?" I said. "I asked you why you were in therapy. With me." I could tell she heard me. But didn't make eye contact.

"Is that a question?" she said, finally.

"Sure."

"He's what I thought he was. But not the way it's turned out."

"You're talking about your relationship with one of the men?"

"Sure. Let's call it that. A relationship."

"You want to call it something else?"

I could not discern the game from the resistance. Or either, from the truth.

She looked away from me, toward the window. She

hesitated for a prolonged period before she said, "Maybe eventually. I admit it's a seductive tangent, even for me— it's that little side road that leads to a deserted beach. At sunset." Her eyes softened. "Hard to resist, yes? But no, that's not why I'm here."

Another minute passed. I said, "Is this when you tell me why you *are* here?"

"If I knew," she said. "Yes, this would be a good time."

Her tone caused me to wonder if her answer was intended to placate me, or to lead me astray. I fell back to the question I had not asked at the very beginning of treatment: "How can I be of help, Amanda?"

Her eyes teared. She offered a bittersweet smile that was absent the dimple that had gone to heaven with her brother.

# THIRTY-SIX

After work I sat down across the kitchen counter from Lauren. She was grating ginger for a sauce to go with dinner. *"Ponzu?"* I asked.

*"Ponzu,"* she confirmed.

Lauren and I had eased into a culinary phase where we prepared Japanese food at least twice a week. I queried Lauren about her day while I contemplated the ingredients on the counter and tried to solve the entrée puzzle.

Lauren said, "I went to Frederick this morning. That manner-of-death case won't go away." She seemed to mistake the look of alarm on my face for confusion. "The suicide that might be a homicide?"

"Yeah," I managed.

She said, "Have you ever been to Frederick?"

I almost choked on the water I was sipping. I managed

to say, "I have. Sometimes I ride east when I'm not in the mood for hills. It's a nice little town. I like to imagine it pre-I-25, before all the development."

"You cross I-25 on your rides? I did not know that."

"Not often, but once in a while."

I was apprehensive at the way the conversation was unfolding. I couldn't tell if my wife was engaging in casual chitchat about her day, or if she was setting me up to see if I'd dissemble or make some disclosure I might regret. I tried to assure myself that Lauren didn't operate that way, at least not with me.

I then thought that the fact that she didn't typically operate that way constituted a behavioral promise not to operate that way in the future. Unless . . .

I desperately wanted to come clean. I wanted to tell Lauren that Justine Winter Brown, the woman Sam knew as Currie, had been threatening to kill our daughter. That Sam had no choice but to do what he did.

That I had no choice but to protect Sam.

I couldn't come clean. By telling Lauren the truth, I would increase the number of us locked in an impossible place from two to three. Other than momentarily sating my need for understanding and forgiveness, nothing would be gained from that arithmetic. But an essential thing would be lost: Lauren's innocence.

I considered myself an honest spouse. My honesty to Lauren had always been my promise to be forthright again in similar circumstances in the future. Unless.

Sam killing Currie became the unless. Did that make me a dishonest spouse?

Or an honest spouse with an immutable unless?

I went back and forth on that.

The kids disappeared to the basement after we ate teriyaki cod. The *ponzu* was dribbled over grilled vegetables served with sweetened rice. I decided to risk a return to the place where I was feeling so exposed before dinner. I asked, "So, why did you have to go to Frederick? Isn't that way out of your jurisdiction?"

Lauren sighed. "We ended up with a dead end trying to ID that cop in the cell phone photo. Even after enhancement, we couldn't make it work. The description we got from the friend could fit fifty different Boulder cops. Beyond Boulder? An almost infinite number.

"Our investigators are stretched to a breaking point. Elliot came close to having me bag it. If he's going to invest staff in a cold case, he's going to pick one that could help him politically at home, not an already-closed case in another jurisdiction.

"His counterpart in Weld begged him to send someone out to Frederick before he pulled the plug. You know Elliot these days—he's a politician as much as he is a prosecutor. He wants the Weld DA's support when he decides to run for attorney general."

"Or governor," I said. Elliot Bellhaven, Lauren's boss, was the current Boulder County DA. And probably, I feared, the someday-soon state attorney general, and then, a term or two later, the future governor of Colorado. Elliot and I had once been friends, but we did not have a good recent history. I did not wish him well in elected office.

"He'd have to be elected AG first," Lauren said. "A governor from Boulder? A gay governor from Boulder? Colorado isn't ready yet. Elliot needs a stepping-stone."

"He sent you to Frederick?" I said.

"To keep the peace with his colleague. I met the Weld prosecutor—young guy, aggressive in an off-putting way, but idealistic and probably well-intentioned. He believed he could convince me I would see something I couldn't ignore."

I began loading the dishwasher. I said, "Did you?"

"There's no new evidence. All the commotion is being caused by a little boy that locals have convinced a sheriff's investigator and this young prosecutor is some kind of . . . savant about how and when the woman died. But here's the thing—the kid has never actually talked to anyone in law enforcement. Not a word. Not once. Not back then, when she died. And he's not talking now.

"Everything they have is hearsay twice removed from a barely nine-year-old boy. You can't build a homicide case that way. I met him briefly, this morning. He was home sick from school. Friendly, talkative, engaging. You know Gracie's friend Avi? From dance? He reminded me of Avi. That kind of smart, chatty kid.

"I shook hands with the boy's grandfather across his fence. Gruff guy. Taciturn. Kind of guy who could look mean petting a puppy. He was polite, but he made it clear to me the same thing he's apparently made clear to everyone else—that he doesn't want the boy involved, and he won't let him be interviewed by law enforcement. Says it will just stir up things that are better off staying buried."

I was confident that Lauren was talking about Elias Tres and his grandfather, Big Elias. I said, "Did the boy actually witness something that night? Are you talking about that kind of traumatic experience? Did he see . . . the gunshot?"

"I don't think so. But then nobody really knows. The hearsay is that he saw a car. And he saw a guy walking toward the cottage where the victim died. And he maintains this all happened on a different night than the ME determined after the autopsy. The boy says the timing is off by a day."

"Is that possible? That a postmortem could be off that much?"

"Anything is possible. Everyone was thinking suicide. She had a bullet through her brain stem. How important was a day back then, either way?"

"Even if the boy is right," I said, "couldn't the two events be unrelated? The boy saw what he saw one night, but the death occurred another?"

"I asked the same thing. But the local lore is that everything about this kid is special. His memories about things are just not questioned by people who know him.

"And this death, the suicide or homicide, occurred only a few days after the kid's father was killed in a fire-fight in Afghanistan. His dad was a marine. The body was due back in town the next day, the day after the boy says the woman died down the road. Can you imagine what that entire time was like for the family? For him?"

I said, "It is hard to imagine." But I could picture almost every detail.

"The way I see it, the way the grandfather sees it, is that everything is all wrapped up together too tightly for this boy. His father's death? God, in combat. Six weeks before the end of his tour. Military honors. Flag-draped casket. Somber marines everywhere. The impending funeral. Getting ready for a big gathering at the house. Imagine, Alan.

"Then this . . . this death, whatever it was, happened just across the road. Down a little bit. Hundred yards away? One fifty?

"For the kid? Remembering back that far? Testifying? I think it's way too much to ask. He's apparently just turned nine. Back then, he was, what, barely six? Basically, the Weld County DA wants us to rely on the distant memories of a nine-year-old boy, when everything he might recollect about that awful day has been contaminated by what I hope to God turns out to be the worst events of his life.

"I don't think there's a prosecution there. Imagine what a defense attorney could do—would be forced to do—to that little boy if he testifies."

"Did you talk to anyone else in Frederick? Or was it just the kid?"

*Anyone named Izza?*

"My counterpart introduced me to a lot of people. Almost everyone on that lane. All the farmers and ranch-ers. The landlord of the cottage where the woman died is a young woman. Twenties. Met her. But she lives in Greeley. She wasn't there that night and she didn't know the tenant well. Her father lives on the property and was there that night, apparently. But he's been quite ill for a long time. He didn't hear anything. Didn't see anything. I didn't actually meet him."

I allowed the conclusions to settle. "Dead end?" I said.

Lauren wasn't quite ready to go there. She said, "The grandfather's protective instincts may be the correct ones. The kid needs to continue to heal, to move past whatever happened during that period in his life. Not to go back and relive all of that again. Think about Jonas, babe. What he went through in that short period of his life right after Adrienne died? In my mind, it is kind of the same thing. Don't you think?"

Our son Jonas had witnessed his birth mother's violent death in Israel at almost the same time that Elias Tres lost his father to war. I wondered if Lauren had recognized the way the dates aligned.

She finished her glass of wine. "We've tried to allow Jonas to move on, right?"

I got distracted for a moment as I reflected on the magnitude of our adopted son's losses. But Lauren was impatient for my conclusion. She said, "You know a little something about all this, Alan. Come on, what do you think?"

Lauren's phrasing jolted me. I didn't know if Lauren was suggesting that I knew "a little something about all this" because she was somehow already aware that I did know what happened that distant night in Frederick. Or if she was referring to my—much more benign—parental or professional knowledge about the best way to approach children who have suffered multiple losses and traumas.

I feared that my guilty knowledge about Frederick was threatening to bust out of my skull like some grotesque monster from a bad horror movie.

I said, "My instinct is to agree with you, but I would probably need to hear more about the boy. For Jonas? I think we did the right thing."

Lauren stood. She spoke with an unexpected edge. "That's all you got? You sound like an expert witness parsing his words during a tough cross. What's that about?"

*Is she teasing?* I couldn't tell. The thought crossed my mind that Lauren already knew what happened in Frederick. *What's one more lie?* "Yeah, for now that's all I have. If you can tell me more, I'll have more."

"I told Elliot to let it go. The evidence Weld County would *like* to have may scream homicide to them. But the evidence they *do* have says suicide to me. I think any more resources that our office invests in the investigation will be wasted."

I tightened my grip on the countertop. Lauren's conclusion left me feeling light enough to float. I edged over in front of the sink to begin cleaning up. I held up the serving dish from dinner. "Can this go in the dishwasher?"

Lauren gave me a how-many-times-have-you-asked-me-that face before she said, "That's ceramic. It's one of the ones you have to wash by hand."

I began to wash the platter. As casually as I was able, I said, "So is that it for you and Frederick? Has Elliot covered his ass politically?"

Before Lauren could reply, Gracie called—okay, Gracie yelled—up from the basement in a voice that indicated rapidly accelerating distress. But to my well-tuned paternal ear the timbre of alarm she was using was more Off Broadway than *Friday the 13th* part whatever. I was reading my daughter's squeal as a high-volume announcement that she wanted help because she was in the process of losing an argument to her brother, who was likely rubbing it in, the way he did sometimes.

And the way she hated every time. Lauren saw things the same way. Without giving any indication that she was buying into the urgency of Grace's 911, she stepped toward the top of the stairs to referee. The walk from the kitchen counter to the basement stairs was short, but Lauren managed it not only without her cane, but also with some physical grace.

From a point of view of the management and progress of her MS—and of her prolonged recovery from a distant exacerbation—I was encouraged by that short stroll.

I couldn't see my wife's face—her head was directed down the stairs—but I could hear her clearly as she said, "Yeah, I think Elliot has seen enough."

Gracie yelled, "Jonas! You heard her. Mom says she's seen eee-nough! Stop it! You heard her! Now stop!"

I couldn't see my daughter, but I knew from previous

experience that she had just stomped her right foot. And that Jonas's face had broken into the slyest, most knowing grin at his sister's predictable affectation. He'd undoubtedly been shooting for the foot stomp. In his eyes, Jonas had claimed victory.

I began drying the little platter. Once I set it down, I pumped my right fist into the air, and I mouthed, *Yes!* I couldn't wait to finish cleaning up so I could take the dogs out on the lane. I wanted to trek to a specific spot down the lane where my phone had five bars, so I could reach out to Sam with the good news.

I was thinking we were halfway in the clear. All that was left for us to do was to deal with Comadoe.

In my heart, I knew Comadoe was up to something. In my head, I didn't know what.

The man was dangerous. I wouldn't underestimate Comadoe.

Outside later with the dogs, I called Sam. He didn't answer. I left a message that I had good news about Weld County, but that I had a bad feeling about Comadoe.

An hour later he texted me that he was working on something.

# THIRTY-SEVEN

I woke at dawn to the sound of my daughter dancing through the house in her Halloween costume, enthusiastically humming the tune of Girlyman's "Everything's Easy." It was Grace's third morning in a row wearing her costume before school.

I was hoping the outfit—Gracie continued to regale me with the Hermione-inspired details—would survive intact until the big day, five days hence.

Jonas had his arms curled around a book at the kitchen table. He would not don his hotshot getup—his chosen costume was an homage to the crews who had snuffed the Fourmile Fire—until the calendar told him to. He had buds in his ears to help him remain oblivious to his sister and a huge serving spoon in one hand to shovel cereal into his mouth as fast as he could chew and swallow.

The family tableau felt like performance art. Like most

performance art, I feared it was well over my head. I did feel gratitude that all the performers were mine.

I rushed to get out of the house just in time to see a new patient at seven thirty. His name was Daniel Shelton. He hadn't said much on the phone while setting up the appointment other than that he wanted to talk about his marriage.

Though I had only seen him once before—briefly, on the night that Sam and I met Comadoe for the first time—I recognized him in the waiting room. Daniel was the widower of the statistician from the Commerce Department labs, the woman on whom I'd performed CPR while humming "Stayin' Alive."

The marriage Daniel wanted to discuss with me was the one that had ended on the first day of the Fourmile Fire. His.

His name had rung no bells when he had set the appointment. He and his wife had different surnames—something my patient had never had a reason to mention in therapy.

Daniel was, it turned out, as focused a patient as his wife had been. Daniel's final words to me at the end of that first session were "I think I have a lot of work to do."

I said, "Yes, we do."

Daniel's history was a toxic mix of neglect, abuse, loss, and perversion—an alloy of toxic components that had, until that morning, been beyond my imagination. My words to him about the work ahead were an understatement.

\* \*

The moment he was out the door after his session, my cell vibrated.

It was Lauren, timing her call to the minute in order to catch me between sessions. At eight fifteen in the crazed morning routine at our house she would be attempting to corral the kids into the car to get them to school on time.

"What's up?" was how I answered. I knew something was up. Lauren didn't often call during the workday; she knew that she could reach me more reliably with a text. I made a guess that one of the kids had complained of feeling ill and that Lauren and I would need to negotiate juggling our work schedules for the rest of the day so we could play nurse. I began to review the day's caseload in my head to see what I could reschedule.

Lauren said, "There's a new fire behind town. I think it just started. We can see the smoke clearly from up here. Have you heard anything?"

My first thought? *It's almost November. It's too late in the season for a wildfire.* I immediately recognized it as wishful thinking. The area remained under a Red Flag Warning.

During the latter half of my session with Daniel I had noticed a few sirens erupt in the direction of Canyon Boulevard. I had not given them a second thought at the time. "I heard sirens out there," I said to Lauren. "But I didn't—" I paused and listened. *Jesus, there are a lot of sirens.* "Yes, I do hear sirens. They're on Canyon." Canyon Boulevard, only a hundred feet away, was the main route west into Boulder Canyon. "Does it look serious?"

I asked, knowing damn well that during Red Flag Warnings along the Front Range there were no inconsequential wildfires.

Lauren said, "There's a lot of smoke."

"Location? Can you tell?"

"It's closer to town than Fourmile was. Jonas spotted it from downstairs. He says it's near Boulder Falls. I think it's closer to the city than that."

"Did you call it in?"

"Yes, but nine-one-one put us on hold. They already know."

The number of sirens outside seemed to double. "Yeah," I said, "they know."

We had friends who lived up Boulder Canyon and along the panoramic ridges in the neighboring watershed, in nearby Sugarloaf, or up Magnolia. Boulder Canyon is a steep, rocky canyon. Beyond the main roads, access is a challenge. Any fire near Boulder Canyon would provide firefighters a daunting combination of wilderness, tough access, lack of water, and depending on location, many difficult-to-defend homes. With years of beetle-killed pine dotting the hillsides, and a season's worth of dry grasses and chaparral waiting for the smallest spark, Boulder's mountain backdrop was as volatile as a fire pit already set with kindling and doused with lighter fluid. If winds blew in hard from the west, a nascent Boulder Canyon fire could jump quickly to the foothills' residential enclaves. From there, any gust could carry embers over the final ridges separating the Rockies from Boulder proper.

I carried my mobile out the French door that led to the yard. From my office, a mere eight blocks from the rise of the first jutting foothill of the Rockies, I would not have the luxury of the perspective that Lauren and the kids had from their elevated perch near the rim of the other side of the Boulder Valley. I didn't see flames or smoke.

I sniffed at the air. I said, "I just stepped outside. I can't smell it."

"It's blowing up fast," she said. "You'll smell it soon."

"Is it windy in the canyon? Can you tell? It's not bad down here."

Lauren said, "It's windy. The smoke is being sheared north-northeast as soon as it rises out of the canyon. I think it's doubled or tripled in size since we first started watching. It's . . . exploding, babe. Just like Fourmile did."

I watched a pumper truck speed west on Canyon.

*Northeast.* I worried about Diane. In so many ways. Could she cope with another wildfire and evacuation? I thought it might be too much for her. I said, "Can you tell how far north it is? Does Diane have anything to worry about up Lee Hill?"

"I would say no, not yet, but . . ." Her pause gave me chills. "Most of the smoke is rising on the north side of Boulder Canyon. I would guess that Sunshine is involved, or in jeopardy. If I had to pinpoint it, I would say that the fire is burning between Boulder and Sunshine, heading north. If it crosses into Sunshine, especially if it stays as close to town as it is, Pine Brook will be in its path. Wonderland, Wagonwheel Gap, and Lee Hill are only, what, another small ridge or two away? There's nothing along the city side of those hogbacks but dry grasses, so a fire could motor north fast. Everything depends on the winds. If they blow from the west or southwest . . ."

Lee Hill was vulnerable. Diane might be in danger. Again.

Hundreds of homeowners would be in jeopardy before the fire got to Lee Hill or Olde Stage. Sunshine Canyon snakes out of Boulder only a few blocks north of downtown. In places, only a solitary hogback separates the watershed canyons. Because of the topography—near its mouth, Sunshine Canyon is neither as deep nor as steep as Boulder Canyon—Sunshine was home to more prime residential mountain real estate than was Boulder Canyon, which meant there were more homes to protect, or to lose. I presumed many residents had already received their reverse-911 orders to evacuate.

"You going to work?" I asked.

"For now, yes," she said. "After I drop the kids at school."

"If you hear anything official, let me know."

"Of course. If you talk to Diane, tell her she can come stay with us, okay? She can have the whole downstairs. We'll move the kids up for a while."

"Yeah. Thanks. I love you."

"Me too. Oh," she said, "I almost forgot. Sofie called. She confirmed her trip. I am so excited to see my baby."

Any denial I had been holding on to about the seriousness of the alarm Lauren had raised was completely fractured by the acrid smell of smoke that blew over downtown in the next minute.

On Canyon Boulevard a seemingly endless stream of emergency vehicles carried mobilizing firefighters into Boulder Canyon. I could watch the operation unfold from my office window.

I wasn't able to reach Diane. I left a message on her home's landline and another on her mobile. I texted Raoul, too, to let him know what was going on. He texted me back immediately. He would monitor things from Chicago.

I texted him again, asking if he had spoken with Diane. He didn't respond.

The second time Lauren contacted me that morning, a couple of hours later, seemed more innocuous than the first. Her text read, **Have a few minutes? Can I stop by during your next break?**

I read it just moments after ten, but she'd sent the text message about twenty minutes earlier. I don't check messages during my sessions.

By the time I read Lauren's note, evacuation orders were in place for the foothills and mountain communities closest to the fire. Everyone west of Broadway in Boulder had been placed on evacuation alert. That included my office. The Justice Center, where Lauren worked, was between my office and the entrance to the canyon. I was certain the complex was being prepared for evacuation, too.

My eleven o'clock had left a message canceling her appointment so she could help her parents evacuate. They lived in town, on Highland up near Fourth.

I wrote back to Lauren, **Free from 11 to 11:45. Does that work? Things OK?**

Lauren replied, **See you @ 11.**

She didn't do it often, but Lauren occasionally stopped by with a gesture of affection during the workday. Once, a bear claw in a pink bakery box. A single stem of red ginger in a tall vase. The most memorable was a she-did-not-say-a-word-but-got-down-on-her-knees blow job that I would recall for the rest of my life.

I sniffed the air. The smoke. The gloom. This wouldn't be that kind of visit. What kind of visit would it be? I lacked the energy for guesses.

*Damn,* I thought. I recognized that I might have created an awkward situation. My ten fifteen patient that morning was Amanda. At eleven, she would be exiting my office at the time Lauren would be arriving. Given my growing concern that Amanda might turn out to be a crucial factor in Diane's and Raoul's marital woes, I didn't think that an inadvertent waiting room encounter would be the ideal way for my wife to be introduced to her.

I typed out a fresh text for Lauren. **Can you do 12:30 instead?** But before I could hit SEND my cell buzzed. It was an attorney with whom I'd been playing phone tag. I'd been trying to convince the lawyer not to depose me as a witness in the divorce proceedings of the parents of a sixteen-year-old boy I was seeing for depression.

The lawyer and I wasted some precious minutes talking about the fire—her sister lived up Sunshine. Once we got to business the conversation went back and forth. As my available time butted up against the ten fifteen start of Amanda's session, I knew I hadn't convinced her. We agreed to speak again.

Amanda was distracted. For the first time since I had begun seeing her for treatment, I watched her skip from topic to topic. The procession felt random. I sensed no grand scheme to distract me with either prurience or private jets. I recognized no theme to tie together threads of content or process. Instead, she seemed to have no affective attachment to anything she discussed. I followed her from place to place the best I could, wondering what the aimlessness meant. I was tempted to blame it on the fire, but I thought it was more likely a psychological retreat from the power of the prior session.

At one point I wondered aloud about her apparent avoidance of an issue she had previously raised. "The pregnancy?" I asked.

She said, "I'm not ready to talk about that."

Our minutes ticked away. Over Amanda's shoulder I could see the red light beaming near the door. The indicator told me that Lauren had arrived in the waiting room.

Amanda sensed our time was up. She grabbed her bag and scooted forward.

"Are you parked nearby?" I said. "I have a favor to ask."

"Have you started validating?"

It was a fine retort. Congested parking near my office was a chronic complaint among my patients. Boulder's meter-reading posse was legendary—in my experience they were the most efficient segment of city government. I smiled to acknowledge her joke.

She said, "I found a spot right across the street, in front of Bitter Bar. Downtown's empty. Probably because of the fire."

I said, "As you know, the architecture of this old house precludes having a separate exit for patients. That can present a privacy problem. Every so often I get a request to exit after a session using this door"—I gestured toward the solitary French door that led to the yard—"instead of through the waiting room. I try to honor those requests. On even more rare occasions, I will suggest to a patient that it might be preferable to use this door instead of the front door. This—"

"—is one of those occasions. I understand," she said. "I'll just sneak out the back." She grinned. "Won't be the first time in my life."

My guess was that what she understood, or misunderstood, was that I was trying to minimize the risk that she might run into Raoul's wife, Diane, in the hallway or in the waiting room. I didn't offer a clarification—Amanda had never acknowledged knowing either Diane or Raoul. Nor did I offer an honest explanation, that I would rather Amanda not meet my wife in the waiting room.

Amanda stepped toward the French door.

I said, "The driveway is to your right. It will take you to your car."

She wriggled her fingertips at me. "I have a mani-pedi at

the St. Julien's spa first. But I may just use this door from now on. Bye," she said, gazing back over her shoulder at me.

She stopped midstride. With wistfulness in her eyes, she said, "He never offered me a future with him. That was never going to be part of what we were doing."

Then she hopped down the two steps and disappeared around the corner.

I recognized her parting line. She had used its mirror image to begin the session the last time we'd met. *I never offered him a future. That was never going to be part of what we were doing.*

That first time she had been talking about her brother.

This time? I didn't know whom she was referencing. *Her brother again? George? The Buffer?* I set it aside.

I stepped down the hall to greet Lauren. Diane's office door was closed.

Lauren was in one of her serious suits, which meant she was scheduled for court that day. I told her she looked seriously hot. She nodded a distracted acknowledgment of my compliment as she preceded me down the hall. Her bag was on her shoulder. It was a small one that could fit inside her briefcase. The hand without the cane was empty.

*No flower today. No pastry today.*

She was not using her cane for support. Even as recently as the Fourmile Fire, it had been a necessity and not an accessory. Her limp down the hall was barely noticeable. I allowed myself to hope that the cane was becoming a figurative crutch—that she was, finally, showing signs of enduring recovery from her most recent serious exacerbation.

I said, "Did you walk over here? I'm impressed."

She said, "I needed the air. I really needed the air."

"Smoky air," I said.

"True," she said. "This fire has me more spooked than the last one did. They're talking about closing the Justice Center. Evacuating everyone." She stepped into my office ahead of me. She took my chair.

At home I didn't feel any possessiveness about a particular seat. I didn't have a designated Daddy chair at the kitchen table or a reserved spot in the family room. But at my office, I did. My office had one doctor's chair, the one where I sat during therapy sessions, with my back to the door and with a clear view of the clock on the wall behind my patient's seat. My chair had a high back that was kind to my cervical spine, and an ottoman at a perfect height for pampering my lower back.

Lauren's choice wasn't an accident. I tried to guess how sitting in my spot fit into her plans. I drew a blank.

"Sit, babe. Please," she said.

Her voice was sober. Not pretend sober. Not flirty sober. Sober sober. I felt wary.

"Time is tight. There is no good way to have this conversation. So I will just begin." Her demeanor was causing a deep chill up my spine.

"First, I need to say that I shouldn't be talking to you. I am here out of love. I can't stand the thought of you learning what I am about to tell you from anyone else. You can't repeat any of this. Not a word."

I thought, *Holy shit.* I said, "Of course."

# THIRTY-EIGHT

She paused as if she were waiting for me to say something more. I obliged. I said, "You're frightening me."

She shook her head, dismissing my fear. She said, "Are we good?"

*Good? What?* I was moving air in and out of my chest, but I wasn't sure my lungs were managing the processing-oxygen part of the process. I said, "Yes, we're good." I wondered if my words sounded as meek as they felt. "I love you."

Lauren took the kind of deep breath that is intended to fortify. "When I got to work this morning—I was late because of the fire—a woman was waiting. She did not have an appointment. Her name is Isabel Kane. I mentioned her once. She is from Frederick, the daughter of the man who owns the rental cottage where Justine Brown died. Izza—she prefers Izza—helps her father, who is ill."

Despite my emotional vertigo, I heard many things in that little speech. Some of what I heard Lauren said. Some of what I heard she didn't say. Lauren had not paused after speaking Izza's name. Her failure to pause to gauge my reaction meant that Lauren was not anticipating that I would be familiar with the name. If Lauren had not yet connected me with Izza, I wondered why she and I were having the conversation we were having. My worst fears, when I heard her mention Izza and Frederick, were predicated on Lauren having made a connection between me and Frederick, and me and Izza.

*And me and Sam and Justine Brown.* If those connections remained secret, I couldn't come up with any explanation for Lauren's visit.

I had also heard Lauren say that Justine Brown had "died" when she could have chosen instead to say "killed herself." Suicide had been the default descriptor the last time Lauren and I had talked about it. If the default option about Currie's manner of death had changed from suicide and become the generic *died*, that would speak unfortunate volumes about the nature of the evolution of Lauren's thinking about that night in Frederick. The specific direction of change in Lauren's thinking—from suicide to died—was causing my fright to approximate terror. Died was much closer to homicide than killed herself was to homicide.

Homicide was where we were heading. Homicide was where the truth was.

Homicide would lead to Sam. And then to me.

I forced my chin down and then back up to form a

nod. I hoped that Lauren would continue speaking on her own, without any prompting. I had no confidence I was capable of making sounds that wouldn't mimic a small farm animal.

"Izza Kane wasn't alone this morning. She was with that young boy, the one I told you I met briefly when I was in Frederick. The one who reminds me of Avi, Grace's friend? His name is Tres. Elias Tres. Elias . . . the Third.

"He is Izza's . . . neighbor." Lauren shook her head as if she were clearing an errant thought. "Izza asked to go outside to talk. She has an aunt near Nederland, and she wanted to be able to monitor the fire. I suggested the Boulder Creek Trail. We sat on a bench. What was going on up Canyon was already crazy."

They had been sitting in the same general location where Sam and I had been walking the day Comadoe had first visited my office.

"Tres played near the creek. Izza said that Tres wanted to speak with me—he remembered me from my visit to Frederick—but that she understood that Tres's grandfather wasn't allowing him to talk with anyone in law enforcement.

"I explained that Tres's grandfather, as guardian, was within his rights—that I couldn't interview Tres without his grandfather's permission.

"Izza said she thought that there were exceptions to that rule. I asked what she had in mind. She said, 'If, by refusing to let his grandson talk to you, Tres's grandfather is covering up his own wrongdoing? Would that be an exception?'

"Izza is a criminal justice major at UNC. She knows more than a little about criminal investigation. She might be right about the exception. A guardian likely cannot obstruct an investigation that otherwise would reveal his own criminal activity, but I told her I had to do some checking."

My dread doubled, something I would not have considered possible.

*My wife,* I thought, *might be here to arrest me.*

She looked at her watch. "Some quick history. Izza's mother left her husband and daughter when Izza was a toddler. The family story has been that she ran away with another woman. Izza hasn't believed that for a while, but she didn't learn the actual reason her mother left until the night that Justine Brown died.

"Izza's father, the one who's ill? He's been in the U.S. illegally for over thirty years. He never left the U.S. after his original visa expired in 1972. He's from Ireland. His papers are fake. Now? He's been fighting leukemia since 2005. Only a couple of people outside the family know his immigration status. His onetime best friend, Elias Contopo, Tres's grandfather, knows."

She wanted me to acknowledge my grasp of the facts. I said, "Okay."

"The night before Segundo Contopo's body was due home from Afghanistan—" She stopped. "You remember we talked about his funeral?" I nodded. "That same night Izza was visiting the Contopo family to pay her respects and to keep an eye on Elias Tres. She was concerned about him. She knew that Elias Contopo—she calls him

Big Elias—wouldn't be at his best while he waited for his son's body to be delivered by the marines. Elias Contopo has a history of problems with alcohol.

"It turned out that her concern was warranted. Elias Contopo was drunk and agitated when she got to their house. Elias Tres seemed frightened. Izza got Tres to go to his room on the second floor while she tried to get Big Elias to stop drinking and go to bed. He wouldn't. At some point he began yelling. He threw things.

"He told her to leave, to go home. She said she would if she could take Tres with her for the night. Big Elias wouldn't agree. They went back and forth for hours. At one point, he popped the magazine from a handgun and walked around with the pistol.

"Elias Tres was watching all this from the top of the stairs. Izza kept telling Big Elias she wouldn't go without Tres. She'd feed him breakfast and bring him back.

"At some point, Big Elias said something like 'You want the orphan? No! They got my son. You can't take my grandson. I wouldn't let your mother have him. I won't let you have him, either.'

"Izza demanded to know what Big Elias meant. What the grandson part had to do with the comment about her mother. But Big Elias wouldn't say. Izza told me he's always been a provocative guy. Kind of a bully, especially when he drinks. That night, they kept going back and forth, arguing about Tres. She'd seen Big Elias agitated before. She wasn't about to leave the boy there.

"Finally, Big Elias sat down, exhausted. He told a long, rambling story that revealed to Izza that Segundo—the dead marine, Elias Tres's father—was her little brother. That Segundo's son, Elias Tres, is her nephew. And then he fell asleep. Izza took Elias Tres home with her.

"At Segundo's funeral, Izza learned the true story from her mother's sister. Izza's mother felt she had no choice but to leave when she learned she was pregnant with Big Elias's baby. She knew the baby would have Hispanic features. Her Irish husband would know he wasn't the father. He would suspect his friend Elias, who had always been a jerk around his wife. Izza's father would never accept the truth—that his wife had been blackmailed into sleeping with Elias to protect her husband's immigration status.

"Elias had threatened her into having sex with him since shortly after Izza was born. When she learned she was pregnant with her second child, Big Elias gave her money to leave town, told her what story to tell. Seven months after she left, she gave birth to a son. Elias showed up in Florida, confirmed that the baby was his, and took him. When he got back to Frederick with a baby boy, he told everyone in town he was still screwing his ex-wife, that she had delivered his baby in Santa Fe. The math didn't add up, but nobody in town challenged Big Elias."

I wasn't sure I understood. "That baby was Segundo? Not Elias Tres?" Lauren nodded. I said, "Big Elias admitted to serious crimes that night. Rape, yes? Why didn't Izza go to the police? Why didn't her aunt?"

"By the time Izza learned what happened her father was already sick. In and out of the hospital. Izza believed, and her aunt believed, that Big Elias would retaliate against her father if they said anything about what Elias had done to Izza's mother. If Big Elias went to the INS, Izza feared her father would be deported. She was sure it would kill him."

"Why is Izza talking now?" I asked. I wanted to know the answer. Badly.

"She says there is nothing left to lose. Her mother is dead. Her father is dying. He just began receiving hospice services in his home. That's the main reason. Another? After I visited Frederick, Elias Tres told her about things he saw the night of Justine Brown's death. Izza decided it was time to get everything in the open."

"Elias Tres?" I asked. "He is Izza's . . . half brother's son?"

"Her nephew," Lauren said. "I think she would like to raise him."

I began to trace the new version of the family tree in my head. I got lost as I sketched new branches that wound up and down that little lane outside Frederick. I am notorious for lacking the brain structures necessary to identify distant relations. Lauren knew that about me.

"I tried to buy time with Izza this morning. I told her I had to consult my boss before I could talk to Tres. Izza told me that it was my one chance to hear Tres's story. She couldn't guarantee she would have the resolve to do it all again. I decided to go ahead and speak with Tres about what he remembered about the night that Justine Brown died. If it turned out I overstepped—legally overstepped—a judge would throw out what I learned. I might get censured. I can live with that." She shrugged before she crossed her arms, each hand grabbing the opposing biceps hard enough that her knuckles whitened.

"Tres sat between us on the bench. He is a smart boy—verbal—with a vivid memory. He confirmed the story about the argument inside the house. What he heard about his grandmother. And then he told me what was happening outside his window as he waited for his father to come home that night.

"Mostly I listened." Lauren's voice cracked. "Izza and Tres left, went back to Frederick. I went over the story Tres told me, and then I tried to decide if I had any choice about what to do next. I decided I didn't. Have a choice." My wife looked at me with eyes as sad as I'd ever seen on her face. "That's when I texted you."

Again she seemed to want acknowledgment. I was too paralyzed to offer it.

"I'm here to tell you that when I leave, I am going to provide information to Elliot, and to the Weld County DA, implicating Sam Purdy in the death of Justine Brown. Sam will be picked up today."

By then I'd guessed what was coming. "Sam? Arrested?" I said, barely getting the words past my lips. I didn't wipe away the tears bulging in my eyes. I said, "Sam? Really? What did that boy see that could . . . involve Sam?"

My questions were frauds. I knew it was Sam. I knew it was real. And I knew why. Disingenuous? Damn yes. Sitting with my wife, the prosecutor, I felt like the most transparent fraud in the world.

By word, and by my behavior, I had promised Lauren

honesty in our marriage. I was either breaking that promise, or I was living an unless.

My unless was this: *unless my honesty will leave my children without their mother.*

I considered confessing but realized my confession would not only compromise Lauren's position at work, but it would also needlessly put both of our children's parents in legal jeopardy. My rationale? One parent in prison was better than two parents in prison.

I was trying to convince myself that there was room to find doubt in Tres's story. I needed to hear exactly what he thought he saw that night. I couldn't accept that the three-year-old eyewitness testimony of a small boy would be sufficient to put a decorated detective behind bars. *Never.* I was sure I could find a crack in what Lauren thought she knew.

*The Tyvek? God, did Tres have Sam's Tyvek?*

Lauren said, "Tres heard all the yelling. He shut it out as best he could by sitting at the window, waiting for his father. Tres knew his father was dead. Big Elias had told him that. But he didn't believe his father was dead. He sat in the dark at his bedroom window on the lookout for a proud, solitary marine who would march in his dress uniform down their country lane, enter their gate, and salute his son at the window.

"That's what Segundo had done the previous time he came home from a tour. Tres was too young to understand that it would be different, that his father's homecoming would be nothing like the last time. That there would be no reunion. That his father would be in a box.

"Tres finally spotted someone parking a car on the road between his house and town. The car came from the west and did a U-turn before it stopped. He thought it was his dad, of course. He seems to remember everything that happened after that like it's a favorite video he's watched a hundred times. The man got out of the car. Grabbed a gym bag from the back. It was an Avalanche bag, Alan." Lauren paused. She allowed the Avalanche part to sink in. The Colorado Avalanche play hockey.

"The man was wearing a baseball cap. Tres knows baseball, plays second base in Little League. The cap was a Minnesota Twins cap."

Sam Purdy was an Iron Ranger by birth, born and raised in the rugged mining country of northern Minnesota. His allegiance to the sports teams of his native state was mitigated only by his ardor for Colorado's franchises. Especially for the Avalanche.

*Why couldn't you wear a Rockies cap, Sam? Even a damn Broncos hat. Dime a dozen around here.*

"Segundo was a big Rockies fan. Tres didn't understand why his dad would wear a Twins cap. The man walked past Tres's house to the east. Then he cut down the dirt path that leads to the cultivated fields behind the cottage where Justine Brown died."

Lauren kept her eyes locked on mine. She was, I feared, searching for signs of recognition. For familiarity. For guilt. I didn't know if she saw what she hoped she would see, or if she saw what she feared she would see.

She went on. "I saw that dirt road when I was in Frederick. It's just an access . . . thing for the farmers. Tres said the man stopped about halfway down. He pulled on a white suit that was inside the gym bag. Tres said, 'He became like a ghost. *Espíritu.*' That's the word Tres used. A spirit."

*Damn Tyvek.*

"Tres didn't see the man go into the cottage—the back door isn't visible from his window. He doesn't know what happened inside. He saw the ghost again later. Tres knows the time—after two o'clock. The man removed the white suit before he got back to the main road. He got in the car. He drove away toward the mountains."

There had to be more to the story. Lauren didn't have enough. "Why Sam?" I said. "The Avalanche bag? The Twins cap? Is that all?"

Lauren was a prosecutor presenting her case. My questions were inconsequential. She said, "While the man was gone from his view, Tres drew a picture of the car parked nearby. He drew a boxy thing, the shape of a station wagon or SUV. In his drawing, he used two numbers and two letters from the license plate."

I saw more holes. There are thousands of dark Jeep Cherokees on Colorado's roads, and tens of thousands of look-alikes. Had Lauren checked the partial plate and matched it to Sam's car? Even if she had, it was only a partial. That meant doubt. "You ran the plate?"

"I didn't have to. I recognized the car."

*From a child's drawing? No way. Not possible. An old navy Jeep Cherokee? It was way too common a car along the Front Range.* Trying not to sound defensive, I said, "Sam has a very common car."

She nodded in agreement. "Elias Tres didn't draw Sam's car, babe. He drew mine. He drew our Audi. The car in the picture has three interlocking circles on the front. Tres called them 'the rounds.' The Audi logo has four."

*Not enough. No.* Audis, even wagons, are plentiful along Colorado's Front Range.

But my heart rate didn't slow. Lauren wasn't done. I could tell she had more. *God.*

"Tres's picture shows a ball on the back of the car. Gracie's pink soccer ball decal? Tres even colored the ball pink."

*There are not many Audi wagons with a pink soccer ball on the back.* I couldn't imagine a way to explain the soccer ball.

"The Audi wagon he drew?" Lauren said. "It's a white car."

The moment she mentioned the car's paint color, I knew my long subterfuge was over. I could almost hear an extended drumroll accompanying the pregnant pause Lauren inserted before she added, "But it has a black design on its roof."

I stood. The act felt involuntary, as though I were a marionette and fate had yanked my strings.

# THIRTY-NINE

More than a year before Frederick—long before Adrienne died, long before Sam killed Currie—I had gotten ambitious around the house, as I was prone to do. My home repair initiatives were frequently misadventures, often to everyone's amusement, occasionally to someone's regret. The precipitant for my industriousness that time was that our garage door opener had failed. I was determined to install a new one myself. The guy at McGuckin cheered me on, convinced me I could do it. But the repair didn't go well. Or, in a more optimistic appraisal, the repair went well but its success was short-lived.

The heaviest part of the new machine fell from the garage rafters onto the roof of our Audi wagon three days post-installation, putting a significant dent in the car's top.

Our mechanic, an ever-resourceful Scot, arranged for

a cousin of his to pop out the dent. We elected not to pay him to repaint the car. By then, our Audi had almost a hundred thousand miles on the odometer. Lauren and I planned to drive the wagon to its death. A contrasting blotch of primer on the roof would be an inconsequential scar visible only from helicopters and from the cabs of eighteen-wheelers. We asked our mechanic to tell his cousin to sand and prime the damaged area to prevent rust, but to stop there.

The blotch of dark gray primer formed—either by the cousin's intent or by divine accident—a shape over two feet wide. Everyone I showed it to thought the design looked like a five-point star.

We'd ended up with what I suspected was the only two-toned Audi A4 wagon roof in all of Colorado, certainly the only one with a primer stain in the shape of a star. I never thought that fact would make a difference to anybody.

Our car had to have been in Frederick the night that Currie died.

I didn't *know* how our car got to Frederick that night. But I thought I could guess how our car got to Frederick that night. Murphy's Law had something to do with it.

The day before Sam killed Currie, Jonas and I were driving to New Mexico to pick up his new puppy from a Havanese breeder outside Los Alamos. The puppy was a gift that Adrienne had arranged for her son in the months before her tragic death. My car back then was a Mini Cooper. The initial plan had been for Jonas and me to

take the Mini to Los Alamos; it was a more reliable vehicle than our other car, the aging-quasi-gracefully Audi
wagon. The puppy's travel kennel would be a tight fit in
the Mini, but I was hopeful I could make it work.

The Audi scoffed at our plans. While Jonas and I were
packing to leave for New Mexico, Lauren's wagon refused to start. She was due in court in thirty minutes.
Adrienne's big Land Cruiser was a possible solution to
the problem, but Lauren's MS was in a phase that made
climbing in and out of the tall vehicle difficult, and potentially dangerous. I told her to take the Mini to work;
Jonas and I would use the Land Cruiser for our trip. We
delayed our departure until a flatbed arrived to haul the
Audi to the mechanic's shop not far from my office.

On the way out of town I stopped to have the oil
changed on the big Toyota. While that was happening, I
called Sam Purdy to ask him to please retrieve the Audi
from the repair shop and leave it at my office, so that
Lauren could have her car once Jonas and I were back
from New Mexico.

I didn't know the reason, but after Sam had retrieved
the Audi from the shop he had decided to take it to Frederick instead of using his Cherokee.


I raised my hands, palms up, toward Lauren. I was preparing to beg. For understanding? Certainly. For forgiveness? Yes. For freedom? Maybe.

She said, "Yes?"

I said, "I know."

Her head snapped as her eyes found mine. She had not expected an admission. "You know what?"

In that moment—on that spot, faced with the truth—it was beyond my capability to devise a fresh layer for the too-complex subterfuge I was living.

My unless, I knew, had spawned its own unless. I sat down.

I said, "I know Sam was in Frederick that night. I did not know until right now that he had our car."

Lauren seemed steady. She was a litigator, accustomed to hearing unexpected words from witnesses. I knew she was good at appearing steady even when she wasn't.

I went on. "The woman? Justine Brown? She was doing Michael McClelland's bidding. She's the one who broke into our house and ransacked Grace's room. She's the one who beheaded Grace's teddy bear."

Puzzlement clouded Lauren's eyes. She had expected something specific, but not that. "She what? What are you saying? Back then? That was her? And you knew all this?"

"She was threatening Simon and Grace. McClelland had sent her. Sam and I caught her following us. We ended up with her camera. We have the pictures she took. She had been stalking Grace and Simon."

With an exotic note of bittersweet in her voice, one I had never before heard, my wife said, "Alan, do I need to Mirandize you?"

She wasn't getting it. "No, you need to understand that Sam didn't have a choice that night. He was—"

"Oh my God, oh my *God*! Alan, stop! I think you should call Cozy."

I didn't know how the conversation would end, but it wouldn't end with me calling my lawyer. "Sam was protecting his son and our daughter. Justine Brown would have killed them. We had no time. We were out of options. He couldn't put together enough evidence to make a case. There was no other way to protect our children."

Lauren's expression was of profound disbelief and an equal measure of disappointment. The disappointment sliced through me. Her violet eyes were wide, her lips parted. She said, "Sam was the Boulder cop, the one she was dating?"

"She got close to him. Yes. It was part of McClelland's plan."

Lauren returned to the beginning. "Grace? This woman was threatening Grace?"

*Good*. I nodded. "She's the one who broke into our house. Ransacked Grace's room. She stalked the kids. Sam's son. Our daughter. McClelland had already failed to get us. You, me, and Sam. Justine Brown had tried to get Sam and me, too. When that didn't work, McClelland sent her after our kids. She would have killed them. I have no doubt."

"You have no doubt? Are you judge? Or are you jury? Or wait, both?"

Defending myself from Lauren's scorn was a fool's errand. I said, "Sam told me later that she admitted it."

Her eyes screamed belief and disbelief at once. "She confessed?" she said.

"I only learned that recently. Sam didn't tell me in advance about his plan. I thought we would do something to stop her after I got back from New Mexico. Something together."

She pounced. "You didn't know? Sam didn't tell you he was going to kill her?"

I heard that question for what it was: a lawyer's question, not a wife's question. Not a mother's question. She was eyeing ways to diminish my culpability.

The distinction she was drawing wasn't important. Even if I didn't know, I *knew*. I said, "He told me right after. But not the details."

Lauren's eyes lost their fire. She said, "That's when you should have told me. That's when we should have gone to the police."

It was my turn for disbelief. "To turn Sam in?"

She didn't hesitate. "Yes."

"For saving our daughter's life?"

"For killing a woman. Murder, Alan. Homicide."

"For saving our daughter's life, Lauren. Please." She exhaled twice, with no breath in between. "That woman would have killed Grace and Simon," I said. "Maybe even the next day. Sam confirmed it with her."

"We don't know that," Lauren said. "Not for sure."

"Sam knew it. I couldn't risk it," I said. "Could you?"

She stared at me. The meter between us became the Grand Canyon.

I had asked an impossible question. She had no answer. Instead she moved on to a different accusation. "You knew that Grace was in that kind of danger? And you didn't tell me? Her *mother*. We could have found a way to solve this. Together."

I didn't know exactly what I was being accused of not telling my wife.

That I was complicit in Justine Brown's homicide?

Or that I knew that Justine Brown was an imminent danger to our daughter?

Nor did I know, in Lauren's eyes, which omission constituted the greater sin.

# FORTY

---

Lauren said, "You didn't trust me, Alan."

I had imagined a version of this conversation with Lauren many times since the night Sam went to Frederick. Each imagining took me to the same spot on the edge of the same perilous cliff. In each version, on that rim, my balance impaired, Lauren would challenge me about trust.

*"You didn't trust me, Alan."*

I always got stuck formulating a reply. From her perspective, a dichotomy would be clear. I would either trust her. Or I would not.

But I never felt the luxury of black and white.

*Would trusting Lauren mean believing she would act, as I had acted, to protect our family, our daughter, at all costs? If I trusted that Lauren would act to protect our family, then after I confided in her—whether that was three years* earlier, or that day in my office—she, too, would have remained silent about Frederick.

*Or would trusting Lauren mean believing she would do what was right, what she was sworn to do, what she was ob-ligated to do?* If I trusted that Lauren would act legally and morally, then after I confided in her she would have acceded to the law's requirements. She would have felt compelled to turn Sam, and me, in to the police.

I had known all along that I would never have the freedom to blend the two versions of trust. At the end of some day—the day I chose to trust her, or the day that fate required that I trust her—I would be left knowing only one essential truth about my wife, and about trust.

Had I made a promise about trust? Had she? If so, what were the unlesses?

I'd gone back and forth scores of times. But I never settled the debate.

Of course, by being honest, I had promised to be honest. By not murdering previously, I had promised not to murder. But there was always an unless. *Right?*

*A gun, figurative or literal, to my daughter's head.* This was that unless. A best-in-class unless.

All marriages have stories. In my office that day, I still did not know what trusting Lauren would mean. From our beginning together on a softball field in north Boulder, trust had always been part of our stories. Our promises. Our unlesses.

Softly I said, "What would you have had me do? Knowing the consequences?"

"I would have had you trust me," she said. "About this, you should have trusted me." She made it sound like an uncomplicated plea between lovers. But as a simple plea, it had never been engineered to carry the weight of the burdens of the lives of children.

"I do trust you," I said, meaning it, and not knowing what it meant.

"This? Now?" she said. "This is you trusting me?"

It was. But by then, after Frederick, I was Gulliver, and I knew Lilliput. I was Alice, and I knew Wonderland. I was Dorothy, and I knew Oz.

To Lauren, who knew none of the places I'd been, my perspective was unimaginable. She couldn't see what I needed her to see. She couldn't believe what I needed her to believe. She couldn't know what I needed her to know.

Lauren saw a simple promise broken. A promise about trust.

She could not know my unlesses. I wanted to believe that was on her. But I knew it was on me.

She said, "What would you have me do? Now that I have this?" She pulled Tres's folded drawing from her purse. She threw it onto the coffee table between us.

I lifted the paper into my hands, glancing at it long enough to recognize that I was holding the evidence that would indict Sam. The three-year-old testimony of a savant kindergartener? That alone would not convict him. Never. Not without corroboration.

But this drawing, from that night? With the detail I was seeing?

A jury would eat it up, and would convict Sam Purdy

of murder. And a jury would convict me of something close enough to murder that the difference would make no difference.

Lauren said, "You asked me what I would have had you do. Well, it's my turn. What would you have me do with that drawing now?"

"You were never supposed to know," I said. I felt relief, lightness, saying the words, shedding the secret of my secret. "I wasn't distrusting you. I was . . . protecting our family by insulating you from what . . . Sam and I did.

"For the kids' sake—for all of them, Simon, Grace, now Jonas—Sam and I knew that one of us would need to have clean hands. Always. Sam and I . . . don't."

She seemed startled at the reality I presented. "Clean hands," she said as she gazed at her elegant fingers. Maybe I was imagining it, but I thought she was trying to get a feel for the words, and for my predicament. I presumed, too, that she was deciding whether she could trust me about trusting her.

"It was never about trusting you," I said. "I believed you would do what was right. That you wouldn't risk Gracie. But one of us—you, me, or Sam—has to be able to deny everything. One of us has to be standing at the end, no matter how badly this blows up. One of us has to be able to care for the kids.

"I have been, and I am, prepared to go to prison to protect our kids. I can live with that outcome. I couldn't have lived with the alternative. Now? You need clean hands. Gracie and Jonas need that."

"Clean hands?" she said again, her eyes completely

puzzled. "My *car*, babe? Sam used my car to commit a murder. How am I supposed to have clean hands?"

I reached to touch her. She pulled away. I said, "I didn't know until right now that he used your car. I swear."

"Where are my clean hands now, Alan?" Her voice had turned plaintive. "Who the hell is going to take care of our kids? Sam has Sherry for Simon. Who is going to take care of our babies?"

I could tell from the horror alighting in Lauren's eyes that she was recognizing the dark reality she'd discovered that morning by meeting with Izza and with Elias Tres. Having met with them she was left with but two real choices. Any second she would understand what I already understood, that only one of those choices would leave her with anything resembling clean hands.

Her first option? Lauren could strike a match, a literal match, and hold the flame to the corner of Elias Tres's drawing. Together she and I would witness the construction paper turn to ashes. A little more smoke on a day when Boulder was choking on the stuff.

Lauren was a seasoned prosecutor. Despite its allure, she would see the flaws in that solution. Witnesses would be left behind. Izza would know she handed Lauren the drawing. Elias Tres would know that Lauren had it.

Lauren's other remaining choice was the one that would leave her with clean hands. She could pick up her phone and arrange for the police to arrest Sam Purdy and me for questioning in the murder of Justine Winter Brown.

We would be prosecuted a world away, in Weld County.

Sam would attest that he took Lauren's car that night without permission.

Sam and I would, separately, agree to plea bargains. We would embrace any deal presented to us so that Lauren would have clean hands.

"No matter what? McClelland wins," Lauren said as she began to get her arms around the only resolution. "He's still standing."

I couldn't argue with her analysis. Michael McClelland would win this round. "The kids will be safe," I said. My words were intended to acknowledge our rival's victory but also underscored the enormity of our consolation prize.

"Safe?" she scoffed. "Not safe. McClelland isn't done. He won't stop."

*Sam and I will go to prison. Lauren will have clean hands. The kids? The kids will have a life without their fathers. Each will endure another loss. God.*

*And Lauren? She will awaken each morning with no safety net beside her.*

It wasn't the outcome that Sam and I had wanted. But it was the one we were ending up with.


I heard a click and then the sound of someone trying to turn the doorknob on the door that led from my office to the hallway. Because I was sitting in the seat where my patients usually sat, I was facing that door.

Lauren heard the noise, too. "Don't tell me you're

expecting someone?" she said. "Not now. Make them go away." The frustration in her voice was so thick it fogged the air between us.

"I'm not expecting anyone." I was sure that I had locked the door after I followed Lauren into the office. For me, it was reflex. "No one should be here. I will—"

I heard the sound of a key sliding into the lock. I said, "Shit."

Lauren puffed her cheeks. I knew well what exasperation looked like on my wife's face. That's what I was seeing. Complete, end-of-her-rope exasperation.

I thought, *Comadoe. How did he get my key?*

I reached for a weapon, grabbing a heavy crystal turtle from the table.

# FORTY-ONE

The door opened. It wasn't Comadoe.

It was Diane. Her intrusion stunned me. In our many years as partners she had never walked into my office un-invited. Not once. My instinct was that it had to be the damn fire. She must have been evacuated yet again.

Diane was not dressed for work. She was wearing grubby chinos and an open shirt over a simple camisole. She had used a spare key—we each had the other's key for emergencies—to enter my office. I could see the familiar fob poking from the dead bolt.

Something terrible must have happened. *The fire. She must,* I thought, *be in full panic mode*. I worried that her fragile grip on adjustment had failed. I feared she had gone ahead and torched the grasslands adjacent to her home on Lee Hill.

*God,* I thought, *not today. Be an arsonist tomorrow, or next week. Damn it, Diane, not today.*

Across from me, Lauren had closed her eyes. She couldn't take any more. She didn't lean forward to look back toward the door. She didn't stand.

Lauren's reaction to the intrusion was an instinctive one for a practiced therapist's spouse. Lauren had to be presuming, reasonably, that a patient had burst into my office. She knew that if she stayed seated, and anonymous, the person at the door couldn't see her. She figured that if she maintained anonymity, it would be easier for me to resolve the situation, whatever the situation was.

I was praying that Diane would recognize how inappropriate her intrusion was and head immediately back out of the room. But she did not.

In as compassionate a tone as I could muster in the circumstances, I said, "The fire? I'm so sorry, but this isn't a good time. Maybe in a little while, we can—"

Before I could finish the sentences, Diane narrowed her eyes and raised her hand. It had been slightly behind her. In it she held a handgun, a blocky semiautomatic that fit her hand like a glove. With no hesitation at all, she fired three shots into the back of the chair five feet in front of her.

She kept pulling the trigger until she had pulled it five times. The last two pulls the gun only clicked.

Gravity began to force Diane's hand down. She regrouped. She lifted the muzzle back up, toward me.

She said, "This wasn't how you were supposed to help."

I thought that's what she said. My ears were ringing too much to be certain.

Ba, ba, ba, ba. Ba, ba, ba, ba.

*Stayin' alive.*

I listened for breath sounds. I heard gurgles. I felt for a pulse.

I told myself that the second she stopped breathing I would start chest compressions.

I would hum the brothers Gibb's disco anthem and I would embrace the *ba ba ba ba* beat and I would compress my wife's chest, over and over, for as long as it took.

I must have called for an ambulance.

The rig must have been parked nearby. EMTs arrived within moments of my first Bee Gees musing.

Only later would I learn that a passel of ambulances was staged six blocks away at Eben Fine Park near the entrance to Boulder Canyon in case the rigs were needed to transport casualties into town from the fire that was blowing up in the canyon.

"Weak and thready" was what a slender, freckled EMT with kind green eyes called my wife's pulse as she worked to stabilize her on my office floor. I was so grateful that Lauren's pulse had a description other than absent that I would have laid the deed to my home at the freckled paramedic's feet in gratitude for her words.

It took no longer than two minutes to get from Walnut Street to Alpine Street. I had no recollection of climbing into the ambulance at the beginning of the trip.

The rig must have run with the siren blasting. I never heard its wail.

I was the last to exit. As I jumped down, Lauren's gurney was disappearing through the ER doors.

The Emergency Department at Community Hospital was crammed with a legion of nursing, medical, and surgical specialists. The hospital's disaster plan was in effect in response to the fire.

Lauren was the first serious casualty of the day. In seconds, she was surrounded. I tried to stay beside her. The triage nurses would have none of it. They blocked my path. They noted that I was covered in blood. "Where were you hit?" one asked.

My vital signs were truly important to the nurses, an interest I didn't share. "Where does it hurt, sir?" one nurse kept asking. His clear baritone was so distinctive that I thought I recognized him from an impromptu group bicycle ride up Left Hand early in the summer. *Clayton? Crandall?*

"It's my wife's blood," I said to Clayton or Crandall. "All of it." I kept insisting I wasn't hurt, that it wasn't my blood, and that if Lauren had lost this much—my clothes were covered—she must need more.

"Sure," Clayton or Crandall said, placating me. "We're on that."

I finally got one of the nurses to listen to what I had to say. "Listen to me," I begged. "Please."

Her ID read MARCIE. She leaned toward me, touched the side of my neck with her gloved fingers, and made eye contact. "I am listening," she said. It was a slightly exasperated "I am listening," but I was grateful for it.

I said, "I am not hurt. I was not shot."

"Okay," she said. She walked away and returned seconds later with clean scrubs. The drawstring on the pants had to be untied before I could put them on. The fisted little knot of cord turned out to be the most impenetrable of puzzles.

Marcie noted that my hands were shaking. She took the pants from me and untied the knot. She pulled my bloody shoes off my feet. My socks were next. One was soaked with blood, the other not so much. Finally, she helped me peel off my bloody trousers.

She wanted to wash the tacky blood from my legs and feet before I pulled on the scrubs. "Later, please," I said. "It doesn't matter." I was grateful that she relented.

As I started to pull the scrub pants over my bloody legs and feet, she said, in a perfectly even voice, "That is an exit wound."

I assumed she was talking about someone else. I stood to pull the pants up.

"Sit!" Marcie barked. "Your wife is on the way to the OR. So sit!" I thought her change in demeanor felt contrived. I started to lift a leg into the scrubs. "I said sit!"

The rest of the big room quieted for a beat or two in reaction to her yell.

"You going to sit?" she asked. "Or do I need to help you sit?"

I sat. She looked back over her shoulder. In a much

calmer voice, she said, "Dr. Jansen? Janelle? Take a look at this guy's calf. Looks like a GS, entry and exit."

Dr. Jansen looked up from a computer screen across the room. She said, "Through and through?"

Marcie said, "Appears to be."

*GS? GS?* I'd spent considerable time in ERs in my career. I thought I knew the lingo. That one? *GS?* I was drawing a blank.

A man in a tie with a stethoscope around his neck stood next to Dr. Jansen. He closed his mobile phone and announced in a game-show-host voice that the fire had just jumped a firebreak and was burning in Sunshine Canyon. From the upper floors of the hospital, flames were visible on the ridgetop above Knollwood.

The geography he was describing is familiar to anyone who has lived in Boulder for long. The ridge above Knollwood—a luxury residential enclave on a narrow slice of land at the entrance to Sunshine Canyon—rises only a couple of hundred feet in altitude. That ridge is but a segment in a series of hogbacks and ridges that make up the vertical separation dividing the historical core of Boulder from the Rocky frigging Mountains.

Not far from the ridge above Knollwood the mouth of Sunshine Canyon opens into Boulder. Not into the foothills *near* Boulder. The mouth of Sunshine Canyon protrudes into the city at Fourth Street. Four blocks *into* Boulder.

Knollwood is on the city side of the ridge. If the wildfire flames consumed the homes in Knollwood, historic

Mapleton Hill would be next. If Mapleton Hill burned, downtown, two blocks away, would literally be in the line of fire.

Someone asked, "How are the winds? Are they still from the west?"

Winds from the west would blow the fire into town.

The man with the game-show-host voice said, "Gusty."

A woman with lovely gray hair climbed on top of the counter at the nursing station. She called for quiet. It took her a while to cut through the chatter and get the attention she was seeking. She instructed all staff to contact their supervisors and to begin to review hospital evacuation protocols. Immediately.

*GS*, I finally remembered, meant "gunshot."

*Diane fucking shot my wife, and she shot me.*

Through and through.

# FORTY-TWO

A quick X-ray confirmed that my bones were undamaged and that my leg was fragment-free. Dr. Jansen began to clean and dress my wound.

I told her I didn't understand. The gun had never been fired at me.

"Maybe a ricochet," she said. "It's not perfectly round, could have been a fragment." She asked a question about the muscles in my calf. I told her I was a cyclist.

She said she rode, too. She warned me that at some point soon "this thing is going to hurt like the dickens."

In my head, I repeated *the dickens*. The point she warned about—the hurt-like-the-dickens point—hadn't arrived.

"A single stitch at each end should do it," she said. "Maybe two."

My mind got tangled up rhyming the phrases *maybe two* and *through and through*. I had enough observing ego left to recognize that my focus was not what I needed it to be. I had important things requiring my attention. I needed to be in three places at once, and none of the three included that particular corner of the ER, rhyming inconsequential phrases with Dr. Jansen.

I had to be at Lauren's side.

I had to be at my kids' school to meet them, and hold them, and comfort them.

And I had to let Sam know that Lauren knew everything. That she knew all about Frederick. That he was about to be picked up for investigation of murder.

Marcie came back into the treatment room. She told Dr. Jansen that two police detectives were waiting to speak with me about the shooting. Marcie handed me a business card.

One of the detectives was Amal Sengupta. I'd met him once before. Sengupta was a pleasant enough guy, but I had been hoping for Sam or Lucy.

Dr. Jansen asked me if I was ready to speak with the police.

"Can you give me ten or fifteen minutes?" I said. "To gather my thoughts?"

"I'll try," she said. She covered my sutured bullet wounds with the same kind of bandages I would use to dress my daughter's scraped knee.

In the pocket of my bloodied trousers, I found my cell

phone. Marcie handed me my wallet. "Better to have this with you than leave it here," she said.

I scrolled to Cozier Maitlin's name. On those rare occasions that I needed an attorney with his skill set, Cozy was my lawyer. At six-eight, he was also my first choice for a teammate in pickup basketball games. His assistant put me right through. Cozy had already heard details of that morning's shooting.

I said, "I don't want to talk to the police today, Cozy. Can you help me? They're right outside the door. So it has to be, like, now."

"I am truly sorry, Alan. But I have been retained to represent the . . . accused."

I was surprised that my first reaction was relief. I said, "They found Diane, Cozy?" I almost asked how she was doing.

"We were retained by her husband."

Cozy could have made me guess that information. I was grateful for his indiscretion. He offered to provide names of other attorneys who could help me prior to my interview with Detective Sengupta. I declined. I already had a plan B.

It took me longer to get past Casey Sparrow's receptionist than it took me to enlist her help. She, too, had heard about the shooting. I decided to postpone telling Casey about Frederick, and about Sam. I did tell her about Cozy's involvement with Diane. Cozy and Casey knew each other well.

I read her Amal Sengupta's contact information from his business card.

She said she didn't know him. She would do what she could.

When I poked my head outside the treatment room fifteen minutes later, no detectives were in sight.

# FORTY-THREE

Lauren's surgeries lasted over four hours. She was in recovery for ninety minutes.

Sam tracked me down in the ICU shortly after Lauren was wheeled into her room. Hearing him say, "Hey," was the first sign I got that he hadn't yet been picked up.

He waited outside the door as two nurses completed the process of settling my wife into their care. They made double sure that the monitors were monitoring and the pumps were pumping and the IVs were dripping.

The nurse that I thought was Lauren's primary appraised Sam suspiciously. He was hovering the way cops hover, something few found reassuring. The nurse said, "No visitors at this hour. You want him here?" I nodded. "I'll give you five minutes."

I was sitting by Lauren's side with her limp hand in mine. Her hand was too cool for my comfort, but not cold enough to spawn any greater panic than I'd been feeling all day. I felt no indication Lauren knew I was by her side. I hoped I was wrong. I kissed her. I whispered, "I love you."

With the exception of a wrenching trip across town to pick up the kids at school so I could tell them a PG-13 version of what had happened to their mother, and to arrange for their care for the evening, I had spent the day at the hospital, waiting for any sign that things were not as bad as they seemed.

My optimism, like my wife, was on life support. All afternoon I expected to hear that Lauren had died on the operating table. But she had made it off the operating table. Then I was told that the next twelve hours were crucial.

Those dozen hours were passing with neither speed nor grace.

Whenever I managed to focus beyond the hospital walls, I realized that the Dome Fire loomed above town. Flames were racing through dry grasses, torching pines and spruce, living and dead, while consuming relics of cherished memories without mercy.

Ashes floated into town like funeral confetti.

The smell of it, altogether, was the aroma of dread.

Hundreds had been evacuated. The hospital remained on alert, awaiting the development of some secondary tragedy that would deliver multiple casualties. In the vacuum created by the waiting, rumors of imminent evacuation of the hospital complex raced through the corridors at regular intervals.

A consistent piece of news? The fire had not dropped down the ridge into the mouth of Sunshine Canyon. Knollwood hadn't fried. Yet. The fire wasn't in town. Yet.

A subtle wind shift got most of the credit for the good fortune. Valiant firefighters got the rest. I heard a few of the more devout offering thanks to God. For the moment, the devout seemed to be in the minority. Most people were thanking the prevailing winds.

The strangers around me were wary of me but kind. The wariness could have had to do with the fact that I was zombie-ing through the hospital hallways in scrubs stained with dried blood wearing shoes that squished with each step I took.

I wouldn't have known what to say to me.

The critical care nurses finished up their duties with Lauren and left the room. I stood to greet Sam. He hugged me, holding the embrace for a long time. "How are you?" he said.

I was determined not to cry. If I started, I feared, I couldn't control what would come next. More tears, of course. It was the what-else besides the tears that had me worried. I lacked the imagination to predict the manner I would disintegrate.

Sam stepped back. He kept a hand on each of my biceps, as though he suspected I might need to be held up. He said, "I heard about the shooting late morning, but I didn't know it was . . ."

*Lauren.* At first, he didn't know it was Lauren.

"This fire has the whole town completely . . ."

*Whacked*. It was one of Jonas's words. It seemed to fit.

Boulder, I guessed, had spent the day doing what I'd been doing. Pacing, awaiting tragic developments. Praying for miracles from the same inattentive God who had been careless enough, or callous enough, to permit the figurative or literal match to be struck—and the trigger to be pulled—in the first place.

During one of his frequent philosophical/spiritual forays, my old friend Peter, Jonas's biological father, had told me that if there was indeed a God responsible for planet Earth, he was certain it was a kid God, an adolescent God, a young, distracted deity who spent most of His time in celestial amusements—playing in a garage band, trying to get laid—that had nothing to do with His more somber God-ish responsibilities.

That meant that we on Earth ended up being the room He didn't get around to cleaning. The homework He didn't get done on time. The dog He didn't get around to feeding.

At intervals all day long, I'd been rehearsing a conversation I wished to have with that kid God of ours. The conversation started with "Excuse me. God? *God?* Excuse me. What the fuck were you thinking?"

Rumors were that God had a vengeful streak. I was pretty sure my impertinence and profanity would earn me an extended stay in purgatory. I was well beyond caring. My fate, it seemed, included a stint doing time somewhere.

\*     \*     \*

To Sam, I said, "I know it's awful out there."

"I want to hear about Lauren. But first I don't want you to be surprised if you hear something—I was picked up today."

My first thought was *Oh God, here it is*. My second thought? *Then what the hell are you doing here?* I said, "Picked up by whom? For what?"

"IA."

*Internal Affairs*. That made no sense. If Sam was picked up for what happened in Frederick, it would have been his detective colleagues who did the apprehending, not his distant professional relations who made their living investigating police misbehavior.

"What did IA want?"

"There are some allegations." Sam looked around.

"Come on," I said. I had no patience to spare. If Sam was feeling parsimonious with details, he could do it with someone else. "I have to talk to you about—"

He stopped me before I could say "Frederick."

"I know you do. We'll get there. You need to know this. Okay? IA got an anonymous tip that I had an unregistered handgun and some pilfered drug evidence in my personal vehicle."

*What?*

"They asked for permission to search my car. I granted it."

I couldn't fit these pieces into the story I knew. *Had Lauren called IA? Had she initiated the search?* I said, "Sam, wait. You need to—I really need to—"

"I know. I'm almost done. Then I want to hear everything. Remember the break-in of my Cherokee? Right after, I searched the car trying to figure out what had been stolen. Identity? Registration? Anything.

"Nothing was gone but a few dollars in coins. I concluded the guy had been scared off, remember? Then I got to thinking. Couple of nights ago, I couldn't sleep, got up, went out, turned the car inside out. High in the springs below the driver's seat, I found that old thirty-two. The one from the intercom in my kitchen."

I thought I was beyond surprise at that point in my day. I was wrong.

"In the back, duct-taped to the underside of the jack, I found a bag with a couple of ounces of white powder in it. I think it's meth. Could be coke, but I think it's meth.

"The gun? Jesus. I was sure it had my prints on it. I mean, it was my gun, right? If IA had found the stuff during their search, I could have, maybe, argued that the drugs were planted during the break-in in the parking lot, but . . . the weapon? That would be hard to explain. How could I convince IA that an asshole had busted into my car and planted a throwdown with my prints on it in my personal vehicle?" He shook his head. "I would have been screwed. Comadoe made a good move.

"But I made a slightly better one. The IA search came up clean."

Despite the high stakes, Sam's successful thwarting of Comadoe's attempt to set him up with IA didn't feel like it had much to do with my reality. It was kind of like hearing about the outcome of a parliamentary election in Belgium on the BBC.

Sam didn't know it yet, but he had bigger worries.

Sam could tell I was unmoved. He said, "Thought you needed to know."

My eyes were full of tears. "Maybe some other time I will appreciate the—"

"Lauren? In the hall earlier?" He sensed it was past time to change the subject. "One of the doctors said that Lauren's surgery went well. That's good, right?"

I nodded. To me, it meant that Lauren survived the operations. That's all.

Sam said, "Ophelia has the kids at the DW. She's frying chicken. It's good, her chicken—almost like that time I was in Georgia. And her biscuits? Hey, how about I send a car up there to get you a plate. Does that sound good?"

It didn't. I shook my head. "Simon?" I asked about Sam's son.

"With a school friend. He's fine."

I was grateful for Ophelia's kindness to my children. The loss-accounting in each of the kids' lives had reached critical sums. I didn't know what Lauren's shooting would do to their fragile holds on adjustment. Jonas was the most vulnerable. *How,* I wondered, *can he survive this day after all the awful days that came before?*

I looked at my wife and felt a pain that bored beyond my core. It was at once hollow and sharp. Without looking up, I said, "Lauren knows everything, Sam."

I thought he grunted. The grunt puzzled me. I turned my head.

It hadn't been a grunt. Sam had choked. His wide eyes said, *What the f—?*

My nod provided the confirmation he feared. He poked his tongue into the side of his cheek while he weighed the consequences. Sam stood. He wrapped the nurse-call device in a spare blanket. He taped a fat round of gauze over the microphone below the speaker panel behind the bed.

It was all déjà-something, for him and for me.

Sam pushed both his open palms down in the direction of the floor. He was the conductor, controlling the volume of his orchestra of one. Me.

As directed, I went pianissimo. "Lauren had a visit at her office from Izza this morning. And Elias Tres. You remember him?" Sam nodded. "Turns out that Tres saw you that night. You parked near his house. He was up because he was waiting for his dead father's body to come home from Afghanistan. His dad had been killed a few days before in a Taliban ambush. Tres was also up because he'd just heard his drunk grandfather tell Izza the true story of his father's conception. A story about the rape of Izza's mother."

Sam's mandibles hardened into golf balls.

"The boy drew a picture of the car you were driving that night." I examined Sam's face for a twitch, a sign. Nothing. No indication that he realized he'd screwed up.

"Tres has this great . . . memory. Like a savant, people say. He remembered the gym bag you pulled out of the back of the car. A damn Avs bag, Sam. And the cap you were wearing? The Twins, Sam? Jesus. The drawing he did even had two digits and two letters from the license plate."

Sam's everyday pink complexion began to fade to hospital-sheet white. He stepped outside the room. He stuffed his hands into his pockets. He gestured to me with his head to join him in the hall. I stepped out. Sam made doubly sure the door was closed.

He had completely lost faith in unconscious people.

He looked toward the nursing station, in the direction of the seated clerk. I had not noticed, but it was Imogen. He leaned in so close to me he could have compared the relative sizes of our heads in a hand mirror. In a barely audible whisper, he said, "It was my understanding that the grandpa wouldn't let him talk to . . . law enforcement."

I whispered back, "Turns out there's a way around that. Because of the rape."

Sam pondered that news. "Lawyer wizard shit?" he asked.

Sam wasn't too fond of attorney magic. "Pretty much."

He stretched his neck back as though he were maximizing the exposure of his flesh in anticipation of his imminent beheading.

I said, "Right after Lauren met with Izza and Tres, she came by my office to tell me that you would be picked up for questioning in Currie's death. Lauren came to see me out of love, Sam."

Sam almost emptied his lungs before he said, "Ah Jesus. That's why she was at your—"

"Yeah. She was there because of what we did in Frederick."

"What *I* did in Frederick," he said, correcting me. "Remember that, Alan."

Sam was feeling the wash of a Gaia breeze. I knew the signs, because I'd been feeling the Gaia blow over me all day long.

The Gaia was, for us, the ill wind that blew no good.

The Gaia effect is an attempt to explain how a butterfly flapping its wings in the Amazon rain forest can ultimately influence the weather, and events and lives, on the other side of the globe. Say, in a place like Boulder. Lives like Lauren's, and Sam's, and mine.

What happened that night in Frederick with Sam and Currie was our Gaia, the wing-flap of the butterfly that Sam and I shared with Lauren and with our kids. The forces put in motion that night had, years later, led Lauren to visit my office, so that she would be sitting in my chair, vulnerable to be shot multiple times in the back.

Take away the distant cause—the flap of the wing that included Sam wrapping his gloved hand around Currie's trembling hand while they together pointed a revolver into a specific hollow below her chin—and Lauren would not have been in that chair in my office that morning. She would not have been shot.

I would never have known about through and through.

Sam derided most of what New Age believers professed. In fact, when the day came that a Boulder brewer got around to naming a new light ale "Gaia"—it would

be a light ale, and the day, I was confident, was coming—
Sam would relish the opportunity for ridicule. I had no
doubt that were he and I to discuss Gaia, he would be-
little any who paid homage. But despite Sam's derision,
and maybe because of it, the reality of the power of the
distant influence was smacking him hard right across his
pale face.

# FORTY-FOUR

He said, "Jesus." He kicked a foot so it scuffled on the linoleum. He shifted his weight. He did the kicking, scuffling motion a second time with the other foot.

He said, "Diane? Really?"

He knew the facts. He sought understanding. Failing that, he wanted a perp. But I wasn't quite ready to string Diane up. "She's not well. I think she mistook Lauren for somebody . . ."

"Yeah?" he asked. It wasn't a curious yeah. It was a dismissive yeah. A *so what* yeah. It was his way of saying that lots of people are not well, but that Diane was the one who shot my wife in the back. He asked, "You got somebody particular in mind?"

"I think Diane made an assumption. Time of day. Maybe a car outside. Hair color. Similarities." I heard myself. I was sure I sounded to Sam like someone who was trying to convince himself about something.

Sam wasn't about to cut me any slack with my theory. He said, "But the . . . the misidentification? It involved somebody Diane wanted to shoot? In the back?"

It was a tough point to argue. "She hasn't been well. Not for a long time. I didn't see how bad it was. Or maybe I didn't want to acknowledge how bad it was."

Sam was suspicious of the defense, however tepid, that I was sketching out for my friend. I loved Diane. I also knew that my anger at her would eventually show up, the way that it's always the visitor you don't want to see who arrives with the most suitcases. I knew that when my rage arrived and pounded on my door, it would move in for an extended stay. I knew that my rage would loom large, that it would scream loud, and that despite my efforts to tame it, it would prove mean enough to blow fire.

Until it showed up, I had no plans to go looking for it.

Sam said, "They haven't found her. I heard—Sengupta is the lead detective on this—that Raoul is concerned that she might have, well, you know."

*Suicide?* I hadn't gone there. But the moment Sam raised the issue of Diane's self-destructive risk I gave some consideration to my friend's state of mind. "It's possible," I said. "She could have decided to try to . . ." I hesitated as I tried to think of how and where Diane might take her own life. She was in possession of a hand-gun, obviously. Would she shoot herself with it? I didn't think so. But when I woke almost twenty hours earlier, I hadn't been thinking that she would shoot anyone else that day, either.

*Where might she go to kill herself?* I was drawing a blank on that one.

"You guys checked her house?" I asked.

Sam nodded. "Early on. That whole area's been evacuated because of the fire. Lee Hill and Olde Stage are closed." Those were the primary routes that led to Diane and Raoul's foothills home.

I said, "Raoul is back in Boulder?"

"Sengupta told Lucy he flew in from out of town. Got back around dinnertime."

Sengupta hadn't been a detective for long. I'd met him once. Pleasant guy. Kept his cards close to his chest. I was getting the impression that Sam was taking some incomprehensible pleasure from speaking Sengupta's name. Foreign words didn't exactly roll off of Sam's Iron Range tongue. That he pronounced his colleague's surname with accented grace was apparently a source of simple joy for Sam on a day that was threatening to come to a conclusion without even a trickle of the stuff.

I said, "Raoul was in Chicago, or maybe Cleveland, I think. Did Sengupta say anything else? Had Raoul spoken with Diane . . . since . . . ?"

I thought, but didn't say, *Since she shot my wife.*

Sam shook his head and raised his hands in some don't-blame-the-messenger mime-ology. "Everything I know is thirdhand. From Sengupta, through Lucy, mostly." I swallowed a wry Sengupta grin. "But, no— Raoul says he hasn't spoken with her. As of maybe twenty minutes ago, no sign of her since this morning. Everyone's out looking for her and her car. APB. BOLOs across the state."

*Be on the lookout for a 2008 Saab convertible, metallic gray . . .*

Sam leaned in again. He lowered the volume of his whisper so it was closing in on mosquito-buzz territory. "I know you haven't been outside, but it's not normal out there. Resources are scarce. Because of the fire, and the evacuations, and all the closed roads. Our assets are supporting the firefighters."

"I get it," I said. On another day, Lauren's shooting would have been the biggest news in Boulder. That day? Not even close.

Sam said, "You haven't talked with Diane, have you? You know, after?"

*After she shot my wife in the back?* I had not. As Lauren slumped to the floor, Diane had walked from my office, leaving the spare key dangling in the dead bolt.

Sam's last question left me uneasy. I was ready to go back into the room to be with Lauren. I placed my hand on the door. I paused, turned, and said, "Was that a detective question? Or a friend question?"

He replayed the audio in his head. He winced. "Forget I asked that," he said. "Please. Please. Instinct. I'm sorry."

"It's okay," I said. "Thanks."

Sam said, "Hold on." I stopped. "The fact that I'm here with you? And that I'm not in an interview room on Thirty-third asking for my lawyer? That means it's possible Lauren didn't tell anyone else what she knows."

"Or?" I said. The day had provided me with a wealth of thinking and pondering time. "There's a less optimistic possibility that would explain your temporary freedom."

Sam had no trouble filling in the blank. "I know, or maybe she did tell. And with the fire and everything my colleagues just haven't gotten around to us yet. They don't expect us to . . . scramble."

I nodded. "If that's true—if Lauren had spoken with a colleague before she came to see me—there's a good chance it's not *us* they're looking for, Sam," I said. "When Lauren stopped by, she didn't think I knew anything about Frederick. She knows I was in New Mexico that night—she didn't think I was any part of Tres's story."

"She thinks it was just me?" Sam spoke with profound relief. I found his relief to be generous. I doubled the gratitude I felt at being his friend.

"She thought it was just you. But I told her the truth." Sam narrowed his eyes and shook his head as though the motion could erase my words. "I told her what I knew."

"No," he said. The *you fucking idiot* was understood.

"I told her that I was every bit as responsible as—"

"You told her? What the f—? Are you—"

*Kidding you? Nuts? Does it matter?*

"This is about both of us, Sam. Not about you. I explained to Lauren why Currie had to die that night, that I was part of it, that I would have done the same thing that—"

"No." Sam reached out. He put a hand on my shoulder. It felt heavy, like I imagined one paw of a big grizzly might feel a split second before the other paw swatted my head to the next county. "You were the one who was supposed to take care of my kid. That's how this was supposed to . . ."

We were talking past each other. I said, "Simon has his mom, Sam. The moment Diane walked in? Lauren was furious at me, not at you. She was furious that I hadn't trusted her."

The nurse told Sam his time was up. Sam snorted, then he mumbled, "Almost."

She spread her feet and opened her mouth to assert her authority. She wanted none of Sam's attitude.

Sam hadn't been quibbling with her announcement that his visit was over. Sam's retort—"Almost"—had been an existential commentary. The nurse had no way to know that, of course. If you didn't know Sam Purdy, you wouldn't suspect by looking at him or listening to him that he had an existential streak as rich as a mother lode.

Sam hugged me again before he left. "One more thing. This is *not* a detective question. Has Izza told anyone else about her mother's situation? Or about what Tres saw that night?"

"I don't know," I whispered. "Why?"

He shook his head. "You're not thinking clearly. If Lauren told her colleagues what she learned from Tres before she went to your office this morning, those colleagues don't know you're complicit in Currie's murder. Lauren didn't know you were complicit before she went to see you. So her colleagues can't know, either."

"Which means—"

"In their view, you still have clean hands," Sam said.

Sam was excluding an important variable from his scenario. The unless. I wasn't about to ignore the unless. "That's true," I said, "only if Lauren dies. If she dies, I may have clean hands. Or I may not."

Sam nodded, agreeing. The circumstances felt surreal. If I suffered a loss so great I could hardly imagine it, I might be free.

"If Lauren lives," I said, "she knows I don't have clean hands."

Sam had more comfort with conspiracy than I did. He said, "She knows, but does she tell? I think it depends on whether she told anyone what she knew before she went to see you. If she didn't share earlier, then she's going to have a tough call to make. She can become part of our enterprise or she can turn us in."

"Her best move is to turn us in," I said. "It's the only strategy that guarantees that one of us would be free to take care of the kids. The clean hands would be hers. That's how it should be."

"It is the safest strategy. If she said something to a colleague before she went to your office, even something vague, then she has no choice—she has to turn me in," Sam said. "But only me. She's sharp; she'll recognize that the only way to keep her own hands clean is to sacrifice me for the kids. You? It's not so clear."

The nurse walked by, tapping the face of her watch.

I had promised myself I wouldn't resort to accusation. I couldn't help it. I said, "You drove her car, Sam. What the hell were—"

"My water pump died. I was ready to go. I wasn't sure I could be ready again. I had your keys. I took your car."

"You risked us all."

"Come on. I was risking us all anyway," Sam said. "I didn't expect to get caught. I couldn't have done it if I thought I was going to be caught."

I stared at him with a jumble of feelings in my heart. "The second rule of criminals?" I said. "None of them think they'll get caught."

Sam nodded. He left without another word.

He returned two minutes later. His hands were in his pockets. His eyes were narrow. He said, "I have to ask this. I think you were implying earlier that you know who Diane's real target was when she shot Lauren. Yes?"

My heart dropped so fast I had an urge to lunge to catch it. Immediately, I saw where Sam was going. I didn't move. I didn't blink. I didn't speak.

Sam went on. "That person might need some protecting. Seeing that Diane is not in custody. And that she is likely still armed." He paused to allow me to process the risks. "And in case you're forgetting the rules, this circumstance falls right smack in the middle of one of the exceptions to doctor-patient confidentiality."

"Imminent danger?" I said.

"Yeah. That should cover it."

The nurse who shooed Sam away earlier was jogging toward us to shoo him away again.

Sam reached out and touched my shoulder. He said, "Just saying."

\* \* \*

I left Amanda a voice mail asking her to call me, regardless of the hour. I said it was urgent. I sent her a text and an e-mail with the same message.

Despite my best efforts to stay awake, I fell asleep in the chair beside Lauren's bed.

I woke, completely disoriented, to the sound of her IV pump alarm. For the briefest of moments, the world was one where my wife hadn't been shot by my dear friend. The respite from reality slipped through my fingers in the time it took to blink my eyes thrice.

I threw water on my face as a nurse silenced the machinery. It was almost three in the morning. I had two dozen text messages, almost as many voice mails.

Amanda had not returned my messages. That truly concerned me.

I scrolled for the kids' names in the lists. I checked for Ophelia's.

*No news, good news,* I said to myself. I thought I would try that one on as a mantra.

I stopped scrolling when I spotted Casey Sparrow's name in the roster of text messages. My lawyer had reached out just before nine o'clock the night before.

**I told Det Sengupta he could talk to you tomorrow morning at 10:30. Come by my office on S Broadway at ten. We'll drive together. Sorry, best I could do.**

The nurse asked me if I had eaten. I had to think. I said I had not. She told me to take a break, get something to eat. She said she would text me if there was any change.

I made her promise to be in touch. She crossed her heart.

I kissed Lauren's forehead and went in search of fuel. I hoped something was open on Broadway so I could get a sandwich.

Once I made it down to the first floor, I could see that the western sky was lit in a way that felt obscenely celebratory. The fire was not under control. Billowing clouds of fresh smoke reflected the dancing lights of the flames back toward the city. Ashes floated in the air.

I still smelled dread.

I wondered if there was any way to get up to the hospital roof. I was sure that from up there I could see the precise locations of the flames on the near ridges.

With that thought, I felt an epiphany land on me with what felt like physical mass.

I did next what lost despairing souls have done throughout the ages at the precise moment they are struck upside the head with an epiphany.

I used my mobile phone to call a taxi.

# FORTY-FIVE

The driver I drew in the taxi lottery was a cannonball of a woman far enough north of seventy that her age created doubts for me about the wisdom of her occupation. I wondered whom she'd had to offend to earn the overnight shift in Boulder, which had to involve shuttling a steady stream of drunks from bars and clubs to homes or after-parties.

She was not only round, she was also little. No part of her head extended beyond the lowest perimeter of the seat's headrest. Only about a third of the quantity of hair I expected protruded up from the top of her head into my visual field. My thoughts wandered initially toward chemotherapy, but within seconds I was weighing the possibility of alopecia.

In response to her jolly, "Your cabbist, sir," I began hoping for alopecia. I asked her to please take me to the east end of the Mall. That was as specific as I planned to be.

She surprised me with a quick turn of her head. I

leaned forward and spotted a mouthful of beautiful teeth and a smile as bright as my daughter's. She said, "I don't get too many pleases and thank-yous after the bars close. I am appreciative. That end of the Mall is what, Pearl and . . . Fifteenth Street?"

I had no doubt she knew the geography, but I played along. "I think that's right."

"Pretty sure it's a one-way in the wrong direction. I'd have to circle back—go all the way to Walnut on Broadway, or weave through on Fourteenth and then around. Is Fifteenth and Spruce okay? Or Sixteenth and Pearl? Probably save you a buck."

I smiled, an act that reminded me I'd had the kind of day that caused a smile to feel as though it might fracture something in my face. My cabbist brightened her grin in return. At the hospital my appearance had earned me a few turned heads—I remained styled, after all, in blood-stained scrubs and blood-filled shoes without socks. In response to the pain in my calf, I was limping the limp of an advanced-stage syphilitic.

The driver had to have noticed all that as I approached and settled into her car. Despite it all, she was looking out for me. I was certain she needed the buck more than I did. I would accept the savings graciously and give it back to her as part of her tip. I said, "Sixteenth and Pearl is fine. Thank you."

I explained that I might need to get back to the hospital urgently. She said, "At your beck and call till dawn," and handed me a card with her personal mobile number listed below her job title: Cabbist.

Once she dropped me off I kept my head down as I hugged the storefronts along Pearl Street. Two police cruisers passed during my short stroll, one driving in each direction. The one heading east slowed beside me as I neared Frasca. The officer kept pace, right behind me, until I reached the next corner.

I stopped to tie my shoes, which were loafers. The squad moved on at a crawl. I wondered if *my* presence—and not just the presence of any random, bloody, disheveled pedestrian—had been noted. In a determined attempt to keep my paranoia in check, I tried to convince myself it was just a cop on patrol making a citizen nervous to see how said citizen would respond to the duress. I had witnessed Sam do a version of the same provocation a dozen times. It was second nature to him.

I had told him it wasn't one of my favorite things about cops.

He'd laughed and told me that was a second rule about cops: cops don't care much about citizens' favorite things about cops.

From the moment I climbed out of the taxi I had been trying to recall the silly ditty that Diane had been singing the first evening we'd visited the garish flat off Pearl Street together.

The rhyme came to me as I turned the corner. "*Who you gonna tell? Everybody. What you gonna sell? Sell me, baby!*"

I was prepared to decipher a four-digit code from that song so I could enter it into the lockbox to retrieve the keys that would allow me inside the front door. I might also have to guess an additional code for the alarm system. I had already decided to go with *t-e-l-l, s-e-l-l,* or *b-a-b-y.* My money was on *s-e-l-l,* a sales agent word, for the lockbox, *b-a-b-y* for the alarm.

The next step of my grand plan would be to find the disguised door that Diane had told me was located somewhere behind the staircase, the door that would take me inside the garage. From there, I would use the private elevator to get from the garage into the garish flat. My planning beyond that point lacked specificity. But I was neither alert enough nor in the correct frame of mind to engage in the kind of critical thinking that would have helped me recognize the inherent perils of my unplanned steps.

My anticipatory ditty-singing was for naught. Even from the sidewalk in front of the gallery, I could tell that the door fronting the sidewalk was not quite latched. A quick glance up the stairs confirmed that the door to the flat wasn't even closed all the way—a bar of light the width of a paring knife blade allowed a dull though distinctive vertical gap to glow on the side of the door nearest the knob.

*Diane had to know I would find her.* That's what I was thinking. I was also close to concluding that she wanted me to find her. If I couldn't warn Amanda about Diane, second best was finding Diane myself.

I paused before I began to trudge up the stairs. I thought of calling Sam.

But Sam was a cop. I wasn't ready to have the cops

take over. Not before I had spoken with Diane. I knew well that this might be the last opportunity I would have for an unmonitored conversation with Diane. I needed that opportunity.

I thought of calling Cozier Maitlin, Diane's criminal defense lawyer. Cozy lived close by near Mapleton Hill, only two minutes away by car. But Cozy would most certainly have advised Diane not to speak with me. That would have been appropriate legal advice, given the circumstances. The thing was—I wasn't ready to have Diane suddenly begin to act appropriately. Not quite yet.

I thought of calling Raoul.

But Raoul was suddenly the most wild of wild cards. I didn't know whether Diane wanted to kiss him. Or whether she wanted to kill him. Whatever she yearned to do would distract from my desire to have her undivided attention.

The truth was that I wanted to talk to Diane alone. I needed to ask her why. I needed to learn why she had opened fire in my office. I needed to understand *something*.

I called no one.

My calf grew weary of stair climbing after a measly four treads. Weary wasn't the actual feeling. No burn I'd ever experienced in my quads during the ascent of an impossible grade on a high mountain pass on my bicycle came close to the burn I experienced in my wounded calf after those first four steps. I reconsidered my action plan, hopped back to start, and quickly found the disguised door that led to the garage.

Diane's convertible Saab was inside.

The elevator cab was on the ground level. *Coincidence?* I wanted to think so, but it hadn't been a day when coincidences were falling in my favor. I concluded that Diane had used the keys from the lockbox to unlock the elevator. I would find her upstairs. Waiting.

The elevator and I were on level 0. The control panel had options for 1 and for 2. I didn't have a gut feeling about where in the flat I would find Diane. If she were fire-gazing, the best view of the Dome Fire would be from that expansive deck on the roof. I chose 2 because it was the highest option, and because I'd just learned I was better at descending stairs than I was at climbing them. Moments later, the elevator door opened silently into the short hallway on the bedroom level. The hallway was too dark to navigate. I found the flashlight app on my phone and tried to use it for illumination. *Ha.* All that it illuminated was my location. I turned it off.

The climb up the stairs to the roof was slow and painful. Although I didn't think my presence at the flat would surprise Diane—the unlocked elevator had erased any doubts I had that she was anticipating someone's arrival—I didn't want to startle her with anything sudden. I stuck my head out the door at the top of the stairs and I called her name at a volume calculated to traverse the deck but not to wake the neighborhood.

She didn't reply. I checked to make sure the door was unlocked before I stepped outside. The middle-of-the-night glow that was lighting the sky across the rooftops of downtown Boulder caused me to suck a volume of foul air into my lungs.

For a fleeting second I entertained the possibility that I was wrong about everything, that Diane wasn't in the downtown flat at all—she was back up at her home on Lee Hill, somehow, with a match, or that Army-Navy Surplus flamethrower. The thought didn't linger. My mouth had fallen open at the incongruous sight of flames spinning cyclonically from the tops of torching trees. The flickering night sky seemed almost as obscene as the burning trees. A slight shift of my gaze, only a few degrees to the north, allowed me to see a jagged line of persistent flames assembled like a cavalry of fire, awaiting orders. That section of the burn was scorching the top of the ridge that separated Boulder Canyon from Sunshine Canyon.

Every breath I took tasted like a fireplace with a clogged flue.

I spotted a dark form on one of four sleek teak chaises that were pointed toward the sunset on the far edge of the expansive roof deck. On nine random glorious Boulder nights out of ten, the location of those chaises would identify prime cocktail-sipping territory. This would have been the tenth night.

The form didn't change shape as I approached.

"Hey," I said when I was halfway there.

If it was Diane, she didn't respond.

*Oh God*. I tasted a new flavor of dread. I narrowed my eyes to look for variations in the shadows below the chaise, trying to spot a dark stain on the dark wood in the dark night on the darkest of Boulder's, and my own, dark days.

I was looking for the ripe, shimmering, swollen shape of a puddle of warm, pooled congealing blood. I didn't see it.

I thought, *Diane wouldn't use a gun, she'd OD.* That was how she would kill herself—an overdose. All irony about the day aside, Diane just wasn't comfortable with violence. She was the girl who closed her eyes at cartoonish mayhem at the movies.

There would be, I assured myself, no blood pooling beneath that expensive chaise. If that was Diane I was seeing, and she had chosen to end her life, it would be a still form slowly yielding the last of its warmth after a toxic death.

Slightly louder, I said, "Diane? It's Alan."

Nothing. I stepped forward until I could identify the dark form on the chaise. It was the fake-fur throw from the tangerine couch downstairs in the living room. Someone had carried it up there while they rested on that chaise, eyeing the fire.

Behind me, I heard a noise. I translated the sound as coming from something weighty moving across heart redwood.

I turned in time to see a shadow on the glass panel of the door.

I heard a click.

# FORTY-SIX

I was too clumsy from my wound to sneak up on anyone, so I didn't try. The only precaution I took as I followed whomever I was following was tapping the digits *9* and *1* on my phone. I kept the phone in my hand, with my index finger hovering above the *1* and my thumb hovering above SEND. If I managed some mildly complicated digital dexterity, I was an instant away from initiating a call to 911.

For some crazy reason, I was assuming that the arrival of the police would work in my favor. As I limped down the stairs to the second level, I didn't try to minimize the noise I was making. After every few steps, I called out, "Diane, Diane? It's Alan."

I really didn't think Diane would shoot me again. I wasn't certain, but playing the odds, it seemed unlikely. She and I had a history of thousands of days together when she hadn't shot me even once.

I was nearing the bottom of the staircase that led to the bedroom level when I heard a male voice say, "Down here."

*Really?* I thought. *Screw the stairs.* I took the elevator to the main floor of the flat.

Raoul was sitting on the tangerine sofa. He stood. He moved toward me, his arms extended for an embrace. We hugged as though his wife hadn't shot my wife, as though I didn't have through-and-through GS wounds in my calf.

Our embrace should have been mindful of all that. It wasn't. While Raoul had his arms around me, tapping my back twice with his open palms, he said, "That was me trying to sneak away from you, up on the roof. Thought it would be better to stay invisible. If you found no one here, maybe you would leave. Turns out I'm not so good at . . . being clandestine. I should have known that about myself by now, yes? I went up there to see if the fire is moving north toward Lee Hill. If it gets to Pine Brook or Wonderland, I will have to . . ."

When he chose, Raoul could speak with no hint of his Catalonian roots. He was so choosing. I was disappointed by what he was saying. Chatting about the fire was easy. I was more interested to learn why he was in the downtown flat in the middle of the night.

But mostly I'd been hoping to hear a sincere version of "I'm so sorry." Maybe some insight into Diane's acute emotional decline. Her state of mind. Something.

I limped back two steps. His eyes went wide at my bloodstained scrubs. It was as though he hadn't expected that the consequences of the day would include ill-fitting borrowed clothes and dried bodily fluids.

"She snapped, yes?" he said.

He didn't sound surprised. I didn't have time to have that conversation with Raoul. I said, "Is Diane here? I came to speak with her."

"Did she call you?"

"No. I guessed she'd be here. Didn't know where else she would go. A thousand people must be looking for her."

"She called me from here. That's why I came. This"—Raoul spread his arms wide—"is where she wants us to move, apparently." He made a lyrical gesture with his hands that someone in Catalonia could probably interpret. My guess was that it meant that Raoul didn't love the flat. "She left the door open. Her car is downstairs. But she is not here. There was a note on the door." He retrieved it from his pocket as he grinned one of his charming grins. "It says she will be back soon. See." He held up the paper for me to read. "Diane leaves me lots of notes. I keep telling her she should learn to text."

I said, "She knows how to text, Raoul. She's not the digital illiterate she wants you and me to believe she is."

He shook his head and said, with obvious affection, "No, no. Not my Diane."

I considered telling him about finding her in the utility room of their home with a laptop connected via USB cable to the home network's hard drive backup. I didn't have time or energy for the whole story, so I cut to the headline. I said, "A conjecture on my part? I think she's monitoring your e-mail, Raoul. Maybe through the backup hard drive you have set up on your home network. In that utility room, all the way in back behind the TV room? Or maybe she figured out your Gmail password. I'm not sure which."

"Diane? Non." He wasn't so much being incredulous as he was being dismissive. He was doing it in a way I thought Diane would find condescending. He didn't believe that his wife had any digital deception in her. The reality was that he and I had both been guilty of underestimating Diane. He said, "She can't even manage her own passwords. Try to teach her about case sensitivity. Try." Another Catalonian hand gesture punctuated his assertion. Again, I couldn't interpret it.

The truth was that I had attempted to instruct Diane about password case sensitivity. I thought I had failed. But by that evening I believed that Diane had learned every lesson I taught. "Maybe I'm wrong about the details, about how," I said. "Maybe she installed a keystroke logger on the desktop in your office at home. Maybe she got your admin password that way. Don't know. It doesn't matter how she did it. The bottom line? She's reading your e-mail, Raoul. That is what is important."

Raoul typically carried his age with less transparency than anyone I know. At the moment he was contemplating Diane's deception he looked old.

"Some irony?" I said. "I only know all this because she needed my help rebooting your modem a night you were in Cleveland. She couldn't figure out that part. That's the night I saw the setup. She had a laptop open that was connected with a USB cable to your backup hard drive."

"It is not possible. My Diane is hopeless with, with . . . ," he said. "With electronics. She couldn't find a USB cable in a box of linguine. She can't—"

"Diane's smart, Raoul. She may not *like* electronics. But if she decided to figure something out, she could figure something out. Like I said, I could be wrong. I've been wrong about a lot lately. But I think she wanted to know what you were e-mailing, and to whom. You might want to consider that . . . tonight. If you speak with her."

"Why would—" Raoul stopped himself. "My Gmail? It's all business," he said. "Ninety-nine percent business."

I allowed him a moment to do the arithmetic. Raoul could design complex circuits or do elegant algorithms in his sleep. But he was having some trouble with simple percentiles.

I offered a clue. "What about the other one percent, Raoul?"

He stuffed his hands in the pockets of his trousers. He allowed his always-proud shoulders to slump forward. He stepped sideways, turning his body from mine. He was looking toward the glow from the flames of the Dome Fire, at the haze from the smoke pouring from the property of the already unlucky.

I had a lot of empathy for the already unlucky.

Despite the direction of his gaze, Raoul was thinking, I assumed, not about the unlucky but about that 1 percent. The mental review—the process of determining what content those e-mails encompassed—took him most of a minute.

*Did one of those e-mails come from Amanda? Did it mention pregnancy?*

Finally, he turned his back on me. With an emphasis on her name I heard as almost saccharine, he said, "Tell me, Alain. How is Lauren?"

# FORTY-SEVEN

It was past time for me to return to my wife's bedside. And it was too late in the conversation for Raoul to ask me about her condition.

I said, "Diane is fragile, Raoul. She has been fragile for a long time."

He faced me. "Now? Beyond fragile. This day? I didn't see it coming. Yet I did. You know? You've been a good friend to her," he said.

I wasn't looking for Raoul to bless my friendship with his wife.

I had an abrupt need to sit. I chose one of two matched chairs opposite the tangerine sofa. I'd avoided them on my prior visit because they looked like they were constructed of ice cubes.

"Are you injured?" he said. It was as though he'd just noticed my limp.

"Bicycle accident," I said, digesting that he didn't realize I'd been shot. "A little road rash."

"What do I do now?" he asked me. "When I see her? How do I help?"

I wasn't interested in guessing what cards Raoul had in his hand. I planned to comment only on the ones he had set faceup on the table. "You need to consider calling Cozy Maitlin. Right now. For Diane. I have his mobile number. He lives near Mapleton Hill, could be here in minutes. He'll know what to do. I need to get back to the hospital."

"*Sí,*" Raoul said, acknowledging that my advice was prudent while also letting me know that it wasn't the counsel he had been seeking.

I began to stand. "I have to get back to Lauren," I said.

"There is a woman," he said, flipping a new card for me to see.

I checked the time on my phone. I told myself five more minutes. The ice-cube chair was surprisingly comfortable. I shifted my weight to sink into its cushions. I raised my bad leg onto a matching ice-cube ottoman.

"There have been women. Diane knows that. It's part of us. 'A valve,' she called it. 'Pressure release.'"

Raoul's facility with the English language was suffering a crash. I was thinking, *Bullshit.* I didn't buy his rationalization, but I didn't tell him that. I realized that I had never really witnessed Raoul's ego defenses under major stress. This performance was a first. I was sure his defenses had been stressed when he'd been in Vegas searching for Diane when she was missing. But I hadn't been there to observe him. In our time together, I had seen Raoul mostly as golden boy.

As what Sam had called him—a "ten-ten."

My initial assessment was that Raoul's defenses were a tad creaky. He was not seeing this crisis for what it was.

"Our marriage has been difficult," he said.

*Really?* I compared our experience with difficult marriages. About the best way for a husband to handle hard times. Then I tried to imagine Lauren suggesting that I hire an attractive companion to assist me in gliding over the rough patches in our relationship.

*Yeah,* I thought, *that's what Lauren would do. She would even help me pick.*

"Diane knows I love her. She is not threatened. By the . . . women."

Was Raoul talking one-night stands? Mistresses? Or ASPs? Adult service providers. Escorts.

I said, "Diane has been hurt, Raoul. All the trauma has taken a toll. You should have realized that. Now she is broken." I spoke the words as an admonition. I felt the room needed just a pinch of acidy superego to balance out the cloying narcissism. A taste, at least.

He wasn't ready to hear it. He said, "She knew. The women were not important to her."

*Big of you,* I thought. *A perfect bargain for two. Or three.*

"My heart"—he thumped his fist against his chest—"belongs to my wife."

I half expected Raoul to launch into an explanation of

the cultural differences between us, how he didn't think I could understand the life that he and Diane were living.

If Raoul's argument went in the general direction of European sensibilities, I thought I might lose my cool.

"Las Vegas? The kidnapping? The rape? She was recovering. Yes?" He nodded. "And then Mimi's arrest? What she did?" Raoul sighed. "Lauren knows how bad it was last Christmas. It has all been too much for Diane. Emotionally and physically. For us, as a couple, it's been a challenging few years. Tough."

*The rape? What rape?* After everyone returned from Vegas, I had asked Diane if she had been raped. Diane had assured me that she had not been violated during her time as a hostage. Had she lied to me? Or had she lied to Raoul? Was the rape, real or not, a marital rationalization that Diane and Raoul kept in safekeeping to explain what was going wrong in their marriage? And what did Lauren know? I had no idea where to look to find the truth.

"The trauma was Diane's, Raoul. You were supposed to help her. Not seek solace elsewhere."

Raoul moved to the west-facing windows, his back to me. He asked me, "What's his mobile number? The lawyer's? I have only his office number." His familiar robust tone was hollow.

I heard footsteps on the stairs. Raoul heard them, too.

To Raoul, I said, "I think it may be too late for that now."

*Diane,* I hoped, but my gut said *Sengupta. The guy's timing is not good.*

I knew when I left the hospital that there was a risk I

would be followed, but I had hoped to take my leave from the flat before any cops showed up. I was acutely aware that I had also missed my window to call my cabbist and get back to Lauren's side.

I lifted my phone and quickly found Sam's name in the favorites. I hesitated before I hit the CALL button. Sam couldn't do anything to help Diane. Not with Sengupta and his partner already on the stairs and backup officers covering the exits.

Anyway, I knew I should let Sam sleep. He still had to deal with Frederick.

And with Comadoe.

# FORTY-EIGHT

It was neither Diane nor Sengupta on the stairs.

It was Amanda. I had a pretty good idea how surprised I was to see her. As in, completely. A glance at Raoul's face revealed that he was just as surprised as I was.

Amanda? She was indubitably the most surprised of the three of us.

Her arrival caused a bolus of adrenaline to course through me. The fatigue that had been slowly consuming my energy began a galloping retreat. I knew my adrenaline stores were just about shot; the rush would not endure for long.

Amanda looked at me. Then at Raoul. Then at me, again. Her eyes were warmest when she gazed at Raoul.

*Oh boy.*

I hadn't summoned Amanda. Raoul hadn't summoned Amanda. I was concerned that my god-awful day had taken its toll and I was missing something obvious that might explain her arrival. Part of me was relieved, simply, that she was safe.

The composure I was accustomed to seeing in Amanda's face was absent. She seemed off balance as she tried to ascertain where she fit into a complex puzzle that included pieces as diverse as the garish multimillion-dollar flat off Pearl Street; Raoul, who I guessed was her employer; and me, her psychotherapist.

In bloody scrubs. Had to be awkward for her.

Raoul did not step toward Amanda. He said, "How . . . did—" Then he said, "Who told you that I was—"

Either it was fine acting, or Raoul's self-focus was winning the moment—he was continuing to fail to adjust to the possibility that this impromptu assembly was not about him.

If Raoul had a relationship with Amanda, the allure, beyond the obvious, was beginning to make a little more sense. He was paying Amanda to be all about *him*. It wasn't the sex he was buying—the Raouls and Georges of the world could find that anywhere.

Diane's narcissism—the way it had blossomed post–Las Vegas—had crowded him out of their marriage in a way he couldn't abide.

"What?" Amanda said. "*You* did. I got a—"

Amanda was interrupted by a voice from the direction of the kitchen, a voice I knew as well as I knew my wife's.

"That wasn't him. That was me," Diane said. She directed her next words to Raoul. "I used your iPad to text her an invitation to join you here. I made the text sound all urgent. But . . . this is unexpected. I didn't expect her to actually show up. Right? I mean . . . I thought . . . Well, I had to be sure, didn't I?" Diane smiled in a perplexed way that, for me, underscored the tragedy. "God! I wish I looked like that without my makeup. Your complexion, honey! You and Mary-Louise, I swear. I got the brains, but that girl got the skin. How can skin not have pores? Amazing."

During sane moments, Diane liked to pretend that she was Mary-Louise Parker's older fraternal twin. On good, and even mediocre, mental health days, Diane was in on the jokes about the actress, which she told at her own expense. That night I was dubious.

Diane was standing in the doorway that led to the kitchen. Behind her, the door to the walk-in pantry was open. "Forgot," she said before she raised the pistol I had first seen in her hand that morning. "Forgive me? Turns out this thing helps people focus. Even me." She lifted it to firing height but didn't seem to be targeting anyone in particular.

She had changed her clothes since the last time I'd seen her. The morning shooting outfit—the chinos and the cami layered below the open shirt—had been replaced by cocktail attire. Her strappy dress was purple organza. On her feet were a pair of textured, metallic Jimmy Choos with too-tall heels that she'd modeled one distant afternoon in our office hallway after a FedEx delivery.

Her hair needed some attention, and her eye shadow was questionable. But all in all Diane's appearance was hovering on the outskirts of "fine." Completely inappropriate, but fine. She leaned against the kitchen doorjamb, examining each of our faces. She said, "Everyone knows everyone." Her demeanor had become that of a gracious hostess preparing to offer her guests a choice of beverages. "Amanda, dear? You look . . . lovely. I mean, considering."

Amanda closed her mouth. She shifted her eyes from Raoul to Diane.

Diane addressed her again. "Except us two, right? We haven't been introduced. I am Raoul's wife, Diane Estevez." She curtsied. "He may have mentioned me. I'm the one who . . . Whatever. He thinks I bitch a little. True, that. Maybe you've heard?"

Raoul begged, "Diane, please."

Diane continued as though he hadn't spoken. "So, do tell," Diane said to Amanda. "How on earth did you come to know my dear Alan?"

Raoul had a different idea about how the conversation should proceed. "Diane, give me that gun. Right now."

He said it expecting to be obeyed, which I considered to be illuminative. I had known Diane for a long time; giving her orders had never worked out too well for me.

"Don't," Diane hissed at her husband. "This is a Kahr, with a *K* and an *h*. I like my little Kahr." She moved the gun barrel from the generally threatening position where she'd been holding it to a direct aim at her spouse. She used her trigger finger to caress some engraved lettering near the barrel. "It's a point-three-eight-zero. Though I don't know what that means." I found it eerie that her voice so easily resumed its hostess timbre as she added, "I'd love to discover how Amanda came to know Alan. Has Alan been . . . *straying*?" Diane poked her tongue into the side of her cheek. "Is that how you two, well, came together?" Diane brought the hand that held the pistol quickly toward her open mouth, mocking some horror at the thought of Amanda and me hooking up.

The gesture, and the fact that she had failed to recognize her double entendre, made me much more nervous than did the accusation.

In my pocket I began to finger my phone. Hoping that Sam's number remained on my screen, I hit the button I thought was CALL. I slid the phone from my pocket, trying to keep it hidden at my side. I placed my thumb over the indentation that I thought was the device's speaker.

Amanda saw an opening that might allow her to defuse some tension. She said, "When I decided I needed help, I got Dr. Gregory's name from a . . . colleague. A girlfriend, at Prackfer and Lander. She said he was good."

"Oh, Alan is good," Diane said. "Fine choice. I find him a little prudish at times, though. Don't you think?" Diane nodded, agreeing with herself. "But he's easy to love, right? The man is a positive transference magnet, you have to give him that. Everybody falls for Dr. Alan. Raoul? *Mel*? Did you know about Amanda and Alan? That she was seeing my best friend right next door to my fucking office?"

Diane's use of *mel* threw me for a moment until I recalled that it was a Catalonian endearment.

I assumed that Diane's insertion of Raoul between the proverbial rock and the proverbial hard place was intentional. To reply, Raoul had to choose either to tell Diane—who was pointing a gun at him—the truth, or to fabricate a lie internally consistent with whatever reality Diane might have gleaned from reading his e-mails.

It was a tough act to perform on the fly, especially with a pistol aimed at one's sternum.

Raoul said, "Not at first. Diane, could you please lower that gun? Please?"

That time, it was more of a plea than an order. Diane wanted none of it.

"Where did you get the gun?" Raoul asked, determined to assert something.

She grinned. "I do wish you paid more attention, *mel*. I told you this place comes furnished. *Completely* furnished. There's a built-in gun safe in the master closet."

*And,* I thought, *the idiot owners use the same combination for the gun safe that they do for everything else in their lives.* Diane had not mentioned the gun safe to me during my initial tour of the flat. Oversight? I didn't think so.

Raoul took a half step toward his wife.

"Don't!" she barked. "There is recent evidence to suggest I will, in fact, fire this thing." She smiled. "Next question. Do you know the reason Amanda was seeking Alan's professional care?"

Raoul didn't reply. I assumed he had no facile lie handy. The truth? Problematic.

I thought a different path for the conversation might prove salutary. I said, "Diane? Is this the best time and is this weird condo you want to buy the best place to discuss this? It's late, we're all tired, and—"

I paused when Diane closed her eyes. She left them closed for two or three seconds. When she reopened them, she gestured toward the ice-cube ottoman. She said, "Is that your blood? Did I do that? To your leg?"

I glanced down at my bloody scrubs. I nodded.

"Is it serious?"

I shook my head. I almost said, *Flesh wound*. Instead I chose, "Through and through."

"I am so sorry. *Mmm mm mmm*." She briefly brought the palms of her hands together in front of her chest. For that fleeting instant she looked like a schoolgirl in prayer. Albeit an armed schoolgirl wearing purple organza and metallic Jimmy Choos. Then she said, "Now, shut up, please. We're here. We're doing this . . . *thang*."

Amanda took another stab at deflecting the crazy lady with the gun. She said, "I have issues with my brother's death. That's why I am seeing Dr. Gregory."

"Issues?" Diane said.

I recognized Diane's tone. So did Raoul. Amanda was at a disadvantage; she couldn't know that Diane had turned to high-octane sarcasm.

"Sexual issues mostly. They started . . . with my brother."

Amanda was doing what she did. She was trying to captivate, and distract, with one of her true and prurient stories.

"Really," Diane said. "Incest then? Raoul, did you know your friend has incest issues? Now, there's a loaded gun."

Raoul's face made it clear to all that Amanda's brother-sister sexual issues were news to him. The expression in his dark eyes was a Catalonian variant on *What the fuck?*

Diane had again missed her own joke. Her failure to flash even a self-referencing grin indicated that far too little of her awareness was in our moment.

"Well, amen to issues," Diane said. "Me? God knows I have a shitload. My house for one. And, *ughh,* I have this weird uncle named Oliver who lived around the corner from my grandparents when I was seven. I could kill that asshole. Like with my bare hands. I could literally sharpen my thumbnail and use it to slit his throat. I would do it right now if he was here. Let's see, what else? These damn fires. Right? So tired of the damn fires. Evacuate this, evacuate that. And this flat? Who would expect to find a place like this half a block from Pearl Street in Boulder?" She sighed. "Issues? Oh my—a trip I took to Vegas. My marriage. Didn't used to be an issue, but . . . And social networking? There's an issue. So much money to be made on the VC side. And so much damn money to be lost. And so fast." Diane's chin began to quiver. She wrinkled her nose and pinched her eyes almost closed. She faced Raoul. "I also have baby issues. A husband who . . ." She shook her head with vehemence. "And a womb that . . . And then . . ."

Diane leveled the gun and waved it from side to side until we all felt equally arbitrarily threatened. "See, I'm getting older. Tick-tock, tick-tock. My window to have babies is small. Now, or never. It's one, and then the next second it's the other." She used the index finger of one hand and the tip of the barrel of the pistol to mark a space about the size of a molar. "Little window. Dollhouse window. Amanda? Girl-talk time. *Tu i jo.* Just like me and Mary-Louise." Diane lowered her tone to a stage whisper. "Sorry. *Tu i jo* means 'you and me' in pretty boy's native tongue. So, just between *tu i jo,* in addition to the incest thing—and I don't mean to minimize that, not at all; it's a big, big deal—do you have baby issues, too? By chance? Is this your time, too?"

Diane arrested the swinging arc of the gun barrel and let it settle in the vicinity of Amanda's midsection.

*Oh God.*

Diane hit her forehead with the heel of the hand without the handgun. She said, "Damn, I forgot about the STIs. Talk about issues. Back up! Everyone with an STI, raise your hand."

# FORTY-NINE

Diane raised her hand. At first, she raised the hand that held the weapon. Two seconds later she realized her error and switched hands, pulling the gun back down.

I had missed a chance to rush her while the gun was in the air.

The STI thing had to be a detour. Diane's thinking was impaired, so I doubted the detour was intentional. Her true destination? Amanda's baby. Not good.

"Nobody?" Diane said. "I am the only one here with STIs? How is that possible? We all know it takes two to tango." Diane broke into a little tango. Given the heels, and the semiautomatic, it wasn't bad. "Okay, okay," she said. "Maybe it's a nomenclature thing. How about STDs? Anyone? Hands up!"

Raoul didn't seem to understand the venereal allusions, which I found perplexing. Had he, too, been asymptomatic? Was that possible? I so wished Adrienne were alive. I could have used one of her patented irreverent urological consultations right then—one specifically about the epidemiology and symptomatology of sexually transmitted infections. Adrienne had been a great storyteller.

Raoul said, "What was I supposed to say to her, Diane? What? Come on."

The expression Diane shot his way seemed as dangerous as the handgun she was jostling about. "Let's review," she said in a bright tone. "What you said in your touching fucking e-mail was that there was a time when you couldn't have imagined having a baby, but that now—*now!*—you were having a hard time imagining not having a baby. Words I always wanted to hear from you. But when I heard you say them, you were saying them to *her*"—the gun became a pointer, directed toward Amanda—"not to me."

Diane's affect since her exit from the pantry had displayed the kind of wide range—falsetto to soprano to bass—that would make any singer envious. For Diane, that kind of range in her affect indicated to me that she was dangerously labile.

Lability and loaded handguns go together like *seitan* and fine steakhouses.

Amanda was crying. One of her hands was at her face, pushing away each fresh tear the moment it escaped her eyes. Her other hand rested unself-consciously on her lower abdomen.

I hadn't really expected to be forced to test my theorem that Diane wouldn't shoot me twice in one twenty-four-hour period. But that was what I felt compelled to do.

Wondering not only how many rounds Diane's little Kahr carried in its magazine but also whether she had reloaded since she was in my office, I slid my phone into the pocket of the scrubs, pulled myself to my feet, and limped from the ice-cube chair to a spot on the floor directly between Diane and Amanda.

The ER doc, it turned out, had been prescient: my leg hurt like the dickens.

In between my wonder at the highs and lows of the drama I'd been witnessing since I found Raoul in the flat, I had been busy tracking the progress of the conversation, noting the presence of key words that I wanted to be certain Sam Purdy had a chance to hear at his end of the open mobile phone line. Open, that is, if the number I had dialed blind had indeed been his. And if Sam had not concluded that the call he received was nothing more than a butt dial.

All in all, a lot of variables for one telephone call. If all those things had gone my way, Sam would have already had the opportunity to hear the word *gun* and the name Diane. Those two keywords should have served to mobilize him. He would also have learned that Raoul and Amanda were present in the room with me. I'd also managed to personally toss in the phrase *weird condo* and the word *buy*. I'd been grateful to Diane when she added that we were all only a half block away from Pearl Street.

Would it turn out that all those scavenger's clues, along with any cell tower triangulation magic that could be done on the open call, could combine to provide data sufficient to guide Sam's detective colleagues to the downtown flat?

I had no way to know. I hoped that Sengupta and his crew were finally on their way and that they would arrive any second. The timing was crucial; Diane's pistol was presently pointed toward a much more vulnerable part of me than my calf.

"Move, Alan. Please," Diane implored me. "I don't want to shoot you."

"Diane, I don't think I will move. I don't want you to shoot me, either. You know that shooting anyone isn't a solution."

She looked at me with affection. "You think you understand the problem, don't you? That's sweet. But you can be so naïve." For a moment her eyes brightened. "Do you like my dress?"

I took a moment to settle on a way to respond. "I do," I said. "I don't know anyone else who could pull off that look."

"Mary-Louise Parker could."

To that, I did not know how to reply.

"You know what?" she said. "The outfit doesn't work without the shoes. They tie it all together. I don't want to have to take off the shoes. So please, just move. Get out of my way."

The roar of an explosion almost knocked me from my feet.

I thought, *Fuck, again?* as tiny pieces of porcelain tile began to fall down from above my head. The shards rained fast. And they were sharp—the shower felt more like shrapnel than snowflakes.

I reacted to the ensuing chaos by rushing at Diane like a linebacker, albeit a hobbled linebacker, maybe one with a torn ACL. My shoulder impacted across her upper thighs. I knocked her, literally, out of her Jimmy Choos.

I had felt the floor absorb the force of the back of her skull as it thudded onto the hardwood.

The Kahr scooted from her hand, back toward the open pantry. I hooked it with my foot, kicked it toward my hand, and grabbed it.

Raoul said, "Who the hell are you?" I thought that's what he said. My ears were ringing. I assumed everyone's ears were ringing.

I scrambled past Diane, who was on her back, dazed. She was reaching to grab her head but seemed unable to find it. I peeked out the kitchen door down the hallway that led toward the other side of the flat. I wanted to see whose presence Raoul was questioning.

I was, again, expecting Sengupta. Again I was wrong.

To Raoul I said, "That is Kevin. He's Diane's friend, the real estate agent who showed her this place."

Kevin's wrists had been rubbed raw. The exposed skin on his forearms was as red as fresh-cut beets. The area around his mouth was swollen and pocked with petechiae. The flesh was a shade of pink that didn't look natural on a man. The entire landscape below his nose looked like a cross between Homer Simpson and the butt of a baboon.

I concluded that Kevin had been bound and gagged. I had my money on Diane as the binder and gagger. I suspected she'd chosen to bind him with tape that had a powerful adhesive, an adhesive to which Kevin had the misfortune of being allergic.

Raoul asked me, "What is he doing here?"

*Excellent question.* I knew the answer. I wished I didn't. But I did.

*Were Kevin a forthright man,* I thought, *and were his wrists not bound, he would have raised his hand during Diane's STI quiz.*

I said, "Raoul, toss me a pillow, call nine-one-one, get an ambulance here for Diane. I think she might have banged her head. Hard."

While the standoff continued—my quick count of the shotgun's barrels indicated that Kevin had at least one shell on standby—I kneeled over to tend to Diane. I feared she was concussed, or worse. I was terrified I might have hurt her. I pulled out my phone to call Cozy Maitlin. "Cozy, it's Alan. Wake up. Your new client will be in Community's ER in five minutes." I hit END.

Diane tried to sit up to locate her Jimmy Choos. I wouldn't let her. I put the pillow under her head. I phoned Sam. He hadn't been asleep; he answered after half a ring. I said, "Find Sengupta. Diane is being transported by ambulance to Community. She'll be there in . . . fifteen minutes."

Sam said, "Sengupta?" as though he'd been raised in Mumbai.

I convinced Raoul to tend to Diane while I suggested to Kevin that he might not want to be holding the weapon when the authorities arrived.

"I just escaped. I was held hostage," Kevin said. I presumed he was making an argument for why he should remain armed for the duration.

I wasn't swayed. I said, "Yeah, well, believe it or not, that's not the worst thing that's happened today." I really didn't want to explain the whole progression to him. "You're safe, Kevin. In your shoes"—literally, I was thinking Gucci, and figuratively, I was thinking the progenitor of the damn STIs—"I would go put the gun back where you found it. The police are on the way."

I knew I could get distracted trying to imagine the circumstances under which Diane and Kevin had hooked up. I forced myself to postpone that query until another time.

Kevin stayed put. He kept hold of the weapon. Whatever. I led Amanda to the tangerine sofa. I asked how she was doing.

"She's pregnant, too, isn't she?" Amanda said. She meant Diane.

"I think that is possible, yes," I said. I couldn't tell if Amanda had gotten around to considering Kevin among the potential sperm donors responsible for Diane's possible fetus.

"She didn't know me. What I looked like. My name. I was just . . . a girl, to her. The latest girl."

"Diane?" I said.

Amanda nodded. It took me a moment to realize that she was rationalizing her decision to select me as her therapist. The crazy night had already convinced me that Diane hadn't referred Amanda to me, that Amanda had chosen me on her own.

The fact that Amanda was drawn to the risk involved in seeing a therapist who was so close to the wife of a man who was her employer, or lover, didn't surprise me. I was well acquainted with Amanda's boundary issues.

"He made a promise," Amanda said.

She said it as though that explained everything. "The baby?" I asked.

She nodded before she shook her head. I was left wondering about the identity of the "he." And about the unless. *There is always an unless.*

"Your car is close?" I said.

She said it was.

I reminded her the police were on the way.

"See you next week," she whispered as she turned toward the stairs.

I thought, *Transference.*

# FIFTY

The ambulance arrived first. I explained to the EMTs that I thought their patient could be pregnant and might have been injured in a fall. In a whisper, I added to the more assertive of the two medics that they should be prepared for her to show signs of emotional instability. He asked what I meant.

I suggested that he might want to keep sharps out of reach and restraints handy. The nonchemical kind.

With the arrival of professionals, Kevin chose to lean the shotgun against the wall in the nearest corner. He then announced that he wished to share the ambulance with Diane. In a low voice, I suggested to the paramedics that might not be the best idea of the night. The EMTs concurred with my assessment that Kevin's injuries—although hideous—were hardly ambulance-worthy. I assured them I would put him in a taxi.

I stayed beside Diane until the paramedics pushed her gurney to the elevator. There was not a solitary inch to spare inside the narrow car. Diane raised her head and asked me for her Jimmy Choos. I found them. She cradled them in her arms.

I leaned in close to her. I said, "You and Kevin? Really?"

She winced. "Oh man. Us? A week, maybe. Or twice. You know what, I kind of blocked it out. Like it was Mary-Louise who did it? She is sluttier than me. Same thing, though. Yeah? Genes? Bad day. Bad day."

She pulled me close to her. She said, "How did I miss her this morning? How? How did I miss her and shoot you? You weren't in your chair. Or were you? Was it the little Kahr's fault?" She looked confused. "Were you?" Her eyes grew huge. "How did I miss her, Alan?" She moved her lips to within an inch of my ear. "She's really here, right? I'm not crazy, am I?"

The EMT squeezed in, forcing me to exit the elevator before the door closed.

Did Diane not know she had shot Lauren?

*Wow.*

The Kahr? I could feel its dense presence at the small of my back.

I was packing heat.

I didn't consider it wise for Kevin and Raoul to share a ride to Community. I called the number on the card in my pocket. My favorite Boulder cabbist arrived in minutes to shuttle Kevin to the ER. The sweet driver leaned out the window and asked me what the hell happened to his face. I told her I didn't know, but that it wasn't me. She blew me a kiss when I gave her a twenty for the five-buck fare. I really hoped she was somebody's doll.

When Kevin finally got around to explaining his injuries at the ER, Sengupta's night—certainly no picnic thus far—was going to grow much more complicated.

When I'd originally left Lauren's bedside, I had expected to be absent for thirty minutes. An hour, max. I was desperate to resume my vigil. I felt I was due some good news. A smile on a nurse's face. A squeeze from my wife's fingers. Something.

Raoul drove me to the hospital in his old Mercedes coupe. He cut down Thirteenth off Spruce instead of taking Broadway. In other circumstances, I would have asked why. I didn't. I said, "Diane doesn't know she shot Lauren, Raoul."

"I was wondering about that," he said.

I said, "She's not well." I intended for my assessment to serve as a poignant preface to a necessary conversation between us. Diane's mental collapse. Her possible pregnancy. It did not. It was the totality of our discussion.

My phone vibrated. A text. The ICU nurse wanted me to return "stat." *Shit.*

Raoul left his car at the edge of the ER bay as though he expected it to be whisked away by a valet. Despite my anxiety, or perhaps because of it, I allowed him to enter the building before me. Below his cotton sweater, at the small of his back, I spotted a telltale bulge.

Raoul was carrying a handgun.

The gun caused me to recognize a truth I had been avoiding.

*God. Raoul isn't George.*

*Raoul is the Buffer.* The Buffer was the one of Amanda's gentlemen with the gun in his briefcase.

Instinctively, I rejected the conclusion. *That can't be right. The Buffer is broke. He lost all of his money.*

Raoul and I parted as we crossed through the waiting area of the ER. My mind insisted on replaying the Buffer's story of loss.

*Shit. Has Raoul,* I wondered, *lost his fortune?*

Raoul's unaccented voice intruded into my reverie. He had stopped walking. He said, "Alain? I didn't understand what Diane was saying earlier about diseases. Venereal and the like. Did you?"

I was too distracted to sugarcoat things for him. I said, "You may want to get tested."

The reality hit me like a slap. *Diane and Raoul are broke. Raoul lost all their money.*

*And Diane knows. She may be pregnant with the wrong man's baby. Her dreams, and security, are in flames.*

For her? Which recent insult was the final straw?

I thought I heard Raoul mumble, "What?" But before I could reply, he said, "Alain? There is something that I, I think I should . . . confess." Then he shook his head. He forced his lips together. "No," he said under his breath. "Ah, no."

*He can't tell me the truth,* I thought. I remained unable to digest the preposterous idea that Raoul's empire had collapsed. I had been so sure that he was golden. Perennially golden; that he was George. Absent his admission, I needed confirmation.

As Raoul turned to continue to the ER, I called out, "Enzo!"

Raoul didn't break stride.

*Raoul isn't George.*

As I limped toward the elevators, I passed Sengupta jogging from the main lobby on his way to the Emergency Department. He looked as exhausted as I felt.

I wondered if he was always a little bit late.

# FIFTY-ONE

The intensivist was at Lauren's bedside in the ICU. My wife hadn't stirred during my absence. In lieu of a greeting, Dr. Craig Posner—he'd introduced himself earlier as "Dr. C"—said, "I have concerns about the trajectory of your wife's liver and kidney functions."

I didn't react. I tried to react. But I couldn't react. At that instant, I felt as though I'd just had a double dose of Botox injected deep into my soul.

When we'd met earlier in the evening Dr. C had demonstrated a frank manner, but it appeared he was taking a scenic route to get to his current point. He began explaining, again, that one of the three slugs had done virtually all of the significant harm to my wife. One of the trio had merely nicked Lauren's stomach and lung. Those wounds were repaired without complication, though infection remained a concern. Another, the bad one, had caused potentially catastrophic damage to her liver and had messed up a long section of her bowel.

He added a new detail about compromised blood supply that caused my brain to hiccup.

I knew what all his words meant. *Serious concerns. Trajectory. Catastrophic damage. Blood supply.*

I also knew the expression on his face. For me, seeing what was in his eyes was like the moment near the end of a film when I can tell that hope isn't on the menu, that the director does not intend that the movie come equipped with a happy ending.

I tried to swallow so that I could speak, but my mouth felt like I'd been chewing rope. Dr. C's final sentence found my ears as though he were speaking underwater.

"The third bullet," he said, "went through and through."

*Lauren and I shared that third bullet. It was the one that found my calf.*

The doctor excused himself to continue his rounds of the ICU. I stepped into the hall and walked in a circle because I didn't know what else to do.

I returned to Lauren's side and phoned Sam. He answered after half a ring.

I said, "Please ask Ophelia to bring Jonas and Gracie to the ICU as quickly as she can."

Sam was quiet for three seconds. I imagined him processing my request.

He said he would have Lucy arrange an escort.

One of the nurses poked her head in the door. She pointed to a white plastic bag on the chair beside the bed. "An ER nurse dropped that off for you. She said it's your things—yours and Lauren's—from this morning." I must have looked perplexed. She added, "Does that make sense to you?"

Nothing was making sense to me. I was lost on the edge of a Möbius strip of incongruity. My incomprehension had no beginning, no end.

I remembered how to do polite. "It does," I said. "Thank you."

She stepped away.

I was alone with my wife. I began to cry as I realized it was time to begin to say good-bye.

# FIFTY-TWO

Sam walked in before my children arrived.

Lauren was turning yellow before my eyes.

I stood. He embraced me and held me. He whispered that he had passed Diane on the way up. She was on her way to radiology for a CT scan. He asked if I wanted to fill him in.

"Later. You were home?" I said. "Is that how you got here so fast?"

He held the whisper. "Comadoe rents a house on Hawthorn. I was there." Hawthorn Avenue was only a few minutes away from the hospital. "His real name is David Cohen. Ring any bells?" I shook my head. "His mother is a rabbi in Saint Louis. She's a big gay rights advocate. Go figure."

I did not know what to say about Comadoe being a Reform rabbi's son. I thought his mother was going to be disappointed in him. "You were visiting him at this hour?" I asked as I pulled back from Sam's hug.

I expected more bad news. My bad-news receptacles were overflowing. I did not know where I would put any additional bad tidings.

Sam leaned right back in close to me so that his lips were close to my ear. In a church whisper, he said, "His PO is going to do a surprise visit in a few hours. I had some items I had to . . . drop off before that happens."

I recognized the tracks that Sam was leaving. "Turnabout," I said, "is fair play?"

"Something like that. I kind of let slip to Lucy that I'd heard about the guy still dealing, but that I heard it from a CI I didn't really want to have to burn." Sam kept few confidential informants. He protected the ones he valued like the Swiss Guard protects *il papa*. "Lucy got what I was saying—and she also knew that somebody had tried to set me up with IA. She put the pieces together and she let it all slip to the detective who busted Comadoe last time around that his guy was still dirty. Lucy's discreet; she never mentioned me or my CI. The detective she talked to told Comadoe's PO there was a rumor on the street that his guy was continuing to do business and may have been trying to take down a cop. So . . ."

"The whole setup was very Kevin Bacon–ish. Many degrees of separation."

I wiped my eyes, though I wasn't trying to hide my tears. "What's the PO going to find during the search?"

Sam embraced me again. "An unregistered thirty-two reported stolen in a burglary in 2009. Eighteen hundred and sixty dollars in hundreds and twenties. And an ounce and a half of crystal meth."

"Comadoe goes away this time?"

"Comadoe goes away."

I saw loose ends. "He'll reveal what he heard that night in the ICU, Sam."

"Nobody will believe that shit. Asshole was in a coma."

"You're sure?"

"DA will have him as the guy who tried to set me up." He shrugged. "Has to work. Has to. It's all I got. That, and South America.

"Know what? I'm much more worried about Izza and Tres, what they might say. They can still bring me down."

*Us down*, I thought. "Yeah," I said. "They can. They probably will."

He raised his phone. "I missed your earlier call. Long message. Important?"

I couldn't face explaining the last hour of my life to Sam. "Probably a butt dial," I said. "I need to sit." I sat. I realized that my blood sugar was probably the kind of low that an endocrinologist might find alarming.

Sam went to sit down across from me, but the bag of belongings from the ER was on the other chair. I reached out. He handed it to me.

I put it on my lap. I gasped. The sound from my throat surprised me. I thought I had used up my allotment of gasps.

"What's wrong?" Sam asked.

I raised a hand, shook my head. "I need to think for a second."

Sam checked his phone. "Not too long. That was Lucy. They just turned onto South Broadway. Ophelia and the kids."

Sam was telling me how much time I had to think. The kids were five minutes away. Maybe less, given the hour and the police escort.

I used up one of those minutes before I reached into the plastic bag. The bloody clothing was neatly folded. On top of the pile was a beat-up sheet of construction paper, creased into fourths.

I handed it to Sam. He unfolded it. His eyes grew wide.

"Tres drew this, that night. What you're looking at," I said, "is your—our—Get Out of Jail Free card. Weld County edition."

# FIFTY-THREE

Sam was wise enough not to speak.

I said, "I think—I admit I'm not sure—that Lauren had just handed this to me when Diane walked in with the gun. I figured it was there, in my office, when the crime scene techs showed up. That they collected it. That Sengupta would see it. Izza would come forward, say something. They'd eventually make the connection. It would be over for us."

Sam's wide eyes were red. He said, "But it's here. We have it. And without it, if I'm reading this right, Weld County has no case. No reliable witness to corroborate Elias Tres. A three-year-old memory of a five-year-old boy? Won't fly in court. Doesn't matter if Izza backs him. That's hearsay. The kid's testimony about an old memory? Will not stand without this drawing. This piece of paper is the ball game for the prosecution."

I said, "I must have been holding it when . . . I must have stuffed it into my pocket."

Sam looked at me. Back at the drawing. Back at me.

I said, "Out in the hall. We should finish this out in the hall."

We stepped outside Lauren's room. I said, "Clean hands, Sam? For our kids. It's all about clean hands." I looked through the glass at Lauren. "And it looks like we may be about to lose our last pair of clean hands."

Sam nodded. His eyes were full of tears. He said, "We're it, now. You and me."

I had to force myself not to turn my gaze toward my wife. I wanted to scream at the top of my lungs that she was still here, too. I swallowed it.

*What would she want?* I knew there was another vulnerable kid she wouldn't want left behind.

I said, "Here's the deal. The drawing is yours. But you need to make me a promise. You need to try—try—to find a way to make Big Elias pay for what he did to Izza's mother and to Elias Tres's grandmother. To Tres. You need to find a way to make things right for Elias Tres. That means giving him a chance to grow up with his aunt."

"That's Izza?"

"Yes. That is Izza. You need to try to figure it out. To make it happen."

Sam scuffled his feet on the linoleum. First one, then the other. He said, "Bad idea. We need to stay away from all that."

"I don't care."

"You'll care next week. You'll be thinking clearer."

"Promise me."

He stared at me as he slid his lower jaw from side to side. "If I do it, I do it my way, Alan. You stay out of it. If it gets too risky, I back off."

I nodded.

"Then I promise to try," he said.

*Unless,* I thought. There's always a goddamn unless.

Sam's phone buzzed. He showed me the screen. It was a text from Lucy.

**We're pulling up.**

I took a deep breath.

Sam put a hand on the side of my neck. He said, "You ever heard of something called Gaia?"

"Yes."

"I'm that butterfly," he said. "In the Amazon." His voice was breaking. I had never heard Sam Purdy's voice break. "I did this to you. That night. To us. To Lauren. I am so sorry. Maybe there was another way. I wasn't smart enough to see it."

I was done wiping tears. They streamed off my chin. "You're not looking far enough back," I said. "With Mc-Clelland? I am the butterfly. This is on me." I put my arms around him. I said, "I love you, Sam."

He said, "I love you, too."

Sam moved toward the elevators.

I slipped the little Kahr from the small of my back and stuffed it to the bottom of the bag of belongings from the ER.

I began steeling myself for Gracie to call out, "Daddy."

I didn't know if I had the strength.

# FIFTY-FOUR

The Dome Fire never did the kind of catastrophic damage that the Fourmile Fire had done. The winds cooperated. Ground crews and pilots were heroic. In days, the evacuees returned home.

I paid attention to none of it.

As autumn arrived in reality, and not just on the calendar, I waited for the toxic fallout in my life to settle. I took many long bicycle rides. I took them because they had always helped in the past. They didn't help. But they didn't hurt. On one excursion I tempted fate by riding north through Weld County, but I did not cross Interstate 25.

I did not want to see Frederick again. Ever.

The interstate loomed to my right as I pedaled toward Longmont. Just before I reached the intersection with

County Road 16—a right turn would have taken me into Frederick—I passed a farmhouse adjacent to some shimmering fields of what I thought was young winter wheat. Between the farmhouse and the edge of the cultivated fields, a dormant garden was arranged in a Stonehenge-like circle, awaiting spring.

Smack in the center of the raised straw-mulched beds stood a proud, tall, fat scarecrow on a podium of twisted, welded scrap iron. The scarecrow's left arm was raised in defiance that was intended to deter intruders and scavengers.

The scarecrow was dressed in a Tyvek jumpsuit.

# ACKNOWLEDGMENTS

*Line of Fire* is the nineteenth, and penultimate, story about Alan Gregory, Sam Purdy, and their ensemble in Boulder, Colorado.

Penultimate is a word that anticipates loss. But my feelings about this book, and about the approaching end to the series, are more about gratitude and opportunity. Many long series stall the way a car runs out of gas; I am especially grateful for Brian Tart's guidance and support as I worked to steer this one to a more determined conclusion.

Jessica Horvath's editorial vision is carved indelibly in *Line of Fire*; I thank her for her contributions, her persistence, and her always level demeanor.

Sharp-eyed readers of the series might notice minor inconsistencies between this story and an anticipatory narrative I set up in an earlier book. I could have written this story within the established narrative but I prefer my recent imaginings to the alternative.

*Line of Fire* is not intended to be a history of the Boulder wildfires of the late summer and fall of 2010. The devastating impact of those fires inspired me while I created the Boulder backstory, but I did not allow the facts to get in my way. Locals might also recognize that I reopened Oak on Fourteenth Street long before Oak actually reopened on Fourteenth Street—yet another fire tale that did not limit me.

Robert Barnett and Bonnie Nathan counsel me with professionalism and grace, and they do it in the manner of a friend who has my interest at heart and an affectionate hand on my shoulder. I am most grateful.

I comprehended only a scant fraction of what Peter Ossorio taught in his lectures in my graduate school days. I am left to imagine, fondly, the twinkle that would be in his eyes were he to note how I have applied what I thought I did understand. Thanks for the echoes, Pete. No unlesses.

Terry Lapid, Jane Davis, Elyse Morgan, and Nancy Hall read early versions of the manuscript while hunting for my flaws. They graciously suffered the early drafts so no one else had to. Jane's guidance was particularly astute this time around. Al Silverman was the first publishing professional to ever take a red pencil to my work. Two decades later I continue to be blessed by his guidance. Al's editorial acumen is without peer, and the truth is that he is as fine a friend as he is an editor, which is saying something.

I miss Enid Schantz, who died while I was writing this book. She was a crime fiction pioneer who embodied everything I have come to appreciate about booksellers. She loved the words, the writers, and the readers. But she was never fond of the heavy lifting, and she never suffered fools. If you end up in an afterlife that leaves you in search of something good to read, you know who to talk to.

And to Hank and his handlers, my thanks for being gracious about the cameo.

One session stood out. Our third.

By then I'd left his resistance in tatters. Kidding.

I have replayed the session in my head ten times, at least. It was the day my perspective changed. The day I got suspicious. On occasion I went back over it to see if there was a nuance I'd missed. Other times the loop replayed itself, an earworm, a melody my memory couldn't cut loose. One with lyrics that made no sense.

It's not in my personality to recall moments of assurance with much clarity. What I tend to recall vividly are my doubts and my fears. That therapy loop earned the replays because it was the session when my doubts and my fears began to crystallize, when I went from thinking that I might be in over my therapeutic head to wondering what the hell I might have gotten myself into with Dr. Alan Gregory.

Or as I called him, my patient.

As the end of the session approached, I said, "I don't know what happened that morning. The day of the fire. The morning of the shooting. Moment by moment. You may think I know. You may wish I knew. You may want to proceed as though I know what you need me to know. But I don't know."

He didn't reply. That happened a lot with us.

Early on I'd asked him why he'd picked me to be his therapist. He said it was because he wanted a therapist he didn't know—he knew almost everybody—and because someone he trusted had once said good things about my work. I'd asked him why he didn't go to Denver; there had to be therapists there he didn't know. He said it was too much for him right then. An almost three-hour round trip? He said he couldn't do it.

During that third session I began to think he'd been less than honest. I began to believe he chose me because I was inexperienced. He thought he could manipulate me.

I said, "I imagine it will be tender for you, sharing the story. But at some point, you will need to tell me those details."

He stood. His timing was impeccable; he rose within seconds of the precise forty-five-minute mark. As a therapist he had sat through a million forty-five-minute hours. After the first few thousand or so, he'd undoubtedly internalized the session interval.

I had not. My hours in the consultation chair were still in triple digits. The clock I relied upon was digital. It was not visible from his seat.

"Who does?" he replied. "Know? What happened, I mean."

*Who knows? You're going existential with that? You were there. I wasn't. If I had been there, I would know what the hell happened.*

I kept the rant to myself. I said, "Are you unsure what happened that day?"

*No dissociation, please. I don't have the chops for fugue. Not your fugue.*

His face adjusted into an expression I couldn't interpret. He had a few of those. Then he said, "Am I 'sure'? A lot of certainty is squeezed into that syllable. Certainty is elusive for me. Death? Certain. Everything else? Uncertain."

*God.*

"Okay," he said. "Here's part of what happened that morning that you don't know. That maybe no one else knows." He took a deep breath. "My wife was in my office to caution me about a development in a case she was working. When she came to see me, she didn't understand the implications of what she had learned. She thought she did, but she did not. She was being generous, maybe loving—I go back and forth about that—with her warning about legal action that was coming against someone I know."

"Legal action?"

"Taking that person into custody. For questioning. Or arrest. Like that."

"Thanks," I said. Why I thanked him I did not know.

"But I told her that if she were to start arresting people, she would have to begin by arresting me."

I was disbelieving. I'm sure I looked it. I said, "You?"

He said, "It's complicated. This may help: After Lauren told me what she was about to do, I knew it was time to reveal some secrets I'd been keeping from her. I did that—I revealed some things I had done."

"Things?" *Jesus.*

"Are you being supervised on this case?"

I had never before been asked that question. Few patients know that supervision—oversight of a treatment by a senior practitioner—exists as an option for their therapist. But Alan Gregory knew. He was one of those senior practitioners. In Boulder he was a supervisor.

"This therapy?" I said. "You?" He nodded. "No. I am not being supervised."

"If you change your mind—about supervision—will you agree to inform me? I can't have what I tell you leave this room. Not even to a supervisor. Clean hands?"

"That's irregular. You know that."

"It's essential. Without that assurance, I can't proceed. Won't."

"I need to think about it. We can discuss it next time. What about my notes?"

"I would like you to make them sparse."

"Short? Or . . . or lacking detail? What kind of sparse?"

He nodded. Then he shook his head.

I made a *so-wtf* face. If I'd had a supervisor, he or she would have been directing me to continue to work on maintaining my therapeutic expression. They all did.

He said, "Lacking content. No names. No facts. No he-said, I-said. Process? Go to town. Whatever's helpful."

"I don't show my clinical notes to anyone. Ever. You don't have to worry."

His eyes were dismissive. "I wouldn't be here if I thought you would. I am concerned about people who would look at them without your consent."

I felt a chill. *Huh?* I looked at my hands again.

"Acts."

*That sure clears things up.* "You're being vague."

"Intentionally. I am revealing I have secrets, but I am not revealing those secrets."

"Trust?" I said. Not exactly a therapeutic reach on my part. It was like a meteorologist forecasting rain seconds after she opens her umbrella.

"Yes, Lauren recognized the implications of what I told her. I knew she would, but I had hoped that my admissions might alter the tilt of her heart. In my favor."

To him, his failure to trust me required no exploration. I felt it as a wound.

"I was wrong," he said. "Lauren was angry. Not understanding. All that my revelation changed for her that morning was her thinking about whom to arrest."

Alan Gregory was one of those people who confused me when he told me things intended to alleviate my confusion. By then that wasn't news for me.

I said, "She was going to arrest you? When she was shot?"

"Not at the beginning of the visit but, yes, by the end. When she was shot."

His shoulders fell. Some amount of tension disappeared from his temples and his jaw. He seemed relieved to have breached this wall with me. We made brief eye contact, a connection that left me with the odd feeling that I'd known him since we were children.

The intimacy of it all stunned me. Part of me melted with his glance, as though for that instant our arteries shared the same pumping heart.

He shook his head as though he was as amazed as I was. His breath was shallow. "That morning? The fire up the street? Don't forget the fire."

My breathing was shallow too. The mirroring was not intentional. No, I had not forgotten the fire.

In a way that I don't think I had ever felt before in my limited time as a therapist, I was aware that a patient was sharing a dangerous secret with me. Not just a sensitive truth—that's routine—but a dangerous one. Dangerous for him. And possibly dangerous for me. The danger part was novel for me.

But not for him. Alan Gregory woke to foreboding every morning of his life. To help him, I needed to understand his foreboding. Perhaps even to feel it.

I said, "Could you please sit back down, Alan?" If he considered me a peer, he wouldn't put me in that position. I knew that. I didn't like it.

"Our time is up," he said.

"That's my call. This is my office. I am your therapist." I shouldn't have had to remind him of that. We'd work on that issue later. The list of what we would work on later was becoming unwieldy.

He nodded. But he remained standing.

"Your wife was about to have you arrested for what?"

"Something serious. A felony. I can't discuss it."

"Can't?"

He sat down. "I will tell you what I told Lauren that morning: My caution has to do with clean hands." He looked at his hands as though he couldn't not look at his hands.

With monumental self-control, I managed not to look at my hands. I was aware that his wife was shot not too many moments after he told her whatever he told her that morning. Apparently about clean hands.

"Yours?" I asked. "Your clean hands?"

He stood back up. "No," he said. "Yours."

That did it. I looked at my hands. I said, "Sit please." He didn't. *Shit*. "She had a reason to arrest you? The felony?"

"Yes. Definitely."

"You say 'definitely,' yet you continue to be vague. You seem to be admitting . . . guilt. Yes? Are we talking about trust again? Right now? Between you and me?"

Air escaped his nostrils in a little huff. "Guilt? No question. Right and wrong. Morality? That's murky. Between us? Of course it's about trust."

He paused. I look back now, and I wonder about that pause. I think he was telling me something. But I was missing it.

"Trust is not only an issue between you and me. It was there between my wife and me. Maybe it is there between my friend—or friends—and me. There is a lot on the line here beyond my mental health. Culpability. Survival. Freedom. All of those."

Before I could acknowledge that gravity, he refocused on the mundane. "We need to talk about your notes. Session notes, process notes, whatever. And supervision."

*What?* "Please sit. If you don't, I am going to have to stand." He sat. I said, "Thank you. What about supervision? What about my notes?"

"You may not have experience with those people. I do."

"I don't," I said. With another patient, I would not have admitted that. Alan Gregory was not another patient.

"Those people may know that I am coming to see you for therapy."

It is typically no more a presence in my body than my liver, but my heart suddenly became an entity in my chest. *Bump bump. Bump bump.*

I began to question things I should have questioned sooner. My mind reassembled fragments and pieces he had allowed to leak out along the way.

*A wildfire. Arrest. A gun. Shots in the back. Red soles. An escort. A witness. His partner. A felony. A little boy. Trust. A leg wound. A wife in ICU. A cabbist.*

*Oh shit. And . . . holy shit. The felony. Trust. Guilt?* I realized what he was admitting to me. I began to speak. My breath caught in my throat. I tried again.

I said, "You had a motive? That morning? To shoot your wife, didn't you?"

"If you choose to stop treating me, I understand."

"I asked you a question," I said. *Bump bump. Bump bump.*

He looked out the window. "My request about your notes?"

*Jesus. Did you hear what I just asked you?* "Uh, I will be careful. I will take a look at what I've written. Next time we can talk about what I decide about shredding and starting over. Did—"

"Handwritten or digital? Dictated? I hope you don't have them in the cloud."

"Handwritten."

"If you shred, it needs to be cross shred, not strip shred. Separate the confetti into piles. Dispose of the piles in different places. Or set the shreds on fire. Either works."

My patient wanted me to torch my notes. I added paranoia to his differential diagnosis. *Great. This is great.*

"Alan, did you have a motive to shoot your wife?"

Without any further hesitation, he said, "I did. That's the problem. At some point, they'll figure that out. He certainly will. And he won't let go. That, by the way, is the exact sort of thing that can't go in your notes."

*He?*

*Bump bump.*